W9-CPL-110

DISCARD

praise for
somebody like you

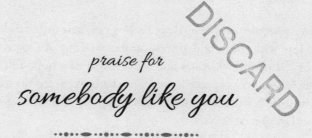

"In Vogt's quietly beautiful inspirational contemporary, two people learn to let go of the past and discover that God often works in mysterious ways. . . . A heartwarming tearjerker about learning what love is."

—*Publishers Weekly* (starred review)

"Beth Vogt gets better with every book. *Somebody Like You* wrestles with the tough topics of widowhood and family while wrapped in the heart-warming cocoon of romance. Bravo to Vogt for coming up with an intriguing concept and executing it brilliantly."
—Rachel Hauck, award-winning author of *Once Upon a Prince*

"A beautiful story of an unexpected second chance at love and redemption by one of my favorite authors. I loved this book!"
—Susan May Warren, bestselling and
award-winning author of *It Had to Be You*

Valparaiso Public Library
103 Jefferson Street
Valparaiso, IN 46383

"In *Somebody Like You*, Beth K. Vogt captures the tender emotions of loss with grace and sincere understanding. An expertly handled story of rekindled hearts and the whisper of a hope-filled future are safe in her very capable hands. For the broken, for the awakening of new love, for the heart that seeks a champion to heal its wounds . . . this is a special book."

—Kristy Cambron, author of *The Butterfly and the Violin*

"With crisp prose, flesh-and-blood characters who live and breathe on the page, and a poignancy that reaches into one's very soul, *Somebody Like You* is not only a must-read for somebody like you . . . but for anyone who loves great fiction."

—Julie Lessman, award-winning author of
the Daughters of Boston series

"Woven with grace and sensitivity, author Beth K. Vogt sheds a tender light on the human spirit in this bittersweet story of love and loss. Beautiful and emotion-packed, the only bookmark for this is a Kleenex, for *Somebody Like You* will tug at your heart in a way that is not easily forgotten."

—Joanne Bischof, award-winning author of *Be Still My Soul*

"*Somebody Like You* is a story filled with characters I adored from the opening paragraphs. At the end, I sighed, longing for just a few more pages with my new friends. A perfect read for those who like a romance with a rich story and heart."

—Cara Putman, award-winning author of *Shadowed by Grace*

"Poignant, intriguing, and not without its lighter moments, too, Beth Vogt's *Somebody Like You* captured me from the first chapter. The unique premise had me curious from the start, but it was the emotional depth combined with heart-tugging characters that had me reading until late at night. A beautiful story, beautifully told."

—Melissa Tagg, author of *Made to Last*

"With a poignant plot and a tenderness that grips your heart, *Somebody Like You* is a story to be savored. Vogt shows how God restores the brokenness in lives for his happily ever after. This engaging read brought tears to my eyes several times, but it concluded with a heart-sighing smile."

—Lisa Jordan, award-winning author of *Lakeside Reunion*

"*Somebody Like You* grabbed my interest from page one and didn't let go. Beth K. Vogt pens this heart-wrenching and tender romance between a military widow and her husband's estranged twin brother with the deftness and assurance of a skilled storyteller, rendering deep emotion without ever dissolving into melodrama. My only complaint is that it had to end! If Beth's first two novels marked her as an author to watch, *Somebody Like You* proves she's here to stay."

—Carla Laureano, author of *Five Days in Skye*

"*Somebody Like You* takes you on an emotional journey to witness the bravery of a widow in the face of impossible circumstances. Beth Vogt has written a book you will not soon forget."

—Elizabeth Byler Younts, author of *Promise to Return*

also by beth k. vogt

Wish You Were Here
Catch a Falling Star
You Made Me Love You: an eShort sequel to
Wish You Were Here

somebody like you

PORTER COUNTY PUBLIC LIBRARY

••••••◆•••• A NOVEL ••••◆•••••

Valparaiso Public Library
103 Jefferson Street
Valparaiso, IN 46383

BETH K. VOGT

FIC   VAL
VOGT

Vogt, Beth K.
Somebody like you : a novel /
33410012908069   05/09/1

HOWARD BOOKS
A DIVISION OF SIMON & SCHUSTER, INC.

NEW YORK   NASHVILLE   LONDON   TORONTO   SYDNEY   NEW DELHI

Howard Books
A Division of Simon & Schuster, Inc.
1230 Avenue of the Americas
New York, NY 10020

This book is a work of fiction. Any references to historical events, real people, or real places are used fictitiously. Other names, characters, places, and events are products of the author's imagination, and any resemblance to actual events or places or persons, living or dead, is entirely coincidental.

Copyright © 2014 by Beth K. Vogt

Scripture quotations are taken from: The Holy Bible, New International Version®, NIV®, copyright © 1973, 1978, 1984, 2011 by Biblica, Inc.® Used by permission of Biblica, Inc.® All rights reserved worldwide. The Holy Bible, English Standard Version, copyright © 2001, 2007 by Crossway Bibles, a division of Good News Publishers. Used by permission. All rights reserved. The Message copyright © 1993, 1994, 1995, 1996, 2000, 2001, 2002. Used by permission of NavPress Publishing Group.

All rights reserved, including the right to reproduce this book or portions thereof in any form whatsoever. For information, address Howard Books Subsidiary Rights Department, 1230 Avenue of the Americas, New York, NY 10020.

First Howard Books trade paperback edition May 2014

HOWARD and colophon are trademarks of Simon & Schuster, Inc.

For information about special discounts for bulk purchases, please contact Simon & Schuster Special Sales at 1-866-506-1949 or business@simonandschuster.com.

The Simon & Schuster Speakers Bureau can bring authors to your live event. For more information or to book an event, contact the Simon & Schuster Speakers Bureau at 1-866-248-3049 or visit our website at www.simonspeakers.com.

Interior design by Jaime Putorti

Manufactured in the United States of America

10 9 8 7 6 5 4 3 2 1

Library of Congress Cataloging-in-Publication Data

Vogt, Beth K.
Somebody like you : a novel / Beth K. Vogt.—First Howard Books trade paperback edition.
  pages cm
I. Title.
PS3622.O362S66 2014
813'.6—dc23
                                                              2013030353

ISBN 978-1-4767-3758-4
ISBN 978-1-4767-3759-1 (ebook)

For the ones who have been broken and whose dreams have been lost . . . and for the One who finds us and restores our dreams

"The Lord is close to the brokenhearted and saves those who are crushed in spirit."
(Psalm 34:18 NIV)

prologue

"We're lost." Stephen tossed the words at Sam's back. "Hey! Did you hear what I said?" Probably not. Sam tromped through the underbrush as if he was fifteen, not ten, crunching fallen leaves and twigs with each step and bending small seedlings under his brown boots, the laces of one trailing in the dirt.

Once Sam crested the side of the ravine they'd been walking along, he stopped and turned to face Stephen, revealing a sunburned nose. "We are not lost."

So his brother had heard him—he'd just ignored him until he wanted to talk. Stephen scrambled up beside Sam, wiping away the sweat that had gathered on his forehead. "Do you know where we are?"

"Not yet." Sam pushed up his Dallas Cowboys Super Bowl baseball cap and scanned right, then left. "Give me a minute and I'll figure it out."

"Well, if we don't know where we are, and if we don't know where we're going, we're lost."

"I told ya, we're on an adventure. If we're exploring, then we're not lost." Sam pulled a crumpled bag of beef jerky from his jeans pocket, offering it to Stephen before taking a few pieces for himself. "We're discovering new things. New places."

Just sniffing the salty tang of the leathery jerky made Stephen's mouth water. "So far the only things we've discovered are a patch of poison ivy, an empty bird's nest, and how long we can walk and not find camp. Dad's gonna let us have it when we get back—if we ever figure out how to do that."

His brother scratched at a mosquito bite on his neck, causing all the itchy spots on Stephen's body to demand attention.

"We'll find it. Do you remember seeing any weird trees or big rocks while we were hiking this morning?"

"I dunno. Where's the creek?" Stephen turned a slow three-sixty. "I know our campsite is somewhere along the creek."

"Yep. And we crossed the creek once, so we—"

"Need to find it and cross it again to be going in the right direction."

"See? We'll figure this out." Sam pulled his canvas-covered canteen around to the front of his body. "Better have some water before we get started again."

"I drank all mine."

"I'll share mine with you—but don't finish it."

Stephen gnawed on the teriyaki-flavored beef jerky, periodically taking small sips of lukewarm water that pushed back the thirst building in his throat. The sun filtered down between the branches of the trees, but even with the lingering coolness of the Pennsylvania mountain air, sweat dampened Stephen's gray cotton T-shirt. "How long have we been hiking?"

"I don't know. I left my watch in my sleeping bag."

"Mom probably made breakfast already—and she promised us blueberry pancakes and bacon." He swallowed a hunk of jerky. "This stuff tastes like I'm chewing on my hiking boot."

Sam sipped more water, wiping his mouth with the back of his hand and leaving a streak of dirt across his chin. "It's this or nothing."

Why had he listened to Sam's "let's go exploring" suggestion this morning? A hike sounded like a good idea then—tromp around the woods a bit instead of sitting around, staring at the remains of last night's campfire while Mom and Dad still slept in the tent. Sam had promised they'd be back before their parents woke up.

Getting lost hadn't been part of the plan.

"Do you think they're going to go tell the ranger? Maybe get a search party?"

"We've only been gone a couple of hours." Sam rolled his eyes, positioning his cap backward on his head. "They won't do anything like that until it's getting dark and we're not back . . ."

"But we'll be back to camp before then, right?"

"Sure we will." Sam hooked his arm over Stephen's shoulders. "It's not even lunchtime yet."

After tucking the now-empty plastic bag in his pocket, Sam pointed toward the steep hill off toward their left. "We're going that way."

"Did we go downhill on the way out of camp, Sam?"

"I think . . . so." His brother had already scrabbled partway up the hillside, his voice floating back to Stephen in short puffs. "I want to get higher . . . maybe we'll see something . . . from up there."

He started to follow, Sam's feet sending small rocks and clods of dirt skittering down the side of the hill and into his face. Stephen coughed, pausing to put some space between him and his brother before resuming the ascent. Maybe when they got to the top of that ridge, they'd recognize something. Maybe they'd see their campsite. Or a big sign saying THIS WAY BACK TO MOM AND DAD.

When his foot slipped on some loose rocks in a patch of scree, Stephen went down hard, his chin hitting something sharp. He bit his tongue, tasting the metallic flavor of blood, and lay with his face sideways in the dirt, leaves, and stones for a few seconds.

"Sam!" His voice was muffled as he held his hand over his chin, his fingers warm and wet. He tilted his head, watching his brother put more distance between them. *"Sam!"*

Sam paused, looking back over his shoulder. The sight of Stephen sprawled on the side of the hill prompted Sam to half run, half slide back down. Stephen closed his eyes against another shower of debris.

Sam crouched beside him. Against the sunburn on his nose, his face looked white. "You're bleeding."

Stephen swallowed the taste of salt and iron. "Yeah. Figured. I banged my chin on a rock or something."

"You want me to look at it?"

Sam hated blood even more than Stephen did. "There's nothing you can do about it. Didja bring a bandana with you?"

"Yeah." Sam pulled a folded red bandana out of his back pocket and handed it to Stephen, who pressed it against his chin, exhaling with a sharp hiss.

"Mom would say to rinse that out."

"Well, first it's gotta stop bleeding."

"Let me see your hand." As Stephen switched hands and held the material to his chin, his brother poured a bit of the tepid water from the canteen onto his fingers. "Think you're gonna need stitches?"

"Maybe." Stephen sniffed, then tried to cover up his tears

with a cough. "Got some dust and stuff in my mouth. You got needle and thread with you?"

"I'm not sewing—" Sam's wide-eyed gaze collided with Stephen's, and he smirked as he realized his brother's joke. "I'm sorry, Stephen."

"For what?"

"For suggesting this hike. We're lost and we missed breakfast and now your chin's busted—"

"Hey, did you think I was gonna let you go hiking by yourself? The Ames brothers stick together, right?"

"Right. And so long as we stick together now, we'll be okay. Right?"

"Right." Stephen held up his right hand, which was damp and still streaked with blood, as Sam mirrored his action with his left hand, which was caked with dirt from his skid down the side of the hill. They did their right-hand-left-hand high five, followed by a quick low handclasp.

Stephen dabbed at the wound. "I'll be okay. Let's get going."

"You sure?"

"Yeah. The sooner we get started, the sooner we get back to camp."

"I'll take it slow."

"Don't worry about it. I can keep up with you."

one

Six minutes.

Surely six minutes was enough time to propose, wasn't it? Returning to where he and Elissa first met seemed so romantic—but Stephen hadn't factored in Breckenridge's high-speed ski lifts.

As the chair lift hit the back of his knees, Stephen settled into the unpadded metal seat. Elissa snuggled next to him, leaning up and brushing a kiss against his jaw. The soft caress of her lips invited him to wrap his arm around her, anchoring his ratcheted-up heart rate to the reality that he wanted to marry this woman. He blew out a huff of air, releasing his death grip on the protective guardrail.

The time was right.

"This was such a good idea, Stephen, riding the ski lift in the summer. You always make our dates fun. I love being with you—I can relax. No pressure." Elissa's husky voice pulled him from his mental mathematics. "It looks so different without any snow, but this reminds me of how we met."

He brushed long strands of her brown hair away from her face. "Only that day we were wearing ski boots and parkas and helmets—and I didn't get to see how absolutely stunning you are until dinner that night."

"Flatterer." Elissa pressed her full lips against his.

Stephen inhaled the scent of Elissa's spicy perfume, savoring the warmth of her mouth and her unreserved affection. It was one of the things he loved most about the woman in his arms— one of the many reasons he wanted to marry her. With Elissa, he knew he was loved.

Elissa lifted her right hand, tilting her wrist so she could admire the tourmaline and silver bracelet he'd bought her just before suggesting the ski lift ride.

As they ascended the mountain, they left behind Brecken-ridge's annual art festival. The parking lots and side roads were packed with cars and trucks, and the trendy mountain town teemed with people strolling through the various craft booths. The jewelry artisan had stood in one of the white tents along the main street, insisting it was as if he'd made the bracelet just for her. By presenting her with one piece of jewelry, Stephen hoped the diamond ring he'd slip on her finger during the next few minutes would all the more surprise Elissa. An expensive decoy, but well worth it. After six months, he knew the woman beside him—and jewelry was her love language.

Stephen swallowed, fighting against the constriction in his throat. This was good. He was ready to move forward. He couldn't wait to see the surprise in Elissa's eyes—the gleam of joy tinged with love as she said yes when he proposed. She always enjoyed it when he surprised her with flowers or a card—a proposal would top all of those.

Slipping his left hand into his jean jacket pocket, Stephen ensured the ring was safe. He'd lugged it around all day tucked in a beribboned box in his well-worn backpack as they browsed the different craftsmen's stalls, switching the ring to his pocket during a supposed bathroom break before he purchased their lift tickets.

After all, if Prince William of England could hike all over Africa carrying some world-renowned family heirloom in a rucksack, waiting for the right moment to propose to his precious Kate, why couldn't Stephen sling a pack over his shoulder and plan a proposal in the Colorado mountains?

And thank you, Elissa, for the fact that I even know that bit of royal trivia. Every woman wants a bit of fairy tale coming true in her life, which probably explained why Elissa followed three different blogs about the future queen of England.

Breckenridge didn't qualify as remote terrain—even if his '66 Mustang was parked in the farthest lot from the main street running through town.

Even as Elissa leaned closer, he pulled away, running his thumb along her bottom lip as she pretended to pout. "As much as I would enjoy kissing you the entire ride up and back down the mountain, I need to control myself for a few minutes."

"Afraid we'll fall out of the chair?"

"No . . . I just—" Why were the words evading him now? He'd practiced the proposal all week, wanting it to be perfect. A memory Elissa would treasure. "I want to talk about . . . I mean, you know I love you . . . and I want to ask you—"

Wait. He wanted to give Elissa the ring as he asked her to marry him. Stephen fumbled with his coat pocket. Maybe by the time he started talking again, he wouldn't stumble over his words like a middle-schooler asking a girl to a dance for the first time. He sucked in a breath. *Relax.* He could do this. "Elissa, would you marry me?"

"What?" Elissa half-turned to watch him, her sculpted brows furrowed over her smoky brown eyes as he pulled the ring from its hiding place. "You're not . . . you're not proposing, are you, Stephen?"

"Yes . . . I am. I did." He'd asked her to marry him. Not flawless, like the half-carat diamond, but he'd proposed.

Wait—wasn't he supposed to ask the question? And wasn't Elissa supposed to say yes? He raised his hand and offered the ring to Elissa. Realized he held the square-cut diamond so that it was hidden from view. Repositioned it so the gem glinted in the late-summer sunlight.

Elissa leaned away from him, one hand gripping the base of the seat. "Why are you asking me to marry you?"

What happened to a simple *yes*? Why wasn't she throwing herself into his arms, causing the lift to sway back and forth, exclaiming over the ring, and kissing him again? Okay, so he'd left his polished proposal at the base of the mountain, but still . . .

With the ring suspended between them, Stephen tried again, ignoring how his heart pounded in his chest like thunder during an afternoon storm. "Elissa, you are amazing. Beautiful. I love being with you. I love you. Will you marry me?"

"What ever gave you the idea that I was ready for you to propose? We've been dating for barely six months!"

He hadn't prepared for a no. Hadn't prepared for her to recoil, to refuse to even look at the ring, much less reject it.

"Stephen." Her warm hand covered his cold fingers. "You're wonderful. I've had a blast the last six months. But—" Her eyes narrowed and she seemed to search for the right words. "—we never even talked about getting married. Where is this coming from?"

He still held the ring out to Elissa, gripping it so it wouldn't slip from his fingers and plummet onto the mountainside below. "Six months is long enough for me to know—"

"To know what? For us to know we want to spend the rest of

our lives together?" Elissa closed her eyes, pressing her fingertips against her temple. "If you knew me at all, you'd know this is not how to propose. Or when."

"I do know you. I know how much you love your work at the boutique. I know how you balance your books to the penny—and never file a paper but can find whatever you need to from all those piles in your office. I know that if anyone took you on in trivia about Kate and William they'd be obliterated."

"That's all information—not what you build a lifetime commitment on." Her eyes skimmed over the ring he'd spent hours selecting. "Please, put the ring away. My answer is no."

"No, you don't want to marry me now—or no, you don't want to marry me ever?"

"Stephen, have you listened to anything I've said the last six months? We've had fun. I like hanging with you. What part of that implies that I'm ready to marry you? I'm still getting my boutique established—"

"Are you worried about finances? We'll be fine. I told you, as soon as the company lands that contract to refurbish the old office building in Denver, I'll get a promotion."

"This isn't about money. This is about our relationship. We've been having *fun*. Skiing. Going to dinner. Hiking . . . but no one said *marriage*." She closed her eyes again, her throat working as if she was swallowing back words. When she spoke again, her voice was soft. Controlled. "Not until today anyway. And that's a topic that should be discussed by a man and a woman before anyone proposes."

"I wanted to surprise you. Propose. Go to dinner. Start making plans."

"Yes, I like surprises—when you brought me flowers unexpectedly. But when it comes to forever and ever, amen—you know I'm a planner. Or at least I thought you did."

Silence settled between them as the chair lift rounded the station and began the descent. Stephen tucked the ring into the small upper pocket of his jacket, buttoning it closed. What could he say? *I'm sorry I proposed? Forget I said anything?* Heat flared up his neck and across his face. If only he could jump out of the chair. Surely a broken leg or two wasn't any more painful than being rejected by Elissa. How would they survive the two-and-a-half-hour drive back to Fort Collins? He'd envisioned dinner overflowing with laughter and all the what-ifs and maybes that go with planning a wedding. Holding Elissa's hand on the drive back, humming along as she sang a duet with Adele on the radio. Insisting on a brief engagement because he was tired of going to his studio apartment after dropping Elissa off at her condo. But now . . .

Elissa sat as far away from him as she could, huddled in the corner of the chair lift. If she wasn't careful, she'd fall off before they reached the base of the mountain. When she spoke again, her words were hesitant. "Stephen, I don't know if I have the right to say this now—"

"I'm listening." Stephen braced himself for whatever would come next. He didn't expect an emotional about-face.

"You say you love me—but I have to wonder what's driving you to propose."

He twisted in the chair lift, reaching for her hand. "I do love you—"

"Let me finish. Please." Elissa shook her head, her hand worrying the collar of her sweater. "I don't know how to explain it, but you always seem like you're looking for something . . . or waiting for someone. I can't explain it. But I wonder if you want me to fill in for someone else. An old girlfriend, maybe."

"There's no old girlfriend, Elissa." His shoulders sagged. This conversation was useless.

Once they reached the bottom of the mountain again, Elissa scooted forward, leaping from the chair as it slowed before continuing its cycle back up the mountain. He straightened his shoulders, easing a breath out between clenched teeth. "I asked and you . . . answered. I think it's best if we just go home."

It was going to be a long, cold drive back to Fort Collins.

"Fine."

His iPhone, which he'd muted, vibrated in his back pocket. After a quick glance at the display, he took a step away from Elissa. "Excuse me for a minute—this is my boss. It's probably about the new contract." At least something was going right today.

"Go ahead." She tucked her hands in the pockets of her white sweater jacket and walked away.

Would she keep going until she got all the way to his Mustang? Stephen turned away, refusing to watch. "Hello, Mr. Talbott. What can I do for you, sir?"

......◆......

Six thirty in the morning—what an ungodly time to meet his boss, especially since he'd stared at his ceiling most of the night, replaying Elissa's rejection and their silent ride back to Fort Collins.

Not even bothering to turn on his office lights, Stephen tossed his leather attaché case onto the chair behind his desk. He could only hope Mr. Talbott had coffee brewing in the conference room. One cup gulped down while he shaved wasn't going to cut it today.

"Good morning, sir." Stephen's voice seemed to echo in the large glass-enclosed room. Where was everyone else? The elongated rectangular table could seat an even dozen, but only he and his boss occupied the room.

"Sit down, Stephen, sit down." The man motioned Stephen to the high-backed leather chair to his right, where an insulated cup of Starbucks waited. "I needed you for a pre-meeting."

"A pre-meeting?" The warmth of the coffee seeped into his palm but did nothing to cut the chill that settled along the back of his neck. What was up?

"No sense in dillydallying. We didn't get the contract."

"That's impossible—our preliminary discussions bordered on a guarantee—"

"Doesn't matter—the only thing that matters is who gets the final approval, and it wasn't us." His boss removed his silver wire-framed glasses, rubbing his bloodshot eyes. "The company can't weather a hit like this, not with the economy we're in."

"What does that mean—practically?" Setting aside his coffee, Stephen braced his hands on the flat surface of the table.

"It means layoffs. I've avoided it as long as I could, but I've got to cut costs until we get more business. I hate to do it, but Jenkins has to go. As my lead architect, you—"

"Jenkins? He's got a wife and twin preschoolers. And if the office grapevine is correct, baby number three is on the way."

"Like I said, I hate to do it—but this is business. Jenkins was the last architect hired, so he's the first to go." His boss broke eye contact. "I'll talk to him before the employee staff meeting this morning. I'm also going to ask Gilberts to go half-time."

Stephen couldn't push his mind past his boss's announcement that he was letting Jenkins go. He tugged at his tie. What could he do? The decision was made. Another solution skittered through his head. Impossible. Mr. Talbott wouldn't approve.

But he had to try.

Ignoring how the oxygen seemed to be disappearing from the room, Stephen sat up straighter. "Excuse me, Mr.

Talbott. I have a suggestion that would allow Jenkins to keep his job."

"You do? What, exactly?"

He rushed the suggestion past the mental barricades being set up by the realistic side of his brain. "Let me take his place."

"You're joking." Mr. Talbott sat with his cup of coffee halfway to his lips.

"I'm absolutely serious—I'll take Jenkins's layoff."

"Why would you do something like that?"

He had no idea. It was irresponsible—essentially walking away from a job he loved. But the thought of Jenkins . . . his wife and kids . . . the man had a family. Stephen had a loft apartment. And no one waiting at home for him.

"I can take the hit, sir. I haven't got a wife and kids."

"I don't know what to say."

"Don't say anything to Jenkins. We have our eight o'clock meeting. Announce that I'm being cut from the team—"

Mr. Talbott dismissed his suggestion with a shake of his head. "Do you really think anyone is going to believe that?"

"Fine. Tell 'em I quit. I'll clean out my desk and be gone before anyone gets here."

"Stephen, I can't give you anything more than I was going to offer Jenkins—a month's severance. Three months' insurance."

Reality sharpened as he realized there'd be no paycheck automatically arriving in his bank account. He stood, rubbing his hands together. He could do this—he wanted to do this. Why, he didn't know. "My dad taught me to save before spending—and I don't have any debt. I'll be fine."

His boss grasped his hand in a firm handshake. "I'll write you a stellar recommendation—don't worry about that."

"Thank you, sir."

"No, thank you. I didn't think men like you existed anymore, Ames."

"Just trying to do the right thing."

"Exactly."

••••••——••••••

So much for going forward.

Stephen pushed back from the drafting table in his loft, his gaze landing on the black and white framed photograph of the Lone Cypress Tree hanging on his wall. It had been one month since Elissa rejected his proposal and his boss accepted his resignation. And what had he accomplished in the past four weeks? The diamond ring sat in the jeweler's box in his backpack, dumped just inside his bedroom closet. He'd updated his résumé, trusting Mr. Talbott's recommendation to be all the entrée he needed for interviews—and a new job. So far, not a single door had swung open for him.

And he certainly couldn't do anything about Elissa's musing that he was searching for someone. Elissa had no idea how close she was to the truth . . . and how far off. Yes, he and his brother hadn't talked in twelve years. But that didn't mean Stephen wanted to go find him—or could change anything even if, by some miracle, he did track Sam down and they managed to have a conversation. He might as well try repositioning the Rock of Gibraltar on dry land. The Ames brothers had disappeared twelve years ago—but Sam still shadowed him. No, Sam stared at him every time Stephen looked in the mirror. He just never said anything.

What was that verse in Romans? *As far as it depends on you, be at peace with all men.* Peace with Sam meant he lived his life and Stephen lived his. No communication meant no arguments. Nobody got hurt.

Returning to his desk, Stephen lost himself in sketching a building, giving himself freedom to daydream with each stroke of his artist pencils. He was unaware of the sky darkening outside the windows until the ring of his phone pulled his attention away from the designs. He picked it up, intending to silence it, when he saw the name of the caller.

His mother.

She always called three times a year: his birthday in May, Thanksgiving, Christmas. Easter, if the mood struck her. It was the end of August—the only things being celebrated were back-to-school sales.

"This is Stephen."

The seconds ticked away in silence, and then his mother cleared her throat. "Stephen?"

"Yes, it's me. Everything okay?"

More silence.

"Mom?"

"I had to call . . ." Her voice trailed off into a choked whimper.

"What's wrong? Are you sick? Did something happen?" He and his mother weren't close, but that didn't mean he wanted her facing a crisis.

"Not me . . . your brother . . ." Another whimper followed by a shaky inhale and a rush of words. "Sam was killed during his deployment in Afghanistan."

two

JANUARY 2013

This conversation wasn't going to be easy.

Haley pulled off the faded fatigue-patterned ball cap, twisting it in her hands as she approached the front counter of the gun club. Thick arms crossed over his barrel chest, her boss chatted with Frank, a club regular.

"Wes, I need to talk to you—"

The man wrapped up his conversation with a gravelly laugh before clapping the guy on his back and focusing on her. "There a problem, Hal?"

A glass display case separated them, filled with two shelves of handguns—ranging from .32 caliber to 9mm—that members could rent for use on the range or purchase. "I need to talk to you about taking maternity leave."

"Now?" Wes stopped prepping to count up the day's take. "I thought the baby wasn't due for a few more months."

"Not until April." She scuffed the faded patch of carpet with the toe of her brown cowboy boot. "But I need to get off the range."

"What's bothering you?" Wes dumped his unlit cigar in a spotless ceramic ashtray.

Haley twisted one of the strands of hair that had slipped free from her ponytail. "One of the women in the gun safety class asked if it was safe for a pregnant woman to be on the range."

"Is that all?" He dismissed her concern with a wave of his beefy hand. "Of course it's safe. We have the best ventilation system in town."

"But what about the noise? I hadn't even thought about that." Repositioning the hat on her head, she rubbed the palms of her hands along the front of her sweatpants. "I wear stuff to protect my eyes and ears—but it's not like I can soundproof my belly. I haven't read a lot of the information online, but I do know unborn babies hear sounds."

"So what are you telling me? You want to quit because your baby might be bothered by the noise?"

"I didn't say quit. But maybe . . . a leave of absence? Just to be safe?"

"You know I'm short-staffed as it is, Hal. Who am I going to get to teach your classes?"

"How about I make a few phone calls? Maybe someone at the Olympic Training Center might know of a competitive shooter looking for part-time work. And maybe I can do some shifts behind the counter. Let's both sleep on it and talk tomorrow or the next day, okay?"

A few moments later, Haley stuffed her gear bag into the backseat of her Subaru Forester, standing to stretch the ever-present ache in her lower back. One more decision to make—and no one to talk it over with. She couldn't even ask someone to help her remember to make the phone calls—except for the virtual assistant on her iPhone.

Why couldn't that woman in her class mind her own

business? Most people didn't even notice she was pregnant, especially when she wore one of Sam's baggy chamois shirts.

Once on the road, Haley shifted in the seat, one hand on the steering wheel, the other hand holding a Three Musketeers bar as she tore at the silver wrapper with her teeth. Even as she inhaled the first whiff of sugary chocolate, she promised herself something healthy for dinner when she got home. Like a banana. Wait. Did she have any bananas? Did she have any fresh fruit at all?

The Forester's in-dash clock declared it was nine thirty. "Sorry, buddy." She patted her rounded tummy underneath her cotton henley top. "But it's not like you're running on a regular schedule in there—not the way you like to roll around right when I want to go to sleep."

Only a few more miles and she'd be home. Was it only two months ago that she'd signed on the multiple dotted lines and bought a house? When she stared down the woman in the mirror brushing her teeth twice a day it took a few seconds before she recognized herself.

Owning a home was one thing.

Being pregnant . . . well, by the time she got used to that life-and-body-altering idea, the baby would be here and she'd be wrestling with the up-close-and-personal reality of motherhood.

And now, four and a half months later, she still shifted under the heaviness of the word *widow*. There was no dodging the truth. But when would the nightmare of Sam's death stop slapping her awake in the early hours of the morning?

Haley rolled her shoulders—backward, forward—in an attempt to ease the tautness that had settled right between her shoulder blades. Until tonight, work had given her a respite from thinking about the what-ifs and the what-nows stalking her. She usually got a kick out of teaching the weekly women's gun safety class.

But not tonight.

Doubt had followed her out to her car and settled in the passenger seat beside her. Some trained professional she was—she hadn't once thought about how being on the range might affect her unborn son. But then, hearing the "Mrs. Ames, we're sorry to inform you . . ." speech from the military representatives four months ago had muted every other reality in her life—even her pregnancy. What kind of mother didn't go to her first OB appointment until she was sixteen weeks pregnant? Had she been too relaxed about being on the range?

Haley crumbled the candy bar wrapper and stuffed it beneath her seat. She hadn't enjoyed a single bite. After months of spending her days staring into the bottom of a bucket—or worse, the toilet—she could eat again, and she wasn't even paying attention.

As if a Three Musketeers bar would give her anything more than—what?—two minutes of enjoyment. Not that something as temporary as a sugar rush mattered anymore. She needed to take care of, well, *everything*—and that included the baby. Her son. Sam's son. And if it meant starting to act as though she was pregnant and taking a leave from her job, then that's what she'd do.

But first she'd grab a banana or a bowl of cereal—something—to eat when she got home. And she needed to surf some of the pregnancy websites she'd found when she first realized she was pregnant. Her friends with kids said there was lots of good information available on the sites. But had they meant the slideshow labeled "Poppy seed to pumpkin: How big is your baby"? Imagining her unborn child as an ear of corn was odd enough. But would she ever get used to the thought that by the end of this pregnancy, she'd be carrying around something—*someone*— the size of a small pumpkin?

Sam would have laughed at the entire fruits-and-veggies slideshow, probably juggled a few of the oranges and apples in the fruit bowl—if they had any—to make Haley laugh, and then suggested they go out to eat.

Haley pulled the car in front of the house—her home—put the vehicle in park, and cut the engine, closing her eyes and tilting her head as if to catch the echo of Sam's laugh. Yes. She still remembered her husband's low, rumbling chuckle that created a crooked half smile and warmed his chicory-brown eyes.

She needed to remember Sam's laugh.

Half in and half out of the car, Haley froze. Why was a Mustang parked in her driveway? Had one of Sam's army friends come to check up on her? But none of them drove a Mustang— Sam's dream car.

She reached over to grab her gun case from the backseat, stilling when a movement on her front porch caught her eye. Who was that backlit by her porch light? Most likely a man, based on the width of the shoulders. She left the gun case where it was, bringing her hand back to check the SIG Sauer 9mm holstered on her belt, hidden by her shirt. Was she overreacting? Probably. But better armed and safe than caught unaware and sorry.

She stepped out of her car, keeping the Forester's front end between her and the house. The heels of her boots tapped on the cul-de-sac's asphalt, and she forced herself to steady her breathing, small white puffs of air appearing with each exhale. A man stood in the pale yellow halo cast by her front porch light. His face was hidden by the darkness . . . but the set of his shoulders, his height, reminded her of . . .

"Sam?" Even as she whispered his name, Haley strained to see past the shadows. It wasn't possible . . . was it? She'd been confronted by a Bereavement Team. Endured alone the rain on the tarmac at Dover, Delaware, when Sam's body came off a plane in a flag-draped coffin. Stood beside his grave surrounded by her family, Sam's mother clinging to her hand, while an army chaplain she barely knew talked about God's grace being sufficient . . .

Haley moved around the car and stumbled toward the specter of her husband as he stepped off the porch.

"Haley—Haley Ames? I'm—"

She would know her husband's voice anywhere.

With a strangled cry, Haley launched herself into the shelter of Sam's arms. "Sam . . . Sam . . . how—"

She'd told herself to wait . . . to not think during the funeral, or about the future without Sam. She hadn't taken a true, complete breath in months. If she sifted through and measured everything she'd lost, she'd become nothing more than one unending, keening wail. She inhaled. Exhaled. The brittleness around her heart began to splinter. Sam was home. *Home.* His heart beat against the palm of her hand, which she'd pressed against his chest. Maybe now her heart would find the right rhythm again.

• • • • • ◆ • • • •

She didn't know.

Even as Haley Ames threw herself into his arms, Stephen staggered back under the weight of realizing she didn't know he existed. Neither his brother nor his mother had told her that Sam had an identical twin brother.

They'd left that job for him.

For a moment, she clung to him, her body shaking—the silence more painful than if she'd sobbed so that the neighbors came running out of their houses. Stephen's arms hung at his sides. He didn't dare comfort this woman—not when the first words he spoke would rend her wound open again.

He cleared his throat. Tried to step back, to put some space between them. "Haley, I'm sorry . . . I'm not Sam. I'm his brother, Stephen."

No response. He tried again. "Haley—I'm Sam's brother, Stephen."

She pushed away from him, her movements jerky. "What?" Her expression twisted around the question. "Sam? What are you saying? You don't have a brother—"

"Yes, I do—I mean, yes, he does. I'm Sam's twin brother. My mother—our mother told me that Sam was killed in Afghanistan. That's why I decided to contact you—"

She backed away from him, her steps unsteady, her eyes wide in the moonlit darkness. "Who are you . . . you look exactly like . . . like . . ." Her voice was high. Frail.

"I know this is a shock. I didn't know Sam hadn't told you about me—"

"Stop talking. Now." She reached behind her back and then positioned her arm beside her right leg. "I don't know who you are or why you look like Sam, but I'm telling you this: I have a gun and I know how to use it. Get out of here."

"Let me explain." A sharp metallic click stopped Stephen before he could find a way to unravel who he was from who Haley thought he was.

"I've released the safety on my gun." Haley took another step back, raising her arms so he could see the gun pointed halfway between his feet and his knees. "Leave. Now."

She was either bluffing or ready to put a hole in him.

Stephen lifted his hands in the universal sign of surrender. "I'm going." He shifted his position in the direction of his Mustang, her eyes tracking him. "Just one thing."

She turned, her aim straight and sure, as he moved right, one slow step at a time, giving her a wide berth. But she didn't respond to his statement.

"I left my, uh, business card tucked in your screen door. Will you at least think about calling me so we can talk?"

Silence followed him as he rounded the front of his car. Opened the driver's-side door. Ducked his head and climbed inside, the chill of the Colorado night air following him into the car. He knew Sam's widow watched him, could almost feel the heat of her eyes trained on him through the car windows—could almost hear the measured pace of her breathing, until he slid behind the wheel and shut the door. Locked it. She remained still as he started the engine and backed out of the driveway. In the rearview mirror as he pulled away, Stephen saw her walk toward the house, shoulders hunched, arms crossed over her waist.

Wait a minute.

There was something eluding him . . . something not right, beyond the fact that Sam's widow had just threatened to shoot him. He hadn't expected a warm "Where have you been all these years?" welcome, but he hadn't imagined being threatened by a pistol-packing mama either.

Mama.

Sam's widow was pregnant.

The few moments that Haley Ames clung to him something had felt . . . *odd* about their one-sided embrace. She was tall. Slender. And yet the woman had a belly. There was no other way to say it. Not a "What have you been eating since Sam died?" kind of weight gain . . . but a firm tummy that indicated pregnancy. Not that Stephen knew a lot about pregnant women. But holding Haley reminded him of hugging his stepmother, Gina, when she'd been pregnant with his half brother, Pete.

What do I do now, God?

Stephen's hand clenched and unclenched around the cool steering wheel. He resisted the urge to slow down, pull the car into the next driveway, turn around, and head back to Haley's house. And then what? Knock on the door, wait for her to answer, and hope she didn't shoot him before he asked her—what? *When is the baby due?*

He'd get settled in his hotel room. Regroup. Pray. And maybe figure out a way to approach his armed and angry sister-in-law tomorrow.

·•◦••·• ◼ •··◦•·

Sam did not have a brother.

He didn't. He would have told her. Husbands and wives told each other things like that, didn't they?

As if she had any right to hold Sam to a standard of honesty.

Haley curled up under a white and gray rugby-striped blanket in the middle of the faded blue corduroy couch that she and Sam had bought off Craigslist, clutching her cell phone to her chest. In the background, John Wayne discovered Maureen O'Hara hiding in his family's cottage. How many hours of movies had filled the backdrop of her life since Sam had died? What had once helped her deal with Sam's back-to-back deployments—fill the empty apartment with a movie . . . and another . . . and another—was now a daily ritual. Anything for background noise—even life in black and white, with a disgraced boxer who escaped his demons by traveling home to Ireland.

She needed to call her mother-in-law.

Right.

She'd call Miriam at ten thirty at night—eleven thirty in Oklahoma, where she lived—wake her up, and ask, "You don't have another child that you and Sam forgot to tell me about, do you? A son who looks just like Sam?"

Absurd.

Gathering the edges of the blanket closer, she closed her eyes—and stared down the image of a man who walked like her husband. Sounded like her husband. Who had her husband's face.

In all the months since a trio of somber men in military uniform had shown up at her door to inform her that Sam had been killed, she'd never once dreamed of him—no matter how many nights she lay in bed and begged God for a glimpse of her husband. And now, when she was wide awake, he had walked toward her.

But he wasn't Sam.

Sam had died last August. And what had happened tonight didn't alter that reality.

Four people had answers. One, she had buried. One, she had chased away at gunpoint. Then there was Sam's father—whom she'd never even talked to. That left her mother-in-law.

She needed to make the call. Get it over with.

As the shrill sound of the phone rang in her ear, Haley prayed that Sam's mother would answer the phone. If not, what would she do? Leave a message? *Hi, Miriam. This is Haley. I wanted to ask you if Sam had a twin brother?*

Miriam Ames's half-asleep "Hello?" interrupted Haley's practice conversation.

"Miriam, it's Haley. I'm sorry to call so late."

"Oh, Haley." It sounded as if her mother-in-law was moving around in bed—maybe sitting up. "Honey, you know you can call me anytime. Is the baby keeping you awake?"

More like an unwanted apparition.

"I'm sleeping okay." She was—when she was able to fall asleep. She shoved her hair back from her face. "I don't know how to ask this. I mean, you're going to think I'm certifiable—"

Miriam's sharp inhale should have warned her, told her to tuck her heart away. Prepare for the blow of the unwanted but expected truth. "Did he call you?"

"Did who call me?"

"Sam's twin brother, Stephen."

She'd read about how people felt as if they'd been verbally punched in the gut. But Miriam's statement felt more like something—someone—had strangled the breath from her throat.

Was she the only person speaking truth tonight? "Sam doesn't have a twin brother."

As if she should have been telling Sam's *mother* any such thing.

The silence between them dissolved into muffled sobs.

"Does he?" Her whispered question couldn't pierce the woman's grief. She tried again, reining in her emotions and raising her voice. "Sam has a twin brother?"

"Yes. Sam never talked about Stephen—" Miriam broke off again, any attempt to talk lost in her tears, forcing Haley to wait. "—and it wasn't my place to tell you if he didn't."

Dear God, help me, help me.

Since Sam's death, all of her prayers had been reduced to that one-sentence plea. God was all-knowing. All-powerful. His thoughts were higher than hers—he could decipher all the hidden meanings in six words. Six syllables.

"Why wouldn't Sam tell me about . . . Stephen?"

"They haven't spoken to each other in years—since they were eighteen. It's as if they erased each other from their lives. I kept hoping and praying they'd figure out a way to reconcile . . . but it never happened."

"Why would brothers—twins—refuse to speak to each other?" Haley pushed off the couch, the blanket puddling at her feet. She needed to walk. Think. She needed answers.

Miriam's reply escaped as a sigh. "Haley, it's such a long, convoluted story. What did Stephen tell you?"

"Nothing." Her crack of laughter brought her up short. "I threatened to shoot him."

"What?"

"I didn't know who he was. How could I?" Haley paced between the living room and the kitchen. She wouldn't find what she was looking for in either place. "Sam didn't tell me that he had a twin brother. I just wanted him . . . gone."

"Oh, Haley, I'm so sorry. This is my fault. I called and told Stephen that Sam was killed. I thought he had a right to know, even if they were estranged. Stephen refused to come to the funeral—said it would shock too many people if he walked into the church."

He'd been right about that. The strength that enabled Haley to stand, to not shed a tear, would have shattered if the man she saw tonight had walked into the church and stood beside Sam's casket.

"And then . . . well, it's been four months. I thought Stephen decided to leave things be."

"You haven't talked to him since then?"

"No. We're . . . not close. And I didn't call him during the holidays—I just couldn't."

Twilight Zone. That was it. She'd been transported to a present-day *Twilight Zone.* There was no other way to explain the fact that she was widowed and pregnant, and that her husband's twin brother had shown up on her doorstep tonight, unknown and unannounced. And now her mother-in-law stated, "We're not close," as if she were talking about the mail carrier.

Miriam's voice pulled her back to the harsh glare of reality. "The divorce—it did awful things to our family."

"I have to go." Haley walked over to where she'd left the blanket, picking it up and clutching it to her chest.

"Haley, let me explain—"

"Not tonight. Please." Haley curled into the corner of the couch. "We'll talk tomorrow."

"I'm so, so sorry."

She disconnected without saying good-bye, but not before cutting off the sound of tears in Miriam's voice.

Miriam was sorry. Would Sam be sorry that the secret he'd kept from her had walked into her life, a living, breathing reflection of him?

Secrets. How she hated them.

three

·····•·····•·····•·····•·····

Just do the next thing.

How many times since becoming a widow had Haley pushed herself forward by saying, "Just do the next thing"? The next thing. And the next. Bury her husband. Confirm her pregnancy. Move out of her apartment. Go to work. Come home. Try to sleep. Go to work the next day. She was an expert at doing the next thing. By saying that simple phrase enough times and staying on emotional autopilot, she got through each day. The not-so-funny thing was, the heaviness on her shoulders never eased.

Not that she would complain. This was her life—and she would manage. Somehow.

And now, here she sat at her got-it-at-a-bargain-price dining room table with Claire beside her, staring down the next "next thing," her hand motionless on the computer keyboard. On the TV, John Wayne held a muted conversation with Jim Hutton in one of her favorite non-Western movies, *Hellfighters*. Why didn't she remember to turn the TV off before Claire arrived? She'd have avoided the whole "How old is this movie, anyway? Did you see the cars they're driving? Their clothes?" drill. And she'd have avoided the way her best friend tried to hide her sympathy behind forced casualness. For all her kindness, how could Claire, who was more than busy with her job as a front-desk receptionist at the Broadmoor, understand the need to block out silence?

"You have to pick a childbirth class, Haley." Claire's voice softened, wrapping around Haley's shoulders like a favorite sweater. Comfortable. Never too tight.

"I know. Why are there so many choices?" And why did she have to go sit in a class with other moms-to-be—and dads-to-be? And would anyone understand the invisible "It's all on me" albatross hung around her neck the day Sam died? "I'm a little distracted because I got a letter from the homeowners' association telling me that I need to edge my lawn."

"What? It's January—no one edges their lawn in Colorado in January."

"You know that and I know that—but I don't think I'm dealing with a rational person. I can accept the warning to turn my porch light off—even if it does freak me out a bit that some guy must be driving around at night checking out porch lights. But it feels like they're trying to find things to hassle me about." Haley motioned toward the garage. "And I still haven't unpacked the Great Wall of Boxes—"

"The what?"

"All the boxes piled up in my garage. And my fence is . . . leaning or something. My bathroom toilet is leaking. The sliding glass doors don't want to slide. The shutters need to be repainted—not to mention I didn't like some of the room colors when I moved in, and I still don't. Orange only works on a pumpkin."

"Haley, you know some of the guys will help you. Let me have Finn organize a work crew."

"I was talking out loud, Claire, not asking for help. Everyone's busy—they have their own families to take care of." She forced herself to refocus on the list of childbirth classes. "Sorry. We were talking about options."

"Whichever works for you, I'll go with you."

"You have a husband, not to mention a job. And if I remember correctly, weren't you talking about training for a marathon? You don't have to take care of me."

"I've already told Finn I'm your coach. It's all settled. I talked to my supervisor and explained the situation, and she's willing to adjust my shifts so I can go to your classes." Claire commandeered the mouse, moving the cursor along the listings. "What about the one offered at the hospital? It's close."

Haley nodded as Claire clicked on the link. Stared at the web page.

"Or . . . there's always the one offered at that instructor's home. She has a lot of experience." Claire switched back to the previous web page. The black and white images of smiling, peace-filled women holding newborns blurred before Haley's eyes.

Just do the next thing.

This wasn't about having the baby. Yet. She was doing what she needed to do to be ready when it was time to have the baby. To be a mom. By herself. Without her husband, who didn't—

Charm bracelet jangling, Claire rested her hand over Haley's where it sat next to the computer keyboard. "I'll be with you, Haley."

"I know."

"For the classes. For labor and delivery. Everything." Claire squeezed her hand.

"I hate to ask you to do all this, Claire." Haley scraped together her confidence, which had been undermined just by looking at web photos. "I can manage."

"You're kidding, right?" Claire grabbed her by the shoulders—gently—and turned Haley to face her. "You are not having your baby alone. End of discussion. Moving on."

Haley allowed Claire to hug her, leaning into her for the briefest of seconds before squaring her shoulders. Inhaling. Exhaling. "Now all I need to do is figure out what kind of classes to take. What do you think?"

"No experience in this category, my friend." Claire masked the shadows Haley glimpsed in her hazel eyes by leaning forward to study the screen, causing her shoulder-length black hair to fall forward like a shield. "So, we're back to you: What do you want to do?"

Haley's troubles were no reason for her to ask careless questions. "Here's what I want: anything and anyone to ensure I have a fast, uncomplicated delivery."

"That's what every pregnant woman wants."

"Then someone should have figured it out by now." Haley closed the laptop sitting on the table with a soft click, standing to stretch her back before moving past the archway into the kitchen. Through the sliding glass doors, the solitary tree in the backyard seemed to lift its branches in supplication to the muted gray sky. "I'll look at that again later. You thirsty?"

"Sure. Hot tea?"

"For you, always. For me, soda." She pulled a Plexiglas bowl of rinsed green grapes and a smaller bowl with some mini squares of sharp cheddar cheese from the fridge. "Look, I cooked just for you."

"Rinsing fruit and opening a bag of precut cheese is not cooking."

"For me it is." She grabbed a bag of cheese-flavored Doritos out of the mostly bare pantry and set a tub of cream cheese beside it. "One of the members at the range said this is delicious."

Claire wrinkled her nose at the chips-and-dip option. "That's all yours."

"Fine." Slipping her hand beneath her long-sleeved denim top, Haley rubbed the faint tightness in her lower back. "So . . . something happened last night."

Claire stopped sorting through the wire basket on the counter that contained the few boxes of tea Haley kept on hand for her friend. "Something bad? Or something good?"

"Something . . . weird."

"Weird? Baby weird?" Claire paused, as if weighing the effect of her next question. "Being-without-Sam weird?"

Haley chewed her bottom lip, leaning back against the counter, gripping the edge of the sink. "Some guy showed up claiming to be Sam's brother."

Claire dropped the box of Constant Comment tea she'd selected, causing it to hit the floor with a dull thud. "Sam doesn't—he doesn't have a brother."

"That's what I thought." Releasing her death grip on the counter, Haley filled the electric teakettle with water, setting it on the counter and turning it on.

"Sam would have told you if he had a brother."

Claire knelt and scooped the tea packets back into the box. Haley pulled a red ceramic mug from the cabinet and placed it next to the electric kettle. She had five more just like it—a bargain at a dollar apiece. "Again—that's what I thought after meeting this guy who looks and sounds exactly like Sam. I mean, why would he have a twin brother—and not tell me?"

Claire looked up from where she knelt—why hadn't Haley swept those scattered dust bunnies and cereal and chip crumbs? "What did you say?"

"I said why would Sam not tell me—"

"No, you said *twin*."

"He's Sam's twin brother."

Claire plopped onto the floor, seeming to abandon all thoughts of cleaning up the tea bag mess. "This gets more and more bizarre."

"Welcome to my personal episode of *The Twilight Zone*. You'll have to be satisfied with a cameo appearance, as it seems I have the starring role."

"Is this guy a—what do they call it—a fraternal twin? You know, the kind that doesn't look alike?"

"He looks *exactly* like Sam."

"No, he doesn't."

"Claire, I was there." Haley refused to allow even a hint of anything—everything—she'd experienced last night to creep into her voice. "When I say 'exactly,' I mean I couldn't tell the difference."

"What?"

"He walks like Sam. Sounds like Sam. If Sam looked in a mirror, he'd see this guy. It was dark . . . but for a minute or so, I thought . . . I thought . . ."

Claire scrambled to her feet, walking over and wrapping her arms around Haley. "How awful. This guy is really Sam's twin brother?"

Haley shrugged out of the embrace. "I should have known it wasn't Sam. The guy called me 'Haley.' To Sam I was always 'Hal'—you know, like one of the guys."

"Your husband did not think of you as one of the guys!"

"You know what I mean. Anyway, I called Sam's mom last night. She confirmed it—although don't ask me why I needed her confirmation. Miriam said she couldn't tell me about Stephen before because it was up to Sam to do it. And he never did."

"What did Sam's brother say?"

A snort escaped her lips. "Not much after I threatened to shoot him if he didn't leave."

"You. Did. Not." Claire gave her space, gathering up the tea packets before tearing one open, positioning the tea bag in the mug.

"I did." She'd collapsed in some strange man's arms—who, even in the muted light, seemed to have the same cleft chin as Sam . . . the mirage had haunted her sleep all night.

"One day, Haley, you *are* going to shoot somebody. Then what?"

"Then, as my brothers would say, I'll have made 'em proud." As the teakettle whistled, Haley poured boiling water into the mug, the water hissing as it flowed over the tea bag. The scent of cinnamon and cloves wafted into the air.

"What did he do when he found himself face-to-face with your gun?"

"He left. I'll give him points for being smart." She picked up the ivory business card with brown lettering that he'd wedged between the screen and the front door. "He did leave me this."

"What? His card?" Claire scrutinized the writing. "'Stephen R. Ames. Architect. Entrepreneur.' Huh. Thinks a lot of himself, doesn't he? Lives in Fort Collins. Sam's twin brother lives in Colorado?"

"Apparently. Two hours away—and he shows up after Sam dies." As the baby moved inside of her, Haley covered her tummy with her hands. "What do I do, Claire?"

"About?"

"About this guy . . . if he shows up again?"

"Hear him out?"

"Why?"

"Because he's Sam's brother, and he's here for a reason."

"But Sam never told me about him, and he did that for a

reason." She paced the kitchen, stopping to stare out into the backyard. "Why should I get to know him now?"

"Have you prayed about it?"

"Yes. And no." Claire's burst of laughter tugged a smile across Haley's face. The first of the day.

"What do you mean, 'yes and no'?"

"If you mean have I said a formal 'Dear God, what do you want me to do about Sam's lookalike?' prayer, then no, I haven't prayed about it." She retrieved a can of Sprite from the refrigerator, taking a sip in hopes of soothing the ache in her throat. "But if you mean have I prayed in a 'God, help me, help me, help me' kind of way . . . then I've been doing that since the day I shut the door when the Bereavement Team left."

"So you have no plans to call Stephen R. Ames, architect and entrepreneur?" Claire wandered back out to the living room with Haley following her and settled on the couch, resting her bare feet on the redwood-and-pine coffee table.

"No." Haley set the chips and dip beside her on the couch cushion.

"And if he shows up here again?"

This was one of the times Haley was glad she'd perfected the tilt-head-and-raise-one-eyebrow stare. "Do you really think some guy is going to want to face the wrong end of a gun again?"

"If he's anything like Sam, he would."

·•●·—◆—·•●·

Maybe in the light of day things would go better.

Or maybe Haley Ames would just have a clearer shot at him.

Sam put the Mustang in park and gazed straight ahead, taking in the outline of the snow-covered Front Range against the pale blue of the Colorado sky. He hadn't expected an armed standoff when he'd finally taken his best friend Jared's advice to go looking for Sam's widow. He knew it wouldn't be easy, but he never imagined outright hostility.

"Pardon me for not closing my eyes, God, but the last time I was here, an irate pregnant woman threatened to shoot me. And, yes, I admit she had reason to be upset. So I'm asking for a little help here. Please let Haley listen." He stole a quick glance at the house. Muted gray siding. White shutters that needed a fresh coat of paint. Faded brown grass waiting for spring to arrive. Nobody looking out the window—armed or otherwise. All clear. "And I wouldn't mind a little heavenly protection, too."

Now, why did a scene from *Gunfight at the O.K. Corral* flash through his mind as he approached the front door? He looked heavenward. No visible angels riding shotgun in the cloudless Colorado sky.

He rang the doorbell, a short, off-key peal, and then took two steps back from the screen door, which needed some repair. Braced his shoulders and straightened his spine. A few seconds later, the front door opened halfway and Haley Ames stared him down through the worn mesh screen. Even with her body shadowed, he saw her jaw clench, heard the swift inhale. She half-lifted her hand—why? To push him away?

"You look just like Sam."

Stephen nodded. "Always have."

"When were you born?"

"May 20, 1983." He wasn't sure what the personal trivia accomplished—just looking at him proved he was Sam's twin. But he'd play along if it kept the woman on the other side of the screen door happy.

"Who are your parents?"

"Joe and Miriam Ames. They divorced when Sam and I were thirteen."

"What was Sam's full name?"

"Samuel Wilson, after the superhero the Falcon." Stephen couldn't hold back a chuckle. "My name is Stephen Rogers, after Captain America. Our dad was a real Marvel comic book fan."

Haley didn't crack a smile. Didn't even blink. "Why are you here? Now?"

He risked taking a step forward, only to have Haley step back behind the muted blue door and start to close it. "Wait. Please. Hear me out." They stared at one another, as if through shadowed glass. Now that he had her attention, how could he explain twelve years of silence? "I wanted to make things right between Sam and me."

"A bit late for that, isn't it?"

Her words, rough as unsanded wood, scraped at the wound Stephen still didn't know how to live with. He could look back and count all the days he'd lost—and could look ahead and see the same: days lost with his brother. "Yes."

"Then why are you here?"

He cleared his throat. Tried again. "I want to know who my brother became . . . and I want to help you and the baby, if I can—"

"If Sam had wanted a relationship with you—if he wanted us to have a relationship with you—he would have contacted you." The door was closing in his face. "And I—*we* don't need your help."

The barrier between him and what he'd come for was back. At least she hadn't shot him. But with her words, Haley Ames had killed any hope of his connecting with his brother.

• • • • • ◆ • • • •

Haley stood with her eyes shut, forehead pressed against the hard surface of the door, hands clenched. Maybe by the time the blood stopped pounding in her ears she would be able to forget Stephen Ames existed.

"You're not going to talk to him?"

The sound of her best friend's voice reminded her that she wasn't alone. At least, not for the moment.

"I said everything I need to say to him." Haley turned, sagging against the door and crossing her arms.

"Really? You caught up on, oh, I don't know, a dozen lost years with Sam's brother?"

It wasn't like Claire to be even slightly sarcastic. Supportive, yes. Kind, yes. "There's no reason for me to 'catch up' with that man."

"Except for the fact that he is Sam's brother—his extremely identical twin brother, from what I could see." She shrugged and offered a smile that didn't even hint at repentance. "Sorry. I peeked through the bay window."

"Mirror twin."

"What?"

"I think they're mirror twins. I looked it up this morning before you came over. Sam was left-handed. His brother's right-handed. That kind of thing." Haley pushed away from the door and reclaimed her place on the couch, dunking a chip in the cream cheese and popping it in her mouth. Crunchy. Creamy. *Yum.* Junk food was always good for what ailed her.

Claire turned her face away. "Honestly, Hal, does your doctor know what you've been eating?"

"My weight gain is fine—I have the metabolism of a hummingbird. And I drink lots of milk." She dragged another chip through the cream cheese, nibbling on it without looking at Claire.

"Never mind—it's hopeless to talk nutrition with you."

Haley waited on the couch while Claire refreshed her tea. When the baby moved, she rubbed the area with her fingers.

It seemed as if the only time she thought about her baby was when he kicked, as if to say, "Hey, I'm in here!"

Claire joined her on the couch, tucking her bare feet underneath her, perfectly manicured toes glinting a soft pink. "Question: Why can't you have one decent conversation with this guy? And then be done with him?"

"Sam didn't want a relationship with him; why should I have one?"

"One meeting." Claire held up her index finger, the fingernail painted a matching pink. "Answer a few questions. That is not a relationship."

Haley motioned to where she'd had her latest standoff with Stephen Ames. "He wants to help me."

"As I heard—sorry, wasn't trying to eavesdrop, even if I was peeking—you already declined his invitation to help you. Again, you're not starting a relationship with the man."

Haley closed the bag of Doritos, the foil crinkling. "I—I can't do it, Claire."

"What can't you do?"

"I can't look at him." Haley's voice came out small. Hollow. She closed her eyes, locking the first swell of moisture behind her eyelids. "The army shipped Sam home in a casket—a closed casket. I got a folded flag. His medals. A coroner's report that I've never read. The last time I saw Sam, he was alive—walking away from me, getting on a plane for Afghanistan. And now . . . it's as if my husband is standing in front of me again. Breathing. Talking. But it's not Sam."

Silence swallowed up her words.

Haley stared straight ahead. "Nothing to say?"

"What can I say to that, Haley?" Claire tried to blink away the tears in her eyes, but not before Haley realized she'd made her cry. "I hadn't thought about it that way."

"And yet—" Haley stifled a groan.

"What?"

"I can't help but wonder what God wants me to do." She ran her fingers through her long hair, shoving it away from her face. "I hate that question sometimes. *What would God want me to do?* It makes me think of other people . . ."

"The whole you're-not-the-only-person-in-this-equation syndrome?"

"Exactly." Haley sat her soda on the varnished surface of the coffee table, which she'd edged with multicolored tiles, twisting to face Claire. "I didn't sleep much last night. And I thought about what if . . . what if two of my brothers had somehow argued about . . . I don't know what. Something. And then they didn't talk to one another for years. I mean, I get that stuff like that happens. What about Jacob and Esau in the Bible?"

"I hadn't thought about it like that—"

"You weren't the one watching the clock last night. At least Jacob and Esau reconciled. But what if one of my brothers died without a chance for them to forgive each other . . ."

"To talk."

"Yeah." Haley stared into her friend's eyes. "I'm one way for Stephen to connect with his brother."

"True."

"Do you have to agree with me?"

"You usually like me to agree with you."

"About where we eat dinner. Or what movie we watch." Haley leaned forward, her elbows on her knees, her chin in her palm. "Am I going to do this?"

"I think so." Claire crossed the room and retrieved Stephen Ames's business card from the breakfast bar. "You know how to reach him."

"Okay. One phone call. One meeting." Haley stood. Chin up. Back straight. Shoulders stiff.

"Exactly."

"To answer questions."

"Yes."

"I am not becoming Stephen Ames's sister-in-law."

"Well, technically—"

"I don't think there's anything technical or legal about this. He's Sam's brother. And that's as far as it goes. I'll answer his questions this one time. And after that, he can talk to his mother."

"But they're not close, right?"

"That's not my problem." Haley took the business card from her friend, rereading the name scripted in plain block letters. "I don't have time to worry about Stephen R. Ames's family problems."

four

The pale winter sun failed to warm her as Haley shuffled through the handful of mail. Electric bill. Milk bill. Weekly neighborhood flyer. Today was her lucky day. It had been an entire week since an ivory envelope embossed in gold from the Contrails Homeowners' Association had lurked in her mailbox. Maybe Sterling Shelton III had decided to leave her alone—or perhaps the association's president was drafting one long list of infractions before mailing another letter to her.

Could she stop dreading going to get her mail—holding her breath when she peered inside her numbered section, heaving a sigh of relief when all that awaited her was normal mail, or muttering to herself when yet another letter from the homeowner's association waited inside? Maybe she should call Shelton again. Try to reason with him. But her first and only phone call had elicited nothing more than a "Read your covenants, Mrs. Ames. You signed the contract. You agreed to the covenants."

A black BMW sedan circled the cul-de-sac, the odor of burning oil staining the fresh winter air as the car stopped in front of her house with a wheeze and a rattle. Unless Sam's brother had a second car, she didn't have to worry about facing Stephen Ames until their agreed-upon dinner tonight.

"Mrs. Ames?" The man waited beside his car, the driver's-side door open. A navy blazer, patterned blue shirt, and basic blue tie gave him a professional—if monochrome—look.

Haley stumbled to a stop, Sam's coat slipping off one shoulder. "Yes?"

He shut the car door. "I'm Sterling Shelton, the president of the Contrails Homeowners' Association."

Of course you are. Haley's body flushed hot, then cold. A letter—even a letter every day of the week—was better than Shelton showing up at her house. "Is there something I can do for you, Mr. Shelton?"

"I thought maybe a face-to-face discussion might help clear up any confusion about your responsibilities as a new homeowner." He offered a smile that thinned his lips across crooked teeth, without ever reaching his dark eyes.

"There's no confusion—and you really should have called before showing up today. My schedule's full." He didn't need to know that the first thing on her list was putting a load of laundry in the washing machine, followed by a midmorning snack and unpacking one box of household stuff.

"Then perhaps you can explain why you have so many violations?" He positioned himself beside her, surveying the house. "Wrong-size house numbers. A stained driveway. Paint peeling off your shutters and porch—"

"I bought the house in this condition." The shrill tone of her voice shocked Haley. She scraped her hair from her face, swallowing the sharp retort that wouldn't change anything— especially the man's attitude. "Why didn't you address these infractions with the previous owners?"

"That doesn't concern you—you are the current homeowner." Shelton rocked back on the heels of his worn black dress shoes. "You do realize I have the authority to fine you when you're in violation of the association codes?"

First there were written threats. Now there were verbal ones? "I just moved in—I haven't even unpacked all of my boxes." If the man saw inside her garage, he'd realize she'd hardly unpacked *any* of her boxes.

"I'm a compassionate man, Mrs. Ames—but to be blunt, none of those excuses are my problem."

Haley tugged Sam's coat tight around her. A never-ending stream of letters and showing up unannounced didn't even hint at compassion. The man was throwing his weight around—and wasting her time. Haley needed to see Shelton for what he was: a bully. She couldn't deck him like her brother David had taught her to do in fifth grade, but she could keep her guard up and not let him hassle her anymore.

"Mr. Shelton, I know you are only doing your job to the best of your ability." Let him think what he wanted about that statement. As she talked, she put distance between them, leaving him at the foot of the driveway. "I am not ignoring the covenants—and will deal with the problems you point out as quickly as I can."

"I'm not finished talking—"

"But I am." She tossed him a mock salute. "Good-bye."

Back inside the house, she tossed the mail in the basket on the breakfast bar between the kitchen and the dining room and dropped her coat on the arm of the couch. She would not look outside to make certain Sterling Shelton III had left. She could only hope the man understood the meaning of *good-bye*—and resorted to writing letters again.

After the unexpected face-off with the man, Haley was thankful Wes had decided he didn't need her help behind the

counter at the gun club. The day stretched ahead of her, empty
of her regular schedule. Fine. She'd list out the home projects.
Unpack a box in the garage.

And, thanks to Claire's prodding, she'd meet with Stephen
Ames.

Powering up the television and the DVD player, she grabbed
a notepad and pen, determined to create the to-be-tackled to-do
list. *So there, Mr. Shelton!* Stretching out on the couch, the dialogue of *Hellfighters* filled the empty rooms. Imaginary people
were better than no one at all. Between the list and the almost-
memorized movie, she'd manage the hours until her meeting
with Sam's brother.

Haley doodled a row of boxes across the top of the page.
Why had she called the man and suggested they meet for dinner? Oh, that's right. Claire had guilted her into it. She repositioned herself, placing a cushion under her knees in an attempt
to get comfortable. She wasn't being fair to her friend. Claire
had made a reasonable suggestion, and she'd agreed to it.

Not that she was going to be some sort of "answer woman"
for Stephen Ames. If he wanted to know how she and Sam met
or how long they dated before they got married—fine. But if he
started asking questions about Sam's life before then . . . well,
Haley wasn't going to be much help. After they'd married, she'd
quickly learned her husband focused on *now*. When she asked
about his family—him and his mom—he glossed it over, saying
things were "typical."

The arrival of his twin brother shattered that word into mirrored shards of truths and lies—and she was left to clean up the
mess.

●•••• • ➤ • ••••●

Five fifteen. No Haley Ames. Was she going to leave him sitting in Johnny Carino's, staring at a basket of cloth-wrapped bread?

Stephen powered up his iPad, opening his Paper by Fifty-Three sketchpad app. He roughed out a tree. First the trunk, then the leafy branches. Next, he outlined a tree house.

Always the same simple tree house.

It had never occurred to him that Haley wouldn't show, although he had no reason to assume she would keep her word. Of course, he hadn't expected Haley to call him half an hour after she'd shut the door in his face, much less suggest they meet for dinner and talk. He'd been too shocked to say "What about lunch?" and had spent the rest of the day bumming around Colorado Springs, finally ending up at a Williams-Sonoma cooking store for an hour. Not that he had anywhere else to go—like a job. He had plenty of tools from Lowe's and Home Depot—he didn't have to defend the fact that he also had a well-stocked kitchen . . . well, the beginnings of a well-stocked kitchen. A guy had to relax some way. He'd limited himself to purchasing a rice cooker, an item that had been on his wish list for a while.

Stephen gulped down some ice water and was debating ordering Italian sangria when the waitress returned to check on him. But how sorry would he look if he ended up sitting in a booth, drinking by himself?

Should he call Haley? See if she'd changed her mind? He tapped the "Recent Calls" button on his phone, scrolling through to find her number.

"Sorry I'm late."

Haley's voice yanked his attention from the phone screen. She slipped into the seat across from him, even as he started to rise to his feet. Her head tilted to the side, an eyebrow arched in a silent *What are you doing?* Stephen settled back against the cushioned booth.

"I overslept." She ran her fingers through her honey-blond hair, which still looked tousled, as if she'd rushed to meet him without bothering to brush it. "I, um, started watching a movie and fell asleep."

"Understandable." Stephen paused as the waitress appeared at the table, two short brown braids framing her round face. "I've gotten all the way to water—" He motioned to the basket. "—and bread. Do you want something else to drink?"

She turned her attention to the waitress. "Sprite or Seven-Up, whatever you serve."

"And we'll need a few minutes to look at the menu, please."

By the time he finished his request, Haley was flipping through the selections, leaving him to do the same. Again. When the waitress returned, they placed their orders and then sat in silence. Haley Ames was not the chatty type.

Fine. He'd start. "Thanks for agreeing to meet with me."

"My best friend, Claire, convinced me it was the right thing to do." She unwrapped her silverware, clinking the forks and knife against the wooden table, and began folding her cloth napkin.

If he knew how to contact her best friend, he'd have thanked her. Maybe sent her flowers. "I suppose I should have called instead of just showing up at your door."

Electric-blue eyes snared his. "You don't think that would have freaked me out, picking up the phone and hearing Sam's voice on the other end? You sound exactly like him. That's what threw me the other night." Haley looked down. Smoothed out the napkin, only to start folding it again. "I mean, I know Sam is dead . . . but there I was, hearing his voice again . . ."

Stephen kept his eyes trained on Haley's fingers as they folded the cloth napkin. Fold. Unfold. Fold again. She didn't mince words. No saying Sam was "gone" or "in heaven" to soften the reality that a sniper's bullet had killed his brother. He blinked once, twice, hoping to relieve the sting of tears at the back of his eyes, the dryness gathering in his throat.

"I hadn't thought about that. And, to be honest, it never occurred to me that Sam wouldn't have told you about me."

"Did you tell people—friends, girlfriends—about Sam?"

Stephen couldn't dodge the questions in Haley's gaze. He remembered all the times he hadn't mentioned Sam, treated him as if he were the invisible man instead of an unadulterated reflection of himself. When someone asked if he had family, he usually mentioned his father, his stepmother—and Pete, his half brother. But not Sam.

Haley had no problem interpreting his silence. "I didn't think so. If you didn't tell people about Sam, why did you think he would talk about you?"

"You're his wife . . ."

"Obviously he didn't want me to know about you. Estrangement ripples out to other relationships."

His pressed his lips together. Now she was some kind of psychoanalyst? "I told my best friend, Jared, about Sam."

"One person."

Why was she excusing Sam and accusing him? Ridiculous question—she'd married Sam and didn't even know Stephen existed until last night. Beneath the table, Stephen clenched and unclenched his fists. He didn't have to justify the last twelve years of his life. That's not what this meeting was about. He just wanted answers.

"So how did you and Sam meet?"

"Oh, that." She released the napkin and moved it to her lap, then tucked a wayward strand of her hair behind her ear. "At a mutual friend's wedding. Sam was a groomsman and I was a bridesmaid—so cliché, right? One of the few times he ever saw me in a dress."

"When did you and Sam get married?"

She closed her eyes, as if mentally calculating. "It was three years last October. We got married in 2009, right before one of his deployments."

"So Sam loved being in the military?"

Her mouth twisted into the semblance of a smile. "Yes. He re-upped a few weeks before he was killed. Another two years. He was good at what he did."

"He went into the military right after high school graduation." Amazing how the memory still caused tightness in his chest.

Haley traced a droplet of condensation on the outside of her glass. "I know. He told me."

"We always talked about going to college together—getting an apartment."

"Plans change." Haley slumped back against the seat, the too-large coat she wore sliding off her shoulders. Sighed. "If my friend Claire were here she would slap me right now—and then she'd make me apologize. Well, actually, Claire's too much of a lady to slap anyone."

Was it too late to invite Claire to join them for dinner?

"But I do apologize." The smile on her face was a mere shadow of the real thing. "Claire would be proud of how quickly I recovered my manners. I'll pretend she's sitting next to me and we'll see if things go better the rest of the time."

"Did Sam deploy often?"

"Yes." She paused when their salads arrived, allowing the waitress to grind pepper over hers. Her hair shimmered in the lamplight when she bowed her head for a moment, eyes closed. Saying grace? If she was, she didn't include him in the process.

Silence settled in the booth as they ate their salads even as the conversation and laughter of other people in the restaurant ebbed and flowed, buoyed by the upbeat music piping through the building. Haley seemed content to let him handle the one-sided conversation. He asked questions. She answered them. And that would be the routine from salad to dessert. And then what? She'd exit the restaurant and never look back? He'd have a sixty-minute sound bite of his brother's life. Was that enough to fill the yawning relational gap between him and Sam? Hardly.

Stephen helped himself to more salad. "What did Sam like to do?"

"Pardon?" She paused with a forkful of lettuce in midair.

"Besides work, what did Sam like to do?"

"Um, I met him the second time when he and some buddies came to the shooting range where I work."

A laugh slipped past Stephen's take-it-one-step-at-a-time approach. "I noticed you're, um, comfortable with guns. What do you do at the range?"

"I participated in competitive pistol shooting in high school and college." For once, the distant look in Haley's eyes disappeared. "I've been teaching gun safety classes at the club."

When she didn't elaborate, Stephen moved the conversation on. "So Sam liked to shoot, too?"

"Yeah." She ate some salad, chewing for so long he wondered if that was all she was going to say. "I mean, he had to pass firearm certification—but he liked shooting for fun, too."

"Did you guys shoot together—you know, as a hobby?"

"No."

Another dead-end topic—and time for a different question. "Sam and I wrestled from middle school into high school. Do you know if he kept that up?"

"He never said."

"What did Sam do in the army exactly?"

"He was a medic."

"Wait . . . a medic?" His hoot of laughter broke the stillness in the booth once again. "Sam hated the sight of blood when we were kids."

"Guess he outgrew it."

"And aren't medics considered noncombatants? Why would a sniper—"

"Do you really think enemy snipers have a code of ethics? Don't be naïve."

"I'm not naïve—"

"Forget it." Haley shook her head, eyes closed. "Believe me, you didn't say anything I haven't thought."

How did she switch gears like that? "Did Sam plan on making the military a career—I mean, was he going to stay in until retirement?"

"I don't know. We hadn't discussed it that much. It was a possibility."

The waiter delivered their entrees: a steaming serving of sixteen-layer lasagna for him, and a trio of lasagna, chicken parmigiana, and spaghetti for Haley. After a healthy dose of grated cheese was applied over both their plates, Stephen sliced half his lasagna into small pieces, relishing the aroma of meat, marinara sauce, cheese, and Italian herbs. He looked up and locked eyes with Haley again.

"What?"

"Do you always do that?"

"What?"

"That." She waved her fork at his plate. "Cut your food up before you eat it."

"Yeah. It's somewhat grade school-ish, I know. Why?"

"Sam did that, too. He also liked to dip his potato chips in—"

"Ketchup. We started doing that when we were kids. Drove our mom crazy."

Haley turned her attention back to her meal. "For his birthday last year, I bought him some of those ketchup-flavored potato chips. He told me they weren't as good as dipping chips in the real stuff."

"He was right. Our parents said we had our own personal language when we were toddlers—no one else understood us."

"Huh." Haley seemed to file away the information. "How long have you had your car?"

"The Mustang? I bought it a couple of months ago." Back when he thought he was headed for a promotion—not volunteering for a pink slip. "It's my dream car."

"Sam's, too. He used to talk about winning the lottery and buying a '65 or '66 Mustang."

"That was always the plan."

"What do you mean?"

"Besides Marvel comics, my dad loves cars. Sam and I used to read his automotive magazines. We decided Mustangs were the coolest cars, so we were both going to get one. Sam wanted—"

"A black one."

"Yep. I said the only color for a Mustang was red."

"You didn't change your mind."

"Nope. So, Sam never got his Mustang?"

"He rode a Harley. The closest he got to a Mustang was the Christmas ornament I gave him the first year we were married."

"I bet he loved that."

"I think so. He was deployed at the time, so I didn't get to see him open it."

"Was Sam excited about becoming a father?"

Haley's eyes searched the restaurant as if looking for an answer. His brother *had* wanted a family, right? Not that he could ask that question out loud.

"We'd talked about starting a family."

"When are you due?"

"The first week in April—the fifth."

Silence.

What was there to say? They were two strangers, eating a meal together, talking about a man they both knew. But Stephen's memories of Sam were frozen in time. For him, Sam was forever a teenager, walking out the door—away from all their plans—to go sign on the dotted line and find his future in the army. Haley's Sam was a grown man. A soldier. The father of her unborn child.

•••••• ••• ••••••

"I'm not sure what you want from me."

Haley decided she might as well be honest with Sam's brother—to a point. Her memories of Sam were few, a montage that started and stopped whenever months of deployments interrupted their marriage. And now Stephen wanted her to put her relationship with Sam on display so that somehow he could feel closer to his brother. Were there enough memories of Sam to create an image of a father for their son? There was no way she could make up for the years Stephen had lived apart from his twin brother. Was that even her responsibility?

"I don't know if Sam would want me to have dinner with you, much less talk with you." She sipped her lemon-lime soda, the glass cool against her hand. "Maybe I'm not the one you should be talking to. I still think you should ask your mother questions about Sam."

She pushed away the plate of tepid pasta, her appetite gone. She'd have the waiter box it up so she could take it home. She'd be hungry later—the baby guaranteed that.

"My mother and I . . . We don't talk often." Stephen seemed to be weighing his words. "She believes I chose my father over her after the divorce—and when my father remarried."

"Did you?"

"No. I just didn't *not* choose my dad's new wife." Now it was Stephen's turn to move his plate aside. "Sam and I lived with my mom for the first two years after our parents divorced, until we were fifteen. We had summers and some holidays with our dad—until he remarried. Sam said Gina tried too hard to make us like her."

"Did she?"

"I don't know. Maybe. Don't all stepmothers try too hard?" Stephen downed the last of his water. "After our first visit, Sam refused to go back. He was all about not upsetting Mom— about not abandoning her. He got angry when I refused to desert Dad. So we . . . we picked sides."

"You with your dad and Sam with your mom."

"Yes. He went to high school in Oklahoma and I went to high school in Pennsylvania. And then Sam decided to go into the army—instead of sticking with the plan to go to college. I got mad. He got mad. And I didn't say good-bye when he went to boot camp."

Haley motioned for the waitress, requesting to-go boxes for her and Stephen, too aware of the man across the table again. Would she ever stop flinching when she looked at Sam's brother? "Well, it might be time to try and get along with your mom, because I can't help you that much. And I need to head home now."

Stephen grabbed the black plastic folder holding their bill, throwing some cash into it and then scraping his lasagna into the Styrofoam container while Haley boxed up the remnants of her entrée.

"Thank you for dinner. I don't know if I was any help . . . Anyway, thank you."

Stephen scrambled into his coat as she slid from the booth and headed for the front of the restaurant and the exit. "Wait. Let me at least walk you to your car. I wanted to talk to you about—"

As she passed a crowded booth, a man called out, "Hal? Hey, Hal!"

The too-familiar voice of one of Sam's comrades brought her up short. He and his wife and another couple sat together, menus in hand. "Chaz. Angie. How are you?"

"We're good. Just having dinner out. How are you doing?" Chaz rose to his feet just as Stephen caught up with her. "Who is—*whoa*!"

Chaz had deployed with Sam—had played a game of cards with Sam the night before he was killed. Been a pallbearer at his funeral. If only she could rewind the last thirty seconds so he wouldn't be staring at Sam's face again.

Even as Angie gasped, Haley put a hand on Chaz's forearm while positioning herself between the two men. "Chaz, this is Stephen Ames—Sam's twin brother."

"What are you talking about?" Chaz's gaze darted from Haley and then back to Stephen.

Haley forced the words past her lips again. "This is Stephen, Sam's twin brother. Sam didn't tell me . . . or anyone else about him."

Chaz rubbed his hand down his face and then refocused on Stephen. "You're Sam's brother?"

"Yes." Stephen stepped up, reaching out to shake Chaz's hand. "Stephen Ames."

"Geez, man, you look exactly like him. I thought I was seeing Sam's ghost." His eyes narrowed. "You okay, Hal?"

"I'm fine. I had dinner with Stephen because he just found out about Sam being killed in Afghanistan. He had some questions. That's all. He's heading back home after this."

"Good thing." Chaz huffed a humorless laugh. "He'd freak out a bunch of people if he hung around here."

Haley watched as Stephen tucked his hands in the pockets of his chinos. "I take it you knew my brother?"

"Yes." Chaz's gaze stayed glued to Stephen's face. "He was one of my best friends."

"He was mine too for a lot of years. I'm sorry to say our parents' divorce changed that."

"Your brother was a good guy. A great soldier."

"Thanks. I'm not surprised to hear that."

Haley found herself between Sam's past and what, only five months ago, had been his present and their future. Time to end this. "Well, I'm heading home."

Angie spoke up from where she sat in the booth. "Let me know if you need anything, Hal."

"Will do."

five

What had she been thinking?

As Stephen crossed the parking lot, Haley took her first full breath in over an hour. Sitting across from Sam's brother had forced her into some sort of macabre, eyes-wide-open nightmare.

Her husband's smile.

Her husband's cleft chin.

Her husband's broad shoulders and strong hands.

She could overlook Stephen's hair, which wasn't trimmed military-regulation high and tight, the way Sam preferred it. But everything else, including the voice, was Sam.

And then, the man sitting across from her would do something different. Something that would shatter the illusion.

Trying to stand when she entered the restaurant? Walking her to her car, even though she assured him that she was perfectly safe? Guys didn't do that anymore. Sam never did that.

Using his right hand, when Sam had been left-handed.

Eating two huge servings of the unlimited house salad after

dousing it in creamy Gorgonzola dressing. Sam would have scorned the vegetables and focused on the bread basket.

"Sam, why didn't you tell me you had an identical twin brother?" Her question broke the stillness of the car, returning her to the present and the reality that she was sitting in a parking lot, freezing. Time to go home. She could reheat her dinner, pay bills, maybe start another DVD to help her fall asleep.

Less than ten minutes later, she pulled up in front of her home. Why had she bought it? Did she even want to be here a year from now? So many people had told her, "Don't make any major decisions during the first year after Sam's death"—and she hadn't. Except for buying this house.

Oh . . . and having a baby. But that decision had been made before Sam died.

Her phone jangled and she answered, knowing it was Claire, checking on her. "I'm fine."

"Are you sure?"

"Yes. We had dinner. He asked questions."

"And?"

Tucking the phone between her ear and shoulder, she opened the door and entered the darkened house. Found the remote for the flat-screen TV and turned it on, restarting *Hellfighters*, adjusting the volume to low. "And I realized how much I don't know about Sam."

"Don't say that—"

"It's the truth." Moving to the kitchen, she tossed her Styrofoam container of leftovers on the brown, faux-granite counter, shrugging out of Sam's coat and hanging it on the back of the bar chair. "You know Sam; he wasn't much of a talker. A kidder, yes. A competitor, yes. A talker, no."

"Could Sam's brother tell you how the two of them got separated?"

"The parents divorced. Initially they were both with Miriam—until the dad got remarried. Then Sam picked his mom and Stephen picked his dad. Some kind of awful *Parent Trap* twist." She opened the lid of the white Styrofoam container, dumping the lukewarm trio of entrées onto a plate and covering it with a paper towel. "I told Stephen if he needed more information about Sam to ask his mother, but I'm not sure that will happen."

"Why not?"

"It's pretty obvious Stephen is closer to his dad." She kicked off her brown, fur-lined boots and padded over to the refrigerator, pulling out a Sprite. "But I am not responsible for patching up things between Stephen and his mother."

"Have you told Sam's mom that you had dinner with Stephen?"

"Just got home." She placed her leftovers in the microwave, programming it to reheat. "I'll call her later. She was talking about going to a Gold Star Mothers meeting last week—the group for moms who've lost a son or daughter in service to the country. I'll have to see how that went."

"What about you?"

The soda hissed as she popped the can open. "What about me what?"

"Have you considered going to a Gold Star Wives meeting?"

"No. They're not for me. I don't do that yadda-yadda sisterhood stuff. You know that. I've got to figure this out on my own."

"You might appreciate being with other women who understand how you feel—"

"Me and strangers? I don't think so. I'm sad. I miss Sam. And I'm going to have a baby in April. There's not much to figure out there. Grieve. Move on. Figure out how to be a mother to this little boy of mine."

Claire giggled. "You know, you could have a girl. I've heard of ultrasounds being wrong—"

"Don't even suggest it. I don't do girls—and they don't do me. The only reason we get along is because you decided to be my friend—although I don't know why." She patted her tummy. "This is Sam's son."

"Are you having any more ultrasounds to confirm that?"

"I've already had two—one at my first appointment when I was sixteen weeks, just to confirm dates. And then they did what they called an 'anatomic survey' at twenty weeks—checking fingers and toes and his heart and other stuff."

"And the 'other stuff' indicated you're having a boy?"

"That's what the ultrasound tech told me—not officially, but she seemed pretty certain."

"Uh-huh."

"I am having a boy—now stop with the *uh-huh*!"

"Fine. Do you have any names picked out?"

"No, not yet. I'll figure something out. I've got plenty of time." She realized the microwave had been beeping to let her know her dinner was reheated. "Time to eat."

"Listen, before you go, did you select a childbirth class?"

"Not yet, but I will."

"You keep saying that."

"I will. I forgot. Ask me after my appointment this week."

"You want me to go with you?"

"No need. I'm good."

Haley stood in the middle of the kitchen holding her iPhone after saying good-bye to Claire. She would be good. She didn't have a choice—and come April, another person would be depending on her to make everything okay, just as Sam had.

If she paused, closed her eyes, she could still see the look of hesitant recognition in Sam's brown eyes over three years ago when he walked up to the counter at the gun club.

"Have we met before?" Sam stood with his hands tucked in his jeans, a gray army T-shirt covered by a blue flannel shirt.

"Maybe." Haley resisted smoothing her hair.

"You going to tell me where?"

"You're a smart man, Sam Ames. Figure it out." She wasn't going to waste her time on a guy who couldn't even remember her name. She hadn't been wearing that much makeup at the wedding two weeks ago. A dress, yes—but that didn't alter her appearance that much.

She walked away to help another customer who wanted to check out some of the guns on display in the glass cases. As she explained the different merits of several models, she knew Sam watched her. Every time she glanced his way, he was standing where she'd left him, a slight frown on his face. At least she wasn't one of those women who blushed or stammered when she was nervous. Growing up with three older brothers had killed any of those outward signs of anxiety. Never let a guy see you sweat—or cry.

Ten minutes later, when the customer left, saying he'd think about the classic .45-caliber Colt M1911, Sam approached her again, his walk easy, slow. "I'd like to see that nine-millimeter." He pointed to one of her favorite models.

"Sure thing." She bent to retrieve the gun. "You interested in adding to your collection—or just starting one?"

"I'd like to try it out on the range today."

"Then I'll need some identification—your driver's license will be fine."

"I'll hand over my license . . . if you give me your phone number,

Haley." A half smile quirked his mouth, deepening the cleft in his chin.

"Remembered me, didja?" After laying the gun on the counter, she held out her hand for his driver's license.

"Jill and Randy's wedding. Yes, I remember you."

She'd given him her phone number—and they'd shared their first kiss the next night after a movie.

Another beep from the microwave reminded her that the leftovers still waited for her. Memories of Sam, when she allowed them to slip past the mental barricade she'd erected, left the salty taste of unshed tears in the back of her throat. She scraped the remnants of dinner into the trash can, closing the metal lid on the aroma of Italian food with a bang.

"Whatcha say, buddy?" Was that a small kick or punch in response to her question? "How about pretzels dipped in Nutella?"

••••••◆••••••

He should have asked Haley what her middle name was.

After spending an hour wrestling answers out of her, he'd go with "Stonewall." The woman was worse than a dead end. She gave up no ground.

Stephen sat in his Mustang, a chill surrounding him, even as a deeper cold—an ache he couldn't relieve—grew in his heart. Years of choices—things said, things left unsaid—separated him from Sam. And now, the chasm between heaven and earth.

He leaned forward, arms resting across the steering wheel, his breath fogging the windshield. He already knew his brother liked to dip his potato chips in ketchup. That Sam wanted a classic '66 Mustang. He could have found most of the other information about Sam if he'd read his obituary. But Stephen couldn't do that. Let Haley Ames be casual about the word *dead* when it came to Sam. He'd been the one to fight back tears, not her.

A tornado of unanswered questions swirled inside, all the larger after spending time with Sam's widow. What kind of woman had his brother married anyway? Honey-blond hair that scattered past her shoulders. Icy blue eyes highlighted by high cheekbones. No makeup that he could see. And no engagement ring or wedding band on her finger either. She hadn't waited long to take off her rings. She'd huddled across the table from him in a quilted green North Face coat that looked like something a guy would wear.

Maybe it was. Maybe it was Sam's coat. She took off her wedding band but wore her husband's coat. *Odd.*

Stephen shifted in the seat, a faint hint of moonlight filtering into the car. He couldn't find Sam by going forward . . . and without Haley's help, he couldn't discover Sam's past. She was a shaky bridge to the twelve years of silence, but he had to try. Her resistance, her silence, impeded his progress. But he couldn't give up yet.

The doors to the white SUV next to him opened, then slammed shut in a rapid one-two-three-four beat, as a family with two preteens entered the car. Their laughter snagged at his heart, an echo of sweeter family times with Sam. What next? The thought of calling Elissa flickered through his mind. Faded. He hadn't spoken to her since his crash-and-burn proposal in Breckenridge. The memory of that day scalded his heart.

"That's it, then?" Stephen waited at the bottom of Elissa's stoop.

She stood with the front door half-open. "What else is there to say? You want something more . . . something I'm not ready for. Honestly, Stephen, it's always felt as if you're searching for something—"

He shook his head, the words tumbling past his resolve not to expose his heart to her again. "No. No, I found what I want. Who I want, Elissa."

"I don't think so." *She reached out, as if to caress his face, but then pulled her hand back.* "I will miss you."

"Maybe—"

"No maybes, Stephen. They're fraught with expectations, don't you think?"

And that was that. And while Elissa wouldn't leave room for maybe, he couldn't deny the ember of hope that still burned. If he settled this thing with Sam—about Sam and himself—then maybe he could go back and make things right with Elissa.

But not tonight.

He hit autodial for his father, who answered on the first ring. "How are you, son?"

"I've been better."

His father's voice was gruff, weighed down. "I still can't get used to the idea that we've lost Sam—"

"I went to see his wife—his widow, Dad."

"What?"

Stephen opened the driver's door, turning so that his feet rested on the bottom edge of the car's frame, welcoming the rush of cold night air on his face. A faint scent of a coming snowfall lingered around him. "I'm sorry. You didn't know that Sam was married—"

"No. Your mother made it clear years ago she wasn't going to answer my questions about Sam. And I didn't press the issue. I kept thinking there'd be time—"

"We both did, Dad. When Mom called to tell me about Sam, she mentioned Sam's wife. So I decided to try and find her. I didn't say anything to you because I wasn't sure what would happen."

"So, how did it go—meeting Sam's wife?"

"Well, just like we didn't know about her, she didn't know about me." Memories of their first meeting rushed back, causing his heart rate to accelerate. "For thirty seconds, she thought I was Sam."

"Stephen, how horrible for you—"

"For me? I wasn't the one seeing her de—her husband." He opted for the abridged version of his interaction with Haley— no need to mention the armed standoff. "Despite all that, Haley—that's her name—agreed to meet me for dinner today. In the Springs."

"Sam was stationed in Colorado?"

"Yes. About two hours from Fort Collins."

"Hard to believe . . ." His father's voice trailed off. "So, what happened?"

"I survived an hour with a woman who didn't want to look at me because I'm an exact replica of her husband. I wanted to apologize . . . or at least drape a napkin over my face."

How could he confess the rest to his father? He'd spent so many years just being Stephen Ames that he'd forgotten what it was like to be Sam's twin brother. The stares of his friends. The confusion.

But now it was worse. He wasn't just Sam's twin.

He was Sam's ghost.

He knew his father was waiting for him to say more. "After dinner, we ran into a couple of Sam's friends—one of his army buddies. The guy was stunned when he saw me."

"I can imagine."

Stephen stood, shutting the door and walking to the front of the car, leaning against the hood, cold seeping through the material of his pants. Cars moved along Powers Boulevard, headlight beams streaming past, the sounds an odd motorized acoustic background. "Maybe I shouldn't have come."

"Do you really believe that? You had to try, son. You may still end up with more questions than answers."

"Haley agreed to one meeting. And I got nothing." He did a quick review of Haley's minimalist answers. "While Sam and Haley were married, it sounds as if he was gone more than he was home."

Hesitancy tinged his father's words. "You could always talk to your mother."

"I don't think so, Dad." The leap from a single phrase written in a Hallmark card to an entire conversation seemed as wide as the Vermont lake he'd tried to swim across when he was eight— and almost drowned.

"I could try calling her."

"This is my journey, Dad. I'll figure out something."

He had to . . . because, really, he still didn't know who his brother was. And he wasn't willing to walk away—or to let Haley walk away. But could he convince her to talk with him again? Was there any other option?

Chaz's words echoed through his mind. *"Your brother was a good guy. A great soldier."*

Maybe someone like Chaz, someone who had worked with Sam, could tell him more.

six

......•—•......•—•......•—•......

It had been good to get out of the house again. After last night's dinner with Stephen Ames, Haley hoped the walk this morning would clear her head of the double images that haunted her sleep. At six months pregnant, she couldn't outrun them, but she could walk fast.

Haley rounded the corner onto the cul-de-sac that harbored the home she'd moved into eight weeks ago. It sat just left of the house in the center. Would Sam have liked it? Today the gray, cloudless sky huddled over the rancher guarded by a tall, leafless tree on the left and a small porch that she'd have to paint come summer. How soon before Shelton notified her about that? Patches of leftover snow dotted the faded brown grass, and she had no idea what, if anything, would bloom in the flower bed beneath the front bay window.

She tucked her hands into the pockets of Sam's coat as a breeze whipped past her. Exercise was good for her and the baby—or so her doctor said. But now she was ready for a nap. Resting was good, too. From what everyone said, she was going

to get precious little sleep once her son was born. She appreci-
ated the few hours each day when she slept soundly and didn't
have to think about her life—what she'd lost and what she had
to face by herself.

Just as she reached her neighbor's house, a red Mustang entered the cul-de-sac. Haley stood and watched as it looped past
her and pulled into her driveway, the shadow of an achingly
familiar face flashing past her in the driver's window.

What is Stephen Ames doing here, God? Hadn't she done the
right thing—the sacrificial thing—by agreeing to have dinner
with him last night? Couldn't the man be grateful and leave her
alone?

He hopped out of the car dressed in a dark jacket and black
jeans, then walked to the back and popped the trunk. Haley
held her ground on the sidewalk out in front of the house. The
first words that came to her mind were *Get off my property.* She
counted to ten. "Don't you have a job?"

A slight improvement.

"Excuse me?" Stephen looked over his shoulder, the winter
sun creating highlights in his dark hair.

"A job. Don't you need to go to work?"

He leaned into the trunk and pulled out a medium-size
brown box, closing the trunk with his elbow. "Not at the moment."

"You need one." Haley kept her voice low as she punched in
the code to open the garage door.

"Sorry, I didn't catch that." Stephen stood behind her, waiting while the garage door slid up.

"Nothing." Haley navigated the maze in her garage. Besides
her car, boxes filled the space to overflowing. She wasn't completely avoiding unpacking boxes—but she was avoiding going
through Sam's clothes and books. Anything that would cause her

to face Sam again. One more huge, heartbreaking thing. There was always one more thing. Maybe by the time the baby was old enough to go to kindergarten she'd catch up with her life again.

Stephen muttered about taking his life in his hands as he squeezed between her car and the teetering pile of cardboard boxes. He didn't answer her "don't you need to go to work" inquiry until they passed through the laundry room, stepping over the pile of dirty towels, and stood in the kitchen.

"I'm job hunting."

"Oh. Good luck." Was she supposed to ask him why—as if she was interested in his life? Right now the only coherent message her brain was telegraphing was spelled N-A-P.

Stephen lifted the box that he held in his arms a few inches. "I brought a present. For the baby."

"What? Why?" Was the man trying to bribe her into talking about Sam?

He kept talking, turning the box so she could see the brightly colored photograph on the front of the box. "It's a toddler swing."

Haley pointed at the photo of a smiling little boy sitting in a bright blue swing, seemingly suspended in midair. "A newborn can't use that."

"I know." Stephen walked to the bay window in the living room. "But the other day when I was here I noticed that great old tree beside the garage. And I thought that it needed a swing, for when the baby's older."

"Oh." Haley shook her head. Exhaustion had reduced her vocabulary to one word. What was pregnancy doing to her brain? Even if she was falling asleep standing up, she could still be polite. "Thank you."

"I read about it online. It got great customer reviews and it's good for kids from nine months to two years old, so you'll get a lot of use out of it. Sam and I had this old tire we used to swing from. We thought it was the best thing ever."

"He mentioned that. Said it hung right underneath a tree fort he built."

"We built it." Stephen deposited the box on the table beside her laptop.

"He never mentioned you."

"I realize that." His brown eyes dulled to the color of unpolished leather. "The summer we were nine, we scavenged all the old lumber we could and asked our dad for nails and hammers. We built the tree house in our backyard. Dad helped when he got home from work, and Mom even cooked a celebration dinner of homemade mac and cheese. We all ate dinner in the fort."

Haley stood silent, listening as the statement "There are two sides to every story" came true right before her eyes. When Sam talked about building the tree house, he mentioned only how *he* built it. Not his father. Or his twin brother. Or his mother, even—and he had a relationship with her. Haley's heart had ached for only-child Sam playing by himself. She'd pulled him close, kissed him until he stopped talking, in an attempt to erase the pain of the past. They'd fallen asleep in each other's arms.

And the story hadn't been true. She felt like the Grimm brothers' Gretel, discovering bread crumbs that she hoped led back home—only to find she'd been deceived and ended up lost, left wandering alone.

Stephen's all-too-familiar voice pulled her back to the present problem. "Sam ever show you pictures of the tree house?"

"No."

"I have some . . ."

What gave Stephen Ames the right to share memories with her that Sam hadn't? "If Sam wanted me to see the tree house he would have shown me the pictures."

Unspoken words stretched between them. *But then you would have learned about me.*

Time to call the man's bluff. "Why are you here?"

Stephen's hand rested on the box. "I told you, I wanted to put a swing up for the baby—"

"You didn't even know I was pregnant before you showed up." Haley fisted her hands on her hips. "Your being here has nothing to do with the baby."

"Fine. I wanted to help you and the baby—and I want to know my brother. You're my best chance for that."

"Don't you think this grand gesture—showing up here after Sam is dead—is too much, too late? If you wanted to get to know Sam, why didn't you try sooner?"

"I did." His admission came through gritted teeth as he approached her until mere inches separated them, but Haley refused to back down. "I don't have to explain my relationship with my brother to you. We were more than brothers before our parents divorced. We were best friends."

"Then what happened?"

Before he looked away, something shadowed his eyes—an ache she lived with every waking moment.

"I don't know."

"Why don't I believe you?" They stared at one another, the all-too-familiar silence looming between them. After a few seconds, Haley shrugged her shoulders and moved away.

"Thanks for the swing. I'll put it up later. But I just came back from a walk and I'm beat." A yawn punctuated her declaration. "So I'm going to take a nap."

"My offer still stands. I can hang the swing while you rest. I'll be outside, so you won't hear a thing. If you show me where Sam's tools are, I'll get out of your way and let you get your beauty sleep."

She shook her head, long strands of hair whispering around her shoulders. "It's more like my baby sleep. And Sam's tools are still packed in one of those boxes in the garage." She waved good-bye. "Be seeing you."

Or not. Please.

Haley prayed she could dispel the image of Sam's lookalike standing in the middle of her kitchen, watching her. Half the time she was with Stephen Ames, she battled to remember he wasn't her husband—merely an unwanted reflection of the man she'd married.

•◦••—◆—••◦•

Stephen stood on the top step leading into the garage and surveyed the mess. How did Haley fit the Subaru in there? Somewhere in the midst of all these boxes were Sam's tools—which he intended to find. Because whether Haley liked it or not—and she didn't—he was putting up the toddler swing. That was his plan and he was sticking to it.

He hit the garage door control, dodged boxes, deposited his box underneath the tree, and circled it. Yep. There was a perfect branch to suspend the swing from. Not too high up. He'd noticed a large tree in the backyard, but it didn't have any low-hanging branches adequate for a swing. And some of the top branches looked . . . old. Brittle.

After opening the box, he read through the directions to figure out what he needed to complete the job—and realized tools were unnecessary. He wasn't going to hang the swing today, not when the directions stated to store the swing indoors when temperatures dropped below freezing. It was only February—still plenty of opportunities for that to happen.

So much for surprising—and defying—his sister-in-law. He

tucked the directions in the box and confronted the disarray in the garage. There was no method to this madness, as boxes were just pushed and piled on top of one another. Words were scrawled on several of them, and a closer inspection revealed them to be labeled LIVING ROOM or BATHROOM or BEDROOM CLOTHES. If he couldn't hang the swing, maybe he could rearrange the boxes into some sort of order.

After forty-five minutes of shoving and repiling, Stephen stepped back to survey his progress. Sweat dampened his shirt, and the layer of dust coating his hands lodged in his throat and nose, prompting mild bouts of coughing. All of the boxes marked BEDROOM were in one area. Kitchen boxes were closest to the door leading into the house. His stepmother had taught him to unpack the kitchen first when they moved into a new house. Boxes labeled CLOTHES were stacked next to the bedroom boxes. And all of the boxes marked GARAGE were piled over by the workbench, with the ones labeled TOOLS on top of the stack. It was a start.

Would Sam have been glad his brother planned on putting a baby swing in the tree? Maybe not. His shoulders slumped. After their father remarried, Sam had made it clear that his life was with their mom—that it didn't include their father. Sam's decision to live with his mom when they'd started high school began the slow erosion of their relationship.

Stephen needed to man up and admit there was a part of him that had heaved a silent breath of release during his high school years. At last, he was just Stephen Rogers Ames. The only Ames brother—except for the few holidays he spent with Sam and his mom, and as those had gotten more and more tense, they became less frequent. The one letter Stephen sent him after college graduation . . . what happened to that? Probably gone missing in the midst of Sam's moves with the army. Or tossed in the trash, unread.

He'd willingly lived a lie—and so had Sam. And now Stephen would pay for their choices for the rest of his life.

•••••—◆—•••••

What time was it?

Haley opened her eyes, shoving her hair out of her face with a groan. Why oh why had pregnancy made her a drooler? She rolled from her side onto her back, wiping the warm moisture from her lips. Lovely. If Sam were here, he'd make some sort of crack about having to rethink why he'd married her.

If only she could dredge up a laugh.

She swung her legs over the side of the bed. No lying around and definitely no lying on her back, not when her bladder insisted she get up. Everything she'd ever heard about pregnant women making multiple trips a day—and all through the night—to the bathroom was coming true. At this rate, she'd spend the last month of this pregnancy in the bathroom.

A few minutes later, she smoothed Sam's ARMY STRONG T-shirt over her tummy. "Try not to use Mommy's bladder as a pillow, okay, buddy?" She stilled as movement fluttered beneath her hand. Most of the time, she could ignore what was happening—how her body was morphing into something she no longer recognized—until moments like this one. This was when she'd have called Sam and placed his hand beneath hers, both of them marveling that their baby, their son, was moving inside her.

And she'd deprived Sam of experiencing a single moment of the pregnancy with her.

I'm sorry. I'm sorry.

How many times did she have to repeat those words before

she felt any relief? Sometimes she whispered them aloud until she fell asleep at night, her arms wrapped around Sam's pillow. But when she woke in the morning, forgiveness still eluded her.

Hunger pushed her thoughts toward food, prodding her toward the kitchen. Maybe grilled cheese again? A bowl of Cap'n Crunch cereal? But sounds from the garage brought her up short. She half-turned, determined to get one of her guns from the safe in her bedroom closet. It was the middle of the day. She took a slow breath and pushed aside the bay window curtain instead.

Why was Stephen Ames's red Mustang still parked in her driveway? According to her iPhone on her bedside table, it was twelve thirty. She'd slept for two hours. Didn't the man understand the words *no* and *thank you*? Stalking to the garage, she yanked open the door, causing Stephen to whirl around.

"What are you doing here?"

"You're awake."

She pushed the tangles of hair from her eyes. "Obviously. Why are you still here? I told you I'd hang the swing myself." Her bare foot tapped against the cool linoleum floor.

"And I told you I'd do it."

Was she going to stand here and argue? She'd learned, growing up with three older brothers, to pick her battles. "It shouldn't take two hours to put up a swing."

Stephen raised his arm, motioning to the garage. "Well, neither of us can hang the swing until the weather warms up. So I organized things for you. Wanted to help."

Haley's eyes tracked the arc of his arm. The towering wall of boxes had disappeared. In its place were the beginnings of space and order. She opened her mouth. Closed it. Tried again. "What did you do?"

"I didn't unpack much—just some of the tools." Stephen

dusted off his hands on the front of his jeans. "Mostly I tried to rearrange the boxes into categories: living room, bedroom, bathroom, office, books, that kind of thing."

Did the man have a superhero complex or something? Why was he so determined to help her? "Why?"

"Well, you have to admit it was a mess in here."

Did he think she was lazy? She stood straighter, jabbing a thumb into her chest. "I was going to get to it."

"When did you move in?"

"Two months ago. I've been busy."

Stephen Ames could do the eyebrow arch, too. "And the baby's due—"

"In April." Haley held up her hand to ward off another appearance of Sam's lookalike smile. "I can do this myself."

"But I'm here." Stephen had the nerve to move a box from one pile to another. Wasn't he paying attention? "I want to help."

"Why?"

"You're Sam's . . . wife. That makes you my sister-in-law—"

"We are not *family*." She gestured between them. "I didn't even know you existed until three days ago, and the fact that you and Sam were close for the first part of his life doesn't require me to have a relationship with you. I answered your questions. *I'm done.* I don't need your help. Now, if you don't mind, I just woke up and I'm starving. I'm going inside and I would appreciate it if you'd leave like I asked you to do before I took a nap."

The two of them faced off across the expanse of the garage. Was the man going to argue with her? That's what Sam would have done—challenged her until he'd backed her into a corner and then kissed her until she gave in or forgot what the argument was about.

But his brother tucked his hands into his pant pockets. Nodded. Offered the faintest hint of a smile that tugged at her wounded heart. "You're welcome."

"You're welcome"?

She hadn't asked Stephen Ames to bring her baby—Sam's son—a gift. And she hadn't asked him to hang the unwanted toddler swing in the tree—just the opposite. And the man had no right organizing her boxes.

She wasn't about to thank him for intruding in her life.

Before she could think of a reply, he was gone. He didn't gun the motor of his Mustang as he backed out the driveway. Didn't grind the gears or peel out of the cul-de-sac. He even tossed a wave in her direction.

seven

·····•···•—•···•—•···•—•···•·

Haley hadn't expected Skyping with her family to make her homesick.

Of course, she'd called on a Wednesday, the night her mom put on a huge pot of taco soup—enough for her adult sons, her "daughters-in-love," and her grandchildren. She issued a no-pressure, open invitation—and whoever could make it was welcomed with her mom's hugs and her father's corny puns.

Haley bit into her reheated Papa John's six-cheese pizza. Yeah . . . didn't quite match her mom's homemade soup, thick with browned hamburger, kidney beans, chopped onions, and taco seasoning. Topped with sour cream, shredded cheese, and crushed Doritos, it equaled a taco in a bowl.

"Hey, Hal! How's my little sister?" David's face appeared on-screen.

"I'm your only sister."

"Yeah, yeah—always talking back to your big brother." David's grin reminded her of all the times he'd teased her growing up. "So, what's up? How'd I manage first place in the Skype queue tonight? Mom's waiting for her turn."

Haley adjusted the laptop screen, centering the computer on the dining room table. Now that she had a chance to talk to her brother, how did she begin? "Is Mom around?"

"No—you want me to go get her?" David half-rose from his seat, his body blocking the screen.

"No! Wait. I need to talk to you privately." She waited as David sat down again, still unsure of how to recount everything that had happened. If she'd learned one thing from her three brothers, it was to say things straight-up. No melodrama. "So I found out that Sam has an identical twin brother."

David's eyebrows rose, even as his mouth hung open. "That is a sick joke, Hal."

"I'm serious. He showed up at my house a few nights ago—I thought he was a ghost."

"What did the guy want?"

"He wanted to find out about Sam—they've been estranged for a dozen years." She wiped her hands on her sweatpants, surprised that they were trembling. "I pulled a gun on him and told him to leave."

"Attagirl, Hal. So that's it, then?"

"Not really. I finally agreed to talk to him, and he's come by once more. But I think he's figured out that there's no sense in showing up here anymore."

"You're okay?"

Her brother didn't need to know about her sleepless nights. "Yeah. Do you think I did the right thing?" She held her breath, waiting for David's answer.

"You're a big girl, Hal. It's your decision to make. Obviously Sam didn't want to have a relationship with this guy, so you don't have to either. Pray about it. If yes is an option, no is an option, too." David leaned back in the rolling desk chair. "You're telling Mom and Dad, right?"

"I have to." The thought of relating the story of Stephen Ames's appearance one more time dragged her down like a water-filled parachute. It would have been easier to talk to everyone face-to-face—but who knew when she'd get home? For now, Skype had to suffice for connecting with family. "She'll worry."

"She's our mom—it's what she does. But you know she prays more than she worries."

"You're right."

"I always am."

And just like that, David had her laughing.

She could still see him tackling the fifth-grade boy who'd hassled her for the first half of the school year. She'd done everything she could think of: confronted him, avoided him, told her parents, told the teacher—but the boy kept on bullying her. David, who was already a freshman in high school, showed up the day the guy actually grabbed her and pushed her around.

David sat on the guy's chest, ignoring the fact that the kid was sniveling and begging for mercy. "You touch my sister again, and I will pound you into the dirt. Got it?"

He walked her home, telling her to stop crying and to not tell their mother what had happened. Right before they got to their house, he stopped her. "Listen, Hal, I had your back today. But I won't always be there. You're a Jordan. You're tough. Don't let guys like that get to you. You're not some sissy-girl."

David was right. She knew the Jordan family rules: *No tears. No tattling. Keep up or go home.* From the time she was a toddler, her three brothers had insisted she adapt to their pace—or not tag along. And she'd have done anything to be with David, Johnny, and Aaron.

The next time a boy hassled her, she decked him. She ended up in the principal's office—but her brothers applauded her. And to this day, the *No tears* rule still worked.

"Hey, Hal, did I lose you?" David knocked on the computer screen.

Haley shook her head, dispersing the memories. "No . . . I'm still here. Go ahead and put Mom on. Just do me a favor, please."

"What?"

"Help her adjust the computer screen. Last time we Skyped I talked to the lower half of her face the whole time."

•••••◆•••••

Sam.

Just the whisper of his name through her mind—no image— scattered the slim façade of sleep.

Haley pulled the blanket up around her shoulders and kept her eyes closed. Opening them would allow reality to destroy the last remnants of rest. Reveal all the stark changes in her life.

The bare taupe walls of the bedroom of the house she'd bought using the life insurance money she received . . . because Sam was dead.

She'd sit up in the bed, push herself to her feet, and walk toward the bathroom . . . and not be able to resist looking over her shoulder and seeing the other side of the bed. Unslept in. And no reason to count the days until Sam's deployment ended.

One toothbrush by the bathroom sink. Just her face in the mirror. Sam wouldn't be in the shower, the scent of his musky soap-on-a-rope lingering on the steam.

Haley squeezed her eyelids tighter.

God, I know you said you'd bring good out of this.

But when?

I know that I have to be patient . . . but if I could get even a small glimpse of the good in being alone. In being pregnant—alone. In doing all of this—today, tomorrow . . . all of the tomorrows piling up in front of me like a lifelong train wreck—alone.

Haley lay in the bed. Waited. The only sound her breathing.

Come on, God. Say something.

She hadn't asked *why* exactly. She wasn't even asking for that all-encompassing peace that passes all understanding.

I'm tired of swinging between numb and overwhelmed, God. Isn't there something in between? Where's the firm ground? Aren't you supposed to be the stability of my times? Some unseen enemy tore my life out of my hands . . . My heart is mangled . . .

Stop.

Haley opened her eyes.

Walls. Floor. Ceiling.

Reality.

In the midst of the brutal starkness, she still believed in God . . . and she wasn't asking for more from him. To have more—and then have it destroyed—was too cruel.

••••• ◆ •••••

It was good to be up early after another night in a Springs hotel. To be outside, catching the first glimpses of the blues and pinks of the sunrise in the ever-lightening sky overhead. Stephen leaned against the hood of his car, the air filled with a bite of frost. The parking lot dug out of a steep Manitou hillside filled up with people intent on getting an early start hiking the Incline. Maybe he should have taken up Chaz's invitation to hike to the summit, but Stephen wanted to talk about his brother, not gasp for oxygen while he ate Chaz's dust. He hadn't even been certain Chaz would return his call when he'd left a message for him at the battalion. They'd talk. Chaz would brave the Incline, and that would be the end of this attempt to find out more about his brother.

It was only seven in the morning and the parking lot was almost full, hikers already tackling one of the most popular trails in the area. He'd never understood the attraction of scaling the wooden ties left over from a cable car that used to take tourists up the side of the mountain. But from the number of people heading up the Incline with backpacks and water bottles or CamelBaks, he was in the minority.

"You sure you don't want to join me?" Chaz appeared on Stephen's left.

"Hey. I didn't see you pull in."

"I had to circle to the far end of the lot to find a parking place. So, are we talking here, or are we hiking up?"

"If you're okay with it, we'll talk here."

"No problem." Chaz settled his CamelBak on the asphalt beside Stephen's Mustang. "Man, it still gets me how much you look like Sam."

Stephen ran his hand through his hair. Same song . . . "Hope it doesn't bother you too much."

"Nah. I'll get used it . . . and it's not like you're moving to the Springs or anything. No offense, man."

"None taken." He might as well get to it. "Haley told me Sam was a medic."

"He was the best. He stayed calm in some bad situations. He saved a couple of guys after a firefight in the mountains in Afghanistan. Nothing ever fazed him. When he was on duty, he was all about the job. He got hit by shrapnel once taking care of somebody. He took care of it himself and wouldn't let us report the incident for a Purple Heart."

Stephen tried to bring into focus the blurred image of his brother. It was as if each word Chaz spoke dialed some virtual microscope so that his understanding of Sam became clearer. "Were you with him when . . . when . . ."

"No." A quick shake of his head stopped Stephen's question. "We played cards the night before. I think he won just about every hand." Chaz stood beside Stephen, mirroring his stance by leaning against the car, crossing his arms over his chest. "Some of the troops on the patrol told me that he'd just started an IV on a wounded soldier after dragging him out of the line of fire. A second later, Sam went down. He landed right next to the guy . . . never said anything . . . The guy Sam rescued survived. They made sure the sniper didn't."

Chaz turned away, his back straight, shoulders tight, and cursed under his breath. He took a deep breath before facing Stephen again. "What else do you want to know?"

Something loosened deep in Stephen's chest. His brother hadn't suffered. He hadn't let himself dwell on the what and how of Sam's death—could barely say the word *died* in the same sentence with his brother's name. "Thanks for telling me that."

"Everybody liked Sam. He was easygoing, always ready to have fun. Wasn't afraid of anything. He and I did our first free-fall jumps together."

"I didn't know Sam skydived."

"We both went through airborne training at Fort Benning. When we ended up out here, he talked me into some civilian free-fall classes. We did about a dozen jumps together. There wasn't much he wouldn't try." Memories seemed to hold Chaz silent as their escapades pulled him into the past, away from Stephen. "We were all surprised when he and Hal got married."

"Really? Why?"

"Nothing against Hal. She's great. But Sam was all about dating a girl three, maybe four times and then moving on, you know? Nothing serious. And we figured that's the way it would go down with Hal. And then the next we know he's marrying her. One of the guys even joked around and asked if Hal was pregnant. We had to pull Sam off of him."

"Sam had a temper?"

"Not really. I mean, you deploy enough times, you can be a bit edgy. But Sam kept a tight lid on things. He loved the army. Said he liked the security of the regular paycheck and the bonuses. Loved being deployed. Some guys sat around and moped. Not Sam. He was the guy who stayed focused. Reminded us why we were there. Found a way to make us laugh." Chaz stopped, staring up at the Incline. "He's missed. A lot."

"Did Sam ever talk about family?"

"No. He wasn't much of a talker. And when it's all about the mission, you don't ask questions."

Chaz's answer didn't surprise him, even as it burrowed deep into the ache inside his chest. "Listen, I know you need to get going." He stuck his hand out, shaking hands with the other man. "Thanks for this—for telling me about Sam."

Chaz shrugged into his CamelBak. "No problem."

"Have a good hike."

"Always do. Sam used to tear the Incline up. Never knew anyone who could keep up with him."

Chaz strolled toward the trailhead. It was as if the man had handed him a half dozen puzzle pieces, each one showing him a new facet of his brother. But when he tried to assemble them, there were huge gaps that left an incomplete picture.

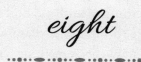

eight

Haley wanted to go home—but escape was impossible with the grip Claire had on her hand.

If Haley allowed her emotions to have their way, she would abandon the childbirth class and go lock herself in the house, sit on the couch with a bowl of mint chocolate-chip ice cream covered in chocolate sprinkles, and let the tears flow while she ate until the spoon clanked on the bottom of the dish. And she'd keep the container nearby for seconds and thirds—and cry some more.

"Let go." Haley leaned close to her friend, tugging her hand away. "I can't feel my fingers."

"Then stop looking at the front door like you're going to bolt." Claire whispered her warning through her lip-glossed smile, even as she released Haley's hand with a warning don't-go-anywhere pat.

"I'm staying."

What choice did she have? Sam's son was arriving in less than three months, and she needed to learn all the tricks to survive labor and delivery. Faking it wasn't an option. She had the "making babies" technique down, but birthing them? Other than that it involved pushing at the end, not a clue.

The ebb and flow of voices seemed to hedge Haley in as other couples—each the appropriate husband-and-wife set—followed the instructor's request to introduce themselves and say when their baby was due. A twentysomething couple who should have been stamped "Too adorable to live." A soft-spoken couple in their late thirties who looked a bit stunned to be attending the class. A Latino couple who were expecting triplets. *Triplets.* When the wife announced it, the husband grinned, even as his skin paled. Only she and Claire were the odd women out. Who knew what the other class members thought about them?

Claire's nudge drew a too-loud "What?" from Haley.

Her friend repeated her whisper-through-a-smile performance, speaking out of the side of her mouth. "Are you going to introduce us?"

"Oh. Sure." Haley focused on the instructor, Lily, who looked more like a yoga teacher in her black leggings and long white blouse accessorized with a flowing, multicolored scarf. Best to just say it. Fast. Pretend she was reading the ingredients on the side of a box of cereal. "I'm Haley Ames. This is my friend Claire O'Dea. She's going to be my coach for labor and delivery, because my husband, Sam, was killed in Afghanistan about five months ago."

Haley braced herself for the murmurs that followed the seconds of silence. She didn't catch what they said. Probably "Oh no!" or "I'm so sorry." That's what people usually said. While the direct delivery was easiest for her, it left other people groping for some sort of adequate response.

As if there was one. If she had been on their side of the conversation, she wouldn't have known what to say, either.

Lily took control, welcoming everyone and turning their attention to the handouts. "The first thing I'd like to do is have each of you show us what you packed in your coach's bag."

Haley looked around the room. Coach's bag? Had there been instructions on the website about assembling, much less bringing, a coach's bag? She'd brought two pillows, but only because Claire told her to, and she wasn't even sure why she needed those. But it seemed as though everyone else had gotten the message, as they unzipped small duffels or backpacks.

"I forgot—"

Claire touched her arm. "I've got it right here. I am the coach, after all."

Right. Claire was the coach. Haley was the mom-to-be.

"All right, Claire." Lily turned toward them. "Do you want to show us what you brought to help Haley during labor?"

"Absolutely." Claire opened the purple floral Vera Bradley messenger bag that Haley had assumed was one of her many purses. "I brought a CD I made of some of Haley's favorite songs—she's a country music fan. I'm willing to tolerate some Keith Urban and The Band Perry while she's in labor. I also brought some of my favorite lotion, because, well, I have no idea if Haley even uses lotion. It's almond scented."

Within five minutes, a pile of coach's supplies lay at Claire's feet: a bright red sock with two tennis balls in it to help with back labor; a brush, just in case Haley wanted Claire to brush her hair; a tiny stuffed bear to use as a focal point; some John Wayne DVDs.

Haley picked up *The Comancheros.* "Movies, really?"

Claire shrugged. "Well, you're hoping and praying for a quick labor . . . but just in case."

The next two hours consisted of the other coaches revealing what they'd packed in their bags—a two-pound bag of peanut

M&M's? Why hadn't Claire packed that?—and then the moms-to-be resting on their sides while their coaches learned how to massage their shoulders, lower backs, even their feet.

Haley wasn't surprised that the instructor sought her out when the class was over. Lily touched her arm as Haley pulled on her gloves. Claire, who could make friends with anyone, chatted with Camilo and Feliciana, the couple expecting trip-lets.

"So, Haley."

"Yes?"

"How was class for you?"

Images of trying to spell her name with her hips replayed through her head. "Interesting. Not sure I'm going to be up for that hula-hip name-spelling exercise when I'm actually in labor."

"It's an option." Lily paused. "You did take my business card, right?"

Haley patted her coat pocket. "Have it right here."

"I want you to know that I understand how you're feeling."

Oh. Another "I understand how you're feeling" person.

Lily's gentle smile hinted that Haley hadn't hidden her reaction. "I mean, I really do. My husband died of a brain aneurysm when I was pregnant with our second child."

Her words collided with Haley's barricaded heart. "How . . . far along were you?"

"Not quite as far along as you are now. Five months." Age lines bracketed her smile, and her gray eyes were clear. Haley's heart seemed to lean toward this woman whom she'd met only two hours earlier. "I didn't know how I was going to have a baby without Tom there with me."

"What did you do?"

"I went from never wanting to have the baby to thinking I'd be pregnant forever." At Haley's soft snort of laughter, Lily's smile broadened. "Believe me, every pregnant woman ends up thinking that."

"Obviously you had your baby."

"My mom was with me when our daughter was born. I held my child and bawled for half an hour. Counted her toes. Her fingers. That's what Tom would have done."

"Claire's my best friend." Haley tucked her hands into her coat pockets. "She hasn't had any children yet, but I know she'll stay with me."

"Well, if you want any more support, just know that I'm available to help you during labor too. Tuck my card in your labor bag."

"I need to pack one first." Haley stepped away as Claire joined them. "Thank you. I'll think about it."

As they walked outside into the darkness illuminated by streetlights, Claire was silent for a few seconds. "So, are you going to tell me what you're thinking about?"

"Lily told me that her husband died when she was pregnant with their second child."

"But her husband greeted us—"

"People remarry, Claire." Other people. Not her. "Anyway, she offered to be a backup coach for me when the baby is born."

"She does have the practical experience."

"But Lily is not you." As they settled into her car, Haley turned to look at the ultrafeminine woman across from her. They'd forged a friendship that ignored Claire's fashion sense and Haley's preference for Sam's flannel shirts and baseball caps. "Friendship trumps experience every time."

"Hey, some birth instructor is not pushing me out of the way that easily. I have first dibs on holding your baby—well, right after you. But if you'd like an experienced mama in the room, I'm okay with that."

"Sure, she's experienced. But she's a stranger."

"Well, let's leave it at you're thinking about it."

"Thanks for covering for me today—bringing the coach's bag."

Claire rubbed her hands together. "It's my job. Now start the car, will you? And turn on the seat warmers, please. I'm freezing."

"Will do, bossy. You interested in some French fries? Buddy's got a craving."

"With a chocolate milkshake?"

"Of course."

"I'm in."

......◆......

Stephen tucked the brown paper bag of takeout from one of his favorite Fort Collins restaurants under his arm, digging in his coat pocket for his car keys. He should have stayed home, cooked dinner for himself. But he was so busy chasing down job leads, he'd forgotten to thaw and marinate the chicken he'd planned on grilling. And after sitting at the computer for six hours, submitting another group of online job applications, he was ready to get outside—if only for twenty minutes while he picked up dinner. One advantage to being back up north: he knew where all his favorite restaurants were—and Café de Bangkok's red curry with beef sounded perfect.

He waited on the sidewalk as a blue Ford hybrid SUV pulled into a slot and both front doors opened. A man with a Roman nose and slicked-back dark hair appeared from the driver's side, and a woman in a brilliant fuchsia coat about Elissa's height stepped out from the other side of the car.

Wait. The woman didn't just look like Elissa. She *was* Elissa.

Stephen stood still as the couple approached, his almost-fiancée so focused on the man beside her that she didn't notice Stephen until she was right in front of him.

"Stephen." Elissa paused at the curb, her arm woven through the other man's.

"Hello, Elissa." His eyes stayed trained on the man with her.

"Eddie, this is Stephen Ames, a good friend of mine."

Nice to know that six months and one rejected proposal earned him "good friend" status.

Eddie held out his hand, forcing Stephen to do the polite thing and shake it.

"Why don't you go inside and see how long the wait is for a table?" Elissa nodded toward the Thai restaurant Stephen had just left.

The man hesitated, looking back and forth between Elissa and Stephen, his hand resting on her shoulder. "You sure?"

"Of course. I'll be right in."

What did the guy expect him to do? Kidnap Elissa?

Elissa watched Eddie enter the restaurant, her head held high, before looking back at him. "How are you, Stephen?"

"I'm good. Job hunting."

"Any prospects?"

"Nothing definite." He eased his grip on the sack of food. "And you? You're doing well?"

"Yes."

She obviously wasn't going to discuss Eddie—and did he really want to know how soon they'd started dating after she rejected him?

"Things going well at the boutique?"

"A little slow after the holidays, but I'm brainstorming a Valentine's Day sale, hoping to attract customers."

"You always were good with marketing."

"Thanks." Elissa fiddled with the belt of her coat, her glance straying past him.

"I should let you go—"

"Yes . . . It was nice seeing you, Stephen."

A few minutes later, Stephen stared at the front of the Thai restaurant, the faint aroma of curry filling his car. One thing was certain: he was going to make a strategic stop by Walrus Ice Cream for a root beer float—for an appetizer.

Elissa wasn't waiting around for him to find what he was searching for—*who* he was searching for. She was starting the new year with a new man. He leaned back, his hands fisted on his thighs. Had he been off track when he proposed? Mistaken his feelings for her? How could he move on, create a family for himself, when his relationship with Sam shadowed him?

All he had to do was figure himself out—find some peace. That's all he had to do.

But he'd ignored the one person who could help him do that for twelve years. Thought he didn't need him. That he was better off, more complete, without him.

When Sam left for boot camp, Stephen never imagined it would be the first day of more than a decade of deafening silence. If he had known that, he would have found some way past the hurt and anger that choked him, that prevented him from saying good-bye—saying he was sorry. From telling Sam he'd miss him. That even though he didn't understand why his brother had chosen the military, he hoped Sam was happy. That he knew Sam would graduate at the top of his class in boot camp.

He didn't mean to destroy their relationship. In Sam's eyes, Stephen may have thrown down the gauntlet when he chose to stay with their dad, but Sam had retaliated by requesting his mom be granted sole parental rights.

"*I can't believe Dad's getting remarried.*" *Sam lay on his back, arms folded underneath his head, staring up at the roof of the tree house, where sunshine sliced through the uneven spaces in between the boards.*

"*You're kidding, right?*" *Stephen sat with his back up against one of the walls, a bit of a summer breeze whispering through the window.* "*This has been coming for a long time. Why do you think he wanted us to meet Gina when we were here for Christmas?*"

"*She's like . . . what? Thirty? Dad looks stupid dating her.*"

"*He's happy.*"

"*He and Mom were happy. They should fix their marriage instead of going off and getting married to other people. What happened to all that 'till death do us part' stuff they probably said at their wedding?*"

"*I dunno, Sam. It's not like we can tell Dad and Mom to go to counseling or something.*"

"*Why should they listen to us? We just have to deal with their stupid decisions.*" *Sam rolled over onto to his stomach so that he could look at Stephen.* "*Well, I'm not going to do it this time.*"

"*Not going to do what?*"

"*Just because Dad's getting married doesn't mean I have to like it or that I have to come to the wedding. This is gonna upset Mom.*"

"*You not coming to the wedding won't stop it.*"

"*I know that. But I'm sticking with Mom. She's been hurt enough.*"

"*The divorce wasn't all Dad's fault—*"

"*Who had to move, huh? Mom. And she had to start working again because she said Dad doesn't pay her enough child support. And she cries herself to sleep at night—can't you hear her?*"

Stephen heard her. And he could still hear the echoes of his parents' fights—the screaming, the yelling, the accusations.

"Dad needs us, too, Sam. I like Gina. I want to give her a chance."

"I don't want a stepmother. Dad can get married if he wants—I can't stop him. But I don't have to like it."

Their standoff in the tree house had been the first of many. Each showdown seemed to shove him and Sam a few feet farther apart as they spent less and less time together. Talked less. Understood each other less. And then Sam left for the army.

And now there was no way this side of eternity that Stephen could reach his brother.

nine

•••••••◆••••••◆•••••◆•••••

*N*esting. What a ridiculous term for this all-consuming desire to ransack and reorganize every dresser drawer and closet shelf in her house. The urge to straighten out her kitchen cabinets pulled her out of bed at four in the morning. She should have been sleeping, not sorting through what few kitchen utensils and Tupperware she'd managed to unpack.

What had Claire said? *"You're getting ready for that little one to be born. Like a mama bird."*

Didn't getting ready for the baby mean creating a room—a nursery—for him? Covering up the orange walls with something more appealing, like plain old white? Putting together the crib? Hanging curtains? Maybe even washing the few infant clothes Haley had purchased because, well, once again, Claire insisted the baby needed to wear something?

"Oh, Haley, look at this adorable sleeper! It has a zebra on it." Claire held up a white sleeper with bright blue, red, and yellow stripes. "And this one has penguins. Aren't penguins fun? You need to get these."

For a woman who hadn't birthed a child yet, Claire had no problem spending Haley's money in Gymboree.

She surveyed her almost-empty cupboard, plastic containers all in a row, the lids stored in a separate container. For the first time in her life, she felt domestic . . . and ridiculously pleased that her cabinets were organized. While she'd been up, she'd tackled her linen closet, too. But if she focused only on towels and Tupperware, her son would sleep in a laundry basket beside her bed.

Of course, if the baby was going to sleep in a crib, she needed to conquer her fear of a toolbox, specifically a screwdriver, for this project. Her dad taught all her brothers how to handle the tools in his workshop—and included Haley in the instruction by the time she was old enough to follow him around asking, "Whatcha doing, Daddy? Can I help?"

But while she could take on her brothers in tackle football—and had the scars to prove it—and bested them on the shooting range, she failed completely when she picked up tools. Any and all tools.

She'd have no problem *unpacking* the crib from the box in the spare bedroom, where the deliverymen had hauled it when it arrived yesterday. Bless her parents for surprising her with the gift. But hauling Sam's toolbox into the room? Reading the assembly directions? Attempting to put the thing together?

A waste of time.

She patted her tummy, which seemed to have popped out even farther overnight and stretched against the limits of Sam's T-shirt, which doubled as a maternity top. Maybe she needed to actually walk into a maternity store. *No.* She'd gotten this far utilizing baggy sweatpants and loose tops and sweaters. No need to spend good money on pants with elastic panels that she'd never wear again.

She walked down the hallway and opened the door into the room next to her bedroom. A window, the blinds closed to the winter sunshine, was set in the wall across from her, with not even a basic set of curtains to soften the stark outline. The walls, marred with wear, were painted the pale autumn orange that the previous owners had selected. Maybe she should have insisted the owners repaint. Did she have the time to paint? The energy? Would her ob-gyn approve?

Haley ran a hand along the rectangular cardboard box leaning against one wall. Did she dare try her luck? Maybe Claire's husband would help her put the crib together. Maybe she should have asked the deliverymen to assemble it—

The out-of-tune doorbell interrupted her internal litany of questions.

But first she'd answer the door. And it better not be Stephen Ames showing up with another unwanted, unneeded, unasked-for baby gift. True, he hadn't been around in three days. But she found herself wondering where he was—and if he would show up on her doorstep again. She wasn't waiting for him . . . just on her guard.

Dusting her hands off, she walked to the front door, giving a quick glance out the front window. Why were cars parked in front of her house? Somebody in the cul-de-sac must have been expecting company.

As she opened the door, Claire's jubilant "Surprise!" caused her to stumble backward.

"What? Who are you surprising? It's not my birthday."

A stream of women, all carrying gift bags or boxes and dishes of food, followed Claire into the house.

Claire blew her an air kiss as she passed. "Surprise for you— and that little guy we get to meet here pretty soon."

Haley watched as Emily, the wife of one of Sam's friends,

breezed by with a cheery "Good morning!" and a wicker picnic basket dangling from her arm. The woman moved the laptop to the breakfast bar, depositing the pile of homeowners' association letters into the wire basket. Then she unpacked the hamper lined with red-and-white checked material, covering the table with a white lace tablecloth. Within seconds, Emily pulled coordinated pale blue plates, napkins, cups, and plastic ware out of the basket and began arranging everything on the table.

Hugging her, Claire nudged Haley toward the kitchen. "Happy baby shower."

Haley tried to process the cacophony of women's voices filling her house, drowning out the sound of the movie playing on her TV. "We didn't talk about a baby shower."

"I know we didn't." Claire squeezed her hands. "I also know how you feel about parties and all that 'fuss,' as you call it. But every mom deserves a shower."

They both sidestepped Sara, who carried a round cake decorated with pastel-colored polka dots and the word *Baby*. Cheryl, Faith, and Sandy, three other wives of men in Sam's battalion, stood at the kitchen counter, arranging croissant sandwiches on a platter and unwrapping fruit and veggie trays. *Whoa. Talk about moving fast.*

"What do you want me to do?" Haley stood in the steady stream of women flowing from the kitchen to the living room and back again, all stopping to hug her as they set up for her party.

"You are the guest of honor—you and baby-to-be." Claire, perfectly put together in a coordinated pair of leather boots, skinny jeans, and a white cardigan sweater set with a gold scarf, turned her around and pushed her toward the living room. "Sit. Relax."

"I can't let you do this."

"As if you have a choice."

Haley lowered her voice, standing close to her friend, who was emptying ice into a fancy silver bucket. She must have brought that with her—Haley didn't own anything silver. "Claire, I've never had a baby shower, but I do know it's usually not a 'show up on the mom-to-be's doorstep' affair. Besides, I wasn't expecting you to—anybody to—"

Claire wove her arm through Haley's and tugged her down the hall. She raised her voice so that it echoed back into the living room. "Yes, I'd love to see what you've done with the baby's room."

"But I haven't done anything."

"Show me the room."

"Fine. I'll show you the room—and everything I've done." She opened the door, stepped inside, and did a quick turn around. "Which is nothing, besides being surprised by the delivery of a crib from my parents."

Dancing a brief jig, Claire clapped her hands like a toddler. "Happy baby shower from your mom and dad!"

Haley would have sat down—if there'd been anything to collapse onto besides the floor. "My parents knew about the baby shower?"

"Of course they knew. I invited your mom, but she said she's coming out once the baby's born. She did want to send a gift, though." Claire gave the room a quick once-over. "You don't want to bring your son home to this room. There are no curtains—"

"I know that. I just haven't gotten around to painting yet. Or choosing curtains. Or a dresser."

All the things she needed to do—and hadn't—rose up and accused her. *Please, don't let Claire ask what I do all day.* She couldn't tell her. Dodged Shelton's letters. Napped. Filled the silence with nonstop DVDs. Went to the bathroom too many times. Avoidance took up a lot of time.

"You're not going to use the crib right away. Most of the time, a newborn sleeps in a bassinet or a cradle near the parents' bed."

"Why can't I just use the crib?"

"Do you really want to be traipsing back and forth from your bed to the baby's crib during the night?"

"No. But my baby isn't going to keep me up at night."

"Spoken like a delusional first-time mom-to-be. No newborn sleeps through the night." Claire eyed the window. "Do you sew?"

"Not even a button on a blouse. If something rips, it ends up in the thrift store pile." She stared Claire down. "What? We each have our talents. Can you drive tacks with a Glock at twenty yards? Disassemble and reassemble a Walther PPK in under a minute?"

"I don't even know what you just asked me. But I doubt either of those skills is going to help you get ready for this baby."

As if Claire needed to tell her that.

"Do you know what color you want to paint the room?"

"Blue?"

"Original."

"Blue is a boy color."

"Hundreds of years ago, boys wore pink. Did you know that?"

"No—and I am not painting this room pink. What would Sam think if I painted his son's room pink?"

Her question thudded against the walls. What would Sam have said about any of this? Would he have wanted a son or a daughter? He'd been denied the chance to experience fatherhood—and her stubbornness had stolen what few moments he could have savored.

"Hey, you okay?" Claire's question pulled Haley back from an emotional abyss. Grief was one thing—remorse could crumble the fragile ground beneath her feet.

"Sure. I'm fine."

"Missing Sam?"

"Yes." She switched off the light, moving back into the hallway. "There's a part of me that always misses Sam."

"I planned this shower to encourage you, not to upset you."

"It's not the baby shower." The words piled up in the back of her throat. If only she could let them tumble out . . . find release. "It's just . . . everything. All the things I have to do before the baby's born. All the letters from the homeowners' association. Never mind."

"Haley, how many times do I have to tell you the guys are willing to help?"

"And how many times do I have to tell you I can handle it?" Laughter sounded in the living room. "Even if Sam were here, I'd be the one painting the baby's room. Come on, let's go enjoy this baby shower you surprised me with—but I'm warning you, I don't play games. Got it?"

·••··•··◄►··•··•·

Well, she couldn't say the baby didn't have stuff.

Haley sat in the middle of the baby's bedroom, surrounded by the gifts the women had given her. A stuffed yellow duck with a neon orange bill snuggled in a car seat. Bottles of baby shampoo, baby wash, and baby lotion overflowed from a blue plastic baby tub, nestled against a pale green terry-cloth towel with one end that formed a hood that looked like a turtle, and a pile of soft pastel washcloths.

Could she wash a newborn without breaking him?

She picked up a teddy bear covered in soft golden fur. How many stuffed animals did one baby need? A duck, two bears, a lamb, a cow that rattled when she shook it, and a floppy striped tiger—she was well on her way to a zoo for her unborn son. If she put all these animals in the crib once she assembled it, he would have nowhere to sleep.

Depositing the bear back in the menagerie, she touched the bundle of tiny clothes lying near her left knee. Would her baby really fit in these? Her finger traced the stitching on a pint-sized jean jacket. Sam would have loved this, especially paired with the BORN TO BE WILD onesie. Claire had instructed her to wash all the clothes and blankets—a glimpse into her future of nonstop laundry once the baby was born. Time enough for laundry tomorrow. She still needed to attack the piles of her own dirty clothes she'd been ignoring.

Ignoring things. That seemed to be her modus operandi since Sam had been killed. If possible, she would have shut the door in the stoic faces of the men who'd shown up almost five months ago to tell her Sam had been killed. Not that they had to say anything—just seeing them standing outside the apartment, so formally dressed, so still, so *sorry* . . . She'd known.

"He's been killed, hasn't he?"

"Ma'am, may we come in?"

"Just tell me."

"Please, ma'am, may we come in?"

Fine. They wanted to be inside the apartment before telling her what she already knew. She moved out of the way, her hand still clenching the doorknob of their second-floor apartment. Followed them into the small living room. Sat in the chair she'd reupholstered during Sam's first deployment after they'd married while all three men sat on the couch.

And waited.

They'd expected tears.

She'd been polite. Controlled. She knew what was expected of her as an army wife. Sam never worried about her when he was gone . . .

A sharp twinge at the base of her belly caused Haley to wince. Rubbing the area, she eased herself to her feet. Braxton Hicks contractions—that's what Lily had called them. A physical reminder that motherhood was imminent. Single motherhood.

No tears. No tears.

I can do this. I have to do this. I will do this. I won't let you down, Sam.

Dispersing her thoughts with a shake of her head, she retrieved a white rectangular plastic basket from the laundry room, bending to pile the clothes and blankets, towels and washcloths into it, and then carrying it back to the room between the kitchen and the garage and placing it on top of the dryer, kicking at the pile of dirty jeans on the floor.

"I'll see you in the morning." She muffled a yawn with her hand. "I need a snack and some sleep."

In the kitchen, she noticed her iPhone sitting in the wooden fruit bowl between two yellow bananas just beginning to sport brown spots. Okay . . . what was it doing there? Where was her brain? If she couldn't keep track of her phone, how was she going to take care of a baby?

When she picked it up, she noticed she had a message from Sam's mom. It'd been a couple of weeks since they last talked— the night of their "Do you have another son?" conversation.

Captured in a voice mail, Miriam's voice hesitated. "Haley? Why aren't you picking up the phone? I hope you're okay—that you're not too angry with me. Has Sam's brother contacted you again?" Haley deleted the message and checked the time. Nine o'clock. Still early enough to call. But first, she tore into a bag of mini candy bars, filling a cereal bowl with an assortment of Snickers, Milky Ways, Three Musketeers—and setting the Twix aside for Claire. Then she poured herself a glass of milk—plain—and settled onto the couch to talk to Miriam.

Her mother-in-law answered before the second ring. "Haley? Oh, Haley, I'm so thankful you called me back."

"Is everything okay?"

"I'm fine. I want to know how you are—you haven't called me since . . . since . . ."

"Since Stephen showed up here?" Were things so bad that Miriam couldn't even say her son's name?

"Yes."

Haley swallowed half a mini Milky Way chased with a sip of cold milk. "Sorry. Having a before-bed snack. Sam's twin showed up here a couple of times. I finally agreed to meet him for dinner and answer some of his questions."

"What did he want to know?"

"Basic things. How long Sam and I were married. Did Sam like the military—that kind of thing."

"How did he look?"

"Just like Sam—"

"No, no. I mean, did he look happy?"

Now, why did Miriam expect her to be able to answer that question? "We weren't talking about him. He asked questions about Sam. I answered as best I could. Miriam, can't you call him? Is it so hard—so bad between you both? I mean, he told me that you were the one who let him know about Sam."

When Miriam didn't respond, Haley voiced the question lurking in her head. "Did you and your ex-husband make some sort of agreement that you'd take Sam and that he'd take Stephen? That you wouldn't talk to Stephen?"

"No, nothing like that."

"Then call him. You must miss your son."

"I—I wouldn't know what to say."

Haley unwrapped another candy bar, but she'd lost her appetite. "Well, that seems to be the problem that kept Sam and Stephen apart all these years. Maybe it's time to say something—anything."

"It's so complicated."

"So are all the unsaid things—the things you can never say once someone's dead." Now whom was she talking to—her mother-in-law or herself? "I'm sorry, Miriam. You've got to decide how to handle this. I'm no relationship expert."

"Are you getting together with him again?"

"I don't plan on it." She stirred the mix of chocolate bars with her fingers, swirling them around in the bowl. "What's the point?"

"Well, if you do . . . will you tell him I asked about him?"

"Of course."

But that would be yet another message left undelivered.

ten

Stephen was 100 percent certain that his oh-so-reluctant sister-in-law was going to hate his showing up again. He'd thought about it all the way from Fort Collins to Colorado Springs. And yet, he wanted to do this. Had to do this. Why else would he drive over a hundred miles? But Haley? His actions might be grounds for another potential "click, click, bang" episode.

He pulled the car into the driveway to the left of the house, his glance straying to the leafless tree that looked even barer now that his plans to hang the baby swing had been thwarted by the unpredictable Colorado weather. He'd be lucky if he got to hang the swing before May—if Haley didn't hang the swing herself.

He grabbed a small white envelope from its resting place on the front passenger seat. Not that heavy, but then again, you couldn't always judge the value of something by how much it weighed.

Would Haley even be home? Was she going to work once the baby was born? If he asked her any more personal questions, she'd hit him over the head with a virtual NO TRESPASSING sign. It wasn't as if a once-absentee brother-in-law and uncle-to-be had any say in how she raised the kid. Sam's son or daughter.

Cold heightened by a biting wind cleared the cul-de-sac today. The bare tree branches rattled as a gust of air tossed Stephen's hair and nipped his neck and ears. The front door swung open, and Haley stood with the screen door separating them.

"I don't need anything else for the baby." Haley stood with her arms crossed over her rounded tummy, which was evident beneath a long-sleeved brown T-shirt adorned with the simple slogan LIFE IS GOOD in muted orange letters. Did she believe that?

"Hello to you, too." Stephen held up the envelope. "I wanted to show you something."

She didn't budge. Haley Ames redefined the word *stubborn*. "May I come in?" Another gust of wind shook the screen. "At least one of us is going to get cold."

"The cold doesn't bother me." When he remained standing in front of her, she unlatched the door. "Fine. Come in."

He watched her as he entered the house. Should he remove his coat? Leave it on? The coat stayed on. She'd said to come in, not sit down and stay awhile. She hadn't issued an invitation to watch whatever was playing on her TV. Was that John Wayne? *Huh.* "You're a John Wayne fan?"

"Absolutely." Haley tucked a wayward strand of hair behind her ear. "You're not?"

"I didn't say that." Stephen studied a stack of half a dozen westerns next to the DVD player. "Although I may not be as huge a fan as you are. How've you been?"

"If you're really interested, I'm doing all right—for a woman who hasn't slept through the night in weeks." A full-on yawn punctuated her statement.

"Sorry to hear that. I'm still job-hunting." Not that Haley had asked. He was finding his way around an almost nonexistent relationship.

She nodded toward the envelope in his hand. "So?"

"Oh, yeah. I wanted to show you something." *Okay. Enough chitchat.* Since it looked as if she had no intention of inviting him to sit down, he risked standing beside her.

"And this is . . . ?"

"I found this in a box of things I've kept since I was a kid."

She reached out her hand, tracing the edge with her finger. "And why would you bring me something from a box of your childhood memorabilia?"

At this moment, he wasn't even sure why. He'd sorted through a white box hidden on the top shelf in his bedroom closet, sifting through boyish treasures. His Eagle Scout medal. A carved wooden car that had taken first place at a Pinewood Derby competition. A watch that Sam had given him one Christmas—and he'd given Sam an identical one. An arrowhead. A shark's tooth. A purple geode he'd bought at a rock store during a family vacation. The first pocketknife he'd ever owned—his dad presented both Sam and him with knives on their tenth birthday. A pile of photographs, where he'd found today's offering. He pulled it out of the envelope, taking the time to smooth out the bent corner. "Here."

"What is this?"

"A picture." So much for stating the obvious. "Of me and Sam the day we finished the tree fort."

Did Haley realize her hand shook as she took the picture from him? She turned it over, as if looking for a date or inscription. Stephen knew what she'd see: two boys, standing side by side, wearing identical jeans, identical T-shirts—only his was green and Sam's was blue—and identical grins. Sam's cowlick in his bangs twisted one way, while Stephen's flew the opposite. They stood at the base of their brand-new tree fort, one on either side of the cockeyed ladder they'd nailed into the tree trunk.

"You don't have to prove anything to me." Haley held the photo out to him.

"I'm not trying to prove anything. I thought you might like to see Sam when he was younger—" Stephen tucked the flap of the envelope back down, closing off the treasure of his past. For a moment, the only sound in the room was John Wayne, as G. W. McLintock, shouting, "Don't say it's a fine morning or I'll shoot ya!"

Ironic.

"I wanted to show you that photo of me and Sam. I don't know . . . Let you see a glimpse of my life with him." He resisted clenching the envelope in a fist, a sigh dragging out of his lungs. "And I admit it: I lost my brother for twelve years. My fault . . . his fault . . . I'm tired of arguing about that. I still need answers. And you have them."

His unspoken plea for help hung between them.

The blue of Haley's eyes resembled that of a pair of faded, worn-out jeans. "You didn't lose Sam—you let him go."

"Are you trying to make me feel guilty? I do. But Sam stopped talking to me, too. We're both to blame." What could he say to get through to her? "Please, Haley. Help me find my brother again—the man you married. I should have been standing beside Sam on your wedding day."

She stared past him for a few seconds, seeming to wrestle with a decision. Her shoulders relaxed. "Have you had breakfast?"

"Is that an invitation?" The coffee and bagel he'd eaten had burned off an hour ago.

"If you're hungry, then yes, it's an invitation. I could scramble some eggs, and we could . . . talk."

"How about I make breakfast? I make a great omelet—if you've got the right ingredients."

"Well, there's one way you're not like Sam. He was lousy in the kitchen—but great at picking up takeout. Cheddar cheese and some of that precooked bacon good enough?" She motioned toward the kitchen. "I may have the remains of an onion or green pepper in the bin . . . but there's no guarantee."

"I'll make do. You can't make an omelet without cheddar cheese and bacon."

"That's what Sam told me, too." Their eyes tangled for just a second before Haley padded over to the kitchen.

Stephen shucked off his jacket, hanging it on the back of one of the mismatched dining room chairs. How did Haley manage to make four different chairs look as if they belonged together? "Dad taught us how to make omelets. He used to let my mom sleep in on Saturdays, and the three of us would have breakfast, watch cartoons, and then we'd make Mom an omelet and bring her breakfast in bed—for lunch."

"Sam mentioned making omelets with your mom." Haley carried an armful of ingredients over to the counter: a package of shredded cheese, a half-used package of bacon, the remnants of an onion in a plastic bag, and a shriveled red pepper tumbled onto the counter. "Why did your parents divorce?"

"Didn't Sam tell you?" Stephen brought the carton of eggs over to the counter next to the stove.

"Not much. Sam wasn't a talker. He liked sports. Participating in them and watching them. He liked to be on the go—talking about the past, not so much. All he said was that your parents argued all the time and that your dad left."

"That's not the whole story."

"I didn't think it was. I figured he'd get around to telling me more details . . . later." She placed a paper towel on a dinner plate, added a layer of bacon, covered it with another paper towel, and then put it in the microwave. "And that's my contribution to breakfast."

"Thank you. Now go sit down and relax." Stephen waved her over to one of the tall wooden chairs tucked around the breakfast bar. "From what my dad told me, our parents married young—and without my mom's parents' approval. I don't know what their marital problems were. Religion maybe. My dad's job. Mom had a couple of miscarriages. Then Sam and I were born, and she had to have a hysterectomy after that. I don't know why. I'm not sure if it was one of these things or all of these things that caused cracks in their marriage. This all new to you?"

"Yes."

Another trademark Haley Ames one-syllable response. She acted like a spectator at a sporting event—somebody way up high in the bleachers who wasn't all that interested in the game. "My dad got promoted when we were in middle school and traveled a lot. That was either when the tension started or when it increased to the point that they weren't able to hide it from us."

As he talked, Stephen chopped onion and red pepper, making separate neat piles on the plastic cutting board. The salty aroma of bacon blending with the pungent onions filled the kitchen.

Haley sat with her elbows on the counter, chin resting in her upturned palms. "What did your parents argue about?"

"How much my dad was gone. How much money my mom was spending. She got addicted to those home-shopping shows—boxes arrived every day. It got to the point where she didn't even open them, just piled them up in their bedroom or the den."

"Sam said your dad had an affair."

"That's what my mom said." Stephen kept his voice even, cracking six eggs into a clear Plexiglas bowl. Even this many years later, the accusation stung like an unexpected slap across the face. "My dad said it wasn't true."

"How do you know your dad wasn't lying? A lot of men who travel fool around on their wives."

"Did Sam fool around?"

"What?" A deep groove appeared between Haley's eyes.

"Sam traveled, right? He deployed with the army—"

"My husband did not fool around!"

He was losing any ground he'd won with her—but it was worth it to make a point.

"Neither did my dad." Stephen deposited the remnants of eggshells into the metal trash can, the lid clattering shut, then lathered his hands with lemon-scented soap, rinsing them under a stream of warm water. He dried his hands on a plain white cotton towel before he spoke again. "I know both of my parents were at fault in the divorce—but I also know my dad didn't cheat on my mom. I'm sorry for what I said about my brother."

He worked in silence for a few moments, adding a little water to the beaten eggs and then pouring half the mixture into the pan he'd preheated on the stove. If he was going to spend time with Haley Ames he needed to get used to silence. "You want everything?"

She failed to hide another yawn behind her hand. "Yes—and double the cheese, please."

At least she was still speaking to him. He let the conversation lag as he whipped up the omelets, enjoying the familiarity of cooking. Different kitchen, but the same motions: slicing, chopping, stirring, mixing. The same smells: onion, butter, bacon, cheese. Time blended into a mixture of present and past—making breakfast for Haley and Saturdays with Sam and his dad. Laughter. Sharing a meal. Family.

Ten minutes later, they sat next to one another at her dining room table, the papers shoved to one end. After two bites, Haley raised her glass of chocolate milk in salute. "You weren't lying—you make a great omelet."

Stephen returned the salute with his cup of orange juice. "An Ames never lies."

Instead of responding in kind at his attempt to keep things light, Haley's face paled. She pressed her lips together, her blue eyes shining with unshed tears.

"You okay?"

She shook her head, her blond hair moving against her shoulders. *Yes. No.* Covered her face with her hands.

What was wrong?

••••••◆••••••

Stephen's offhand comment shoved her into the past.

"What did you say?" Haley wished she could risk twisting around to face Sam, but she stayed still, his arms wrapped around her, no longer seeing the view from Pikes Peak.

"I said I love you, Hal." His throaty whisper against her ear caused a delicious tremor to course through her body as he pulled her closer.

She tilted her head so she could look into his eyes, his scruffy chin scraping against her face, the now-familiar scent of his favorite soap teasing her senses. *"Do you mean that?"*

"An Ames never lies."

"Haley?"

A breath shuddered through her. She lowered her hands, her eyes scanning his face. When she reached out to trace the outline of his jaw with shaking fingers, he inhaled. Held his breath.

"An Ames never lies . . ." Haley whispered the words. "Did you . . ."

As her fingertips grazed his lips, Haley leaned toward him, her eyes starting to close in anticipation of his kiss.

He pulled back just as her lips brushed his. "Haley. Stop."

She stilled. Her eyes flew open; their gazes locked. This was Stephen. Not Sam. "Stephen . . ." She bit down on her bottom lip when it trembled.

Haley bolted up, knocking the chair backward and causing Stephen, who was rising from the table, to stumble sideways. He scrambled to follow her, but by the time he reached the front porch, she was down the driveway.

"Haley, wait! You don't even have shoes on."

She didn't look back. Just raised her hand and waved him off—and kept walking down the sidewalk in her bare feet.

••••• ◆ •••••

She'd kissed Stephen Ames.

Almost kissed him. Almost.

An Ames never lies.

What was that? Some sort of family motto? Stephen and Sam didn't even live together. Hadn't spoken to one another in twelve years.

A blast of wind blew her hair about her face, long strands tangling around her eyes and mouth. Unshed tears scalded her eyes.

She wouldn't cry. Tears meant you were weak—and Jordans were strong. Her brothers taught her well. *No tears. Keep up.*

She was doing her best to keep up with the unrelenting demands of people like Sterling Shelton III and her unborn baby and her husband, who probably watched her from heaven and shook his head.

Stupid family mottos.

"Please, Haley. Help me find my brother again."

Why did she let her guard down? Were the Ames brothers her Kryptonite?

How was she supposed to help Stephen find his brother again? Being around him made her lose her way. She was trying to move forward, not backward.

The soles of her feet scraped against the pavement. When a gust of wind tugged at her hair again, she pushed it away from her face. The scent of lime lingered from when her fingertips grazed Stephen's jaw.

So much for the truce. Sam's brother had to stop showing up at her house.

Stop asking questions.

Stop confusing her because he was so much like her husband.

And yet not him.

eleven

..... ● ..... ● ..... ● ..... ● .....

Until attending childbirth class, Haley had never thought much of the super-sized bouncy balls she'd seen in the gym.

"Should I invest in one of those?" She nodded toward the mass of multicolored rubber exercise balls corralled in the corner of Lily's family room. "I could sit on one the entire time I'm in labor."

Claire zipped up her red down vest, tugging her half gloves from a pocket. "Maybe I'll bring one along for each of us. We'll just bounce our way through your labor and delivery."

"Well, by the time I'm ready to deliver this little guy, I think I'll want to be in the birthing bed." Haley slipped on Sam's coat, tugging on the zipper when it stuck halfway.

"Good point."

The hum of conversation quieted as the other couples said good-bye, carrying their pillows and calling out, "See you next week" and "Practice breathing."

Haley took one last sip of the cold orange-and-lemon-infused water Lily served to the class. "Who knew water could be so refreshing? It can't be that hard to cut lemon and orange slices and add them to water—right?"

"First you'd have to locate the produce section in the grocery store."

"Hey—"

"Well, what did you think of class this week?" Lily rearranged a few cushions on the extra-long sofa before joining Haley and Claire. She wore jeans and a black blouse accented with a turquoise and silver necklace and earrings.

Claire gathered up Haley's pillows. "I got through another birth video, so I figure I'll survive the real event."

"She was talking to the mom-to-be, not you. And half the time you had your hands over your eyes. You planning on doing that when I'm in labor?"

"No. That's why we're doing the classes—trial run and all that." Claire crossed her heart. "I'll be the best coach ever."

At the front door, Lily paused in the tiled foyer decorated with a single large ceramic vase. "No children yet, Claire?"

"No. I'm ready, but . . . my husband wants to wait. It's okay. We've got time."

Haley caught the hitch in her friend's voice. And here Claire was, coming with her, when being with a bunch of pregnant women probably reminded her of what she wanted and couldn't have—yet.

"What about you, Haley? Are you ready?"

"Sure. I mean, as ready as I can be. I've got six and a half weeks yet. Plenty of time to get prepared. Pack my bag." She waved a folded piece of blue paper. "Practice those breathing techniques you taught us today. With your instruction and Claire holding my hand, I'll do just fine."

She choked back the confession—all the days, weeks, and months stretching into years and years scared her more than a few hours of labor. Birthing a baby was nothing compared to raising a son without Sam.

Lily's soft voice scattered Haley's thoughts. "Remember, I'm happy to be a backup, just in case something happens and Claire can't be there. After my husband died, I decided I wanted to be by myself in the delivery room. I figured the nurses could help me."

"And?"

"I planned on doing it all by myself, but my mother said she'd come in and hold my hand, take pictures, pray for me, whatever I needed. She was a smart woman—I needed the prayers more than anything else."

"You're a believer?"

"I couldn't teach these classes and not be. The miracle of birth just confirms over and over again that there's a God, don't you think?"

"I believe in God . . . I just don't feel that close to him right now."

"Not surprising. The walk of grief is different for each of us." Lily seemed in no rush to have them leave, her relaxed posture echoed in the oval mirror hanging on the far wall. "Sometimes our emotions are so numb we think that means we no longer believe in God. That our faith has fractured. Or been destroyed altogether."

"I want to be strong, to trust God in all of this . . . in Sam's death. But right now strength seems to mean not thinking about it. Not . . . feeling. Praying feels like trickles of water coming out of a hose when someone has tied a big knot in it somewhere. I can only manage a few words every once in a while." Even as the pent-up confession escaped, Haley couldn't believe she was telling a virtual stranger things she wrestled with when she lay awake in her dark bedroom. But this woman had walked the same path Haley was on—and she hadn't given up on life.

"You are trusting God each day that you get up and try again to live your life without your husband." Lily rested a hand on her arm. "You haven't quit. You're taking care of yourself and your baby."

"That's all I am doing—the next right thing."

"Sometimes that's all God is asking us to do: make the right choice—over and over again. And before you know it, you've walked into the future and hope he has waiting for you."

"So not wanting to think about Sam is okay? Feeling numb doesn't mean I'm doubting God?"

"You think about your husband more than you realize. And numb is normal when your world has been rocked by an emotional nuclear blast like the one you've experienced. You need time to heal."

Haley gripped the cuffs of her jacket to keep her hands from trembling—but that didn't stop how her heart thudded in her chest. "Do you ever heal from this?"

"In time—but I can't tell you how long it will take for you. You need to accept that you have to wait."

"Be still and know he's God, right?"

"And believe that he didn't lose sight of Sam or you when your husband was killed. Somehow, some way, God will make sense of it—he already has made sense of it. Don't try to force it."

"You sure you're not a counselor?"

Lily responded with a light, musical laugh. "Childbirth instructor, counselor, mom—sometimes they all flow together. May I share a verse with you? It helped me after my husband died."

Haley nodded. "Sure."

"'He tends his flock like a shepherd: He gathers the lambs in his arms and carries them close to his heart; he gently leads those that have young.'" Lily's laugh sounded again, probably because of the look on Haley's face. "Wondering how that applies to you, aren't you? You're the lamb—and you're going to be a mom soon. And God, your shepherd, is carrying you close to his heart. He's leading you in all of this."

"To be honest with you, I haven't . . . liked where he's led me so far. It's scary to keep following." She could hardly look at Lily as she admitted her struggle and instead found herself staring at her reflection in the foyer mirror. Who was that woman?

"I know. That's where trusting him—knowing that he loves us despite the circumstances he allows in our lives—comes in."

As they left, Lily hugged Haley, and Claire offered the woman an embrace, too. Haley knew the instructor watched them as they exited the warmth of her home. After driving in silence for a few moments, Haley glanced over at her friend, who sat staring out the window. "Not your typical childbirth instructor, I'm betting."

Claire continued to look out the window. "You're probably right."

"You okay?"

"Me? Sure. I'm not the one having a baby."

"And that's a problem, isn't it?"

"What? No. I'm good—"

"Claire, I heard what you said. That you're ready to have a baby, but Finn's not."

Her friend sniffed. Gave a quick shake of her head. "It's no big deal. We're not the first couple to disagree about having children."

"He does want kids, right?"

"Down the road. Maybe."

"But you talked about this before you got married."

"I was so crazy in love with Finn, I didn't care back then." Claire huddled in the passenger seat. "When I told him I wanted a large family, he said he wasn't sure about kids—and I knew I could change his mind. I mean, I've wanted children forever."

"You don't have to do this, Claire. If it's too hard to be my labor coach, you don't have to come to classes with me or to—"

"Of course I'm doing this. I want to do this. You heard Lily. You are not having your baby by yourself. I'm going to hold your hand and make sure you breathe, and I'll take pictures and pray and count the baby's fingers and toes . . ." Claire's voice cracked and trailed off.

"We'll be okay, Claire." Haley reached over and grabbed her friend's hand.

Claire squeezed her fingers. "Yes, we will. Speaking of us . . . How are you doing?"

Haley trained her eyes on the road. "We're talking about you, not me."

"We were talking about me—now I'm asking about you. You're quiet."

"You're the talker, not me."

"More than usual. You look sad." Claire twisted in the seat to look at her. "A different kind of sad."

Before Sam died, Haley never knew how many facets there were to sadness. "I'm tired. This little guy doesn't let me sleep at night." She could tell her friend wasn't buying her excuse. But she wasn't talking about what had happened with Stephen Ames—the crazy moment when he morphed into Sam. The almost-kiss. Not Claire—or anybody else. So she'd give her what she wanted. "And yes, the thought of having the baby without Sam makes me . . . sad."

"I'm sorry, Haley."

"I know you are. And your being with me in the delivery room is going to help so, so much." She reached over and turned on the radio, allowing the toe-tapping beat of "Boot Scootin' Boogie" to fill the car. "Now, what about a late dinner? I'm starving. You pick—my treat."

"Deal—except it's my treat. How's Noodles and Company sound?"

"Perfect. And we'll see who manages to pay the bill first."

twelve

......•......•......•......

Haley stood, her hands folded and pressed against her lips, staring at the business card stuck into the bottom corner of the kitchen cabinet. *Stephen R. Ames. Architect. Entrepreneur.*

He'd shown up at her door three times. Asked for help. And she'd agreed to his request—his plea—to help him discover who Sam became during the past dozen years.

But then there'd been that where-had-her-brain-gone-wandering moment when the present slipped into the past and Stephen became Sam.

And that was the end of Stephen Ames and his questions.

So why was she contemplating calling him?

Pregnancy hormones were blamed for all sorts of behaviors—forgetfulness, sleeplessness, anxiety . . . but did they cause stupidity?

Haley raked her hands through her hair, a groan escaping past her lips. She'd had no intention of calling the man ever, ever again—until another bout of nesting had her dragging one of the bookcases in from the garage so that it now sat against the wall in the dining room. The ache in her back warned her it wasn't one of her brightest decisions, but once she got the thing lugged into her laundry room, she couldn't leave it there. A morning of emptying boxes of books—carrying small armfuls from the garage—and she had half the shelves stacked helter-skelter with books. When she found Sam's high school year-books, she couldn't help but stop and sit on the cement garage steps to flip through the pages. Cold seeped through the seat of her sweatpants as she searched for photos of her husband.

And then she'd discovered the faded sketch of a diagram la-beled "TREEHOUSE."

It was a rough drawing, lines erased and redrawn, but there was enough detail to see the plans for the steps leading up to the "door" in the floor and the windows in two of the walls. The words *saw*, *nails*, *hammer*, and *wood* were scribbled on the back in a boyish attempt at a shopping list.

Stephen Ames deserved to see this—to have the sketch. She wasn't a coward; she refused to tuck the paper back into its hid-ing place.

Haley exhaled when his phone went straight to voice mail. "This is Stephen Ames. I'm sorry I missed your call. Please leave a message and I will call you back."

"Stephen." She cleared her throat. "This is Haley . . . I found something I think you should see. I'll be around this weekend, if you want to stop by."

Maybe she should have said, *And I won't do anything crazy like think you're Sam and try to kiss you*. But she hoped that was implied. Now all she needed to do was wait and see if he called back.

She could always unpack more boxes—maybe something more lightweight, like clothes. Other than Sam's winter coat and some of his shirts that she wore as makeshift maternity tops, everything else was still packed away. But her rationale that it'd be easier not to think about Sam if there were no reminders of him in the house was false. He never invaded her dreams, but he lingered just on the edge of her thoughts.

It was as if Sam watched her and she couldn't fail him. She'd let him down once in such a terrible way—not that he knew that—and she needed to regain her footing as a reliable, capable military wife. Be strong. Be a good mom. How many times a day did she repeat the scripture in Proverbs about a wife doing her husband good *all the days of her life*? Sam was gone, but she still had a responsibility to make him proud.

She gathered Sam's yearbooks from the garage. The brothers hadn't gone to the same high school, so maybe these would satisfy Stephen's curiosity. Stacking the books in her arms, she headed back to her bedroom, passing through the laundry room. For once she didn't have to step around piles of dirty laundry. Nesting had its advantages. In her bedroom was the one memento she'd kept out when she packed the apartment for the move: a framed photo from their wedding day.

Sitting on the edge of the bed, she retrieved it from where it was half-hidden behind a stack of books—advice on what to expect before and after the baby was born, what to name a baby, how to take care of a baby.

Her fingers touched the image of Sam in a dark suit, white shirt, and muted gray and green tie that he'd borrowed from Chaz. She stood beside him on the courthouse steps, wearing the beaded white dress Claire had talked her into buying. She'd waved away her best friend's insistence that she wear high heels, opting for a comfortable pair of sparkly white ballet flats. If she was saying "I do" to Sam Ames, she wasn't going to worry about falling flat on her face. The two of them looked happy in the photograph. They were happy.

"Hello, Mrs. Ames." Sam followed his whispered greeting by wrapping his strong arms around her waist and pulling her close, placing a lingering kiss against her neck. The man's touch, the sound of his voice, was a heady combination that always ignited a slow spark of desire inside Haley.

"Hello, Mr. Ames." She slipped her arms around his waist, closing her eyes as he continued to press warm kisses along the curve of her throat.

"Three weeks, Hal."

"What?" His words weren't the romantic endearment she'd anticipated.

"Three weeks until my next deployment. I'm so glad you said yes when I proposed—now it's all about saying yes." He pulled her toward the bedroom in his—their—apartment, past her suitcase containing her carefully chosen negligee, not stopping until the two of them tumbled onto the bed.

Did he have to mention the deployment now? On their wedding night? Couldn't they forget about the army—and what his job demanded—for just one night? She had said yes because she loved him, not because he was deploying.

●●●━●━●●●

Should he have called again? Of course, Haley hadn't returned any of the messages Stephen had left her the past two days. And it was a bit late now, since he was pulling up in front of her house. Again. He was beginning to memorize the mile markers along I-25 between Fort Collins and Colorado Springs. If this kept up, maybe he'd need to invest in audiobooks. Or satellite radio.

Haley had to be home. The garage stood open, and it looked as if she'd managed to un-organize the boxes he'd rearranged the last time he was there. Stephen still couldn't believe that she'd called him—not after walking away from him. And not after . . . well, what happened before she'd abandoned him in the house. He had waited almost an hour for her to come back. Cleaned up the breakfast mess, storing the leftovers. And then realized that maybe the better part of valor was a retreat.

All the "I can do it myself" stubbornness had disappeared from Haley's face in those few seconds when she'd almost kissed him. Her eyes had closed, hiding the bright blue, lashes skimming downward . . . her touch gentle when her fingers grazed his jaw. An unexpected warmth had kindled in his skin . . .

And he had no right to think about his brother's widow that way—to imagine what it was like to kiss Haley.

Which was why he hadn't figured out how to reengage with her until the phone message. He needed to make certain he settled his mind on why he was seeing Haley again: to reconnect with his brother. Nothing more. Not that showing up unannounced made things easier. He would take his cue from her—and that was the only plan he had.

Stephen rapped his knuckles against the door leading into the laundry room. "Hello?"

Nothing there except a small mound of white bath towels. Haley didn't like doing laundry. He stepped over them and rapped on the door leading into the main house. "Haley? It's me, Stephen."

A quick look around showed that the living room and the kitchen were both empty—which left the bedrooms and bathrooms.

Great. Both his mother and his stepmother had drilled it into him that you did not bother a woman when she was in the bathroom or the bedroom. Maybe he needed to head to the Mustang and regroup.

A thud as something hit the ground stopped his exit. Was that a yelp? He double-timed it down the hallway, stumbling to a stop on the carpeting outside an open door. Haley was on her knees, wrestling with half of a baby crib.

Muttering.

Her hair was piled on top of her head in a messy ponytail and she narrowed her focus on the jumbled pieces of the collapsed baby crib. "You are an inanimate object and I'm smarter than you." Haley ground out the words through clenched teeth. "Tools or no tools, I am going to put you together."

Stephen swallowed his laughter. "Need some help?"

At the sound of his voice, she dropped a screwdriver into the pile of wood and metal. "Stephen!"

"Let me get that." He stepped over the toolbox and the tools that were scattered over the carpeting. "What do we do next?"

Haley hesitated—but then he'd come ready to gauge her reactions to him.

"I hate to admit it, but it's probably time to look at the directions."

"So, you're a no-following-the-rules kind of woman?" He pulled the directions out of the cardboard box that she'd propped against the wall.

"No following the *directions*. That's different from not following the rules." She released her hair from the elastic band so that it fell down past her shoulders, only to scrape it together again and capture it back on top of her head. "My brothers said reading directions is tantamount to cheating."

"How many brothers do you have?" And why did his sister-in-law keep hair the amber color of honey in a scrambled mess on top of her head?

"Three—all older than me." A laugh bubbled up from her throat. "David, Johnny, and Aaron. They were my heroes—and my favorite playmates."

Stephen had to force himself to stay with the conversation.

Had he ever heard Haley laugh? "No tea parties with the other girls in the neighborhood?"

"Why waste my time with that kind of girly stuff when I could climb trees and play football?"

"Full-on?"

"Is there any other way to play the game?" Haley tilted her chin up, running her finger across a faint scar. "I got my first touchdown and my first set of stitches on the same day. I was eight."

"Interesting." Stephen mimicked her pose. "I earned a similar scar when Sam and I got lost during a family camping trip. Five stitches. Sam never did match it."

"I only needed four." She settled back on the floor, sitting cross-legged. "Did you guys like being identical twins?"

"When we were younger . . . yeah, we did."

"Did you do the typical twin prank of switching classes on your teachers?"

"Of course. It was expected of us." He moved to the window. Stared out into the small backyard. "At first, it was fun. But I'll admit that hearing 'Are you Sam or Stephen?' got old."

"So being a twin isn't all fun and games?"

"No." He focused on the faded wood fence. Some of the boards looked as though they were listing to the left. He needed to check that. "Sometimes it felt like I had the word *and* tacked on my name. Stephen and Sam. The twins. You get one with the other. A matched set. Why couldn't people take the time to figure out who was who?"

A quick look over his shoulder showed that Haley watched him from where she sat on the floor. How much should he say? He was here to find out about Sam, not talk about himself.

"There was a part of me that was . . . relieved when Sam chose to stay with our mom when our dad got remarried. In high school, I was Stephen Ames—no *and*. When Sam was fourteen, he stopped talking to my dad, and when I chose to live with Dad and Gina, things got dicey between Sam and me. I stopped visiting as much. We stopped talking as much." Stephen faced forward again, leaning against the windowsill. "I still thought we were sticking with our plan to go to college together. I know that was stupid. What was I thinking? When I was visiting him and Mom during spring break, Sam announced he was joining the army after high school graduation."

"But you liked being on your own."

"I didn't say it made sense." Stephen consulted the directions before beginning to lay out the pieces of the crib in order. "A college campus would be big enough for both of us, right? But we never had to figure that out."

"Did you miss Sam?"

"More than I realized." Stephen kept his eyes trained on the unconstructed crib. "Someone told me that when she was with me it felt like I was searching for something . . . or someone."

"Sam?"

"I waited so long to try and fix things between my brother and me. Sure, I sent him a letter when I graduated from college—I even called him. Never heard back. I don't know if he even got the letter. But I could have done more. Tried harder. I regret the years I lost with Sam, but not as much as I regret losing the chance to look my brother in the eye and tell him that I love him." Stephen stood, wiping his hands on his jeans. "Looks like we'll need a Phillips screwdriver as well as the straight-edge one you have there. I don't see one in the toolbox."

"Um . . . Sam had another set of tools."

"Right. I think I saw it in the garage. A red box?"

"Yes."

"Got it. Be right back."

••••••━━••••••

What was Haley supposed to say? She couldn't even handle her own mixed-up, repressed emotions about Sam—and they'd been married only three years. And Sam was gone more than he was home. She certainly couldn't help Stephen unravel so many years' worth of choices and regrets. She'd have a better chance at figuring out how to assemble the baby crib.

Who was the unnamed "she" who encouraged Stephen to try to reconnect with Sam? A friend? A girlfriend? She crossed the hall to her bedroom, pulling a blue plastic box off the top shelf of her closet, a soft grunt escaping her lips. Heavier than she remembered. Of course, when she shoved it up there, she'd been only four months pregnant. Setting the clear plastic box on the bed, she removed the lid.

Inside was the flag that had covered Sam's casket, folded into a triangle, the red and white stripes hidden beneath the blue field covered with white stars. She brushed shaking fingers across the white threads, remembering how a somber, white-gloved member of the honor guard presented her with the flag. How she'd clasped it to her chest, her heart hammering against it. Beneath the flag lay a shadow box displaying Sam's medals. Underneath that was a laminated copy of his obituary Miriam had sent her, insisting she'd want it for their son one day. Haley had read it once—when she'd composed it. Chaz and Angie had sat with her, along with Finn and Claire, helping her distill Sam's life into too few words. Each sentence, each paragraph typed, felt like a virtual shovel full of dirt on Sam's grave. She was burying her husband with words that scorched his death into reality in her heart.

Tucked in the side of the box was a brown manila envelope—the coroner's report detailing how Sam had died. She'd opened it when it arrived weeks after Sam's death, but only to shove her engagement ring and wedding band along with Sam's band in among the folded papers. She wasn't ready to read the black and white reality of how Sam had been killed. She knew he'd been assisting a wounded soldier. Knew he'd been taken down by a sniper.

"Sam, you should have come home." She weighed the packet of papers in her hands—so light, and yet it contained life-changing information. "I was waiting for you. We were waiting for you."

Some things were too precious to let go of, even for just a little while. Tucking the medical report in her top dresser drawer, she stored Sam's medals and the American flag back on the closet shelf. Then she piled Sam's high school yearbooks back into the plastic box, placing the tree house diagram on top of everything and replacing the lid. It was a start.

As she carried the box into the living room, Stephen walked toward her. "Let me get that."

"It's not that heavy."

"No arguments. You're already carrying a load." He stopped, the tips of his ears reddening and a matching red flushing along his cheekbones. "I apologize. That did not come out like I meant it to."

Stephen Ames blushed? "Be careful. The last thing you want to do is upset a pregnant woman."

"So I've heard." He hefted the box into his arms. "Although when my stepmother was pregnant, she was reasonable most of the time."

"You have a—"

"A half brother. He's thirteen—a great kid."

"I didn't know."

"I figured if Sam hadn't told you about me, he also hadn't mentioned Pete. As upset as he was about my dad remarrying, he was even more upset when he found out Dad and Gina were having a baby."

They stood in the hallway, uncovering family details she should have known—if life had been normal. "You told him?"

"Yes—I thought he needed to know, that my mother needed to know. She locked herself in the bedroom and cried all evening. And Sam threatened to take me down if I ever mentioned it again. So I didn't."

Divorced parents. Going to one high school while his identical twin brother went to high school in another state. A stepmother and stepbrother he wanted nothing to do with. Just what part of any of this fit the word *typical*, which Sam had used to describe his family?

Haley eased past him. "I know there's not a lot in the box, but I thought you could begin with this. Those are Sam's yearbooks. When I was looking through them, I found something unexpected."

Stephen placed the box on the coffee table and sat beside her. He didn't rush her, just waited while she retrieved the drawing of the tree house. "Remember this?"

He scanned the front of the paper, then turned it over and read the scrawled list before flipping the page back over again. "Where did you find this?"

"Inside one of Sam's yearbooks."

"I can't believe he kept this."

"Which one of you is the artist?"

"I am—although I won't claim the title *artist*. Sam was the mastermind, and I sketched out his ideas." He traced the outline of the tree house. "As you can see by the erased and re-drawn lines, it took a couple of tries before I got it right."

"Finding that got me thinking."

"What about?"

She stood and walked to the sliding glass doors in the kitchen that led to the backyard. "See that big old tree back there? Don't you think it'd be perfect for a tree house?"

Stephen came to stand beside her, his steps easygoing. Slow. Sam would have jumped up from the couch and been out of the house and halfway to the tree by now. "Hmm. It's substantial—a strong base. But . . . doesn't that tree look kinda funny to you?"

"What do you mean?"

"Look at those upper branches—they're grayish brown and don't have any leaves on them."

"Well, of course they don't. It's March. In Colorado."

"I get that. But look at the base of the tree—there's new growth down there. Why aren't there at least leaf buds on the branches?"

"I didn't know you were a tree guy."

"Arborist."

"Excuse me. *Arborist.*" She continued to analyze the tree. "I think it's perfect. I'll re-create the tree house for Sam's son—for our son. I've got the plans and at least a basic list of what sup-plies I'll need."

"When are you due again?"

"April fifth. Why?"

"Shouldn't we concentrate on putting the crib together—and put a tree house on the back burner?"

"I didn't say I was going to start today, Rogers."

"What did you call me?"

"Nobody ever called you by your middle name before?"

"Just the typical 'Stephen Rogers Ames' when my mom meant business."

"Well then, *Rogers*, let's get back to the crib. You can keep the original sketch. I made a copy—" She motioned to where she'd anchored a piece of paper to the side of her fridge with a COLORADO magnet. "—for handy reference."

"Sounds like a plan. I'll take this other stuff with me and look through it." His smile disarmed her. "Haley, thank you for giving me the tree house sketch. It means a lot."

She pressed her hand to her throat, quelling the swift choking sharpness. It was a simple childhood sketch. "I thought it would."

"Let me put this in my car. Then we'll tackle the crib. And if you're interested, I'd be glad to help you organize the garage, maybe unpack some of the boxes."

"That's okay, Stephen. I don't want to take advantage of you."

"I offered." He stood in the archway, tossing a wink at her over his shoulder. "I'm going out of town for a couple of days, but when I get back, I'll check into a hotel down the road and we'll clear out the garage. I'll even paint a room or two if you want."

"Not crazy about the orange?"

"Are you?"

"I can't say I am."

"Well, choose another color, then. If you need painting done, I'm your man."

No, he wasn't.

His words punctured her heart with the swiftness of a well-aimed bullet even as the familiar scent of lime lingered after Stephen left. Why did Stephen prefer what Sam would have called "men's perfume" while Sam stuck with a no-frills soap-on-a-rope that his mother gave him every Christmas?

thirteen

······•·····•·····•·····

Haley carried her laptop into her bedroom, waiting for her brother to respond to her instant message. She settled against a pile of pillows, the computer resting against her baby bump. Well, it was more than a bump, with six weeks to go.

Her message remained unanswered in the white box on the lower right-hand part of the Facebook screen. She'd typed *You want to Skype?*

She tapped her fingers on the keyboard, checking her e-mail while she waited for David, flipping back and forth between tabs. Finally he responded.

Sorry, Hal. Don't have time to Skype.

Got a few minutes to IM?

Sure. How ya doing?

No complaints. Unless you want to hear about how many times I go to the bathroom at night.

NO.

Didn't think so.

You keeping your guard up?

She shook her head, mustering a half laugh at his big-brother way of reminding her to be strong, to not let life take her down.

Always.

Seriously, Hal—you need anything?

Haley paused with her hands over the keyboard. She needed advice. The kind only a big brother could give.

I'm good. Sam's brother has been hanging around some.

Why?

He wants to talk about Sam. Helped put up the crib. Wants to paint the baby's room.

Are you okay with all that?

Sure. Shouldn't I be? It's okay for me to help Sam's brother, isn't it? For him to help me?

You tell me, Hal. Didn't you say the guy looks just like Sam?

He's not exactly like Sam.

Identical twins, right?

Okay, they look exactly alike. But they have different personalities.

You're confusing me.

How to explain this to her brother over instant messaging?

I've noticed differences. That's all.

Whatever you say. So long as it doesn't weird you out, I don't see a problem with it. Maybe he feels bad that he wasn't around more when his brother was alive and wants to help you now.

That's what he said.

Guys are uncomplicated, Hal. He's helping you because he
misses his brother. You okay with that?

Sure.

David signed off a few moments later.

Was she fine? There was no easy way to answer that. Most
mornings the remembrance of what she'd lost—whom she'd
lost—jerked her awake. And then she'd have a morning like today
when sleep disappeared in slow blinks of her eyes and emptiness
lay soft in her heart, forcing her to weigh it and find a way to balance it with yesterday, today, and all the tomorrows without Sam.

She clicked on the folder labeled "Sam's E-mails," searching
for the one titled "Follow Up" and dated a few weeks before his
death.

> I miss you, Hal.
>
> I know you're upset that I re-upped. But we talked about it
> before I left. And I thought about it all the way over here. Talked
> about it with some of the other guys. The bonus is just too good
> to pass up. You get that, right? We can save it for that house you
> keep talking about.
>
> Just because I reenlisted for a couple more years doesn't mean
> I'm going to make a career of the army. We'll talk about that. I
> promise.
>
> I need to cut this short—have to go train.
>
> I love you. Take care of yourself. I know you will. You always
> do.
>
> S

Why hadn't she responded? Told him she loved him, too?
Told him that she thought she might be pregnant?

She'd filed the e-mail and waited for his next phone call—and then acted as if everything was fine. Let him talk about his day. His buddies. And when he brought up reenlisting, she said, "I get it, Sam. Decision made."

Even though she didn't get it. She was married to a man who seemed intent on leaving her . . . again and again and again.

Why, God? Did Sam really prefer being deployed over being home with her? Wasn't she enough for him to come home to?

She slammed the laptop shut.

She didn't want an answer. The truth might rip the flimsy bandage off her shredded heart, allowing her to fully feel the pain she'd suppressed for months. The emptiness that had stalked her even before Sam's death.

fourteen

....•....•....•....

The warm fluid trickling down her thigh didn't mean anything. All pregnant women had a little bit of incontinence.

Right. Haley would lock herself in the bathroom that needed to be painted, the fixtures updated, for the next six weeks and keep telling herself a lie. This is what Kegel exercises were for: stopping that bothersome third-trimester leakage when you sneezed. Or laughed. Or coughed.

Only she hadn't sneezed. Or laughed. Or coughed.

She had gone back to her bedroom to get a pair of shoes because Stephen Ames, bossy man, told her that she couldn't work in the garage if she was barefoot. She bent over to get her tennis shoes and felt something . . . something *wrong*.

Haley stood in the bathroom off her bedroom, gripping the edge of the chipped porcelain sink, and refused to look at herself in the mirror. Questions piled up like a mental traffic jam in her head—questions she couldn't answer.

Was that amniotic fluid?

If it was amniotic fluid—and it wasn't!—what happened next?

Could she ignore what was happening?

Stephen called her name from the living room. "Sorry, Rogers. You're going to have to figure out whatever you need by yourself." She was a little busy right now trying to determine if the baby had found a new position on her bladder or if she was leaking amniotic fluid.

Which she wasn't.

She couldn't be in labor. Yes, her back was a bit tweaky this morning—but it had bothered her on and off for the last month. She wasn't having *contraction*-contractions. It was too early. Lily had given the class a brief rundown of the potential complications of preterm labor last week. Haley had joked with Claire that she'd be the woman who delivered two weeks past her due date.

Claire! She needed to call Claire . . . who was in Vail this weekend with Finn to celebrate their anniversary.

"Go on," Haley had told her. *"I won't do anything but gain weight while you're gone."*

Where was her phone? Back in the garage, where she and Stephen were going to spend the day unpacking boxes. Fine. She'd walk out there, pick up her phone, and come back to the privacy of her room and call Claire. She took three steps and felt another warm gush of fluid.

No. No. No. Please, let me have wet my pants.

Haley pulled a light blue towel off the rack and, one slow step at a time, moved from the bathroom to the end of the bed. She laid the towel over the comforter before sitting down. So far, no more fluid. It was probably nothing. Nothing at all.

"Stephen!" When he didn't answer, she raised her voice. "Stephen!"

Nothing. Of course; he was still in the garage. Like it or not, she needed to walk at least as far as the living room.

"God, I'm asking you to please, please, please don't let me have this baby."

She held her breath as she stood and inched her way from the bedroom and down the hallway. When she stood just inside the living room she tried again. "Stephen Rogers Ames!"

A quick pounding of footsteps preceded Stephen's appearance. "Did you just use all three of my names?"

She must have sounded like his mother. "Sorry. You didn't hear me when I called from the bedroom. Could you get my phone, please?"

He cocked his head to the side. "You okay?"

"Yeah." She wasn't lying. Not really. She didn't know if there was anything wrong yet.

She leaned against the wall and counted up to ten and back while she waited for him to return. As she took the iPhone from him, Stephen scanned her up and down, his eyebrows drawn together over his so-familiar brown eyes. "Why don't I believe you when you say you're okay?"

"Maybe it's because I'm standing in a puddle in the middle of the hallway?"

"What?" He looked down at her feet and then up at the ceiling, as if he expected to see a leak. "There's no puddle."

"I'll explain in a minute." She half turned away, then looked back at Stephen. "Would you get me a glass of water?"

"Sure. But you're not fooling me. If you don't want me to listen to the conversation, just say so."

"Fine. I don't want you to—" She gasped as more fluid trickled down her leg.

Stephen froze. "Haley, tell me what's wrong. Now. Please."

The man was polite even when he was being forceful. "I think my water broke."

The next thing she knew, Stephen had picked her up and carried her to the couch, but he didn't release her. "Wait. Do you want to rest on the couch or on your bed?"

His face was inches from hers and she could see the scar that ran along his chin. "Here is fine."

He settled her on the couch, disappearing down the hallway as she hit the speed dial for Claire. "Pick up. Don't be skiing. Don't be napping. Don't be . . . doing anything else."

Claire picked up on the third ring, sounding half-asleep. "Haley, you better be calling me to tell me that you gained ten pounds."

Haley gripped the phone so tight her fingers hurt. Right now she'd take the extra ten pounds without a complaint. "I think my water broke."

"What? No, it didn't. We agreed nothing was going to happen while I was gone, remember? I'm in Vail. You're not going into labor."

"I'm not in labor." She paused when Stephen reappeared with at least half the towels in her linen closet in his arms, motioning for him to wait. "And I said *I think*—as in *maybe* my water broke. Maybe."

"Did you call the hospital?"

"No. I called you." She closed her eyes when Stephen tried to mouth something at her.

"Haley, I can't do anything but worry. Call the hospital and then call me back."

"But, Claire—"

"Hanging up now. Wait—is anybody there with you?"

"Stephen Ames is—we were organizing the garage."

"Let me talk to Stephen."

"Why?"

"Because."

Haley held her phone out to Stephen. "She wants to talk to you."

"Who?"

"My friend Claire."

He dumped the towels on the end of the couch and took the phone, pacing the living room, nodding his head while saying, "I will," and shaking his head while saying, "I won't," over and over to Claire before hanging up.

Haley rested her hands on her tummy, forcing herself to relax her shoulders. *Stay put, buddy. I'm not ready yet. You're not ready yet.* She cut off the internal monologue with her unborn son when Stephen hung up the phone. "What did she say?"

"She told me to make sure you called the hospital. And then she told me to not let you have the baby until she got back."

"That's it?"

"Yes—she kept repeating herself until her husband took the phone from her, told me to call back as soon as we knew anything, and then hung up."

Five minutes later, Haley stared at the phone in her hand, refusing to look at Stephen, who stood at the end of the couch watching her. She could obey the nurse's instruction to come into the hospital and be examined—or she could sit on the towel and ignore whatever was happening in her body.

"What did the nurse say?"

"She told me to come in and get checked out."

"Then let's go."

"I didn't say I was going."

"Haley—"

"Stephen, I am not having this baby yet. I'm not."

He knelt down next to the couch and covered her hands with

his, lowering his voice to a whisper. "Fine. You aren't having this baby yet."

"You don't know that."

"I'm agreeing with you." His thumb rubbed across the back of her hand. "It seemed like the best thing to do."

"I don't want to be in labor. Not yet. I'm not ready." She covered her face with her hands, muffling her words. "I haven't packed a bag. I haven't figured out how to do this without Sam. I'm not ready to be a mother."

Stephen clasped her hands with his, easing them away from her face. "All we're doing is going to the hospital to check things out. That's it. Now, come on, let me get you to the car."

"I can't go like this."

"What do you want to do—change into something more formal?" Stephen's smile invaded a corner of her heart that she'd walled off, even as it encouraged her to relax. To believe that things would be okay.

"I'm . . . damp—" Oh, she never thought she'd say those words to a man. "I need to change into some dry clothes."

She moved to stand, but Stephen pressed a hand against her shoulder. "Tell me what you want and I'll get it for you."

"For goodness' sakes, Stephen, my legs still work."

"Just tell me."

Their stare-down lasted a full minute—and she blinked first. "Fine. Get me a pair of my sweatpants from the bottom drawer in my dresser. And a hand towel from the linen closet in the hallway."

He motioned to the pile of towels at the end of the couch. "Won't one of these towels work?"

"Just get me the hand towel."

When her phone rang, she greeted Claire without even looking at the display.

"Well?"

She sucked in a breath. Exhaled. She would do this. Get checked. Come back home and laugh at the false alarm. "I'm going to the hospital."

"Are you in labor?" Claire's voice rose with each word she spoke.

"I sincerely hope not, but the nurse insisted I come in and get checked." Haley brushed her hair out of her face. She should have told Stephen to get her a clip for her hair. "I'll be back home in no time."

"We're heading back to the Springs."

"Don't do that!"

"Are you kidding me? I'm your coach!"

"And this is your anniversary weekend."

"Finn already talked to the manager and added an extra night. We're leaving everything here, just getting in the car and coming your way."

Haley eyed the hallway. How long did it take for Stephen to find a pair of sweats and a hand towel? "Let me go to the hospital and get checked, Claire. Sit tight. I'll call you in an hour, okay? Even if I am in labor—and I'm not—I won't be having this baby right away, according to Lily."

"All right—but only if you promise to call me as soon as you know what's going on."

"I promise."

When Stephen came back with her replacement clothes, she considered her options. "Why don't you go start the car?"

He stood at the end of the couch, hands on his hips. "What?"

"I need some privacy." She shook the gray sweatpants in the air.

"Oh—right. Call me when you're ready."

•·•••·•─◆─•·•••·•

From his position in the center of the kitchen, Stephen watched the minutes tick by on the microwave. At the five-minute mark, he paced toward the living room. "Are you—"

"Do not come in here, Rogers. I will kill you."

He froze. "Right. Not coming in. Hey, you're not planning on taking any of your guns with you, are you?"

"What kind of question is that?"

"I've seen you handle a gun, Haley. I want to know how serious your threat was."

"Very funny." The sound of Haley's too-rare laugh followed. "Actually, that is funny. Did I ever apologize for threatening you?"

"Nope."

"Remind me to do that sometime when I'm not busy."

"Deal." How serious could things be if Haley could joke with him about their first meeting?

"All right. I'm decent."

When he reentered the room, she'd moved to the edge of the couch. "Can you hand me my keys? They're hanging by the—"

"Haley, don't be stupid." He scooped her back into his arms. "I'm driving."

She leaned away from him. "Did you just call me stupid?"

"Yes. Don't make me say it again."

"I am not getting in a car with a man who insults me."

He shifted her so that she was closer, her hand resting against his chest. "Doesn't look like you have much say in the matter. Remind me to apologize sometime when I'm not so busy." He ignored her huff of air. "Where's your suitcase?"

"I don't have one. I'm not in labor. It's too early. As far as I knew, I still had a few weeks to get my delivery bag packed."

"If you get admitted, I'll come home and get what you need."

"Claire can do it."

"Didn't you say that she and her husband went to the mountains?"

"Yes, but she's on alert to come back." She leaned forward and opened the front door.

"I don't suppose this would be a good time to ask if they checked the weather report. It's been snowing up at the Eisenhower Tunnel for the past couple of hours."

"Did not hear that. Did. Not. Hear. That." Haley closed her eyes as if she could block out his words by not looking at him. "Maybe I should have brought a towel to sit on."

He paused beside the Mustang's passenger door. "Why? Don't answer that. You want me to go get one?"

"No. Yes. No. Let's just go. And if I soak your bucket seat, I'm sorry."

"I'm not worried about the seat, Haley."

fifteen

·••••—•—••••—•—••••—•—••••·

"Mr. Ames?"

Stephen pulled his attention away from his iPad—and the Weather Channel's view of the mess of snow and ice and backed-up traffic along I-70—and stood, closing the space between him and the nurses' desk. "Yes?"

"The doctor decided to admit your wife."

"Haley isn't my wife." He rested his hands on the counter. "She is—was—married to my brother."

The nurse flipped through some papers anchored to a plastic clipboard. "Oh. That's right. Mrs. Ames is a widow. My apologies. Then your sister-in-law is being admitted to L and D."

"She's in labor?"

"I'm sorry. Your sister-in-law will have to authorize any further release of information."

"You're kidding, right? I drove her here!"

"Being someone's chauffeur doesn't automatically give you access to legally protected medical information." The nurse slipped the chart back into a slot on the desk.

"I'm the baby's uncle. They're okay, aren't they? Has anything happened since I dropped them off fifteen minutes ago?"

"I'll go back and check with your sister-in-law, and if she's okay with it, we'll let you know what's going on—or even bring you back to see her."

"Thanks."

Thanks for nothing. He was consigned to one of the padded mustard-yellow chairs lining the walls at the entrance to the hospital birthing center. The woman was doing her job—and she was as effective as a five-hundred-pound defensive lineman in a set of purple scrubs. All he could do was wait, watch the Weather Channel to gauge if there was a chance Claire could make it back, and keep praying.

It was a good half hour before the nurse escorted him to Haley's birthing room. During that time the weather in the mountains only got worse. Stephen paused outside the door.

Please, God, help me know what to say—and what not to say.

In the muted lighting, Haley rested, half-reclined in a hospital bed, with her head back against a pillow, her tummy covered with a soft-looking white blanket. Wires came out from underneath the blanket, connected to a briefcase-size machine beside her bed that was spitting out a paper graph covered with lines forming a continuous flow of peaks and valleys. Stephen trained his eyes on her face, noticing how the lashes of her closed eyes rested against her skin. How her top teeth worried her full bottom lip. That way, he could ignore the needle lodged in her arm, with a tube running to a clear bag of fluid hanging from a metal stand at the head of her bed.

"Hey, you."

"Hey, Rogers." Shadows deepened Haley's blue eyes. "Looks like I'm staying until this little guy is born. I'm premature—just barely. I'm waiting for the doctor to come in and pronounce my official sentence."

"How you feeling?"

"Unprepared."

He might as well tell her straight up—that's the way Haley liked it. "Claire's stranded in the mountains."

"What?" Haley's attempt to sit up was hindered by all the monitoring paraphernalia. "Was there an accident?"

"No—nothing like that. But there is snow—enough to close the tunnel. I've been watching the Weather Channel and checking updates on my iPad."

"I'm not in active labor, so it's okay." Even as she spoke, a wince marred her face.

"Is there such a thing as inactive labor?"

"Very funny."

The door swung open and a woman wearing sage green scrubs and a long white coat entered the room. She glanced at Haley and Stephen. "Mr. and Mrs. Ames, I'm Dr. Axelson—"

"I'm the brother-in-law."

"He's the uncle."

The physician paused, as if processing the information. "Okay, then. Mrs. Ames, I'm Dr. Campbell's partner—and the OB on call. I want to discuss your current situation and our plan for you."

"All right."

"Obviously we admitted you because your membranes ruptured and you started to leak fluid. You're still only two to three centimeters. Our goal is to try and stop your labor, if we can, while giving you some medication through the IV to fight infection and also to help your baby's lungs mature."

"I'm not really in labor, am I? I'm not having contractions."

"Mrs. Ames, that roller-coaster pattern on the paper indicates you're having contractions—albeit irregular ones. If we don't do anything, it's probable you'll go into actual labor. Even if we can buy two or three more days, we give the medicine a chance to work and mature your baby's lungs faster."

"And if the baby's born now?"

"Then we're equipped here to deal with premature births."

Haley's gaze never wavered. "What kind of problems are you concerned about?"

"At this altitude, the more mature a baby's lungs, the less likely he'll need oxygen or have breathing problems." The doctor offered a smile. "But that's not our concern now. Based on our preliminary exam, it looks like you might be dilating. I'd like to order an ultrasound to assess that more accurately."

"Whatever you need to do." Haley pushed herself taller in the bed, as if gaining a better position to battle premature labor. "Does my doctor know what's going on?"

"I'll keep Dr. Campbell updated."

After the doctor left, Stephen moved closer to the bed, resting a hand on the curved railing. "Need anything?"

"Probably need that going-to-the-hospital suitcase now. I'm going to try and call Lily—she's the instructor for my childbirth classes. She volunteered to be available if I needed her when I went into labor. I'll ask her to be on alert."

"Sounds like a plan. I can go get the suitcase for you." Driving back to her house, picking up a suitcase—that was simple enough. "Just tell me where it is."

"I already told you: *I didn't pack one yet.*" She stopped. Inhaled, long and slow. "Sorry. I'm a little tense. It was on my to-do list—the one I hadn't gotten around to writing. But I could use a toothbrush and toothpaste. And my robe. My childbirth instructor gave us a list of things to bring—for me and for the baby—but don't worry about that yet. Maybe one outfit and a baby blanket. Do you think you should put the car seat in the car?"

"Let's just get through today, okay? The baby's not riding in a car today. Do you want anything to eat?"

"I'm on a diet of ice chips—and whatever that stuff is." She motioned to the fluid in the IV bag. "But get yourself something to eat. I'm good here."

Stephen wanted to say something to reassure Haley. Comfort her somehow. He reached over and touched the side of her face, causing her to startle. He drew his hand back.

"I'll be back as soon as I can."

"And I'll be right here." She motioned to her cell phone where it lay on the side table next to a plastic pitcher of water. "I need to call my mom. My brothers. I'll check in with Claire. Hassle her for missing the fun. Looks like I've got some phone calls to make."

Stephen backed toward the door. Should he offer to pray for her when she'd just rebuffed a slight touch meant in brother-in-law kindness? "You make your phone calls. I'll go grab your toothbrush."

"Thanks."

"That's what I'm here for."

••••—◆—••••

During the drive to Haley's, Stephen debated calling both his parents—opting to beg God to stop Haley's labor.

As he walked through the garage, he grabbed a backpack hanging on a hook. That would do for a suitcase. Now all he needed to do was figure out what to pack. The basics were easy: toothbrush, toothpaste, shampoo—and women liked conditioner, too.

Wait a minute. Hadn't he seen a hospital bag checklist posted on Haley's fridge? He found it next to a schedule for the shooting range, which was next to the tree house diagram; grabbed a few Ziploc bags from the pantry; and headed for Haley's bedroom.

After tossing the list on the bed, he collected Haley's toothbrush, a tube of Crest, dental floss, and deodorant in a gallon-size Ziploc bag. Put shampoo and conditioner he found in her shower in another one. Where was Haley's robe? Nothing on the back of the door. He rifled through the clothes in her closet. Weren't women supposed to have closets packed tight with clothes? Haley obviously didn't know that rule. But among the few hangers of tops and pants—did the woman own a dress?—he found a robe. It had to be Sam's. What woman wore a blue Turkish cotton robe fraying around the hem?

Okay. Time to consult the list.

Nursing bras.

Nursing pads.

Maternity underwear.

He scanned the list again. Swiped his hand down his face. Folded the list in half and tucked it into the backpack. *Not going to happen.* Once it stopped snowing in the mountains and Claire got back into town, he'd hand off the list to her.

Stephen got all the way to the car when he realized he had nothing for his nephew. He tossed the bag in the front seat and ran back to the baby's room. A laundry basket piled with infant-size clothes sat beside the crib. He grabbed the outfit on top—something with grinning monkeys all over it—and took a blanket, too.

A quick check of his phone confirmed it had been almost forty minutes since he left the hospital. No time to stop and get something to eat. He grabbed a jar of peanuts, an open bag of M&M's, and a can of Sprite from the fridge, and ran back to the car.

He'd backed the Mustang halfway out of the driveway when he realized he'd forgotten one of the most important things of all. He shoved the car into park, ran into the house again, and returned with Haley's camera, which he'd found after ransacking both her bedroom closet and front hall closet. When his nephew arrived, he'd make sure to get pictures. Lots of pictures.

sixteen

......••••••• ••••••• ••••••••

"Haley, what is going on?"

At the sound of Stephen's voice, Haley's eyes darted to his face and then back to the silver-rimmed clock hanging on the wall at the end of her hospital bed. "Not . . . talking . . ." She zeroed in on the second hand of the clock, huffing short breaths of air as the contraction peaked.

Stephen was wise enough to be quiet, remaining at the foot of the bed. When Haley closed her eyes, Nikki, the labor and delivery nurse helping her through the contraction, encouraged her to rest and then lowered the volume on the fetal heart rate monitor before leaving the room.

"The medicine's not slowing down my contractions." Haley hoped she sounded nonchalant. "I'm not sure how far dilated I am now, but my contractions are getting stronger and closer together."

"You're having the baby?"

"I'm not in charge." She knew another contraction would pounce within minutes. "Dr. Campbell has been alerted. The anesthesiologist came by to talk about the possibility of an epidural. But I'm going to try and do this the old-fashioned, no-medication way—or at least no more than what they've already pumped into me. The L and D nurse said she'd coach me . . ." She paused, the tightening increasing from her back and progressing around to the front of her stomach. "Sorry . . . gotta focus . . ."

All of her attention centered on the circular path of the clock's red second hand, each tick counting off a second of the contraction—and the now very real possibility of her baby being born. Today. Or tomorrow.

Too soon.

Just do the next thing. Survive the next second. And the next.

The nurse reentered the room as the contraction waned. "Now that your husband is here—"

Haley interrupted the assumption. "Brother-in-law."

"Uncle." Stephen's pronouncement overrode hers. "The baby's uncle. Her husband was my brother."

"Are you coaching her?"

"No!" Haley struggled to sit up. "I'm good on my own. You're here. And Dr. Campbell should be coming in. I'll be fine."

"I'm here because I drove her to the hospital . . . and then I went back and got her stuff—well, some of it." Stephen motioned to the backpack he'd sat in the corner of the room.

Stephen Ames was babbling. Just a bit—but babbling nonetheless.

The nurse stayed framed in the doorway. "I came to check on you, but since your—"

Haley and Stephen spoke in unison. "Brother-in-law."

"—brother-in-law is here, I'll check on my other mom-to-be, okay? Press the buzzer if you need me."

"Will do." Haley had never expected a clock to become her lifeline. And couldn't everyone just stop talking . . . stop making assumptions . . . or at least stop expecting her to be part of the conversation?

After readjusting the strap around her tummy and reading the strip of paper being spit out by the machine beside the hospital bed, Nikki left, the door to the birthing room swishing shut. Stephen stood at the end of the bed, blocking the view of the clock.

She stared at Stephen. Nope. She couldn't see through him. "I need you to move."

"What?" Stephen looked right, then left.

"You're blocking the clock—and I'm using it as my focal point. I need it. Now."

"Sorry."

He moved to the head of the bed, standing beside her like some silent sentry as the contraction ebbed and flowed. When she closed her eyes and took a long inhale, she realized Stephen was patting her shoulder.

"What do you want?"

"I'm just . . . patting your shoulder."

"I know that. Why?"

"I thought it would help."

"It doesn't. Right now I don't want anyone to touch me, much less pat me."

He stepped away, hands dropping to his sides. "Okay. No more patting."

"Sorry. Labor is a bit rough." How many times would she have to apologize to Stephen before this was over? She stretched her neck—left, then right. If only she dared to ask him to rub her lower back. But that was something a husband did—not a brother-in-law. "The ice chips are nice, though."

"I'm your man."

No. No, he wasn't. Why did he keep saying that? She hissed as another contraction attacked her body. "Whoa.

Somebody just upped . . . the ante." When she gripped the metal bed rail, her hand collided with Stephen's. He adjusted the position of his hand so she could clasp his fingers and squeeze, tightening her grip with each passing second of the contraction. When she exhaled, he exhaled with her, shaking out his hand.

"Quite a grip you've got."

"Sorry."

"No apologies needed. I'll have feeling back in my fingers before the next contraction—I think."

"Not that I'm holding your hand again."

But when she tensed for the next contraction, Stephen took her hand in his. "Squeeze as hard as you like."

Haley didn't argue. When the contraction ebbed, Stephen shook his hand in the air, as if he was trying to get the blood flowing to his fingers again.

"Very funny, Rogers."

He hid his hand behind his back. "So did you talk to Lily? Is she going to be here?"

Haley averted her eyes. "I left a voice mail."

"What?"

"She didn't answer—there's nothing else I could do. I left a message, explaining what was going on. It's fine. I'm fine. Like I said, the nurse and Dr. Campbell will get me through this."

She tensed as another contraction hit, repeating the pattern of starting in her back and wrapping around her stomach. At least Stephen couldn't ask any more questions now—and if he brought it up again, she'd tell him how unwise it was to argue with a laboring woman.

Twenty minutes later, they had established a pattern, complete with Stephen matching her breath for breath.

"You coach a woman through childbirth before?" She savored

the cool relief of ice chips, licking her lips and wishing she could gulp down an entire glass of water.

"Nope. You're my first."

"You sure act like you know what you're doing."

"Faking it. I saw what you were doing—and I'm just reminding you to keep on doing it."

A few minutes later, Nikki returned, watching as Haley and Stephen performed their contraction hand-clutch routine. "She's going to bring you to your knees."

Stephen didn't waver. "I'm still standing."

"They use techniques like that in torture, but we don't encourage it during labor. Next contraction, just cross your middle finger over your forefinger so the knuckles aren't next to each other, and let her squeeze those two fingers."

As Haley released a breath, Stephen shook out his hand. "Thanks. Duly noted."

Haley gathered the fragments of her sense of humor. "I am not torturing this man. He volunteered."

An hour later, when Dr. Campbell arrived, life had faded to nothing more than the span of the clock face and the sound of Stephen's voice.

"I hear you're doing great, Haley." The doctor shook Stephen's hand. "I understand you're the substitute coach. It's obvious we haven't stopped your labor, Haley. You're contracting every three to four minutes on the monitor. And the expression on your face tells me the contractions are painful and strong."

". . . Not going to argue . . . with you on that point."

"We'll stop the medicine; then I'll get the nurse so I can examine you and see how far dilated you are. You two keep up the good work until I get back."

After the doctor's exam, Stephen reentered the room, his gaze straying to the waiting baby warmer.

Haley rushed the words before the next contraction. "Looks like I'll take it from here. The doctor says I'm at six centimeters, but because I'm early, I only need to get to about eight. After that, I'll start pushing." She drew in a slow breath, forcing a smile, ignoring how her bottom lip trembled. "Nikki's here to coach me. Thanks for all the help."

"Haley, I can still—"

"No. I've got this." Tears blurred her vision. *Stupid contraction.* "Next time I see you, I'll introduce you to your nephew."

Stephen looked as if he was going to say something else, but she looked away, back at the clock. Time was up. She was going to become a mom—and she was going to face that moment without Stephen Ames.

Without Sam.

The reality seemed to press against her with the same force as a contraction—only if she gave in to it, she'd birth the sobs that had been building inside of her for months.

She needed Sam here. She needed him to tease Nikki about whether she had a boyfriend. To come back into the room, after visiting the vending machine, munching on a package of Oreos and a bag of Fritos, telling her that he'd save the Three Musketeers bar for her until after the baby was born—and they'd both know he'd eat it.

She needed Sam to tell her that she could do this.

•••••—◆—•••••

Stephen paced the hallway outside Haley's birthing room. He took two steps toward the door. Stopped.

God, this is not right.

But there's nothing I can do. You know I don't belong in there with Haley—that's Sam's role. Not mine.

But no woman should be alone while she has a baby. Sure, the doctor is there. The nurse. But they aren't family—or even a friend like Claire. Will anyone remember to take pictures?

He turned his back on the birthing room.

If I walk through that door, God, Haley is going to rise up off the bed, grab me by the front of my shirt, and throw me back into the hallway. That would be a memorable moment.

A nurse interrupted his conversation with God.

"Excuse me, sir, you can't just stand in the hallway outside the birthing room. I need you to go to the waiting room down the hall."

Okay. That settled it. He'd do what the nurse asked. Pray. Wait for the invitation to meet his nephew.

That decision didn't last long.

What if Haley were my wife, God? What if I'd died and Sam were here, willing and able to help Haley—instead of leaving her alone during the birth of our first child?

He'd want Sam in there.

He'd want his brother to ignore Haley's protests . . . ignore any I-can't-go-in-there-because-I'm-not-married-to-this-woman protests . . . and stand beside his sister-in-law and hold her hand.

"Being out here while she's in there is wrong." Stephen stood with his hand pressed against the wooden door. "Even if she kills me, I'll die doing the right thing. And the odds of her killing me right now are low. She's a little distracted."

He eased the door open a few inches.

". . . I can't do this." Haley's voice was thin, ragged. "I can't. I want my husband. I want Sam."

Her words halted Stephen's advance.

He wasn't Sam.

He stiffened his shoulders.

But he was the next best thing.

He shoved open the door, striding into the room, his eyes locked on Haley's.

"Stephen—"

"You're not doing this alone." He walked forward and took her left hand, which was clenching the blanket, positioning it around his crossed fingers again. "Here. Squeeze."

"Get . . . out."

"I'm not leaving."

"Go—" Her voice broke.

Nikki interrupted the verbal tug-of-war. "Mr. Ames, if she doesn't want you here, I'm going to have to ask you to leave."

Stephen knelt beside the bed, lowering his voice. He had one chance to get this right—and only the time until the next contraction started. "I thought about Sam. What he would want me to do. He wouldn't want you to be alone. Please, let me stay. Let me help. I'll hold your hand. That's all."

Whether she gave in because what he said swayed her or because the next contraction overtook her, Haley stopped resisting him. Her eyes filled with tears, which she blinked away. Did the woman ever cry?

"Did I ever tell you that Sam and I were born six weeks early? That I'm older than Sam by four minutes—"

"No labor stories . . . kind of busy with my own . . . right now . . ."

The pressure on his fingers increased. "Got it. We'll focus on you. Trade stories later."

The next hour passed much like the previous one: contraction, breathe, rest, contraction, breathe, rest. The murmur of the doctor's voice behind him when he came in to check on Haley's progress was mere background noise, blending with the nurse's softer tone as she moved between Haley and the physician—asking questions, helping Haley adjust her position, encouraging her to keep her eyes open as she conquered contractions. Again. And again. And again.

How many contractions did it take to move a baby from inside a woman to outside? What time was it? He wanted to look over his shoulder, check the clock on the wall, but he continued to keep his back to the "business end" of the bed, his eyes trained on Haley's face. During each contraction, her gaze returned to him, a compelling glow in her blue eyes.

When she licked her lips, he offered her the ice chips.

"I feel like I've been ridden hard and put away wet."

He pressed a damp cloth against her forehead, thankful Nikki had suggested another way to help Haley. "You're beautiful, Haley. You're doing great."

After another exam, during which Stephen stood behind the striped privacy curtain near the door, the doctor announced, "This baby wants to be born before midnight. Thankfully, it's tolerating labor well. I'm going to have you start pushing—but only with every other contraction—and see how it goes. Nikki will be helping you."

Thirty minutes later Nikki, who had stayed on past her shift, called the doctor on her cordless phone and said, "It's only going to be a few more contractions."

Releasing the guardrails, Haley collapsed against the pillows, eyes closed, her mouth drawn. "One more push. I've got one more push in me."

"You can do this—however many pushes it takes." Stephen brushed the damp hair off her forehead.

The sound of the birthing room door swishing open and closed heralded the arrival of Dr. Campbell. "Looks like we're going to have a baby."

Haley managed a weak half smile. "I'm the one having a baby."

Out of the corner of his eye, Stephen saw the doctor roll a metal table of instruments over beside the bed and heard Nikki break down the bed to accommodate the doctor during the delivery. He refocused on Haley—that's what he was there for. "Ready for me to count?"

Two minutes later, Haley's push was accented with a "Come on, come on" that ended in a drawn-out groan.

"Okay, Haley, the baby's head's out." Dr. Campbell's voice was calm. Soothing. "Stop pushing just for a second while I suction the mouth."

For all the huffing and puffing he'd been doing with Haley, Stephen found it impossible to breathe.

"One more little push, Haley."

Stephen and Haley exhaled at the same time, her face reddening with exertion, and then she released his hand. Waited.

"You have a daughter, Haley."

Haley's eyes flew open, and she gripped the handrails, struggling to sit up. "No. No. I have a son. The ultrasound said I was having a boy."

"Nooo, I'm certain I delivered a girl." Laughter laced the doctor's reply.

"But the ultrasound—"

"This is why I told you the ultrasound is just a picture of reality—not reality itself. Ultrasounds can be wrong."

"But I don't do girls." Haley fell back against the pillow.

"You do now."

seventeen

....•....•....•....

A daughter. She had a daughter.

As the nurse covered her with a thick, warm blanket, she felt a shift in the atmosphere of the room. Heard the door open and close. Open and close. A low chorus of voices.

But the one thing she didn't hear was her baby's cry.

"What's wrong?" Haley looked around the room until she found the small group of hospital personnel gathered around the baby warmer off to the left. "What's wrong with the baby?"

Nikki separated from the group and came over, adjusting the pillow behind Haley's head, her eyes kind. "Your daughter is having some difficulty breathing. You remember what we talked about earlier today—how preemies can have issues that need extra care. We're giving her some oxygen before we take her to the Neonatal Intensive Care Unit. That's the NICU."

"Is she going to be all right?" Stephen, who still stood beside her, asked the question forming in Haley's mind.

"The neonatal nurse-practitioner will do a thorough exam."

The nurse's voice was soft. "Let me bring your daughter over so you can say hello to her for a moment."

The sound of a weak cry pulled Haley's attention back across the room. "That's her—that's a good thing, right?"

"Yes—but she still needs extra help. Let me see if she's ready to meet you."

Within seconds, Nikki settled her daughter in Haley's arms, wrapped within two layers of warm baby blankets, so that Haley could only see her face.

She touched the edge of the blankets. "Can I look at her?"

The NICU nurse, who'd introduced herself earlier, touched Haley's hand. "We have to keep her wrapped up because she'll have trouble keeping herself warm."

Haley didn't dare touch the thin, clear plastic tube that encircled both of her daughter's cheeks and ended with small prongs that were inserted in her nostrils.

"That's a nasal cannula. We're giving her oxygen."

"She's so tiny . . . and I haven't counted her fingers and toes yet."

"Ten fingers. Ten toes." The nurse pulled back a corner of the blanket, exposing a tiny hand for a too-brief second. "I counted for you."

Haley pressed a kiss on the baby's forehead, inhaling the warm newborn scent of her daughter. "You were supposed to be a boy. Clint Barton. I don't have a name for you."

"There's time for that." Stephen's words didn't pull Haley's attention away from her daughter.

"We'll be taking this little one to the NICU now. No need to worry. You can come check in on her once you're recovered from delivery." She nodded toward Stephen. "Dad, you can go with us, if you'd like."

Stephen stilled beside her. Was this the time to go into the

"He's not my husband" routine? There were more important things than correcting yet another person who was jumping to conclusions.

"Stephen." Haley reached up and grabbed his forearm. "I need you to go and be with her. I don't want her to be alone."

"Of course I'll go. You relax—well, do whatever the doctor and nurses tell you to do—and I'll keep you posted."

"Don't leave her. I'll get there as soon as I can. Just stay with her. Please."

......●●....●....

Stephen wanted to turn around, go back, and hold Haley's hand. To assure her everything would be okay—that her daughter would be fine. But he also knew he had to keep walking to the NICU because Haley had asked him to stay with the baby. And that's what he'd do.

He followed behind the nurse and the woman who identified herself as the neonatal nurse-practitioner, trying to discern their quiet murmurings, his eyes trained on the Isolette, which reminded him of a space capsule. The tiny form that was his niece lay on her back, bundled in blankets to keep warm, her face obscured by the oxygen tubing, a thin cord protruding down by her feet indicating the compact oxygen monitor attached to one of her toes.

When they came to a set of windowless double doors, the nurse used her ID card to gain access to the NICU. They rolled the Isolette down the carpeted hall lined with small rooms housing warmers with monitoring equipment mounted on the walls—most of which were occupied by small babies. The adults who weren't wearing scrubs Stephen assumed were family members. Another nurse greeted them and led them to the "pod," where Haley's baby would be cared for—a ten-by-ten-foot room with a window for observation from the nurse's desk, a rocking chair, and the required monitors.

Stephen watched as they transferred his niece to a bed with bright lights above it. As one of the nurses came near, he saw his opportunity.

"So what do I do? Stay out of the way?"

The woman offered a gentle smile and motioned him forward. "No—if there's a hand or a foot that we're not using, go ahead and touch her. Talk to her. It will help calm her. We think it even decreases a baby's perception of pain."

He could touch this minutes-old miracle?

The nurse continued to talk. "We're going to get some preliminary labs and eventually do a chest X-ray. Even though she may just have premature lungs, we always have to rule out infection or other potential causes of her breathing problems, especially since she was preterm."

"Why would being preterm indicate a possible infection?" He'd just ask questions until he was brave enough to touch the baby.

"Well, premature labor happens for a reason—often some type of infection, even if the mom doesn't show any symptoms like fever." As she spoke, the baby was being weighed and measured. "We can treat infection, so until the cultures we draw are negative, she'll be on IV antibiotics."

Stephen eased himself closer to Haley's daughter. Sam's daughter. He was here because they couldn't be . . . yet. He wanted her to know she wasn't alone.

The nurse leaned close. "Don't forget to wash your hands."

"Yes, ma'am."

After scrubbing his skin pink, Stephen stood beside the Isolette again. He held his breath as he rested his pinky on her oh-so-tiny palm . . . exhaling as her fingers curled around his finger in a stronger grip than he'd imagined.

She was a fighter, like her mother.

Everything, everyone around him faded into the background as he bent over the Isolette, modulating his voice to a whisper. "Hey, sweetheart. Welcome to the world. You arrived a little sooner than we expected—but we sure are glad you're here. Your mom's getting cleaned up from a busy day and your daddy . . ." Stephen stopped. Swallowed. Waited until he could speak again. "Your daddy's watching you from heaven. Just think of that— you've got someone watching over you all the time. I'm your uncle Stephen, and if it's okay with you, I'm going to be hanging around a lot now that you're here."

He watched as her eyelids opened once, twice . . . his niece had his brother's rich brown eyes. Haley would look at her daughter and see her husband.

eighteen

· · ·· ·•·· ·· ·· ·•·· ·· ·· ·•·· ·· ·· ·

She couldn't put her daughter in the pale blue sleeper adorned with whimsical monkeys, no matter how adorable it was. She'd be swimming in it.

Haley sat in the hospital bed, the blanket drawn up around her, the newborn outfit spread out on her lap. She touched the soft material, shaking her head, a soft sigh disturbing the silence of her room.

"I have a daughter." She folded the garment's arms. "A daughter—and nothing for her to wear."

She wasn't even sure when they'd release the baby to go home. And even more important than clothes, her baby needed a name. She couldn't keep saying and thinking "my daughter" and "the baby."

At the sound of a soft knock on her door, Haley expected yet another visit from a medical tech to check her vitals. But Stephen stepped into the room. "You're supposed to be with her."

"I know." He pulled a chair up beside the bed. "They're doing a chest X-ray, and I had to leave the room anyway, so I came see how you're doing. And bring you this."

Haley watched him pull the camera from his coat pocket, followed by an Almond Joy candy bar. "I forgot about the camera."

"I figured as much. I also thought you might be hungry."

"They brought me dinner—wait." Haley accepted the chocolate, unwrapped it, and took a bite. Chocolate and coconut. Oh, this was the perfect after-labor treat. "Have you had anything to eat?"

"I made a quick run to the cafeteria before it closed." He settled into the chair, running his fingers through his hair, disheveling the long ends. "And then I double-timed it back here."

"Thank you for staying with her, Stephen."

"No place on earth I'd rather be."

Haley ignored how his words warmed her, focusing on the camera instead. She pressed the button so that images from earlier today flashed onto the screen: she saw herself sitting in bed, giving a thumbs-up; a view of the heart monitor strip; one of her holding Stephen's hands, her face marred by a grimace.

"Oh, that's lovely. Not one of my best moments."

Echoes of his "You're beautiful" whispered in her mind.

"We can delete it."

"No, no. I can always use it later—show her the pain I went through to birth her when she's giving me a rough time during the teen years."

"Very wise. See, you're getting the hang of this mothering business already."

She didn't respond to Stephen's teasing, as her attention was centered on the next photo, of Dr. Campbell holding a newborn baby. Her baby. Her daughter.

"Wait—you were facing me and the wall the entire time. How'd you get this photo?"

"I didn't take that. Nikki and I got pretty good at passing off the camera. You were too preoccupied to notice."

There were several photos of the baby in the warmer and then one of her wrapped in a blanket, snuggled close against Haley's chest.

"I barely got to hold her before they took her to the NICU." She touched the photo with her forefinger, closed her eyes, and inhaled, as if she could recapture the warm scent of her daughter when she'd pressed her lips to her soft forehead. "She's so tiny. I don't even know how much she weighs."

"A whopping four pounds, five ounces."

"I've handled guns heavier than that."

"She'll gain weight." Stephen paused. "She has Sam's brown eyes."

Haley looked up from the camera into eyes identical to Sam's. "I wasn't expecting that. I thought all babies had blue eyes."

"Not this little girl." He swallowed, his Adam's apple bobbing in his throat. "Just for a moment, it was like looking into Sam's eyes again. I think he'd like that—knowing his child looks like him."

"He didn't know."

"Of course he couldn't know the baby would look like him—"

"No—he didn't know about the baby."

Stephen's one eyebrow rose, a crease forming between his eyes. "Why wouldn't Sam know? I mean, he was still alive when you found out you were pregnant, right?"

Why hadn't she kept looking at the photos of her daughter, Sam's daughter? Why didn't she talk about what to name her or how an hours-old baby girl already faced the "I have nothing to wear" dilemma?

"He deployed. We were talking about whether he was reenlisting or not." Haley turned off the camera, setting it on the

bedside table, next to the infant sleeper. "I wanted Sam to finish his commitment and get out of the army so we could settle
down somewhere."

The words spilled out, tumbling over each other. If she kept
talking, then Stephen couldn't ask any more questions. "Right
after he deployed, he called . . . told me that he reenlisted.
Two more years. The bonus was too good to pass up. I was so
angry . . . another two years of watching Sam leave. Another
two years of putting our plans—our marriage—on hold . . . I
thought I might be pregnant, but I didn't tell him. He was all
about convincing me that he'd made the right decision."

"But why didn't you tell him that you were pregnant the next
time you talked?"

She had asked herself that same question thousands of times.
"When he called the next time, I knew I was pregnant. I hadn't
seen a doctor—but a home pregnancy test was positive. I was
still hurt, and I thought, *Wait until you Skype*. I mean, wouldn't
it be better to tell him face-to-face—or sort of face-to-face?"

"And then—"

"And then the team showed up at my door. Told me Sam was
dead." She stared at the wall, the clock still counting off seconds, minutes, hours. "I know they thought I didn't cry because
I was in shock. But I kept thinking, *I need to tell him about the
baby*."

The only sound in the room was the TV, which Haley had
turned on low. Nothing as good as a John Wayne movie, but
noise to fill the space. "I hate that Sam died without knowing
about our baby. I didn't mean for it to happen . . . You understand, don't you?"

She waited for him to say something. Something to lift the
burden from her heart.

But Stephen refused to even look at her.

•◦•••◦ ◀▶ •◦•••◦

His brother hadn't known about the baby.

How awful. Simple choices—Sam's to reenlist, Haley's to wait and tell Sam she was pregnant—could lead to regret. How sad to realize, yet again, what waiting to communicate with someone you love could cost you.

When Sam chose to stay in the army, he was doing what he thought was right—for him and for Haley. And Stephen understood why Haley wanted to share the news via Skype. Haley telling Sam that she was pregnant wouldn't have stopped that sniper's bullet. No. But his brother would have died knowing he was going to be a father. And Haley could hold on to the comfort that Sam knew about the baby. Their baby.

Even as he processed all of these thoughts, another one reared up and pushed him away from Haley.

Why was she telling him about her sin of omission? Was he nothing more than a substitute for his brother? An alternate Ames so Haley could confess her mistake, express her regret, and then move on with her life—without him?

Stephen pressed his fingers to the bridge of his nose. It was happening again—he was changing places with his brother, only no one was asking him if he wanted to be involved with the charade.

"Why are we even talking about this?" He squared his shoulders, meeting Haley's eyes, ignoring the shadows in their depths. "You're tired—understandably so. Don't overreact, Haley. It's in the past. If you'd had more time, you would have told Sam. Mistakes happen."

Did his words cause Haley to flinch? What did she want him to say? *Oh, that's right.* That he understood.

And he did. He understood how Sam could have died

without knowing he was going to be a father. That all made sense.

What didn't make sense was why he wanted his brother's widow to see him for himself—not as some stand-in for Sam.

"I need to get back to the NICU. Check on the baby. That's what you want me to do, right?"

"Right."

"You need anything before I go back?"

"No."

"I'll let you know if anything changes. Try and get some sleep."

"Sure."

He left Haley sitting in the hospital bed, arms empty. Her gaze heated his back. Once the door closed, he leaned against the wall. Two women walked by in scrubs, their conversation muted. A phone rang at the nurses' station, once, twice, before being answered, and a woman's voice said, "L and D, how can I help you?"

Stephen pressed his fist against his chest, as if he could stop the burning pressure building inside. This was absurd. This wasn't about him. He had no right feeling anything for Haley—no right to want more. He had come to the Springs to find his brother's widow so he could discover who Sam had become—not to become involved with her.

He closed his eyes, only to see Haley's face appear in his mind. Sam had loved her . . . kissed her . . . been with her in the most intimate of ways. He needed to keep his distance from Haley, despite having just shared something so unforgettable with her.

"How do I do this, God?"

"Are you okay, sir?"

Stephen bolted upright, his eyes latching on to the woman

with short-cropped red hair standing in front of him. "I'm fine. Just been a long night."

"Understood. Your first?"

"Yes. No." He rubbed his forehead. "It's complicated."

"Children always are. I have three." The nurse's calm demeanor seemed to surround Stephen. "Wait until they're teenagers. But they're worth everything from labor pains to late nights waiting up for them to come home."

"I can only imagine."

"You might want to go home and get some sleep."

"I need to get to the NICU—she's having some problems breathing."

"What's her name?"

"She doesn't have one yet. We thought she was a boy."

"It happens—not often, but it happens. Don't rush picking a name. And don't just feminize the boy name you had picked out. You'll know when you find the right one."

"Not sure how you'd feminize Clint Barton."

"Hawkeye from Marvel Comics?" The nurse raised an eyebrow, reminding him of Haley's stare-down tactic.

"Exactly."

"Did you know there was a female Hawkeye character? I think her name was Kate. I'd have to Google it to be sure."

"How'd you know that?"

"Longtime Avengers fan."

"I'll check it out. Thanks."

Kate. Did the baby look like a Kate? Would Haley like that name? It was really her choice. But he could look up the names of Marvel superheroines on his phone—unless the staff in the NICU agreed to let him hold his niece.

nineteen

........•....•....•.....•....

Why had she confessed to Stephen that Sam died before she'd told him about the baby? No one except Claire knew she hadn't told her husband she was pregnant.

Haley curled up on her side in the hospital bed, pulling the blanket up to her shoulders. Her body ached from top to bottom—literally. No one warned her about the post–labor and delivery aches and pains. Her body was stretched out and bruised in places unmentionable—and now her heart seemed to beat with a limp. If she pushed the call button, would the nurse be able to give her some sort of medication for that?

She'd survived childbirth.

"Sam, I did it." The words, breathed aloud, surprised her. "I had your baby. Our baby. She's beautiful—but I thought she was a boy. And I don't know what to name her."

Oh, this talking to a man gone missing was crazy.

But Sam wasn't missing. She knew where he was, didn't she? Didn't she?

She and Sam hadn't talked about the very real possibility of his death that much. He'd shown her where he kept his insurance papers and will, explaining that he'd made her his beneficiary. Assured her that she'd be taken care of if he died.

"Don't you worry, Hal. You'll be fine if something should happen to me." Sam tucked the folded papers back into the fire safe, locking it, and putting the key back in the wooden box inlaid with ivory on his dresser.

"I don't worry about me. I worry about you."

"Me? Why? I'm well trained—and protected by the Geneva Conventions. No need to worry." He wrapped his arms around her. *"I've got this—and God's got me."*

"You believe that, Sam?"

"Of course I do." For once no mocking half smile appeared on his face. *"It's the only way I could do what I do. And I don't worry about you. You're strong—and I've taken care of all the other things."*

"I don't want the money. I just want you to come home."

"I promise."

Sam believed God "had" him. Was that why he could walk away from her and onto the plane—never looking back—each time he deployed?

But he also promised to come home. A promise he couldn't keep.

Maybe a promise he never should have made.

She startled when her phone rang. Retrieving it from beside her bed, she saw her brother's face appear on the screen. Talking to him was better than talking to her dead husband.

"Hey, David."

"Hal—has the baby arrived yet?"

"I wouldn't be answering the phone if she hadn't."

"Great! Mom said it was too late to call, but I told her—wait a minute, *she*? I thought your doc said you were having a boy."

"And this is why—and I quote—'the ultrasound is just a picture of reality, not reality itself.' Believe me, I had a daughter."

"Wow. You. And a girl."

"Hey!" Haley had to protest, even if he was only saying what she believed.

"You gotta admit, life in our family didn't set you up too well for frills and frou-frou."

"Who says my daughter is going to be frills and frou-frou?"

"Point taken. How are you feeling?"

"Beaten up. Labor and delivery are grueling. But I'm more worried about my daughter. She's in the NICU because she's having trouble breathing."

"Oh, wow. Mom's going to want to get on the next plane out there."

"No—no, convince her to wait until I find out what's going on. I don't know how long she'll be in the hospital. I don't know when I'm going home. I don't even know her name."

"Well, you better get on it. You know Mom, she's gonna ask me all the basics: toes, fingers, height, weight, eye color . . ."

"Brown eyes. She has Sam's brown eyes."

"That's pretty cool."

"I think so." Haley maneuvered onto her back. Wow. She could lie on her back again. "And she weighs four pounds, five ounces."

"Tiny little thing, isn't she?"

"Yeah. But not surprising since she was six weeks early."

"Got any pictures? Mom's going to ask about that, too."

"Yes. The nurse took some and Stephen did, too—although I'm deleting the one where he had no right to be pointing a camera at me."

"Stephen? As in Stephen Ames, Sam's brother?"

"Yes, that Stephen. My friend Claire is stranded in the mountains because of a snowstorm."

"Are you telling me that Sam's brother was with you while you had a baby? Sam's twin? That had to be surreal."

"It was . . . comforting. I didn't even think about the fact that he looks just like Sam. I mean, he does. But he's different, too. Sam had this cocky, where's-the-next-challenge attitude. Stephen's quiet—like some sort of soldier who won't abandon his post."

"But this guy saw you . . . have a baby."

Haley couldn't help but laugh at the obvious disgust in her brother's voice, followed by a quick groan of pain. *Wow.* It hurt when she laughed. *Great.* "Actually, he didn't. He held my hands and faced away from all *that*."

"Huh." David seemed to be puzzling out that reality. "All right, if you say so. Figures you'd do the whole having-a-baby experience different from other women."

"What's that supposed to mean?"

"Nothing, Hal. Don't overreact. You just had a baby."

Haley knew when one of her brothers was baiting her, and she knew better than to let David's teasing bother her. She was an adult now—a mother. She needed to stop reacting like a ten-year-old. Or maybe she was just too exhausted to defend herself.

"Listen, I'll call Mom and the guys and report in. And tell Stephen I want a copy of that photo."

"What photo? Oh, no. You'll post that to your Facebook page."

"Me? You're thinking of another brother."

"Right."

The conversation with David allowed Haley to head to the bathroom with a little less regret trailing behind her. Her big brother always had a way of infusing laughter into any situation—sometimes inappropriately.

But even though she tried to ignore it, his comment about not being like other women stung like the first failed tries for her IV line. So she wasn't girly-girly. That came with growing up—and keeping up—with three brothers. And Sam had fallen in love with her as is.

Had she been enough for Sam, really? If he'd lived, would he have felt as if he had settled, marrying her? That he'd missed out on a traditional, more feminine woman? Someone like Claire?

She stood in the dark bathroom, staring at her shadowed reflection in the mirror. Is this what motherhood and raging hormones did to a woman—make her doubt herself, compare herself to her best friend? The only thing she knew for certain was she didn't have what it took to be the single mother of an only child.

•••••—◆—•••••

Where was he?

Stephen swiped his hand down his face, muffling a yawn, stretching his back, which protested the movement. He turned his head . . . and remembered.

From where he'd stretched out on the mini-couch in the hospital room—probably put there for exhausted fathers—Stephen could see Haley, curled on her side, asleep. Her hair splayed across the pillow like spilled honey, her hand tucked underneath her cheek. She looked about sixteen years old.

Why her, Sam? Why did you marry her?

Of course, he had no way of knowing what kind of women his brother would like. Before the estrangement, they'd been young teen boys. They'd talked about girls. Sam even said he'd kissed a few, while Stephen hung back in the wings and waited for his chance to come onstage and be a part of the whole romantic adventure.

Had Sam dated a lot before deciding to propose to Haley? Were all his girlfriends the all-American, athletic, bordering-on-a-tomboy type? From what he'd seen, Haley never wore makeup. Didn't own a dress. And was very possibly more comfortable with guys than girls.

But she must have been Sam's type. He'd fallen in love with her. Married her.

Not that Haley wasn't attractive. When she let her guard down, when she smiled, her eyes shimmering with laughter, she intrigued him—lured him closer—in a way that Elissa, for all her primping and posing, never had.

He pushed himself to a sitting position. Enough of that kind of thinking. He was obviously overtired.

"I'm here!"

A quick glance at his sister-in-law showed she'd managed to sleep through Claire's triumphant, albeit late, entry. He held up his hand, positioning one forefinger over his lips, as he rose to his feet. Then he motioned for Claire to follow him back out into the hallway.

Claire backed up, standing on her tiptoes, trying to see around Stephen. "But I want to see Haley."

At least she whispered.

"You did see Haley—and she's asleep. Let's keep it that way. She's had a rough twenty-four hours."

Claire paced the hallway, unwinding a feathery purple scarf from around her neck. "And I missed it. I failed her."

"You didn't fail her—"

"We got here as fast as we could. We left this morning, as soon as we heard traffic was moving through the tunnel again." There was a distinct quiver to the woman's voice. "And I didn't even wait for Finn to park the car when we got here—I jumped out before he came to a full stop."

"Claire." Stephen stood in front of her, clasping her shoulders. "Do you want to see the baby?"

"The baby!" Her eyes widened. "Can I?"

"Come on, I'll take you to the NICU. Then we'll come back and check on Haley. She's only been cat-napping."

Claire double-timed it down the carpeted hallway next to him. "What's wrong with the baby? Is she getting better? It's not serious, is it? Did Haley pick a name yet?"

"She had some breathing problems early on, and they think it's because she's premature, but they can't be sure for a couple of days."

"They aren't sure if she's premature? She showed up six weeks early—"

"That's not what I said. They think she's having breathing problems because she was premature, but they're not sure if that's the reason why. We can ask questions when we get to the NICU. And no, no name yet. Clint Barton is a no-go, that's for certain."

"Is she okay?"

"The baby? I just told you—"

"No, Haley. Is she okay about having a daughter?"

"Well, after the initial 'it can't be a girl' battle with the doctor, I think she's accepting it pretty well."

"I would love to have been there—and not just to see her face when that happened."

"I'll never forget it, that's for sure."

Claire stopped ten feet from the doors that led to the NICU. "Stephen."

"What?"

"Thank you. Thank you for being there for Haley."

"Like I told her, there was no place else I'd rather be. I did it for Sam—and for her, too, of course." He moved forward. "You ready to meet the most adorable little girl in the world?"

It had been less than twelve hours since his niece had been born. But he still couldn't believe how seeing her look around, react to people's touch, even calm down when he spoke to her, tugged at something deep in his chest, centered right where his heart was. He thought of his love for Elissa—why else would he have planned on proposing? And he resisted examining too closely the jumble of emotions attached to Haley. But what he felt for this baby girl who looked at him through his brother's brown eyes . . . it was pure. Uncomplicated.

"Claire, meet Peanut."

"Peanut?"

"Well, I couldn't keep calling her 'the baby,' could I?" The baby's eyes were hidden from him as she slept. "And she's so little, 'Peanut' seemed to fit."

"She sounds like a snack food."

Just that moment, the baby yawned and then opened her eyes.

With a small gasp, Claire tucked her hands to her chest and leaned close. "Oh, she has brown eyes like you!"

"Like Sam. Brown eyes like Sam."

"Of course—and you, too." A soft smile curved Claire's lips. "So when can she come home?"

"No one is saying yet. It's all about tests and levels . . . I think the doctor is going to talk to Haley later today. They haven't let Peanut eat yet because she's still breathing so fast, but that's improved in the last couple of hours."

They both stepped aside as a nurse approached the warmer. She listened to the infant's heartbeat and respirations. Claire continued their conversation in a low voice. "What does breathing fast have to do with letting her eat?"

The nurse finished checking Peanut and then answered Claire's question. "There's a number of reasons, but probably the easiest to understand is it's hard to swallow when you're breathing about sixty times a minute."

Made sense.

"I'm going back to the room to check on Haley." Claire touched Stephen's arm. "I'll let her know you're with Peanut."

"You can keep that nickname between us."

"Sure thing, Uncle Stephen."

After Claire left, Stephen washed his hands under the warm water, lathering and relathering his skin. He couldn't be too careful with a newborn. She lay on her back, an unbelievably small diaper covering her bottom.

The moment he put his finger on her hand, she circled it with her fingers and held on. As she breathed, her tummy rose and fell, rose and fell. *Wondrous.* The sound of the machine keeping track of her heartbeats faded into the background and he closed his eyes and just focused on Peanut's breathing, allowing himself to exhale. Inhale. Exhale. Inhale. Each breath a prayer for this little girl who in some inexplicable way contained a part of his brother. Yes, she had Sam's eyes. But at her very essence, she was Sam . . . and Haley . . . and God's amazing creation all woven together into ten toes and ten fingers and brown eyes and the barest smidgen of a nose and lips that quivered, and a muted cry that burrowed into his heart and lodged there.

twenty

•••••—•—•••••—•—•••••—•—•••••

Giving birth was becoming a bit of a blur. How was that possible? Her daughter was two days old, and the pain, the pushing, the "come on, come on" longing for the baby's arrival, the shock of having a daughter no longer mattered. Maybe that was why some women had more than one child.

Not her, not since she'd lost Sam. But other women.

Even as the details of labor and delivery faded, Haley could still remember holding on to Stephen's hand. The way he stood beside her hospital bed, never complaining, no matter how hard she squeezed his fingers. The sweet relief when he pressed a cool, wet washcloth to her forehead and neck as she rested between contractions. The deep timbre of his voice assuring her that she could do all her body demanded of her. And how she almost believed him when he told her she was beautiful. How funny that the first time a man ever told her she was beautiful she was panting, sweating, and struggling to give birth!

Of course, Stephen would have said anything to help her. She knew he didn't mean it—not when she wore a nondescript hospital gown that was damp with sweat and who knew what else. But still . . . she had taken the next wave of pain with renewed strength.

Haley's memories scattered when a nurse entered her room "Haley?"

"Yes?"

"Would you like to go see your daughter again? It's quiet up at the NICU."

"Absolutely." The nurse's question expanded the now ever-present warmth in her heart into a tiny flame of longing. "Let me get my robe on."

"Do you need any help?"

"No, I'm fine."

She slipped into Sam's old Turkish robe, which still held a faint hint of his familiar scent, belting it around her waist— well, where her waist used to be. She hadn't even thought about what her post-pregnancy body would look like. She looked as worn out as she felt.

Once she settled into the rocking chair beside her daughter's Isolette, which was labeled with BABY GIRL AMES, a nurse placed the baby in her arms. She was wrapped like a four-pound burrito, her tiny hands tucked just against the top edges of the blanket. Haley tried to block out the ever-present sounds of the machines monitoring infants' heart rates, respirations, and oxygen levels. She touched one tiny hand, smoothing the fingers with the translucent nails over her forefinger after pressing a soft kiss to the wrinkled skin.

She tucked the baby closer to her, ignoring the pressure building in her chest. Would she be able to breast-feed? So far all she could do was pump and store breast milk for future use. The lactation instructor had come by, encouraging her to persevere despite not actually nursing yet, and despite the warning that preemies sometimes had difficulty nursing. She had to ignore the voice that labeled herself a walking "milk factory." She was a mom, doing what needed to be done. For now, she needed to be content with holding her daughter and hope the doctor let her go home soon. And if not, then she'd fight to stay in the hospital with the baby. She had no reason to go home— and one life-changing reason to stay here.

Haley closed her eyes, rocking back and forth, savoring the warmth of the baby in her arms, the soft lilt of her breathing.

"I need to name you, you know." She nuzzled the baby's head, which was covered in a soft pink knit cap. "You don't look like a Clint Barton."

"I did some research on that."

The sound of Stephen's voice interrupted the sweet reverie of motherhood. "I was talking to myself."

"No, you were talking to Peanut."

He looked . . . good. As if he'd slept. Showered—his hair still damp around the long ends that curled around his ears. "Peanut?"

"That's what I started calling her." A smile deepened the cleft in his chin. "I couldn't just keep saying 'baby' or 'her' or 'that one over there.'"

"You did not call her 'that one over there.'" Haley kept her arms still and strong around her baby. No patting. No stroking. Nothing that might irritate a preemie.

He knelt beside the rocking chair. "Well, no, I didn't call her *that*. But don't you think 'Peanut' fits her? She's so tiny."

"It doesn't feel like I'm holding anything—and yet she's the most precious thing in the world."

"So, about her name . . ." Stephen's gaze lingered on the baby she held in her arms.

"You have suggestions?"

"Well, since you'd planned on continuing the whole Marvel-comic-book-hero tradition started by my father, I printed up a whole list of Marvel superheroines. I figured you didn't want any villainesses."

"True." She shifted so she was turned more toward Stephen, who remained crouched beside the rocking chair. The scent of his aftershave slipped past her defenses.

"But I did want to tell you one interesting bit of Marvel trivia." His finger stroked the baby's hand where it rested on Haley's hand. "Did you know there was a female Hawkeye?"

"No, there wasn't."

"An Ames never—" His jest faded into silence.

Oh. Yes. An Ames never lies. And the last time he'd said that, she'd been so sleep-deprived, so overwhelmed, she'd twisted him into some living, breathing apparition of Sam.

She kept her eyes lowered. "I know. So . . . you were going to suggest a name?"

His glance skimmed her face. Mouth. Eyes. Back to the baby. "I printed up the papers—left them on the table in your room. The female Hawkeye's name is Katherine Elizabeth, and she goes by Kate." He brushed her daughter's cheek with the back of his fingers. "She looks like a Kate, don't you think?"

"Kate. It might work. Or Kit. Kate Ames. Kit Ames." She watched her sleeping daughter, her eyes closed, her eyelashes and eyebrows barely visible. "Is that your name, hmm? Kit?"

"So, any news on when you and Peanut can head home?"

"Not yet. I'm waiting for the doctor to come talk to me. I have a feeling we're here for another night." Kit's silent yawn was the sweetest moment. What were she and Stephen talking about? "And if she has to stay for another day or two, I'm told there's a boarding option available so I can stay in the hospital with her."

"You can trust the doctor to do the right thing—and it's good to know they don't plan to throw you out." He rose to his feet, twisting from side to side, accentuating his trim build. "I hope it's okay that I let both my parents know about the baby arriving a few weeks early."

Miriam! In the midst of the craziness, she hadn't even thought to call Sam's mother. "Oh, Stephen, thank you—I can't believe I didn't even think—"

"Nobody expects you to handle all the phone calls, Haley." His yawn was a grown-up version of her daughter's. "Claire tells me that your mom is on her way to help."

"That's the plan."

"Well then, I'll just say good-bye here and let you have some time with this little girl."

"Good-bye?" She forced her voice lower. Calmer. "Where are you going?"

"Back to Fort Collins." He tucked his hands in his pant pockets. "This has all been fun, but I've put off job-hunting long enough. And Jared e-mailed me a few ideas."

"Oh." Haley concentrated on Kit, who squirmed and fussed in her arms. "Well, then. Thanks for everything."

"Glad to be here."

Her throat was dry, the words scratchy. "I'll talk to you—"

"Of course. Sometime."

"You've got my number."

"Yep."

He bent low, and for a moment, Haley expected him to press a kiss to her cheek. But instead his lips grazed Kit's forehead.

"Good-bye, Peanut. Behave for your mom, you hear? Don't keep her up all night." His brown eyes searched hers. "Take care of yourself."

"You, too. Thank you . . . for being there."

"Anytime. That's what uncles—and brothers-in-law—are for."

She thought about reaching out and giving him a hug. Just a gesture of thanks. But she didn't.

Instead, she watched him walk out of the NICU. His gait steady, his posture straight. Just like Sam's—only slower. As if he were more confident in who he was. His dark hair glinting under the hospital lights. Just like Sam's—except for how the ends brushed his ears and the nape of his neck.

She'd miss him.

Not like she missed Sam.

But she'd miss him all the same.

·•●•· ◆ ·•●•·

Stephen surveyed his work from the middle of the bedroom. Fresh air blew in through the open window, diluting the odor of paint. Would Haley like this color for Peanut's room? He'd steered clear of anything close to pink, hoping she would approve of a warm, muted yellow. It was a little late to worry about the choice now that he'd spent the day taping, spackling, and layering two coats of Sweet Chamomile onto the walls.

He picked up the paint tray and brush, dodging the crib, which was covered with a clear plastic drop cloth. Time for clean-up, and then he'd head back up I-25 to Fort Collins.

Twenty minutes later, he abandoned the paint supplies in the tub when he heard the front door open.

"Stephen, are you still painting?" Claire's voice grew louder as she neared the bedroom.

"Just finished up." He turned off the water, half-rising to his feet. "Were you able to get the cradle?"

"Yes—it's perfect." Haley's friend appeared in the doorway,

wearing a deep red cape coat. "You want to help me carry it in?"

"Don't even try to bring it in. Let me wash my hands and I'll be right there."

Claire stood beside her Cabriolet convertible when he walked outside. "I didn't put it in my car. The woman who sold it to me asked her husband to load it in the back for me."

Stephen was already second-guessing himself. "What do you think Haley will say when she sees this?"

"It's beautiful—and it's exactly what Haley needs. She just doesn't know it yet. Her plan was to have a son who slept through the night in a crib in his room when he was three days old." Claire pulled open the hatch. "You can already see how her plans are working out."

"I half expected her to ask someone in the NICU about whether they do trades." Stephen hauled the cradle out of the car. "But then I see her holding Peanut and I know that's not going to happen."

"Hardly. That baby is all she has left of Sam." Claire, who was ahead of him, stopped, looking over her shoulder. "I mean, there's you of course, but—"

"I get it, Claire. It's not the same thing." He carried the white cradle into Haley's room, setting it beside the bed. "Is this a good place to put it?"

"Perfect. Oh! Let me go get the bedding—it's all pink. The woman included it. No extra charge."

Fifteen minutes later, Claire found him in the bathroom, bent over the side of the tub, rinsing and rerinsing the paintbrush. "So, what are your plans now, Stephen?"

"Plans? Well, I'm going to get cleaned up and then I'm heading back to Fort Collins."

"It sounds like the baby is staying in the hospital for up to a week—and that means Haley, too. At least, that's what she said when I talked to her on the phone earlier. And then her mom comes next week, so it's okay. I was all ready to help, but I'll just keep hanging out at the hospital."

"Everything's falling into place, then." He set the brush in the paint tray. Stood, and walked over to the sink to begin scrubbing yellow paint off his hands. He'd deal with whatever he'd gotten in his hair when he got home. "Everything's getting covered."

"What you've done—it's amazing, Stephen."

"I'm only doing what Sam would have done if he were here."

"No—no, this is way more than Sam would have ever done—" Claire clapped her hand over her mouth, her green eyes wide.

"What are you saying, Claire? That my brother wouldn't have helped Haley with the baby?"

"Oh, sure, Sam would have been there for the delivery—if he wasn't deployed or training or something. But all of that—" She motioned back toward the baby's room. "—the painting and finding a cradle—he would have left that to Haley."

Stephen nudged the hot water hotter. "Wouldn't they have had fun doing that together?"

"That's just it: Sam and Haley didn't do a lot together. We always joked they were 'married singles,' you know? It wasn't that they didn't love each other—I mean, why would they have gotten married if they didn't? But Sam's biggest compliment to Haley was always how much he loved not having to worry about her."

Stephen turned off the water, shaking his hands over the sink to dry them off. "Can you go find me an old towel in the garage, please? I saw some in there when Haley and I were organizing it the other day." He motioned to the blue towels hanging on the rack. "I don't want to get these dirty."

"Sure thing. Be right back."

After Claire left, Stephen turned and leaned against the vanity, his arms at his sides. What kind of marriage did his brother and Haley have exactly? Not that he had any right to ask the question—or any way of knowing, except based on what Claire said. And she was an outsider looking in. Except for when Haley broke down during labor—and she didn't know he'd heard her say she wanted Sam—she'd hardly mentioned his brother.

Married singles.

What kind of marriage was that?

twenty-one

Stephen couldn't put his life on hold forever. He lived in—needed to be in—Fort Collins.

He'd been back home for four days, and his rolling suitcase still sat just inside the door to his apartment, next to his laptop bag, which he'd let slide off his shoulder and land on the floor beside it.

He'd managed to sleep—some—the last three nights, but the exhaustion that had trailed him north from the Springs lingered. And somehow the gravitational pull that tugged his mind, heart, and body back toward a tiny bundle of a baby with his brother's brown eyes—he refused to admit how easily he could recall the blue depths of Haley's eyes—only got stronger with the passing of every hour.

He needed to shake it off—whatever this was. He needed to focus.

It was nine thirty in the morning, and the day demanded more from him than inactivity. What should he do first? He could unpack his suitcase and start laundry. Or he could get his laptop out of his messenger bag, power it up, and restart his job search. Or he could go online, find out if Haley had a Facebook page, and if she did, send her a friend request in the hopes that she'd forget all the reasons to ignore him—including the fact that he'd barged into the delivery room—and friend him. And then he could hope she'd posted photos of his niece so that he could spend the next hour looking at them.

Stephen retrieved his iPhone off his desk, hit Jared's contact info, and FaceTimed his friend.

He started talking before Jared's face appeared. "I blame you for this."

"Well, hello to you, too." The face of Moses, Jared's Great Dane, appeared on-screen as Jared positioned the phone. "What am I being blamed for, exactly?"

"You were the one who told me to do it. And I did. And now look!"

Jared shoved his dog away and moved the iPhone so Stephen could see him. "I am looking—and all I see is your ugly mug up close on my phone screen. Be specific."

"Let Elissa go. Find Sam's wife . . . widow . . . who is—*was*— pregnant. And now I have a niece, who was born six weeks early—"

"As I recall that conversation—and don't quote me because it was months ago now—we were eating dinner and you asked me if you should try to find Sam's widow. And I said, 'Yes.' And now you're blaming me because your nice, orderly life is a mess."

"I didn't have a nice, orderly life." Stephen reached over and pulled the bag of beef jerky he'd opened hours earlier closer so he could reach it without falling off the couch. "I had also just gotten laid off before all this started. Or had you forgotten that?"

"No, I hadn't forgotten that. And also as I recall, you volunteered yourself out of a job, buddy. Only I don't see that as a problem. That, my friend, is your open door to walk into a new business opportunity with me. When are you going to wise up and realize that?"

"When are you going to accept that I don't want to do the whole 'let's start up a company' experiment? That I'd like the security of a real job?"

"As if there's such a thing in today's economy."

"Very funny."

"I'm a funny guy, Stephen. But I'm being serious." Jared's face was obscured behind the bottom of a plastic cup while he gulped something down. "Have you read your own business cards? The word *entrepreneur* is on there for a reason—and no one forced you to add it after *architect*. So, are you about taking risks or not?"

Stephen stretched out on his couch, the cushion offering little comfort, holding his phone at arm's length. "I didn't call to talk business."

"We always talk business. We have since we were in college. It's how we roll. But I'm sorry things didn't go so well with Haley."

"I hoped to know Sam better when I was done, you know?"

"And you don't?"

"No. And I don't feel like I'm anywhere close to being done. But there's no reason for me to go back down to the Springs. I've asked questions. Haley's given me answers. And now she's going to be busy with Peanut—"

"Excuse me? Who or what is Peanut?"

"Peanut is my niece—and don't ask me what her real name is, because I don't know. It might be Katherine or Kit, but I'm not sure."

"Isn't there some sort of law that you have to name a child—"

"She's got a name. I just don't know what it is."

"That's pathetic."

"You're telling me." Stephen popped a hunk of jerky into his mouth, the saltiness overpowering his taste buds.

"But I can fix your problem."

"You can tell me what my niece's name is?"

"Better than that." Jared's grin filled the phone screen. "How'd you like to take a trip back down to Colorado Springs?"

"And why would I need to do that?"

"I have a friend—a friend who just inherited a significant chunk of change, by the way. And he's interested in investing in our company."

"We don't have a company, Jared."

"Yet. We don't have a company *yet*. But given the right investor and the right product and the right name—"

"Those are a lot of blanks to be filled in."

"So we brainstorm. Are you interested in meeting with my friend Joe? He'll be at the Broadmoor next week. Lunch or dinner at the Summit?"

Stephen eyed his suitcase. All he needed was to change out a few items, do some laundry, and he was good to go. "I'm in. E-mail me the intel, and I'll call you back in an hour to talk strategy."

"Done. And make sure you let me know what that baby's name is, okay?"

"Done. Talk to you later. I need to go unpack so I can re-pack."

●-●●●-◆-●●●●●

People should know better than to call mothers of newborns.

Her ringtone came around for a second playing of "Hello World," and by the time she settled Kit in her cradle and sprinted down the hall, whoever it was would have left a voice mail—another response backed up in the queue, thanks to her automated request to "Please leave a message, and I'll call back as soon as possible."

The chance of her ever returning those calls now that she was a mom? Slim to none.

"Stay asleep . . . stay asleep . . . stay—" Kit's whimper interrupted her whispered plea. "No. No. No. You're asleep. Please. Mommy's tired, too . . ."

Within seconds the whimper ascended into a wail, and all of Haley's hopes for sleep disappeared. That was one phone message she was going to listen to—because when she found out who had called and woken up her daughter, she was going to call them every five minutes for the next twenty-four hours.

Haley gathered Kit into her arms, covering her with the blanket, her body rocking back and forth. "Sh-sh-sh, Peanut. You're just tired. Go back to sleep and you'll feel all better. And Mommy will feel better, too."

But Kit was having none of it.

Ten minutes later, Haley had swaddled Kit and walked up and down the hallway a dozen times. Kit seemed enthralled with every inch of the ceiling. Her brown eyes were open wide—and she looked as if she had slept the afternoon away.

"Great. You're awake. And I'm dragging here." Haley slumped onto the couch, cradling Kit in her arms. "How about we just sit for a few moments, huh?"

Kit's face screwed up and her tiny lips trembled, a sure sign a mini-squall was in the making. As Haley stood, half her hair tumbled down around her face. Maybe she'd get a shower tomorrow.

When someone knocked on the door, she shifted Kit up onto her shoulder. Bless Claire—her ever-ready lifesaver, stopping by when she got off from a shift at the Broadmoor. Would she stay long enough for Haley to get cleaned up—at least into a clean pair of sweatpants and a fresh T-shirt? Who cared if it was after nine?

She pulled open the front door. "Can you stay long enough for me to—?" She stumbled into silence at the sight of Stephen Ames standing on her porch, thankful she hadn't completed her request.

Stephen cocked his head to one side, eyebrow arched. "I don't know—long enough for you to what?"

Haley leaned against the door, the cool night air against her face a welcome relief. She rested a hand against Kit's tiny bottom as the baby began to fuss, squirming inside the swaddling blanket. "What are you doing here?"

"I thought we were well past that stage in our relationship. It doesn't sound like my niece is all that happy." He patted his broad chest as he stepped past her into the house. "At your service, ma'am."

"No, seriously. What are you doing here?"

"I was in town for a business meeting."

"Did you get a job?" Kit's discontent increased to out-and-out wails, prompting Haley to switch her to the other shoulder, all the while rocking back and forth.

"No. And I decided to stop by—"

"Then why were you at a business meeting?"

"Wooing a potential investor. So I wanted to check on Peanut—"

"Investor? For what?"

Stephen eased Kit from Haley's arms. "You need sleep. This conversation is garbled."

"Sleep?" Haley brushed her hair from her face. How bad did she look? "What's that?"

"My point exactly." Stephen snuggled Kit up against him, his hand cradling her head against his heart.

"I'm going to bed as soon as I convince my daughter to go to sleep." Haley escaped to the kitchen, in search of the can of soda she'd misplaced earlier in the evening. Was it here? Or in the bedroom? Or the—oh, how she hoped not—the bathroom? Oh, never mind. She'd find it sometime. Until then, she'd just start over with a new one. Opening the fridge, she grabbed a Sprite, the can cold against her skin. "Want something to drink?"

"I'm good. I had dinner at the Broadmoor."

"How nice for you. I had Oreos—double-stuffed. And a glass of milk."

Stephen filled the archway, her traitorous daughter quiet in his arms. "Oh, that's a nutritious meal for a new mom. Want me to make you some dinner?"

"No, but thanks for the offer." She slipped past him—and no, she didn't notice that he smelled good. She could only hope he didn't notice that she smelled like baby formula and something that could only be described as "worn-out mom." "How did you do that?"

"What?"

"Get her to be quiet?"

Stephen's smile echoed Sam's ever-present self-assurance. "She missed me. I'm here now. She's happy."

"Right." Haley only meant to sit on the couch, but her body insisted on going horizontal, the sofa pillow beneath her head. The yawn that interrupted their conversation refused to be silenced.

"Wasn't there something you needed to do?"

"It can wait. My plan got disrupted when somebody called about half an hour ago and woke Kit up right when I'd just gotten her to sleep."

A telltale red appeared on Stephen's ears and along his cheek-bones. "Thirty minutes ago?"

"Yes." Haley's head came up off the cushion, her hair falling in her face. *Stupid hair.* Maybe she should cut it. "Did you—?"

"Did I hear you call her Kit?"

"What? Oh, yes. Katherine Elizabeth—I took your Marvel Comics switcheroo suggestion. But I thought Kit was a cute nickname."

"It is." He tucked Kit into the crook of his arm, swaying back and forth. "But I'm partial to Peanut."

"She's still Peanut for her uncle Stephen." His lazy back-and-forth rhythm, all dressed up in a dark pair of pants and suit jacket, starched white shirt, and a silver and blue tie, lulled more than one Ames girl to sleep. Haley struggled to keep her eyes open. "I'm sorry . . . did you need something? I haven't looked through any more of the boxes of Sam's stuff—"

"No." Even Stephen's voice was hypnotic. "I was in town having dinner with a potential investor, and I wanted to come by and see you—see how my niece was. That's all."

"Oh. Well, welcome to my world." Haley gave a halfhearted wave around the room. A leaning tower of diapers sat atop the breakfast bar, and several baby blankets were draped over the backs of the stools. "A house decorated in 'Early American Newborn' is my new normal."

"I thought your mom was coming out to help you."

"She is—tomorrow, as a matter of fact. Because Kit was in the hospital for a week, I asked her to push the trip back." Another yawn punctuated her conversation. "Claire's husband, Finn, is picking her up at DIA in the morning. Saves me a trip. I'm not ready for the whole car seat routine with Kit yet."

"How long is she staying?"

"Ten days—at least. I'll be ready for any and all help when she gets here. I may lock the door and never let her leave."

"Listen, just relax. I've got Peanut, and she seems pretty content."

"Showoff."

"You just prepped her for me." He walked over to the TV, which, for once, sat silent. "I'll pop in a movie—quietly—and do uncle duty for a little bit."

Haley knew she should protest. Drag herself off the couch and do the right thing. Be the mom. Instead her eyes drifted shut as Stephen sifted through the stack of DVDs on the table.

"*True Grit* . . . *Rio Bravo* . . . *El Dorado* . . . Do you own anything besides John Wayne?"

"Sure. I have a nice collection of Bruce Willis—all the *Die Hard* movies. *Lord of the Rings.* If it has a car chase in it, I own it."

"I don't recall any car chases in *The Lord of the Rings.*"

"Ha-ha." She could hardly keep up with the conversation.

"So, on movie nights, you don't insist on a chick flick?"

"Pfffft." She nestled into the couch. "My brothers wouldn't have allowed it."

A few minutes later, the opening scene of *Hatari!* played across the TV. Stephen interrupted the opening dialogue. "I haven't seen this one."

"You're kidding, right? One of my favorites." Was she forming the words right? "John Wayne heads up a group that traps wild animals in Africa . . ."

"I read the back cover copy on the DVD case. Relax, remember?" Like a grown-up lullaby, his voice invited her to doze off. "I'm going to get something to drink. You need anything?"

"Hmmm . . ." Did she need anything? No, not anymore.

twenty-two

....••••••■•••••■•••••■•••••....

Stephen stood in the kitchen, the soft warmth of Kit against his chest seeming to seep all the way into his heart, deepening the beats. The last time he stood here, he'd been searching the pantry for snacks as he headed back to the hospital, unaware that Haley was in active labor. Now he held his days-old niece.

Sam's daughter.

He tipped his head forward, inhaling the delicate scent surrounding the infant mixed with a hint of lavender that reminded him of Haley. Just as Sam and he were intertwined, Sam and this baby were connected. In Kit, his brother lived on.

Miracle.

The realization stole over him with a swirl of emotion—joy intertwined with regret—that he tried to hold, to balance.

His parents' choices. His choices. Sam's choices. And yet, he was the one who had stayed locked in the bedroom the day during spring break when his mom took Sam to sign up with the army recruiter. He had laid the first brick that eventually became the wall that separated him from his brother. And he hadn't called to say good-bye when Sam left for boot camp. And then with each passing year, he let the wall grow higher. Wider. One letter. One phone call. Paltry efforts to make amends. Sometimes the scale of guilt tilted heavily in his direction. Other times he knew Sam had made his own choices, adding invisible bricks to the wall between them. All he knew now was death had demolished the wall—but he was still separated from his brother. With Sam's death, he'd lost all hope of ever seeing him again, this side of heaven.

But holding Kit . . . in a sense, he touched his brother. Embraced his brother. When he looked in her innocent brown eyes, he saw Sam's eyes staring back at him.

"You don't know me yet, little one." Stephen ran his forefinger across the faint outline of her eyebrows. "But I know you. And I know your daddy—oh, the stories I'll tell you about him."

A few moments later, he peeked around the corner to where Haley lay on the couch. "Just as I thought. Your mom's asleep." He watched the rise and fall of his niece's breathing. "And so are you. I have quite a way with the Ames females, don't I?"

Holding his breath, he managed to get to Haley's bedroom and deposit Kit into her cradle without waking either the baby or Haley. The bedroom mirrored the living room—only worse. Two laundry baskets sat at the foot of the bed—one full of crumpled, used baby clothes, one filled with clean, waiting-to-be-used baby clothes. Several unopened packages of diapers sat next to Kit's cradle. A pile of discarded sweatpants, jeans, T-shirts, and sweatshirts sat in front of Haley's dresser.

Stephen arranged a soft pink blanket around Kit's petite form, debating the wisdom of picking up the bedroom. Best not to chance waking Kit—or angering Haley. He walked halfway down the hallway. Stopped.

Wait. What if Haley didn't hear Kit wake up? Should he help Haley back to bed? Carry her back so she'd be closer to Kit?

Yeah, that would go over well.

He paced back to the bedroom. Sure enough, there was a blue and white baby monitor on the bedside table near Kit's cradle. It stood next to a photo of Haley and Sam. Stephen picked it up. This had to be their wedding day—and look at that: Haley Ames was stunning in a beaded white dress next to Sam—wait, where were they? The couple stood on marble steps in front of a building. Had they gotten married at the court-house? Haley's hair hung in loose curls around her face, her bril-liant blue gaze focused on Sam, not on the photographer. His brother's smile had converted to laughter, his arm across Haley's shoulders, one hand raised in triumph.

He set the photo back in place. He wasn't here to look at wedding photos—well, *a* wedding photo. He needed to find the other half of the baby monitor. A quick, quiet search of the house revealed it sitting in the bathroom on the counter, next to a can of soda.

O-kay . . .

He carried both back into the kitchen, emptying the soda into the sink, and then walked over to where Haley slept, her breathing deep and even. He'd leave the monitor on the coffee table and be on his way.

He set the monitor down. Walked to the door. Turned around and walked back to the couch. Picked up the monitor. Put it down. Haley slept with one hand tucked underneath her chin, the other cradled the sofa cushion beneath her head. Long, light-colored eyelashes rested against her high cheek-bones, and the dim lighting in the room hid the golden high-lights in her hair. Stephen fought the urge to search the linen closet for a blanket to cover her with before he left. He flexed his fingers, resisting the desire to trace the outline of Haley's face—but the memory of how she'd pulled away from him at the hospital stayed his hand. He needed to let her sleep. Rest.

He should leave—but he couldn't do it.

Exhaustion etched dark circles under Haley's eyes. She looked thinner—and she'd been thin even before Kit was born. Well, if she was surviving on Oreos and milk and soda, her mother couldn't get here soon enough. Uncle or not, brother-in-law or not, it didn't feel right to stay in the house alone with Haley . . . but how could he get her even a few extra hours of sleep?

⋯•◦•◦•—◆—•◦•◦•⋯

Haley sat up before her eyes opened all the way. What day was it? Wait . . . wait . . . what was she forgetting?

Kit!

She stumbled to her feet, knocking her shin against the coffee table. "Oh, words, words, words!"

She rubbed her hand against her leg. Where was her baby? What kind of mother fell asleep . . .

Stephen.

When she fell asleep, Stephen was holding Kit in his arms, a mixed-up image of uncle and daddy—what Sam would have looked like if he'd lived.

All she had to do was find Stephen and she'd find Kit. She beelined for the bedroom and found Kit safe and warm—and sleeping in her cradle. The bedside clock said it was one forty-five in the morning. What kind of magic did Stephen work on her daughter so that she slept this long?

And where was he?

Maybe there was a note on the kitchen counter—something to indicate that he'd left. That he'd be back.

Nothing.

Poof! Stephen Ames had pulled a disappearing act while she slept—probably while she snored—on the couch. She could call him and ask him where he was, but there was no need to wake him up just because she'd suffered an attack of mother guilt. Switching off lights, she noticed the now-familiar shadow of his Mustang parked in her driveway. Stephen's car was still here. But where was he? Surely not . . .

Grabbing the throw blanket off the end of the couch, she slipped outside, the pavement cool against her feet, the middle-of-the-night hush enveloping her in a gentle embrace. The Mustang's passenger-side window was rolled halfway down. Stephen sprawled in the driver's bucket seat, the window on that side of the car also halfway down.

Why was he camped out in her driveway?

His hand held the other half of the baby monitor against his chest. What was the man doing?

She reached through the open window, resting her hand on his shoulder.

Nothing.

Sam would have bolted awake.

She shook his shoulder. "Stephen."

Nothing.

She leaned in closer, raising her voice. "Stephen. Wake up."

He mumbled something, adjusting his tall frame as if he was trying to find a more comfortable position. His grip on the monitor never loosened.

"Hey, Rogers. Wake up."

He turned his head, his just-opening eyes dull with sleep. "Morning, Haley."

"It's the middle of the night. Why are you sleeping in your car?"

"Um, yeah." He blinked. Once. Twice. "Wanted to be here in case Kit woke up."

"Did you forget that's why I'm here?"

"No." He shook his head, running his fingers through his hair—the color the same rich brown as Sam's. "But I thought it might be nice for you to get some extra sleep."

"Thanks to your Uncle Stephen magic, I did sleep. I can take it from here."

When Stephen sat up, she dropped her hand from his shoulder. He stared out the front of the car for a few moments, as if he was getting his bearings. "Okay, then. I'll head on home—"

Haley reached through the window again, grabbing his arm. "Are you kidding me? It's two o'clock. You're not driving back to Fort Collins in the middle of the night. Come back inside. You can stretch out on the couch. I'll go to bed."

"Thanks for the offer, Haley." Stephen paused. "But, um, I need to get on up the road and report back in on my business meeting. It was great seeing you . . . and Peanut. If it's okay with you, I'll drop in again—and I'll try to make it a more convenient time."

"Fine. But really, can't you—"

Her words were cut off as the sound of Kit snuffling, followed by a whimper, interrupted their battle of the wills. Stephen held up the monitor. "Wow. Good thing I didn't drive off with this." He passed the monitor to her through the window. "Mom duty calls. And I'm outta here."

She took the monitor, the sounds of Kit's distress increasing. Before he could back the car up, Haley reached through the car window and touched Stephen's shoulder again. "Thank you."

"Hey, that's what uncles are for." He motioned toward the house. "Get on in there before Kit wakes the whole neighborhood."

Haley ignored Kit's demands for attention as she stood on her front lawn and watched Stephen drive away. What kind of man fell asleep in his car, holding on to a baby monitor, so that an exhausted new mom could get some sleep? The same man who'd painted her daughter's bedroom an inviting yellow and surprised her with a cradle so Kit could sleep beside her bed at night.

Kit's cries insisted she stop puzzling over the mystery of Stephen Ames and go rescue her daughter. But the realization of how many times the man had rescued her followed her into the house.

twenty-three

When it came to trying to find his brother, looking through yearbooks was a waste of time.

Stephen sat on the couch in his studio apartment, Sam's senior yearbook open in his lap, the other three high school yearbooks stacked in a cascading pile next to him. High school—when Sam lived with their mom and he lived with their dad and Gina. Their visits with one another becoming less frequent—almost nonexistent. He'd hoped that the books' pages would reveal more of Sam's life during those years. He'd been home for three days before he'd opened the box Haley had given him before Peanut's early arrival.

What had he learned? Nothing really.

He'd seen Sam's hair get progressively shorter. Had known his brother participated in ROTC while Stephen joined the computer club and earned his Eagle Scout rank.

They both wrestled for their respective high schools, weighing in at one seventy-five, but Sam was the brother who went to State in Oklahoma.

He hadn't known that under his senior portrait, Sam listed "join the army" as his life goal and added a quote from General George S. Patton: "Always do more than is required of you."

Well, his brother had lived up to that ideal.

"Why the army, Sam?" He stared at the photo of his brother wearing his letter jacket, leaning against a motorcycle. It had to be a friend's—their mom had vetoed any idea of a motorcycle when they'd first daydreamed out loud about it at thirteen. "We never talked about the military."

And here he sat, talking to his brother's senior photo.

The twelve years of complete silence between him and Sam echoed louder than all the arguments—the accusations, the tears, the slammed doors—leading up to his parents' divorce.

Staying with his dad and Gina seemed like the right choice— just as much of a right choice as Sam's choosing to stay with their mom.

Yes, Sam chose sides first.

Did that make him less wrong than Sam?

He should have said good-bye to Sam when he left for boot camp.

But shouldn't Sam have told him that he'd changed his mind about college—not just announced the decision to go into the army the night before he went to sign enlistment papers?

And then all the years Stephen walked away from who he was. All the years he was just Stephen. Not Stephen *and* . . .

I made a choice, God.

I did.

Win, lose, or draw.

This is where I stand.

Truth is wretched sometimes.

And the question "Why?" taunts me . . . which is so much more painful than haunting me. Taunting doesn't linger out there like some nameless, voiceless phantom. I know who is asking the question. I recognize the voice asking, "Why didn't you do more?"

For the sake of family.

For the sake of brothers.

Could I have done more?

Done more than the "Hey, I graduated from college" phone call? Sent more than the one letter that disappeared into postal oblivion?

Is family worth more than two strikes, you're out?

Seven times seven.

He knew that spiritual multiplication table—and how it equaled forgiveness. And yes, maybe he needed to admit that at first a lack of forgiveness was mixed in the cement that held the wall in place between him and his brother.

But was it wrong to pursue the freedom to be himself? To say, "If they aren't for me—Sam and Mom—then I'm going to be for me"? *They didn't choose me. When Sam chose Mom—when he didn't choose Dad—he also didn't choose me. When he chose the army—when he didn't choose college—he also didn't choose me.*

What happened to the whole "Family is forever" ideal plastered across Hallmark cards? From where he sat, it seemed as if "family" had an awful lot of conditions to it. Do this. Don't do that.

No matter what he chose, somebody lost.

Him.

Sam.

Whatever their family had started out as . . . how did it end up here?

He reached over to where his laptop sat on the glass coffee table and closed it down, discarding the links he'd found to the news articles about Sam's death. Facts and figures—his brother's life reduced to data.

Birth date. Years in service. Rank. Awards. Duty stations in the army.

The only living, breathing thing left of Sam was . . . Peanut. A days-old infant created the one tangible link to his brother. But between him and his niece stood Haley.

What was he supposed to do about Haley? How did he deal with the fact that he missed his niece—and Haley? That he thought about calling Haley a dozen times a day—because he wanted to know how she was just as much as he wanted to know how Kit was?

He needed to get on with his life. Find a job. And remember that to Haley he was nothing more than a walking, talking, un-wanted reminder of the husband she'd lost.

He needed to get out of his head. Stephen dialed his father as he pulled a bag of peppered beef jerky out of the cupboard.

"I was expecting to hear from you." His father's voice poured over him, as welcome as a just-right amount of warm maple syrup over a stack of homemade pancakes.

"What happened to 'hello,' Dad?"

"Just cutting to the chase. Tonight's date night."

"Date night?"

"You heard me. It's something our church small group is encouraging. Couples schedule a date night at least once a month. Your stepmom thinks twice a month is a good mini-mum."

"So what are you and Gina doing for, um, date night?"

"Last time we went to the movies. This time we're going to dinner, which means conversation. Just so long as we don't get onto the topic of feelings." His father's chuckle was a faint echo of his. Of Sam's. "I take it you're back in Fort Collins?"

"Yep. Just wanted to check in."

"The three of us are all good here. How about you?"

"A bit . . . frustrated."

"And that would be because . . ."

"I spent all that time in the Springs, Dad, and I'm no closer to knowing anything about Sam." He picked up Sam's freshman yearbook and then tossed it onto the couch again. "All I have to show for it is a stack of high school yearbooks that I'll have to return."

"And a new niece."

"Well, there is that. There's only so much information in a yearbook, Dad."

"So go back for a visit. Ask more questions."

"It's . . . not that simple."

"You start a new job?"

"That wouldn't be a complication—it would be an answer to prayer." Stephen paced the miniscule living room, ending up seated at his drafting table. "My showing up there only complicates Haley's life."

"Don't you think she's gotten past the shock that you and Sam are mirror twins?"

"I don't know. I hope so. I think we both end up confused when I'm around. I'm not sure if she's seeing me or Sam when she's looking at me—and it shouldn't matter one way or the other, should it?"

"No, it shouldn't. Does it?"

"When I'm here, I miss them, Dad—both of them."

Silence greeted his last statement.

"Say something." Even a laugh in his face would be better than this extended silence.

"I need you to clarify which 'both of them' you mean. Do you mean you miss both Sam and the baby? Sam and Haley? Haley and the baby? And if Haley's name is showing up in the answer . . . well, I think I raised you to be smarter than that, son."

Nothing like saying it straight up, Dad.

"I haven't acted on how I'm feeling . . . I'm not even sure what it is that I'm feeling." He drummed his fingers on the desktop. "It just complicates things."

"That's the second time you've used the word *complicates*. Don't you think Haley has enough complications in her life right now? It hasn't even been a year since Sam died. She just found out that her husband has a twin brother who walks, talks, and looks exactly like him. Just had a baby—six weeks early."

Stephen didn't need a detailed list of everything Haley was dealing with. And he knew that, as far as she was concerned, he was filed in the category labeled COMPLICATIONS.

And there was the word *again*.

"I'm not saying she won't ever get married again. She's young. She's got a little girl who needs a daddy. Now, I know if this were during the times of Joshua or Judges, you could step in and marry her—"

Why did his dad have to bring up the Old Testament law? "I'm not planning on any sort of Levitical thing here, Dad."

"So you're telling me the feelings you have for Haley are brotherly, is that it? Because if that's all it is, then I don't even see why we're having this discussion. Go ahead. Be a brother-in-law to her. Pray for her. Help her."

"What if Haley doesn't want my help?" Stephen swiveled in his chair and stared at the package of beef jerky, realizing he had no appetite for the stuff.

"Wouldn't surprise me. Sam may have married her for just that reason—she is an independent, strong woman. He'd have needed that, if he deployed a lot. If you want to help Haley, then be practical."

"Like repairing the part of her fence that looks like it would topple over if I gave it a push? Painting the shutters?"

"Exactly."

"A brother-in-law would do that."

"Yes."

"A simple offer of help."

"Exactly." In the background Stephen heard his stepmother say something. "Now, if you don't mind, I don't want to keep my date waiting."

"No problem, Dad. Tell Gina and Pete I said hello."

"Absolutely. After dinner."

•••••——•••••

"So am I going to meet Sam's brother?"

Haley stayed focused on the increasing pile of pink, purple, and polka-dotted baby clothes. At least her mother hadn't insisted on her going shopping, too. They didn't "do" shopping. But based on the number of bags she'd hauled into the house, her mother had purchased every single item with a bow, ruffle, or lace ribbon on it.

And now she'd tossed in a not-so-covert question about Stephen.

"I have no idea." When Kit moved against her, Haley shifted her weight in the fabric baby sling. "I didn't think I was going to like this contraption when Sara gave it to me, but it's such a comfortable way to carry Kit. She's calmer when she's up against me and stays warm, too. And it's a hoot that it's called a Peanut Shell. I've got my Peanut in her shell."

"Have you talked to Stephen since I arrived?"

So much for changing the topic. "Mom, you know I haven't. We've spent every minute together."

"Is that a complaint?" Her mother held up two sleepers, turning them to show how both the purple one and the pink polka-dotted one had ruffles along the backsides. "Ruffled bottom every time."

"If you say so. Not that I ever wore one of these."

"You most certainly did."

"Pffft. Mother, don't try to fool me. I know girlie stuff was outlawed in our house."

"Haley Leigh Jordan Ames, I was well aware that I birthed a daughter when you were born." Her mother revealed a pair of tiny patent leather shoes. How old would Kit be when she could finally wear those? "A daughter who eventually was determined to keep up with her big brothers, yes—but a daughter, nonetheless. The 'girlie' stuff didn't last long, but you wore it."

"Huh." She could just see the toes of her washed canvas Rocket Dogs peeking out from underneath the frayed hems of her jeans. Her T-shirt was covered by one of Sam's flannel shirts. "Some women are feminine. I'm not one of them."

"You're a female, Haley, which means you are, by definition, feminine. And behind all the who-cares-what-I-look-like clothes there's a beautiful woman."

You're beautiful, Haley.

Now, what was Stephen Ames doing inside her head? Even though Stephen and Sam sounded alike, her husband had never called her beautiful. Strong, yes. Independent, yes. A good shot, yes.

Beautiful—never.

But his brother held her hand while she labored, wiped the sweat off her face, and told her she was beautiful.

"So what do you think?" Her mother's voice interrupted her thoughts as she sat back and surveyed the mountain of new clothes for her granddaughter.

"I don't think we need to buy another thing for Kit—and I'm not sure when she's going to be able to wear some of these outfits."

"That's not what I asked. My question was: Will Stephen be coming around again?"

"I don't know. When he left a week or so ago, he didn't say. He's Kit's uncle, so yes, probably we'll see him again." Haley eased to her feet, careful not to move too quickly and wake Kit. "When, I don't know. I think he's realized I can't really help him find Sam again. He's got his life. I've got mine. And we're not going to keep crossing paths."

Why did saying that make her . . . sad? She wasn't missing Stephen Ames. She already had enough emotions to deal with—to hold at bay. She didn't need to add anything to do with Stephen into the jumbled mess.

twenty-four

•··•··•·····•·····•·····•·····•··•

Stephen glanced at the backseat of his Mustang. A bag of groceries. And two bags labeled with the bright, primary-color logo of Babies"R"Us.

What was the saying? *Beware of Greeks bearing gifts.*

There was no denying he was going to show up at Haley's house with gifts—for his niece. And then he would offer to make dinner. But he hoped Haley didn't think of him as a Greek—an enemy—anymore.

When he called and said oh-so-casually, "I'm in the Springs. Is it okay if I swing by later?" she said yes without pausing, adding, "My mom asked me earlier this week if she was going to meet you."

If he'd known that, he would have driven down to the Springs sooner. It was only four thirty on Wednesday, so his hope was to ply his niece with gifts, meet Haley's mom—Sam's mother-in-law—and then offer to make dinner. He had all the ingredients for chicken carbonara, one of his specialties. All he could do was be casual and take it one step at a time.

As if he'd ever been casual around Haley.

She'd threatened to shoot him.

Shut the front door in his face.

Almost kissed him.

And then they'd experienced the birth of Kit together—even if he did stare at the hospital wall for most of the event.

So, presents and dinner—no big deal. Except that he hoped it was one more step forward for him and Haley—and Kit, of course.

Should he show up at the door with groceries or presents? Presents, definitely. The one uncomplicated cord binding him and Haley was Kit. How could she say no to a doting uncle?

"What did you do, buy out the store, Rogers?" Haley stared at the Babies"R"Us bags as if they were loaded with contraband. "Aren't you unemployed?"

"Unemployed doesn't mean I'm broke." He set the bags on the couch, turning to face the slender woman walking down the hall toward him with Kit cradled in her arms. "Hello. You must be Haley's mom."

"Yes, I'm Paula Jordan—and you're Stephen." He didn't have to work hard to earn a smile from Haley's mother. "Haley wasn't exaggerating when she said you looked exactly like Sam."

It seemed being straightforward was a family trait. "It was a problem for our parents from the day we were born. My mom painted the nail of Sam's big toe bright blue."

Haley reached for Kit, but her mother shook her head in an *I've got this* kind of way. "And what color was yours?"

"No need to paint mine." He motioned toward the bags. "I picked up a few things for Peanut—" Haley's muffled laugh interrupted him. "—and, if you all like chicken carbonara, I also brought the ingredients with me and would like to offer my talents and make you both dinner."

"I don't think—"

Haley's mom interrupted her daughter's refusal. "That would be wonderful. I, for one, am tired of heating up casseroles or ordering pizza."

"Mom—"

"Great. I'll go get the ingredients." He ducked out of the house. Let mother and daughter find their way back to verbal neutral corners while he lugged in supplies. He was just glad not to be in the ring with Haley for once.

Things were quiet when he returned. Mrs. Jordan sat in a rocking chair—when had that been added to the décor?—bottle-feeding Kit. He laid ingredients out on the counter: a roasted chicken, a box of spaghetti, whipping cream, fresh basil, fresh parsley, pancetta, and grated Parmesan—also fresh. He set a bouquet of white daisies on the counter with everything else. Casual. No big deal.

"Who are the flowers for?" Haley leaned against the arched entryway into the kitchen. She'd pulled her hair into a tight ponytail and added a black ball cap with an army logo. Instead of her usual sweatpants, she wore a loose gray cotton top over a pair of black leggings. Nice look.

"All of you."

"Daisies—nice, no-frills flowers. Thank you." She retrieved a tall glass vase from a cabinet over the fridge. "When you said you liked to cook, you weren't kidding."

"It's something between a hobby and a passion of mine." He found a pot and filled it with water, setting it on the stove to boil. "My stepmom liked to cook, and she let me hang in the kitchen with her. It was a good way to connect. And then, when I was a broke college kid, I discovered dates were cheaper when I cooked."

"Ah, wooed the women with your culinary skills, did you?"

"You could say that. It was a great way to double-date. Jared and I would split the costs of groceries—and eat any leftovers. Of course, at first my specialties were spaghetti and pot roast." Stephen kept opening drawers until he found Haley's knives. "So, I noticed you got a rocking chair."

"It's from my brothers and their families. They gave my mom the money, and she shopped for it once she got here and had it delivered."

"And she put it together?"

"No—she's like me with tools. She paid extra to have it assembled." Setting the flowers on the breakfast bar, Haley motioned to the dinner ingredients. "Can I help with anything?"

"You sure you don't want to go take a nap or something?"

"If you tell me how tired I look, I'll dump that pot of water on you."

"You don't look tired. You look . . . fine." Okay, he needed to concentrate on putting dinner together, not on Haley. His sister-in-law. "How about shredding the chicken?"

"Sure." She moved beside him where he stood chopping garlic, the aroma already tingeing the air. "So how come all this cooking skill never landed you a wife?"

"Who said it didn't?"

"What?" She motioned toward his left hand. "You one of those married men who doesn't wear a wedding band? Or are you divorced?"

"Guilty on neither charge." He kept his eyes trained on the cutting board. "I proposed to my girlfriend Elissa a while back—got a no before I barely finished."

"What? How long had you been dating?"

"Six months. Among other things, she said she felt as if there was something I was searching for."

"She didn't know about Sam?"

"No. No one did—except Jared. I told him one night early in our freshman year, thanks to a keg-induced bout of honesty."

The scent of roasted chicken blended with the tang of garlic. "I still wonder why Sam didn't tell me about you."

"Don't make it about you, Haley." Stephen allowed his attention to stray from food prep and made eye contact with Haley. "Sam's issue was with me and our parents. It wasn't about him not loving you."

"So you came looking for Sam because of your relationship with—"

"Elissa." Stephen finished chopping the pancetta, piling it to the side of the cutting board to sauté it with the garlic in olive oil. "And I waited a month to try to find my brother—and by then, it was too late."

"Oh—that reminds me." Haley stopped talking, biting her bottom lip.

"Reminds you of . . . ?"

"No, go ahead. You were talking."

"No-o. I was done talking. What did I remind you of?"

"Your mom hasn't called you recently, has she?"

What kind of question was that?

"Is it Christmas? Or Thanksgiving? Or my birthday? Then no, she hasn't called. Why?"

"We talked about a week ago—and I just thought she might have called you, too."

"Because?"

"They're planning a memorial service for Sam in Oklahoma in June. They originally scheduled it around Kit's due date in April—giving me a couple of months before I traveled with her."

"And you think my mother would invite me to that?"

"She wouldn't?"

"Obviously she hasn't." Stephen paused, reviewing the recipe to give himself time to prepare his reaction. "And it's for the best. I don't have any desire to play the ghost of Samuel Wilson Ames at the memorial—or any other time."

Before she could answer, the sound of Kit's cry interrupted their conversation. Haley lathered her hands at the sink. "For such a tiny thing, she's got a strong set of lungs. Sorry to abandon you in the kitchen."

"I can handle this."

"Great. I'm not good for much more in the kitchen than chatting with the cook while tearing up a chicken."

••●••◆••●••

Stephen Ames left behind too many piles.

Haley didn't mind the huge amount of leftover chicken carbonara. If she didn't figure out a way to resist the lure of all that cream and cheese and pasta, she'd finish it off as a way-too-indulgent midnight snack.

The stack of not-all-age-appropriate toys—she needed to show Stephen how to check for that—meant she needed to find somewhere to keep them. Kit now owned a musical piano play mat and a set of bath toys she wouldn't use for months. And her daughter might not ever wear the Cinderella princess costume.

And then there were the questions piling up, waiting for answers. Stephen was almost engaged? Was he still in love with Elissa?

"He's very different from Sam, isn't he?" Her mother walked into Haley's bedroom, wrapped in the familiar yellow robe she'd worn for years.

"Once you get past all the ways he's exactly like Sam, then yes, he's very different from him." Haley stood in the master bath, looking in the mirror. She splashed warm water on her face. "I mean, he cooks and Sam was good at opening a bag of chips."

"Oh, it's more than that."

"What do you mean?"

"Sam was all go, go, go—on the move, focusing on the next thing, the next deployment. I don't think I ever saw him sit still for more than five minutes. Of course, I didn't see him that often."

"No, you're right. Sam's nickname was 'Gusto.' I mean, he was a good medic. His buddies told me that. But when he was home, he was restless."

"And Stephen has a way with Kit, doesn't he? Did you see how she settled down for him when he held her?"

"Little traitor. Isn't that always the way it is? I do all the work—pregnancy and labor and delivery—and then she settles down for her . . . uncle."

"Is it hard having him around?"

"Sometimes. Not as much as it was at first." Haley pulled her hair into a ponytail. Released it. No matter what she did with her hair, she looked tired. Frazzled. "He's gone from being a ghost of Sam to being . . . Stephen. I imagine it will be easier with time to accept that Sam is gone and Stephen is here."

"You're doing wonderfully, sweetie."

Haley leaned into her mother's embrace, the scent of her face wash an echo of distant times when she was much younger. "Some days it's minute by minute for me, Mom. And then other days I go to bed and realize I didn't think of Sam at all. How could that be?"

"Do you feel like you're being unfaithful to Sam because you don't think about him every minute of the day?"

"Not unfaithful, exactly."

"Did you think of Sam all the time when he was alive?"

"Of course not. That's not realistic—" Haley stalled out at the look on her mother's face. "Point taken. But my goal isn't to think about Sam all the time."

"What is your goal?"

"I don't want to forget him. I want to make sure Kit knows who her father was."

"Both admirable desires, Haley." Her mother wrapped an arm around her shoulders and pulled her close, the cotton of her robe soft against Haley's cheek. "But your life didn't stop the day Sam died—his did. If yours had stopped, then that precious daughter of yours wouldn't be sleeping in that cradle."

"But Kit needs to know who Sam was."

"And you'll tell her. But Sam will be a part of her past, too—not her present." Her mother pressed a kiss on her forehead, just as if Haley was a little girl again and needed someone to make things all better for her. "I don't mean to sound callous. I know you miss Sam. I know Kit will struggle because she never knew her father. It may be God's will that you remarry someday—"

Haley shifted away from her mother's half hug.

Her mother let her go. "I know, I know. It's too soon for you to even entertain the thought. But you're twenty-eight. You have years ahead of you."

"Sam thought he had years ahead of him. And I thought we'd be spending those years together." Haley paused. Held her breath for the space of twenty seconds before continuing. "Can I be honest, Mom?"

"Of course you can."

"I was always . . . waiting for Sam." Haley closed her eyes but couldn't block out the images of Sam walking away from her so many times. Too many times. "I can't believe I said that out loud. We married less than a month before a deployment.

And then he was always gone—he even *volunteered* to go on a deployment. We said good-bye more times than we said 'I love you.'"

"And?"

"And what?"

"What else aren't you saying?"

"Sometimes I wondered . . . I wondered if I was . . . enough to make Sam want to come home."

twenty-five

"Mind if I join you?"

Stephen looked up to where Haley's mother stood on the top step into the garage. What could she possibly want out here?

"No, you're more than welcome, Mrs. Jordan—but it's a bit, um, cluttered in here." He motioned to the boxes still waiting to be unpacked. Every time he tried to get to the boxes, there was another homeowners' association–sanctioned house project needing attention. He'd edged the lawn. Affixed the approved house numbers beside the front door. Painted the front door and shutters—a job Haley insisted on helping with. During the afternoon, Haley talked about some of her shooting competitions, sharing an occasional glimpse of her too-rare smiles that lit up her blue eyes.

"Please, call me Paula. All my friends do. And from what Haley tells me, you're the reason she can park her car in here."

"Barely."

"Barely is better than not at all. Especially with that snowstorm coming in this weekend."

She came around the front of the car and leaned against the driver's-side door. "May I help with anything?"

"I'm just finishing up for the night, then I'll be heading back to my hotel."

"It was nice of you to come back this weekend and help Haley with those projects—including fixing that leaky toilet. And now this. I hope you'll stay for dinner. I made chicken tortilla soup. It's one of Haley's favorites."

"I didn't want to presume."

"You're family, Stephen—truly."

In the most awkward definition of the word, yes, he was.

"I hope Haley's thanked you for all your help." She motioned to what would have been Sam's tool bench, where all the tools hung in orderly rows.

"Glad to do it." Helping Haley made him feel closer to Sam somehow. He could almost imagine the two of them hanging out in the garage, talking while they put things in order. Catching up on the lost twelve years. "And I'm sure she's told you that my motives weren't completely unselfish."

"She mentioned you're trying to fill in the gaps of the years you and Sam were separated. Having success?"

"Sometimes I feel as if the longer I'm here, the further he slips away from me. Haley's not very talkative." He held up his hands, which still had some paint spots on them. "Today was fun."

"She never was a typical girl, you know."

"I'm catching on."

"I blame myself."

"Blame yourself? What do you mean?"

"When Haley was born, I was one very busy, very exhausted mother of three boys. It was all boys, all day, all night. *Cars and Trucks and Things That Go* by Richard Scarry. You ever read that book?"

"Sure did." Tired of him and Sam fighting over the book, his mom had bought a second copy.

"Haley became her big brothers' shadow. The dresses I bought her? She refused to wear them. So I just stopped buying them. The boys called her 'Hal'—and pretty soon so did everybody else. When we enrolled her in school, she insisted that the teachers call her 'Hal,' too."

"So what do you blame yourself for?"

"Haley is my daughter—but I let her be one of the boys for so long I think she lost herself along the way. She embraced the tomboy persona to the exclusion of everything else."

"Well, it's pretty evident my brother saw past that, isn't it?" He finished breaking down the last empty box and piled it next to the recycling bin. "If he proposed to Haley and married her, he obviously loved her in more than a 'she's a great guy for a girl' kind of way."

"You see past it, too, don't you?"

Stephen froze, striving to keep his face neutral. Why did he feel the same way he had when he'd been caught cheating on a math test in fifth grade? "Ma'am?"

"Haley—she's more than a 'great guy for a girl' to you, isn't she?"

"I don't think now's the time to discuss my feelings for Haley—"

"When is the time? When Kit is one? Three? Six?"

"Haley is still grieving Sam."

"Is she, Stephen?" When Haley's mother came to stand beside him, he recognized how similar in height she and Haley were. "You strike me as a man who's more observant than that. She's sad, yes. She's exhausted—every woman is right after having a baby. And she's lonely. But I get the feeling she was lonely before Sam died."

"Are you saying my brother didn't love Haley?"

"I'm saying love—real love—takes time." Paula Jordan rested a hand on his arm. "And that's not something Haley and Sam had a lot of. Sam already had made a commitment to the military before he asked Haley to marry him—and from the little I know of their marriage, that commitment didn't change after the 'I do's.'"

"You think my brother should have gotten out of the military just because he got married?"

"Of course not. But he needed to make room in his life for a wife—and I'm not sure he'd learned how to do that before he died." The pat on his arm was swift, light. "Haley needs a very special man, someone who sees her for who she is—who she could be. Sam could have become that man, but he's not here . . . and I'm sorry he lost that chance. But now you're here—"

"And I'm Sam's brother."

"I know that, Stephen." Paula moved to the door before she spoke again. Then she paused, the door halfway open, speaking over her shoulder. "Don't let a little thing like that stop you from loving the right woman—if you've found her."

A little thing like that.

••••••◆•••••

What was he doing, living some kind of crazy split life? His home was here, in Fort Collins, but his heart resided straight down I-25, two hours south. Some days Stephen woke up wondering where he was, having to push back the heaviness weighing down his heart when he realized he wasn't in Colorado Springs.

How odd to be back at Elissa's boutique. He'd dated Elissa for half a year—met her here for lunch, walked the surrounding streets of Denver—and yet standing in her office at the back of the store felt odd. Her desk was Elissa-organized, which meant it was a collection of disheveled piles of paper—and she could find exactly what she wanted in a matter of seconds.

"You sure you don't have time for dinner, Elissa?"

"Not tonight. I've got other plans." Elissa leaned against her desk wearing a fitted black dress, leaving him to stand in the doorway. "So, Stephen . . . what's this about?"

"I guess you could say it's about closure."

"Ah." Elissa wrapped the long strand of multicolored glass beads cascading from her neck around her forefinger. "And which one of us is going first—you or me?"

Elissa had something to say about closure? That was news to him. He offered her a slight nod. "By all means, ladies first."

"Did you find what you were looking for?"

"You mean did I discover what or who you said I needed to find?"

"I suppose that's the correct way to phrase it."

"Yes." Now came the challenging part. He rubbed his forefinger across his bottom lip. "Elissa . . . I'm sorry to say I kept something from you when we were dating."

"A secret, Stephen?" She leaned forward. "Is that what this is all about—some hidden part of your past? An ex-wife? A child?"

"A brother."

"I know about Pete—"

"My twin brother, Sam."

Elissa tilted her head, her eyes widening. "You don't have a twin."

"Yes, I do. His name is . . . was Samuel Wilson Ames."

"You said 'was.'"

Elissa always was quick on picking up the finer details. "He was an army medic—and he was killed last August in Afghanistan."

"This is like something out of a movie." Elissa slipped into her red swivel chair. "Stephen, I am so sorry. Were you separated at birth or something?"

"We were separated when we were thirteen by our parents' divorce. Up until then, Sam had been my best friend."

"What—your mom took Sam and your dad took you?"

"Sam and I . . . separated ourselves. When my dad got remarried a couple of years later, Sam chose to stay with my mom and I chose to stay with my dad and his wife, Gina."

"So you're saying Sam protected your mom and you took your father's side. It happens. But why didn't you keep in touch?"

"It's hard to explain." He curbed the urge to pace the office—there wasn't any room. "No. It's not hard to explain. It just sounds bad—because it is."

"I don't understand."

"Sam and I are—were—mirror twins. We looked almost exactly alike. After Sam chose to live with my mom in Oklahoma, I liked being just me. I liked that people in Pennsylvania, where I lived with my dad and my stepmom, couldn't confuse me for Sam. Life was easier. Ultimately, Sam asked for my mom to be his sole parental guardian."

"But surely your father . . ."

"He tried at first—but Sam was so hostile. So he thought he'd bide his time. And then . . . life went on. Phone conversations between them dwindled to nothing. Letters were returned—well, except for the child support. I only saw him on occasion—during visits to my mom on some holidays. It was normal not to be a twin."

"So the thing that was missing, that was driving you, was—"

"My brother Sam."

"And all this time—since we broke up—you've been . . . what?"

"Sam was married . . . I found his widow. I've been asking her questions, trying to find out who Sam became. And I'm an uncle, too . . ." He exhaled. "I'm sorry. I do believe I said 'ladies first.'"

Elissa waved aside his apology. "And I thought what I had to say was going to shock you."

"What?" A small laugh escaped. "You get married or something?"

Shrill laughter erupted from Elissa's pursed lips.

"You . . . you didn't get married, did you?"

"Actually, I did." Stephen saw that she tried to restrain the smile, but it snuck past her control. "It . . . just happened. A crazy weekend drive to Las Vegas. He asked and I said, 'Why not?' and then I was saying 'I do' in one of those so-tacky-they're-cute wedding chapels."

Elissa *married*?

"Who?" That was an abrupt question. "I mean, who's the lucky guy?"

"Eddie Marino. You met him."

"I did?"

"Yes, that night outside the Thai restaurant."

"Him?"

"Yes, him." Elissa nodded her head, looking past Stephen. "*Him*."

Stephen half turned and confronted the guy with the slicked-back dark hair whom he'd met a few weeks ago.

"Nice to see you again." Elissa's husband held out his hand. "Congratulations."

Eddie walked past Stephen, over to Elissa, and wrapped her in a close embrace, causing Stephen to avert his eyes. *Nothing like marking your territory.*

What could he say? It wasn't as if he was coming back here

to try to restore his relationship with Elissa. But married? What happened to the woman who insisted she wasn't ready to get married?

"I know this is a surprise, Stephen." Elissa spoke from within the shelter of Eddie's arms.

"Love often is." He needed to stop talking. He sounded like a character in a chick flick. "Thank you for telling me, Elissa. I hope you're both very happy."

His mouth seemed to be a conveyor belt for clichés.

An hour later, he was back in his apartment. With time, the image of Elissa in the arms of another man would fade.

He wasn't jealous.

Stunned, yes. Jealous, no.

Elissa had rejected his proposal, insisting he was searching for someone and that she wasn't ready for marriage—and gone off and gotten married to someone else.

One thing he'd realized while he searched for Sam was that he didn't want to marry Elissa. His idea to come back and try to revive their relationship hadn't lasted long.

His heart was back in Colorado Springs . . . held in the hands of a woman who looked at him and saw her past—the man she'd loved and lost—and the tiny hands of a newborn baby who didn't even know he existed. Yet.

twenty-six

........•........•........•........

After a whirlwind first couple of months after Kit's birth, Haley had gotten what she'd wanted—the house to herself again.

Haley's father had come to meet his newest granddaughter in mid-March. She'd watched both her parents *ooh* and *aah* over Kit and never once ducked when her father took yet another photo of her as a "baby mama." After two days, Haley had pried herself out of one more hug, shooing her parents toward the rental car and assuring her mother she was fine. That yes, she'd miss her, but it was time for Haley to settle into some sort of routine as a single mom. Time for her parents to go back home—and for her to figure out life on her own. With Kit.

During the next month, Stephen continued his "Uncle Stephen" Saturday visits, the one time each week when she knew she'd eat a decent—no, a delicious meal complete with protein, a vegetable, and salad, accompanied by a no-frills bouquet of daisies. Each time she walked him to the Mustang, she assured him that he didn't have to waste his Saturdays driving back and forth from Fort Collins to check on Kit. And each time he said the same thing: *"I'm not wasting my time. I want to be here."*

The man was so serious about being Kit's uncle. And, if Haley were honest with herself, she'd admit she was thankful . . . because she liked having Stephen around. When he showed up on her front porch, she breathed easier. Stephen would look at the ever-present HOA list and say, "Oh, that won't take long," and then they'd work on the project together. Talk. Laugh. Stephen Ames's presence pushed the loneliness away.

Claire and some of her other friends sometimes called or stopped by, but for now, everyone was gone—except for her almost-two-month-old daughter, of course. Life was all about her and Kit. And she was managing . . . until today, when she'd woken up and realized somehow, some way, she had managed to get the flu.

But that was okay.

She could do this.

All she had to do was keep Kit fed . . . and diapered . . . and dressed . . . and maybe, just maybe, Kit would sleep a little more. She weighed eight pounds, six ounces and looked like a normal-size newborn—and slept better, too.

Haley could tough out a little upset stomach. She had only a slight fever. No need to take her temperature. Nothing to worry about. This is what mothers did—they took care of their children, no matter what. If Sam were still alive, she'd be managing on her own whenever he deployed. She'd just pretend Sam was deployed . . .

So hot. Haley stretched out on her unmade bed, the comforter and sheets rumpled beneath her. She should get up and drag herself to the kitchen and get a Sprite—if she had any in the fridge. Maybe she would call Claire—but that would mean Claire would be exposed to whatever she had. She couldn't do that. No friend deserved the flu—that was above and beyond the call of duty.

Her stomach roiled just as she heard Kit rustle in her crib and let out a cry. *Great.* After sleeping for several hours, the baby was hungry and wet. Well, her daughter would just have to wait a moment or two . . . or five. Forget the Sprite—did she have any Pepto-Bismol? She'd figure that out and then prep a bottle for her daughter.

By the time she'd swished her mouth out with water and dredged up the strength to walk to her bedroom, Kit's cries bounced off the walls. Her daughter was eight pounds of furious.

Haley's head swam when she leaned over Kit's crib. *Breathe. Breathe.* She could do this. If she took it slow—and ignored the fact that slow-motion movements made Kit madder and madder—she could do it. She could change Kit's diaper even if her hands shook. Moments later, Haley leaned against her pillows, settling Kit against her, and picked up the bottle. "All right, all right . . . Mommy's here. Here. Right here." It took her daughter several minutes to vent her frustration in shrill cries and finally relax enough to take the bottle.

She didn't know how long she'd dozed off, waking only when Kit fussed against her.

"Think you're ready to go back to sleep, sweetie?" She snuggled Kit against her shoulder. "Ready for a nap?"

Ten minutes later, she admitted defeat. Who was she kidding? Kit was wide awake, ready to be entertained after a long nap. Couldn't her daughter see that Mommy was not up to this? The living room seemed a hundred miles away, but that's where Kit's play mat was, and that was her best chance of keeping Kit happy.

"There you go . . . Mommy's just going to lie down right here next to you." She turned on the Baby Einstein Takealong Tunes and then pulled a cushion off the couch and rested it underneath her head. Thank God her daughter wasn't crawling or walking yet.

•••••◆•••••

What was that?

Where was she?

Where was Kit?

Haley raised her head off the pillow. She was on the living room floor. Pressure weighed her head down, and her eyes were hot. She turned her head and found Kit asleep on her blanket.

Thank you, God.

Her phone played music, alerting her to an unwanted phone call . . . Now where was her phone? She crawled across the room and pulled herself up on her knees, grabbing her phone just as it stopped ringing. Whoever was calling her, it had better be important. She hit redial.

"Hello?"

She knew that voice. Haley shook her head. *Ouch.* That hurt. Okay . . . she'd been fooled before. That was not Sam. There would be no more phone calls from Sam. "Hello."

Wow—where had her voice gone while she was sleeping?

"Haley?"

"Yes."

"It's Stephen. Are you okay?"

"I've got a virus or something—no big deal." She lay back down on the floor. There. Better.

"How long have you been sick?"

"Just today—it is still Thursday, isn't it?"

"Yes. Is anyone there helping you with Peanut?"

"Just me." She needed to end this phone call. There was no

way she could make it to the bathroom if she kept chatting with Stephen. "Listen, I've got to go—thanks for calling."

She tossed the phone on the ground and, with one last glance to make sure Kit was asleep, crawled to the bathroom. It looked as if that was going to be the routine for at least the next twenty-four hours—bathroom, check on the baby, bathroom, check on the baby. And repeat.

••••—◆—••••

Wait. Haley hadn't hung up the phone.

He could hear her moving . . . was she groaning?

"Haley! Haley, pick up the phone!" Stephen put the phone away from his ear and looked—yep, he was still on the line, but Haley didn't realize that. "Haley!"

He disconnected, his fingers fisting around the phone. What should he do? He could call one of Haley's friends—if he had any of their phone numbers. But had he thought to put Claire's information in his contact list after Kit was born? No.

He stared out the window, tapping the phone against his leg. Colorado Springs was two hours away. If he left now, he'd beat rush hour and be there by four at the latest. No time to waste.

Every driver between Fort Collins and the Springs played defensive lineman, blocking him from getting to Haley's. And then there were the rubberneckers slowing down to look at the three-car pileup on I-25, stalling things even more. But even with the delays, Stephen forced himself to pull into the Safeway parking lot.

The first snowflakes started falling as he ran into the grocery store, grabbed a cart, and dashed through the aisles. Tossed in a twelve-pack of ginger ale. Added a twelve-pack of Sprite. Sprinted several aisles over and tossed in a box of saltines. Stood with his fingers drumming on the cart handle and tried to remember what his stepmother fed him when he was sick. Soup. He needed chicken noodle soup. In the soup aisle, he swept half a dozen cans off the shelf, the cans clattering into the cart and just missing crushing the box of crackers. As he moved on down the aisle, he grabbed a few cans of beef vegetable because he was going to have to eat something, and knowing Haley, he'd be lucky if there was anything more than mac and cheese in the house.

He added a roasted chicken and some celery and carrots and an onion. Canned soup was one thing—once he got Haley and Kit settled, he'd start a pot of good, old-fashioned soup like Mama would make. Well, like he could make.

Kit.

He headed for the baby-product aisle. Tossed in diapers, guessing the appropriate size. Wipes. Added a little plush tiger because, well, he was her uncle and why not?

Wait.

Was the baby sick?

He wheeled the cart over to the pharmacy, waiting while a portly man with a single tuft of white hair on the top of his head discussed a long list of prescriptions with the pharmacist. After five minutes, the pharmacist tossed a smile at Stephen, who could do nothing but shrug. He had to ask the question, despite the minutes quite literally ticking away before his eyes on the clock hanging on the wall behind her.

When the man finally shuffled off with two bags of medications, Stephen moved forward, vowing to up his bran intake and decrease his simple sugars.

"Do you have a prescription?"

"No. A question." He drummed his fingers on the handle of the cart again, trying to remember how he'd rehearsed the question in his head. "What do I do if a baby is sick?"

"Is she running a temperature?"

"I don't know. Her mom is."

"Well, just because the mom is sick doesn't mean the baby will get sick, too. How old is the baby?"

"Two months."

The pharmacist looked at him, glanced at his left hand, as if trying to determine whether he was some clueless husband.

"I'm the baby's uncle." *Oh, great. The "uncle."* "My brother—the baby's father—was killed in Afghanistan." As if the woman needed all this information. "I just talked to my sister-in-law—" Could this get any more convoluted? "—and I found out she's sick." He moved the cart back and forth. "I'm bringing her supplies, and I was wondering what I should take for the baby."

"Oh. How sweet." A smile transformed the woman's face from suspicious to compassionate. "Make sure your sister-in-law stays up on fluids. Tea, water. And you might want to get some Pedialyte just in case the baby does get sick."

"Pedialyte?"

"Let me show you where it is." She came out from behind the counter and led him several aisles over. "Pedialyte is good for preventing dehydration in babies."

By the time he got to the self-checkout line, almost half an hour had elapsed. He passed a display of bouquets. He'd almost forgotten the no-frills flowers.

The snowfall was increasing when he left the grocery store, and by the time he pulled his Mustang into the driveway the roads were starting to slick up. He grabbed a bag of groceries and half walked, half slid to the garage, punching the code into the keypad, depositing the bag of groceries just inside. He made two more quick trips to the car and then closed the garage door.

He shucked off his wet shoes in the laundry room, doing a visual sweep of the living room as he carried in the groceries. The house was still. Quiet. "Haley?"

Nothing—except the musical mat lying down on the ground strewn with toys and one of the couch cushions next to it. And what was that? He strode forward . . . yep, Haley's cell phone. He placed it on the table, but not before noticing she had two missed calls—one from Claire and one from her brother.

First things first.

Haley's bedroom door was closed. Everything quiet.

Now what?

He tapped on the door. Waited. Nothing.

Please let Haley be in bed. Asleep. Completely covered with blankets. He eased the door open. *Please, please, please . . .*

No Haley in the bed. No Kit sleeping in the cradle.

Stephen did a quick check of the bathroom. The only thing there was an abandoned pair of sweatpants and a long-sleeved T-shirt. He scrubbed his hand along his jaw. What had he gotten himself into? He'd come this far to help Haley and Kit— and he wasn't going to let a pile of clothes scare him off. On to the second bedroom.

He tapped on Kit's door. Again, nothing. They had to be in there—unless Claire had called, found out how sick Haley was, and taken her back to her house. That could have happened. But wouldn't Claire have taken Haley's phone with them?

He nudged the door open. Haley lay on the floor beside Kit's crib, wrapped in a blanket, shivering as if she were sleeping on the front lawn in the snowstorm.

Stephen strode forward, kneeling beside her. A quick glance at the crib revealed a sleeping Kit covered in a blanket, both arms thrown up alongside her tiny face. He brushed strands of Haley's hair away from her face, the color muted, her skin hot to his touch.

"Haley . . ." He hated to wake her up, but how much rest could she be getting, shivering on the floor?

"Hmm?" Her eyes opened, their color hazy, and she flinched. "Sam? No . . . go away. Not now . . . I can't see you now . . ." Her voice cracked and tears caused the blue to shimmer.

Her words slipped into his heart like shards of a broken mirror, and his hand stilled against her skin. "It's Stephen." This wasn't about him—who he was or wasn't. Who he wanted to be. He wrapped the blanket tighter around her trembling body and shifted her weight into his arms, preparing to lift her. "Not Sam."

"I'm sorry, Sam . . . I'm sorry . . ." Her hand slipped outside the blanket, clutched his jacket. "I should have told you . . . about the baby."

"Shh, Haley." He rose to his feet, cradling her to his lacerated heart, not certain he could bear the weight of her confession. "I know about Kit."

"She has your eyes." A dry sob tore from her throat. "Your eyes and Stephen's eyes. You should have told me about him. We both had secrets . . ."

"Yes, we did."

Haley quieted as he carried her back to her bedroom, but her body continued to shake—from the combination of the fever and her silent sobs. Bare feet and ankles dangled from underneath the end of the blanket, but he couldn't tell what else she was wearing—or not wearing. He'd tuck her, blanket and all, into the bed and cover her with the comforter. Despite the fever, Haley's teeth chattered.

He settled her on the bed, praying she'd lie still as he pulled the comforter across her body. He leaned close for just a moment, alarmed at the heat radiating off of her. Should he wake her? Ask her to try to sip some of the ginger ale? Take some Tylenol? He'd call the ER—or Gina—and ask what he should do.

Please, God, let her rest. Rest has to be the best thing. When she woke up again, he would insist she drink something. Right now, he'd be thankful both she and Kit were asleep. He'd make some phone calls and prep the soup.

Warm fingers clasped his wrist, tugging him closer. "Stay." Haley's words faded to a whimper. "Please, Sam. You always leave—"

Stephen froze. He couldn't do what she asked of him. Of his brother.

"I can't get warm . . . Hold me . . ." Her request twisted his heart and tore at his resolve.

"Give me a minute." He untangled her hand from his. Walked to the other side of the bed. Took a deep breath as he lowered his body to the mattress and rolled over so that he spooned her form as she lay cocooned in the two layers of blankets. She sighed as he pulled her closer, her breathing easing a bit.

Stephen closed his eyes, trying to still his heartbeat. He held Haley in his arms, trying to quiet the jumbled emotions inside. She thought he was Sam. Of course, she wasn't thinking straight. But still, she wanted Sam . . . not him.

Fine. If she needed him to be Sam . . . so be it.

He settled her closer, pressing the whisper of a kiss against her temple. *God, please let Haley sleep. Please let Kit sleep. And help me remember Haley wants to be with Sam—now and forever. I know the truth. I won't forget. Help me not forget.*

"I've got you, Haley." Stephen closed his eyes, embracing both the woman and the moment. For now, for however long Haley slept, he could hold her. Inhale the lavender scent of her hair. Imagine he had the right to be here. Pretend he was someone else—that he was the right brother. The only Ames brother.

twenty-seven

⋯•••⋯•⋯•••⋯•⋯•••⋯•⋯•••⋯

Haley shifted, coming half-awake. What time was it? And why did she feel so . . . safe? She stilled. Someone held her. Someone breathed in tandem with her. The faint scent of lime lingered in the air.

Stephen?

Why was he here, his body molded to hers, offering her unexpected comfort? Protection. And why did it feel so right? In the dim moonlight she could see the outline of his arm across her shoulder, his hand resting on the pillow near her face. Holding her breath, she slipped her hand out from beneath the blankets and rested her fingertips against the back of his hand.

If this was some sort of fever-induced dream—fine. Haley closed her eyes, willing herself back to sleep. She didn't want to wake up—to lose the fragile peace surrounding her. Not yet.

⋯•••⋯•⋯•••⋯

Kit's cry broke through the heated haze in Haley's mind.

She needed to get up. Somehow she needed to repeat the whole feed-Kit-change-Kit-keep-Kit-happy routine again until her daughter fell asleep. Haley started to move and then realized something—*someone*—was lying next to her.

"I'll get Kit. Just stay in bed, Haley."

Just stay in . . . *bed*?

She forced her aching eyelids to part and turned her head to find Stephen's face mere inches from hers. She was either dead or dreaming or—she reached out and touched the hair tousled against his forehead. "What are you doing in my bed, Stephen?"

"Um, you asked . . . me to hold you. You were cold." The mattress shifted as he stood and walked to the foot of the bed.

Haley shoved tangles out of her face. Even her hair felt hot. "Is this a dream?"

Stephen swiped his hand across his face, something between a growl and a sigh shaking his shoulders.

"No. I called you, remember? And after you mentioned you were sick, I drove down from Fort Collins to check on you—found you on the floor by Kit's crib." His words were overshadowed by the baby's cries. "I need to go take care of Kit. She's probably hungry. I don't think she's sick, but I did buy some Pedialyte because the pharmacist suggested it."

The pharmacist suggested—?

After Stephen disappeared, Haley forced herself upright.

Mistake.

The pounding in her head increased and she pushed back the covers, stumbling to the master bathroom just in time to dry-heave, clinging to the sides of the toilet with shaking arms. After her body stopped rebelling, she leaned against the sink. One thing was certain: she was going to drag those sweatpants back on and pull a hoodie on over her camisole.

"Haley?" Stephen's voice came through the door. "You okay?"

She leaned against the bathroom door. "Fine. I'm fine." And she was lying through her clenched teeth. "Did you change Kit's diaper?"

"Done. Listen, go lie down again. I'm giving her a bottle."

"I won't argue with you."

"You want something to drink? I brought ginger ale and Sprite—with a chaser of Tylenol."

"Ginger ale. No ice. Please."

She counted to sixty and then opened the door and looked out. No Stephen, but she could hear her daughter's frantic cries all the way from the living room. Poor guy. She slipped into a blue Old Navy hoodie and sweatpants and made her way down the hallway, leaning against the wall when Stephen turned to look at her. Kit had quieted, now that she had what she wanted: a bottle.

"Hey there." His eyes still held a look she didn't understand. Or maybe he was just tired.

"Hey. I know. I look awful. I feel even worse."

"You were burning up when I touched you—I mean, when I felt your forehead."

Even with a fever, she felt her body flush at the thought of Stephen touching her. She collapsed on the couch, extending her arms for Kit. "Here. Let me take her."

"No. That's why I'm here—so that you only have to worry about taking care of yourself." He nodded to a glass sitting on the coffee table. "Ginger ale and the meds are there. Need anything else?"

"I'm good."

"I found your physician's number and talked with the nurse. She said there's a virus going around and to keep you hydrated, and to use Tylenol for the fever."

"Well, at least I have a reason for feeling so lousy. Here's hoping it doesn't last too long."

"The nurse said probably a couple of days—and the first day is the worst. I'll finish feeding Peanut, get her settled, and then be in the kitchen. I want to put the soup on."

Put the soup on. Of course he did. The man loved being in the kitchen. Haley leaned her head back against the couch, closing her eyes and savoring the sounds of Stephen in her house. He babbled sweet nonsense to Kit as he settled her into the automatic swing, which he'd positioned closer to the kitchen. Cabinets opened and closed as he gathered his supplies, joined by the sound of running water. And then the lure of his voice as he sang to himself in time to the rhythmic chopping of the knife. The comforting aroma of chicken and seasonings escaped from the kitchen. With Stephen here, the house no longer felt empty.

It felt like home.

A tear slipped from beneath her closed eyelids and trailed down her face to her lips, leaving a faint taste of salt. What was she doing, equating Stephen with home?

The longer she sat still, the more a memory crystallized . . . twisting and turning . . . finding no relief from the chills and ache . . . and realizing a man's arms—Stephen's arms—embraced her. Remembering his whispered, "I've got you, Haley."

He did. Stephen had her heart in a way Sam never had—her disloyal heart that found safety with Stephen Rogers Ames. And rest.

Home.

"Haley?"

She jerked, her eyes connecting with Stephen's warm brown ones as he knelt in front of her, offering her the glass of ginger ale. "Did I fall asleep?"

"You're pretty out of it with that fever. Do you have a thermometer, so we could get a take on just how high your temperature is?"

She sipped the tepid liquid, not surprised that it scraped her throat going down. "In my medicine cabinet."

"Let me make certain Kit's all good in the swing." He bent over his niece, tucking the soft white blanket around her, pausing to coax a smile from her. "Hey there, did you miss your uncle Stephen?"

With Kit content, Stephen came and stood over Haley. "Do you want to go back to bed?"

"What?"

Red stained his entire face. "I mean—if you want to go rest in your bedroom, I've got everything under control out here."

"No . . . here's fine."

"Then I'll get you a blanket and a pillow so you'll be more comfortable. You want the television on?"

"Something like the Home Shopping Network?"

Her joke eased some of the tightness from Stephen's jaw. "I was thinking something more like one of those old John Wayne movies you like."

"Sure—but I'll probably fall asleep."

When Stephen returned with the fleece maroon blanket she kept at the end of her bed and one of her pillows, she obeyed his instruction to stretch out on the couch. He arranged the blanket over her and tucked it around her feet. Even though the thermometer revealed she had a temperature of 101.6 degrees, she needed to release Stephen from babysitting Kit—and her.

"You don't have to stay. I can manage Kit."

He smoothed the blanket over her shoulders, the warmth of his hand reminding her of waking last night with his arm across her— his hand resting on her pillow. She closed her eyes, praying there was no hint of the emotions warring inside of her. "Of course I do. I have homemade chicken soup on the stove. Do you think I'm going to abandon you and Kit when you're in this condition?"

"What was I thinking?" She resisted the urge to lean into his touch. She was stronger than this, flu or no flu. "Stephen."

His eyes searched her face. "Yes?"

"Thank you for being here. For me . . . and Kit, of course."

"You're welcome." His fingers trailed down the side of her face, causing her to shiver. "Still cold?"

"No." She couldn't force her voice above a whisper. "I'm not cold."

"Good. Let me know if you need anything."

"I will." Her breath hitched at the comforting sight of his long-legged stride and broad shoulders as he disappeared into the kitchen again.

She wouldn't be telling him what she needed. She couldn't. Not when she'd just realized that a part of her heart longed for him.

•••••—◆—•••••

At least one section of Haley's fence was a goner.

While snow and ice slicked the secondary roads and I-25, the high winds had sent one of the branches from the tree in the backyard crashing down into the fence. Once "rickety," part of the back fence was now smashed to bits, covered in an ever-increasing mound of snow. And the homeowners' association would have more ammunition to force Haley to remove the tree.

When he turned off the kitchen light, moonlight streamed in through the sliding doors. It was ten thirty. Haley was back in her bedroom, sleeping more peacefully now that her fever had subsided. She wouldn't confuse him with Sam again.

The treacherous roads meant he'd be spending another night with Haley and Kit. He'd already made up the couch with a sheet and some blankets he found among the sparse supplies in the linen closet. And Haley hadn't noticed when he'd confiscated the baby monitor. He'd taken her cell phone, too. She needed sleep, not conversation.

He stretched out on the couch, tugging the blankets up over his shoulders. Too bad he hadn't found a toothbrush in the linen closet. Scrubbing his teeth with a toothpaste-laden finger didn't meet his normal standard of oral hygiene.

He rolled onto his side, his feet resting on the arm of the couch. He'd been more comfortable last night in the bed . . . when Haley thought he was Sam.

But he'd known who Haley was every moment he held her. Even now, the thought of holding Haley . . . cradling her in his arms so she rested against his chest . . . how he woke up to find her turned to face him, her hand resting against the curve of his neck . . . there'd been no going back to sleep then. He'd lain in the bed, his arms around his brother's widow, and embraced being with Haley. No conflict. No tension. She needed him. He helped her.

And yes, he wanted more. He wanted the "all" of loving Haley.

The clatter of her cell phone against the coffee table disrupted his thoughts. Who would be calling this late? He grabbed the phone, glancing at the display as he answered it. David . . . he was one of Haley's brothers, right?

"Stephen Ames here."

Silence.

"Hello?"

"This is David Jordan—Haley's brother." The man's gruff voice was all business. "Should I be concerned that you're answering my sister's phone—and it's almost eleven o'clock?"

"You're her brother—of course you should be concerned." His attempt at humor failed—meeting with more silence. "Sorry. No, you have nothing to worry about."

"Then why don't you tell me why you are answering my sister's phone this late at night?"

Stephen pushed himself upright, the blankets slipping down to his waist. "Haley can't come to the phone right this minute."

"I'm waiting for your explanation for that, too."

"She's asleep—in her room. I'm on the couch."

"And why are you even there?"

"I called to check on Haley and Kit yesterday and found out Haley was pretty sick. So I drove down from Fort Collins to check on her." He scratched at the two days' worth of growth along his jaw. He should have looked for a razor in Haley's linen closet. "Then the storm rolled in and the roads are an ice rink, so I'm stranded."

"Are you telling me nothing inappropriate is going on between you and my sister?"

He thought of the too-brief time when he held Haley as she slept. "Absolutely nothing inappropriate has happened between me and Haley. She's my sister-in-law."

"As if that term has anything to do with how you feel about my sister."

"I think I'm the only one who knows how I feel about your sister." Stephen pressed his palms against his eyes. He shouldn't have said that.

"You're not fooling me, Ames." Haley's brother sounded way too sure of himself. "Look, we're both men. No guy drives a couple of hours just to 'check' on his sister-in-law. We don't talk about relationships and feelings—but my mother does. And she thinks you're falling in love with my little sister. The question is, what are you going to do about it?"

"You seem to forget Haley was married to my brother—"

"Hardly." David's response waved off Stephen's reminder. "And by that I mean, at times it seemed like they were hardly married."

"Were you around to see them together?"

"Enough to know that three years of marriage to your brother didn't change him or her."

Now the man had his attention. "What does that mean?"

"I'm a married man. We all go into marriage thinking we'll stay the same. Ridiculous thought. That's what marriage is all about—changing for each other so you can love each other better. Know each other more." David Jordan's chuckle held an echo of Haley's laugh. "If Haley could hear me, she'd ask me if I've been reading a self-help book."

"Have you?"

"I've been married for seven years—had a few bumps along the way. I learned I had to be willing to do whatever it took to make my marriage work: read a book, talk with a counselor, remember to bring flowers home at times other than our anniversary. My mom thinks your brother died before he figured out what it took to be married to my sister."

Stephen's eyes found the vase of daisies he'd set on the dining room table.

"Let me be straight up with you—"

"Have you been anything else during this conversation?"

"No. That's a Jordan quality. I'm sure you've noticed."

"From the first." Stephen set his feet on the coffee table as he leaned against the back of the couch. "Did you know that when I first met your sister, she held me off at gunpoint?"

David's burst of deep laughter tugged a smile from Stephen's lips. "I would love to have been there."

"The question is, would you have helped me or told Haley to pull the trigger?"

"Depends on why she wanted to shoot you."

"I . . . I frightened her. Showed up on her doorstep—never thinking she didn't know anything about me. She thought I was Sam."

"I don't think she would make that mistake today."

He thought of Haley's feverish tears yesterday . . . how she clung to him, asking Sam to hold her. Not to leave her.

"You want to know my opinion about you and Haley?"

Stephen raked his fingers through his hair. He could use a shower. "No."

"Okay, whether you want to know or not, I'm telling you there's no reason for you and my sister not to at least consider the possibility of a relationship. My mom told me that Haley is . . . what did she say? . . . different when you're around. You bring out a side of her that Mom's never seen; she's willing to let someone help her—to admit she can't do it all."

"I appreciate you saying that. But just because Haley lets me help her with house projects doesn't change things."

"What things?"

"The fact that Haley is still in love with Sam. That she wants to honor Sam. That she wants Kit to know about her father— and I would only confuse her." Each statement seemed to push him further and further away from the possibility of any kind of future with Haley. "That people would have a problem with Haley and me having a relationship—"

"I think you and Haley need to decide what you want—no matter what other people say."

Easier said than done. "Right now, I want to get some sleep. Kit's not a late sleeper."

David laughed. "In other words, mind my own business, right? Fine. Tell her I called and said to keep her guard up."

Keep her guard up? What did he mean by that? "Sure thing."

"Ames?"

"Yeah?"

"I don't like anyone hurting my sister, got it?"

"Yes. Good night."

With sleep eluding him, Stephen debated what to do. Watch TV? Get his iPad out and sketch? He stood by the sliding glass doors, the tree in the backyard cast in the milky glow of the moonlight. The loss of one limb didn't wreck Haley's plans for a tree house—he'd watched a television show where professional tree house builders removed the dead portion of a tree and nestled a tree house into what was left. He envisioned an altered tree . . . a specialized house for Kit. His fingers tingled with the urge to sketch out the beginnings of a design, one that forged old with new.

•••••—◆—•••••

As expected, his niece was an early riser, waking up a few short hours after Stephen crawled onto the couch and fell asleep. But Stephen was becoming quite proficient at changing diapers and prepping bottles, so he was able to get her settled again with a minimal amount of fuss.

"There you go, Peanut." He knelt on the floor in Kit's bedroom and snapped the last clasp of her pink footie pajamas. Right now, he was keeping his niece's wardrobe options simple—and what she already had on still worked. "Ready to face the day. I'm not sure I can manage this sling thingy. You want to rest on the blanket? Or do you just want to hang out with your uncle Stephen?"

As he gathered her into his arms, Kit cooed and reached up to touch his jaw with her tiny hand. Stephen stared into the depths of her brown eyes. This little girl had him tied up in knots that weren't going to let go. He was head-over-heels in love with at least one of the Ames females.

Thirty minutes later, someone knocked at the front door. As he abandoned his efforts to plan something for lunch, Stephen checked on Kit, who seemed happy on her play mat. Opening the front door, he braced for the blast of frigid air. Claire and her husband—what was his name?—stood on the porch, bundled up in coats, hats, scarves, and gloves.

"Stephen? When did you get here?" Claire looked past him, as if expecting to see Haley.

"I came down two nights ago—about the time the storm started."

"Is everything okay?"

"It is now." He moved away from the door. "Come on in." He would have offered to shake hands with Claire's husband, but the guy was busy removing his gloves.

"Finn O'Dea—we met when Kit was born."

Claire interrupted the round of reintroductions. "Where's Haley?"

"She's still sleeping." A quick explanation of his presence was probably best. "I called to check on Haley a couple of days ago and found out she had the flu, so I drove down—"

"From Fort Collins?" Claire pulled off her black UGGs, then unbuttoned her coat.

"Yes. Anyway, I drove down to see if she needed help, and then the blizzard rolled in and I got stranded here." No need to feel uncomfortable. He was here in his official uncle/brother-in-law role. "Good thing, though, because Haley's just now feeling better."

"I think I'll go check on her."

"She's still sleeping, Claire."

"I'll peek in—I won't wake her."

The sound of Haley's bedroom door opening interrupted his verbal give-and-take with Claire. "Stephen—are you still here?"

"Yes. And guess who else? Claire and Finn."

"What?"

"Just checking on you, Haley. Stay in bed. Stephen says you've been sick . . ." Claire's voice faded as she entered Haley's room.

Finn remained by the door, his hands shoved into his wool coat. "It's nice of you to take care of Haley and Kit—but you could have called. Claire and I are close—"

"Believe me, I thought about it, but I didn't have Claire's number in my cell phone."

"You couldn't call once you got here?"

"Things were a bit hectic—Haley was sick and Kit needs more attention than I ever imagined." Stephen worked to keep any defensiveness out of his voice. Finn's oh-so-casual questions reminded him of the midnight conversation with Haley's brother—and he didn't have anything to prove to either of them. "Look, I'm here helping Haley because she was married to my brother—"

Finn held up his hand, stopping any further attempts to explain. "Claire already told me you're an okay guy. That you've helped Haley a lot."

"But?"

Finn nodded, acknowledging he had more to say. "But I'm concerned for Haley."

"Because I'm here?"

"I watched a good friend's widow get married four months after he died. She was all mixed up—trying to be a new wife and a widow at the same time. Haley's vulnerable right now— and she'd be especially confused by you because you're Sam's twin."

Before Stephen could reply, the sound of the bedroom door opening again stalled the conversation. And really, what could he say? Should he even defend himself?

All he had to do today was get through the next hour or so with Claire and Finn. Be friendly. Take care of Haley and Kit. And trust God knew his heart better than he did.

twenty-eight

······•······•······•······

Whated a mess.

Stephen had warned her, but still, the mound of broken branches and fence made it look as if a wrecking ball had taken one huge, dead-on swipe at her backyard.

With one more check of the baby monitor to ensure Kit still slept, Haley stepped outside into the midmorning sunlight. She wrapped her arms around her waist, unable to ignore the way her tummy sagged beneath her jeans. She was back in them—barely. Would she ever regain her pre-baby body?

In the week since Stephen left, she'd noticed the destruction through the glass doors, but she'd never had time to come look at the damage close-up. Correction: she hadn't taken the time. The thought of facing the tree—and what she needed to do—incapacitated her. But with the arrival of yet another letter from Sterling Shelton III demanding she fix the fence and remove the tree, Haley could no longer avoid the situation.

Fixing the fence? That was easy. Stephen had already volunteered to handle the project the next time he came down to visit.

But removing the tree? Where would she put Kit's tree house? The place where they could have picnics in the summer . . . and lie on their backs at night, snuggled together in a sleeping bag . . . and pretend it was a fairy castle or a sailing ship . . . and whisper mother-daughter secrets . . . and remember Sam. Always, always remember Sam.

She ran her fingers along the rough edge where the limb had been torn away from the tree, leaving a gaping wound in the trunk. It was just a tree.

But couldn't she salvage it—or at least part of it? She didn't have to tear it all down, did she?

She wrapped her arms around the trunk, the bark scraping against her skin. It was just a tree. A mostly dead tree—no buds forming on the branches to indicate new growth.

Maybe if she gave it more time? Everybody—everything deserved a little extra time, right?

••••• ◆ •••••

Haley clicked SEND, forwarding her flight information to Sam's mother, as requested. Now Miriam would be able to pick them up when they arrived in Oklahoma for Sam's memorial service in June. She bit back a groan as she closed the laptop and settled back against the pillows on her bed.

Her first trip with a baby. It wasn't quite a two-hour flight—she would handle it. She'd substitute a regular suitcase for her preferred carry-on and accept the check-in fee—leaving her hands free for Kit and the never-go-anywhere-without-it diaper bag. She couldn't miss this last memorial for Sam—not when his mother expected her to be there. She'd discussed details via e-mails and phone calls for weeks. Miriam had asked her preferences for songs and the printed program and what photographs of Sam they should use. Haley had survived Sam's funeral—and back then she'd been ten weeks pregnant, struggling with unrelenting morning sickness and exhaustion. She was still wrung out, but from what more experienced mothers told her, that wasn't going to change until Kit went to kindergarten.

Haley shifted, leaning over the edge of the bed so she could see Kit, who slept in the cradle. Her pink lips nursed her tiny fist, the bedside lamp highlighting the faint wisps of blond hair on her head. Brown eyes like Sam—and Stephen. Blond hair like her.

She rolled onto her back, pulling her hair out of the rubber band that held it on top of her head and running her fingers through strands that fell around her face. Maybe she should cut her hair—really, really short. One less thing to worry about. In a few weeks, Kit would be three months old. Haley needed to decide when she was going back to work—*if* she was going back to work. Thanks to Sam's insurance, she didn't have to worry about a paycheck. The question was, did she want to be a stay-at-home single mom or a work-outside-the-home single mom? At least she had a choice.

When her phone rang, she grabbed it, silencing it even as she prayed Kit wouldn't wake up. "Hello?"

"Hello to you, too." Stephen's voice lowered to match hers. "Why are we whispering?"

"Because if Kit wakes up then I'm the one who has to get her back to sleep again—not you." She slipped off the opposite side of the bed and tiptoed out of the bedroom, easing the door shut behind her.

"Is she still asleep?" Stephen continued to whisper, as if Kit might still hear him.

"Yes—good thing for you." Haley headed straight for the pantry and the bag of jalapeño Kettle Chips calling her name.

One advantage of Kit being on formula: she didn't have to worry about her daughter being affected by anything she ate.

"Well, if I woke her up, I'd just have to come down there and get her settled for the night." Whisper or not, Haley could hear both the laughter and the sincerity in Stephen's voice. "Need to take care of my girls—I mean, my girl."

She wanted to tell him that she didn't mind his verbal slip. That she was getting used to how he cared for her—and Kit. Instead, she kept her emotions hidden behind a veil of humor. "If you wake her up, it'll cost you all right—but I'm thinking more like yard work."

"Hey, I've already volunteered for that. Who edged your lawn?"

"True. Well, we'll have to think of something else when you get down here this weekend."

Stephen Ames had a nice whisper—kind of sexy. And she needed to delete that thought immediately. As she readjusted her mindset, she realized Stephen had continued talking. "I'm sorry, what did you say?"

"I asked, what are you up to?"

"Besides noshing on some chips? I just finalized my flight to Oklahoma for Sam's memorial in June—sent the information to your mother."

"Haley, I've been thinking about that."

"What? The memorial service?"

"Yes. I know we haven't talked about it . . . but I'd like to attend the service."

She gave herself time to chew and swallow the spicy-sweet chip before she spoke. "How long have you been thinking about this?"

"Ever since you told me about it." She could hear sounds in the background. The sound of water running. A door being shut. The clang of metal pots? Was he cooking? Or washing dishes? "I didn't get to attend Sam's funeral—"

"Because you knew that was the best thing to do."

"Yes, and I still believe I made the right decision. But things are different now. Between you and me—"

"But nothing's changed between you and your mother." What did he mean about things being different between them? They danced on the edge of their feelings for one another. At times something simmered just below the surface, something Stephen reined in. Her own emotions were too twisted up in her past with Sam and a future that couldn't possibly include Stephen.

"I realize that. But it's not as if my mother and I don't talk to each other. We're just . . . distant. What if I called and asked her—"

"No." She crushed the bag of chips as she stood. "I don't think that's a good idea."

"Who says you get to decide, Haley?" At last his voice rose to a normal level. "It's not your responsibility to run interference between me and my mother."

"The memorial is going to be hard enough for her, Stephen, without—"

"Without what? Without her other son showing up? Without Sam's twin brother being there? Don't you hear how absurd that sounds? Be honest, Haley. Who are you really concerned about—my mother or yourself?"

His accusation, so unexpected, so unlike the man she'd come to know, hit with no warning. She closed her eyes against the ache centered in her chest, a burning that seemed to spread with each breath she took.

When Stephen spoke again, his words came out uneven. "I'm sorry. I—I didn't mean that—"

"It's late. I'm tired. I need to get some sleep, so I'm ready for Kit when she wakes up."

"Haley—did you hear what I said? I'm sorry. I overreacted."

"I heard. Good night, Stephen. I'll . . . see you this weekend."

She didn't hang up on Stephen—not really. She said good-bye. Told him that she'd see him in a few days. She'd been . . . civil.

But was she being unreasonable?

Stephen was Sam's brother. He had every right—just as much of a right as she did—to be at the memorial service. Maybe more.

•••••◆••••

Haley needed to make a decision—another one.

She exited the shooting range, a dozing Kit on her shoulder, stepping out into the soft sunshine of the early-May afternoon. She'd hoped that coming to talk with her boss would give her clarity on whether to come back to work or not. But their conversation left her feeling as if she were firing mental blanks.

Her boss wanted her back—but he also wanted her to work more hours. Haley missed teaching the women's gun safety classes, but did she want to work three nights a week and one half-day shift? It was still part-time, but the thought of being away from Kit that much unsettled her. If she didn't go back to work, though, what would she do? Just sit around the house and stare at her daughter for hours on end?

As she buckled Kit into her car seat, Haley hoped her daughter would continue sleeping. She tucked a blanket around her body, noticing how her legs were finally getting little rolls of fat on them. Kit looked less and less like a preemie every day.

She backed out of the car—and found herself face-to-face with Chaz. "Oh, wow, I didn't hear you sneak up on me."

"Didn't mean to startle you, Hal." Chaz offered a quick smile. "I saw you leaving the range as I parked my car."

Haley noticed the gun bag Chaz carried. "Getting some practice in?"

"Yep."

"Meeting up with anybody?"

"Not this time. Just a quick hour."

"Well then, I won't keep you—"

Chaz put a hand on her arm. "Hal."

"Something wrong, Chaz?"

"You tell me."

Haley tugged at the brim of her cap, causing Chaz to drop his hand from her arm. "What's that supposed to mean?"

"I've heard some things . . ."

"You've heard *some things*—what, am I supposed to guess what's bothering you?" The thought that people were talking about her and Stephen caused her heart to pound, while a flush worked its way up her neck.

"Are you involved with Stephen Ames?"

"Am I involved with— That's a ridiculous question. He's Kit's uncle; of course I'm involved with him."

"I mean romantically."

"Do you hear yourself? This conversation could be taking place between two middle-schoolers." Haley shut the rear door. Stepping around Chaz, she walked to the front driver's-side door, opening it and starting to slide in. Chaz followed her, preventing her from closing the door by grabbing on to it.

"You're evading my questions, Hal."

"I don't have to answer to you."

"You're smarter than this—at least, Sam always said you were. Do you realize how wrong it would be if you got involved with Sam's twin brother? It'd be like you were dating—marrying—Sam all over again. Is that really what you want to do?"

"I'm not dating—or marrying—anyone."

"You want to explain why Ames spent the night—two nights—at your house?"

Haley straightened up so that she stood eye to eye with Chaz. How did he know that? Did Finn say something? "I do not have to explain anything to you—or anyone else. Stop assuming things." She ducked into the car, hoping Chaz didn't see the red staining her face. Because she and Stephen had slept together—but not in the sleazy way he was thinking. "Could you let go of my door, please? I'd like to get home before Kit wakes up."

"I'm talking to you as Sam's friend—"

"This conversation is over." She slammed the door and started the engine, staring straight ahead until Chaz stalked past her and into the building.

So she and Stephen were now the hot topic among Sam's friends. She shouldn't have been surprised. Hurt, yes, but not surprised. The military was a close-knit family and Sam's buddies cared about her. They'd offered to help her in so many ways after Sam's death—to mow her lawn, help her move, unpack, paint rooms. But her repeated refrain of "I can handle it" had stalled their efforts. After all, she was Sam Ames's wife. He'd told everyone how independent she was. She wasn't going to let him down—in life or death.

twenty-nine

‹‹‹‹‹‹•‹‹‹‹•‹‹‹‹•‹‹‹‹›

Stephen stood on Haley's porch, hands on his hips, and stared at the front door. He'd knocked and waited. Knocked again. Had they gone all the way back to square one, with Haley avoiding him?

They hadn't talked in three days—not that he hadn't tried. All of his calls went straight to voice mail. He'd never thought Haley would be a coward, but what other explanation was there for her avoiding him? She knew he was coming down this weekend—and that he usually pulled into her driveway around ten in the morning. Surely she didn't think he'd back out just because they'd disagreed about Sam's memorial service.

Stephen did an about-face and looked up the street. Sunshine backlit the pale green leaves budding on the trees throughout the neighborhood, the outline of the Front Range stretching across a cloudless blue sky. Was she running errands? Or had she been lured outside by the warm spring weather? Maybe taken Peanut for a walk to the park?

He could camp out on the porch. Or he could get back in his car and cruise around the neighborhood, but the thought of getting back in the Mustang after a two-hour drive from Fort Collins made his backside ache.

Looked like he was going for a walk, which gave him more time to rehearse what he was going to say to Haley. Something along the lines of "I'm sorry" and "Please understand." All they needed was a chance to talk about the memorial service again. He didn't want to upset her, but he did want this opportunity to honor his brother. Surely they could figure out a way to agree.

When he first showed up on Haley's doorstep back in January, Stephen wanted to discover who Sam had become. Now he wanted more—he wanted closure. He knew his brother was gone. Stephen carried the weight of his loss with him every hour of the day—a silent companion that shadowed him, in the same way Sam had shadowed him during all the years of their estrangement. He could only hope if he sat among a group of fellow mourners . . . if he let the ache soak into his soul through someone else's memories of Sam . . . if he leaned into the chords of music . . . if he listened to the truth-filled scriptures chosen to comfort hearts torn asunder by such a violent, sudden loss . . . then he could let his brother go—and embrace the future.

As he neared the park tucked inside the shade of harboring trees, Stephen spotted Haley, sitting on a wooden bench, using her foot to push Kit's stroller back and forth. Her loose hair spilled across her shoulder, shining against the green long-sleeved top she wore over a pair of jeans that were torn at the knee.

How had he fallen in love with this woman?

The question ambushed him so he couldn't deny the truth any longer: He loved Haley. Not as a sister-in-law. Not because she was Kit's mother. But simply because of who she was—an intriguing, independent, junk-food-eating, funny woman who sometimes admitted she needed his help. The visits to check on his niece had become mere excuses to see Haley, to spend time with her.

Did he dare reveal his heart? Was Haley ready to love again— and was it too much to expect that she could love him when he was a walking, talking replica of Sam?

The sound of his footsteps on the sidewalk drew Haley's attention. A smile skimmed her lips, but he saw how she glanced away, unable to hold his gaze. How she grasped the edge of the bench as if to steady herself.

"Hey." Nothing like a basic, nonconfrontational greeting.

"Hey, yourself." Another half smile that disappeared before her eyes met his. "Kit was fussy, so I took her for a walk. I didn't realize how late it was."

"No problem. I found you."

"That you did." She scooted to the end of the bench as he sat down beside her. He was not going to read too much into that. "If you tried to call, I'm sorry. I walked out without grabbing my phone."

"It happens." Stephen nodded toward the stroller. "Peanut enjoying the outdoors?"

"She's sound asleep."

Stephen leaned forward to peek at his niece, catching the outline of her face as she nestled in the stroller, tucked beneath a quilted blanket, her head covered with a pale purple hat. "She gets more adorable every time I see her. I didn't think that was possible."

As he spoke, he turned his head, unaware that Haley had moved forward to look at Kit, too. Any effort to maintain a casual front disappeared as the air around them stilled. Filled with something he no longer wanted to deny—or control.

"Haley—"

"Yes?"

He forced himself to go slowly, watching Haley's reaction as he allowed himself to finally dare . . . to risk . . . kissing her. He reached up, sliding a hand beneath her hair, along the soft skin at the nape of her neck. She stared at him, her blue eyes wide. She didn't move toward him—but she didn't back away from him, either.

For all the reasons the kiss was wrong, the rightness of it overwhelmed him. How had he waited this long to kiss this woman? They watched one another as he urged her closer, tangling his fingers in the soft strands of her hair, until he closed his eyes so he could savor the feel of his mouth against hers. He only allowed himself to touch Haley's hair, the soft curve of her cheekbones, even as he fought the urge to pull her into his arms. Her lips parted beneath his, and he explored how she tasted of something sweet . . . something warm—and how she responded to him, her arms circling around his back and pulling him closer.

•••••••••••••••

There was no urgency in Stephen's kiss.

Haley's eyes closed at the first brush of his mouth against hers, the familiar scent of his cologne tempting her to rest in his arms . . . to acknowledge how much she wanted Stephen to kiss her. She wanted to lean into his gentle caress against her skin, but that would mean interrupting their kiss—and the urging of Stephen's lips creating a sweet longing in Haley for more.

The embrace caught her off guard. Not that Stephen kissed her now—here, in the park. But that he kissed her as if nothing else mattered but them. As if he had nothing else to do but kiss her once . . . twice . . . until she couldn't catch her breath, until their hearts beat together and she felt safe enough to admit that she loved him.

Sam's kisses—their lovemaking—had always felt hurried, as if they could be interrupted at any moment. She'd felt like a disruption to Sam's life . . .

Sam.

She pushed Stephen away. "Stop. *Stop.*"

His arms loosened enough to let her regain her balance, but he didn't release her. When she tried to avert her face, he captured her chin in his fingers and forced her to look at him. "You kissed me—*me*. Admit it, Haley. That kiss was between you and me—not Sam's ghost."

She closed her eyes, resisting the temptation entwined with lime and the morning breeze. Made herself look at Stephen. "I know exactly who I kissed, Stephen. That doesn't make it right."

"Sam's not here anymore. There's no law, on earth or in heaven, that says loving each other is wrong."

"I say it's wrong." She pressed her fingers against her eyes. No tears. "I promised to honor Sam all the days of my life— that's what's in the Bible. Sam never knew he was going to be a father—but Kit is going to know her dad."

His fingers dug into her shoulders. "And you think I would stop you from doing that?"

"How would I explain who Sam was and who you are? Don't you see how confusing it would be to her?"

"Not if we handled it right. We can do this, Haley. Together—with God. We can do this."

"I can't."

As she tried to stand, Stephen gripped her wrist, halting her escape. "What happened to you when Sam died?"

"What do you mean?"

"Did you die, too? Did you bury your heart in Sam's casket?"

"Don't be ridiculous—"

"I'm serious." His grasp held her prisoner, forcing her to listen. "I've never seen you cry for my brother. There's one photo of you and him. *One*. It's almost as if the marriage never happened. As if Sam never existed—and yet, he's the barrier between you and me."

Haley twisted out of his grasp, pushing the stroller away from the bench. "I'm going home."

"Run. Don't fight for our relationship. Is this how you handled things with Sam? Walked away when things got tough?"

His words caused her to turn and pace back to him, the stroke of the breeze in her hair reminding her of Stephen's touch. "You know nothing about my marriage to Sam. Nothing."

"That's right, because you don't talk about it—except when you want to push me away. Did you even love my brother?"

"I did . . . I just don't know why he loved me."

•••••••◄►•••••••

Should he go after her? Should he let her be?

Haley never looked back. Back rigid. Her stride sure as she pushed the stroller ahead of her as the breeze fingered the long strands of her hair. He was all kinds of a fool to have kissed Haley—he was left longing for more, so much more than one kiss. And she couldn't see a future with him because of her past with Sam.

What had she said? *"I just don't know why he loved me."*

What did she mean? Sam had married her—they'd had three years together. Why would she doubt that his brother loved her?

By the time Stephen followed Haley back home, she was nowhere in sight. Again.

Stephen paced slow circles around his Mustang. Should he get in his car and retreat north to Fort Collins? Or should he start repairing the back fence, as he'd promised Haley? If he left, then he was back to phone calls—if Haley even answered. But if he stuck around, made himself useful, maybe they'd have a chance to talk.

He was a man of his word. He punched the code into the garage keypad. He'd make a pit stop, grab a bottle of water, and then make a list of supplies to resurrect the part of the fence that had fallen down in the storm.

As he entered the living room, Haley appeared in the hallway, carrying the baby monitor—and a gun case. Stephen jammed his hands into his back pockets, battling the urge to wrap his arms around her. To woo her with words of assurance and love—and more kisses.

"Are you still planning on working on the fence?" She paused in the archway of the unlit hall, hidden in the shadows so he couldn't see her face, shifting from one foot to the other.

"That's the plan. I'll cut up the dead branch, bundle it up for the trash. Don't want to give Sterling another reason to write you up."

She huffed a humorless laugh. "Oh, that letter already arrived. The man is nothing if not consistent. I think he must drive by my house on a daily basis."

"What's the problem of the week this time?"

"He still wants me to cut down the entire tree in the backyard."

"The tree house tree?" Stephen looked across the room and out the sliding glass doors at the huge tree.

"That's the one."

"Why?"

"He said it's dead—and therefore it's a neighborhood risk."

"So what are you going to do?"

"What do you mean, what am I going to do? You don't think I'm going to let Sterling bully me into taking the tree down, do you? I've humored him for months—but that tree is fine. It just needs time. And I'm going to put the tree house in it."

"Don't you think it looks a little sickly?"

"The blooming season comes late in Colorado, that's all." She shook her head. "I don't want to discuss it anymore. Do you, um, think you could listen in on Kit? I reserved an hour at the range."

So her plan was evasive maneuvers. "No problem." He took the monitor, aware of how she avoided making eye contact with him. "I'll check the fence, figure out my supplies, and go out and get them when you get back."

"Oh. I wasn't thinking—now you're stuck here. I could call Claire or—"

"It's not a problem, Haley. I have other things to work on besides the fence, remember?"

"Fine." She skirted past him with her head down. "Thanks. I won't be gone long."

He risked walking over to her, praying she wouldn't bolt and slam the door in his face. "Haley, what happened at the park—"

"I can't talk about it."

"Then let me say this: I'm sorry I upset you. If you aren't ready for what's happening between us—" He reached out and brushed a strand of hair away from her face, but his action only caused her to startle and jerk away. "—I'm willing to wait. How I feel about you isn't going to change."

"I have to go."

He stepped back. "I'll be here."

"I know."

thirty

..•..••—•—••..•—•—•..•••—•—••..•..

Why did the shooting range feel like home?

After pulling her hair back into a haphazard ponytail, Haley slid the protective glasses over her eyes and then positioned the noise-canceling earmuffs on her head. She'd claimed the lane at the far end of the range and had an entire hour to focus on one thing: the target she'd loaded on the mechanical pulley. She pushed the button and sent the paper with the blue figure of a man drawn on it ten yards downrange.

In the stalls beside her, club members were already taking aim and firing. The sounds of gunfire echoed throughout the area, muffled by her protective gear. Haley set her case on the wooden ledge in front of her, snapping the locks and removing her SIG Sauer 9mm. With deliberate precision, she loaded ammunition into the magazine and slid it into the grip.

Routine. Familiar. Easy.

She settled into her stance and raised her arms, her right hand around the grip and her left hand supporting it, looking down the sights.

Inhale.

Exhale.

By the time she emptied the clip, the one-dimensional, faceless man on the target was dead. What was the use of firing a gun if you didn't shoot straight and true?

With the push of a button, she put the target in motion. Once it reached her, she methodically covered each gunshot "wound" with a piece of black duct tape. Nice cluster of shots right where a man's heart would be. Winged on the right shoulder. Grazed the forehead.

She sent the target back down the range, five feet farther away. With the sounds of other shooters as a backdrop, she pushed the magazine release with her thumb. Reloaded. Positioned herself again, relaxing her shoulders before raising her arms.

"I've never seen you cry for my brother."

The echo of Stephen's voice caused her hand to tremble.

Stephen Rogers Ames needed to get out of her head.

She steadied her hand. Squeezed the trigger.

Not her best shot, but she had plenty of ammo.

Shoot. Tape. Reload. Repeat.

Don't think.

Don't think.

She didn't have any answers. The only person who could answer the questions that haunted her was dead and buried.

She replaced the shredded target with a fresh one. Sent it downrange. Loaded her gun. She still had time . . . and ammo.

"Did you even love my brother?"

She pushed the button so the target advanced toward her. Raised her gun and shot as if the piece of paper was a man who'd invaded her home in the middle of the night and cornered her in Kit's bedroom.

Not one foot closer. Not. One. Foot.

The target stopped its forward motion when it reached the end of the track, inches from the barrel of her gun. She lowered her arms, released the magazine. Checked to make sure the chamber was clear. Laid the gun down. Stared straight ahead, ignoring the tears streaming down her face as she clutched the edge of the wooden ledge.

How dare Stephen ask out loud the question that scared her the most? Had she loved Sam? A man who came and went at the will of the military? Who seemed so happy when he shouldered his duffel bag and joined his comrades and flew thousands of miles away from her? Was lasting love possible when you spent more nights cradling your pillow in your arms than resting in the warmth of your husband's embrace?

She'd never know because Sam didn't come home.

He hadn't loved her enough to walk away from the military.

". . . need to tell . . . something, Hal." Static interrupted Sam's words.

Haley pressed the phone closer to her ear. Wretched connection. "Okay, I'm listening."

"I re-upped. Signed . . . papers yesterday."

Haley closed her eyes, clenching the phone with her fist. What had he said? "But we agreed to talk about the decision some more—"

"The bonus . . . good to pass up, babe . . . you not see that?" His voice rumbled across the phone line. "We put it in the bank . . . when I get out, we can buy that house you're always . . ."

She kept her eyes closed, unwilling to face the reality that she'd be renewing the lease on a ground-floor, 650-square-foot apartment with avocado-green carpeting and an upstairs neighbor who exercised at five in the morning and thought nothing of walking around in high heels at all hours of the day and night. And she could only hope the neighbors next door learned the meaning of the words vocal restraint.

"Hal, did I lose you?"

"No. No, I'm still here."

"Don't be mad . . . did it for us . . . our future."

"I'm ready for you to get out, Sam. I'm tired—"

"We can do this . . . worth it in the end." Sam's voice took on his "attagirl" tone. "You're the perfect army wife, Hal. I don't have to worry about you when I'm over here."

Haley's hand rested on her stomach. All the joy she'd cherished, waiting to share with Sam when he called, evaporated with the cold splash of reality that, thanks to his decision, she'd be spending a lot of days and nights as a single mom.

If she really was pregnant. Maybe it would be better if her suspicions were wrong.

"You doing all right back there, Hal?"

"I'm good. Busy at the range."

"Listen, I need to go. Stay safe, okay?"

"I will. You too, Sam."

"Always. Love you, babe."

The sound of Sam's voice receded, replaced by her raspy sobs.

"You should have come home, Sam." She scrubbed her hand across the tears on her face. "I'm not angry that you died . . . I understood the risk when I married you. But all those deployments . . . every single one . . . it was as if you never ever truly came home to me. Wasn't I worth coming home to?"

●●●●●━●●●●●

Haley expected to find Stephen working in the backyard, Kit nearby in her bouncy chair. Painting the front porch. Or working on the stains in the driveway. One of the many projects outlined by Sterling's continual stream of letters.

But instead he was stretched out on the couch, Kit nowhere in sight.

Haley walked into the room, hoping she sounded casual. At ease. That the red rimming her eyes had faded. "Hey. Everything okay?"

The sunlight from the bay window created shadows across his face. "I've had a wonderful time playing with my niece. She's a charmer—and she's having a much-needed nap."

"Wear her out, did you? She loves her uncle Stephen."

"Are you surprised?"

How was she supposed to answer that? Haley pulled her hair out of its ponytail, running her fingers through the loose strands. "I'm sorry I was gone longer than I expected."

"Not a problem. I had everything I needed. Diapers and formula for Peanut. Junk food for me. I even started thawing some steak—thought I could make dinner tonight." He pushed off from the couch and moved toward the kitchen.

Haley stopped him, forcing herself to look at him straight on. "Stephen."

He stilled, his brown eyes searching hers.

"I've been thinking about the memorial service. I was wrong. What right do I have to say you can't come to your brother's memorial?" She paused, waiting for Stephen to respond. "I'll call Miriam—your mom—and let her know you're coming."

"I can do that."

"Whatever way you want to let her know. I'm sorry we argued about this."

"It's okay, Haley. All's forgiven. About earlier—"

"I think it's best if we don't talk about what happened at the park."

"We can't ignore this, Haley."

"Yes, we can." One of them had to think straight. "I mean, even if there wasn't the whole Sam situation, what about you and Elissa?"

"Me and Elissa?"

"Yes. Aren't you hoping to get back together with her?"

Stephen's burst of laughter contradicted how his ears turned the now-familiar red. "I went to talk to Elissa a few weeks back—to tell her about Sam and to get closure. I assure you, things are over between Elissa and me. She's married."

"What?"

"I guess the right guy proposed."

"I'm sorry, Stephen."

"Haley—I kissed *you* this afternoon. Believe me, I haven't thought about any other woman but you in weeks." Stephen reached out and traced a gentle line from Haley's temple to the corner of her mouth, causing a shiver to course up her spine. "You may be able to forget those kisses, but I can't. The truth is, I've thought about kissing you again all afternoon."

As Stephen urged her closer, Haley put both hands against his chest, blocking the embrace. "I haven't thought about kissing you."

Stephen watched her for the space of a heartbeat. Then his hands slid down her arms, leaving a trail of warmth behind. When he leaned toward her, she refused to move away. The longing for another kiss from Stephen enticed her closer, and she allowed her eyes to close as his lips brushed over hers.

"Liar." The word jolted through her.

"What?"

He released her, causing her to sway backward. "I called you a liar. At least I'm honest about how I feel about you."

"What was that all about?"

"That, my dear Haley, was proof."

"Proof of what?"

"Proof that you want to kiss me just as much as I want to kiss you. And when you're willing to admit that—" He walked to the kitchen, tossing the words back over his shoulder. "—then I'm willing to kiss you again."

thirty-one

•••••—◆—•••••—◆—•••••—◆—•••••

It wasn't the first time she'd celebrated Sam's birthday without him.

But in the past, there was always a phone call or a Skype session to take the sting out of the separation.

Now she had a daughter with her daddy's eyes. Their wedding bands stashed in an envelope next to his death certificate. And a single wedding photo on the bedside table, reminding her of their "until death do us part" promises.

If they'd known how soon they would be parted, would they have done things differently? Would Sam have decided not to volunteer for deployments? Would she have stopped always saying "I'm fine" and admitted to missing him more? But doing so would have tarnished her perfect army-wife persona.

Was a widow expected to visit her husband's grave on days like today—birthdays, anniversaries, holidays? She'd never imagined sitting beside Sam's grave—and do what? Talk to him? Pray? She couldn't do any of that. She'd agreed to Miriam's request to have Sam buried in Oklahoma because, as her mother-in-law said, *"Who knows? You might not settle in Colorado forever—and I'm staying here."*

She finished swaddling Kit, fitting a tiny multicolored hat onto her head before cradling her daughter close. "You want to go outside for a little bit? It's cold—but you're a Colorado girl, aren't you?"

She carried Kit to the red and white cathedral-window quilt she'd spread beneath the tree in the backyard—a wedding present from one of her relatives. She eased to the ground, leaning back against the tree trunk and resting Kit against her raised knees.

"So. Today's your daddy's birthday." Her daughter watched with solemn brown eyes. "I know. It kind of snuck up on me, too. Your daddy's name was Samuel Wilson Ames—after a superhero. That's why I named you Katherine Elizabeth—she's a superhero, too. Family tradition and all that."

One thing was sure: Kit was a good listener.

"Your daddy was in the army. He loved being in the military. He was a medic, which means he took care of other soldiers when they were wounded."

Haley paused, unsure how to continue. Maybe if she practiced this next part now, when Kit was too young to understand, too young to ask questions, she'd be able to say it and face any questions her daughter had later. "You need to know there are good guys and bad guys in the world. Your daddy was a good guy. But . . . he died because . . . one of the bad guys . . . well, because there are bad guys in the world."

Haley adjusted the brim of Kit's hat. Stroked her cheek, causing her daughter to offer her a lopsided smile that reminded her of Sam's teasing half smile. "Your daddy would have loved you very much. He would have taught you to ride a bike—probably skipped right over training wheels. And you would have been his hiking buddy. He knew how to juggle—socks and fruit and golf balls. He would have taught you that, too. He liked chocolate chip cookies dipped in milk for breakfast, and he liked to stay up late watching movies and then sleep in the next day."

Haley's reminisces pulled her back in time.

"Come here, Hal." Sam clasped her wrist, tugging her toward where he sat on the couch, wearing a pair of cut-off jeans and a gray sweatshirt.

"I don't feel like watching a movie." Haley pulled against his hand.

"Then we'll just sit and talk."

"I don't want to 'talk,' either."

He released her, settling against the couch as she sat in the chair she'd bought from a friend when they moved. "You mad at me?"

About time he caught on.

"I don't understand why you had to volunteer for a deployment."

"Come on, Hal. I told you. The other guy just got married—"

"And so did we."

"We've been married over a year—"

"And you deployed right after we got married—"

"You knew who you were marrying when you said yes."

Yes, she did. And she hadn't expected to take first place before the army—but she hadn't expected to feel as if she was in last place.

Sam switched on the television. She left the room, crawling into bed. No tears. Keep up. She cradled Sam's pillow in her arms. He came in hours later, waking her as he wrapped his arms around her and whispered he loved her, kissing her until he coaxed a response from her.

The sigh of something soft against her cheek focused Haley back to the present. She touched the tiny spot of cold, looking up in the sky. What? Sparkles of white drifted down—a glitter here, there, and there. Was it snowing? She watched a minute snowflake land on Kit's face. May in Colorado, and it was snowing. Springtime in the Rockies.

"Time to go, Peanut." She stood, holding Kit in one arm and gathering the quilt up in the other. "We need to make a phone call, anyway."

In her bedroom, she positioned Kit on the bed before lying down alongside her so she could see her wedding photo. Then she put her phone on speaker and dialed Stephen.

"This is Stephen Ames."

"I should warn you, Rogers, that you are on speakerphone."

"Because?"

"Your niece wants to wish you happy birthday."

His chuckle threatened to invade something locked away in Haley's heart.

"All right, Kit, say happy birthday to Uncle Stephen." Silence—and then a soft coo as Kit squirmed on the bed. "Did you catch that?"

"Absolutely. Thank you, Peanut. That's my favorite birthday wish ever."

"And happy birthday from me, too."

"Thank you, Haley."

"Are you having a good day?" Haley patted Kit's tummy, rocking her back and forth.

"Pretty low-key. But I like it that way."

"Me, too."

"When is your birthday, anyway?"

"September."

"You're not one of those women who lies about her age, are you?"

Haley rubbed slow circles on Kit's tummy. "No. I'm the age I am, and lying doesn't change that."

"I didn't think so."

"So no special plans, then?"

"Nope. Just kicking back. I'm good."

"Well, I'll let you get back to your perfect do-nothing birth-day." Because, really, what more was there to say? "Take care."

"You, too."

•••••••◆•••••••

Stephen stood holding the phone after Haley hung up. His hand hovered over the keypad. Why not call her back? Suggest he drive down to the Springs and make dinner for them? Knowing Haley, she would scrounge up a bowl of Cap'n Crunch.

Anything was better than sitting in his apartment, sifting through the too-few memories of Sam. Sketching and resketching a tree house.

How did he celebrate his birthday—their birthday—without Sam? He'd done it for a dozen years, but then he'd known Sam was somewhere, eating a slice of cake and a huge serving of ice cream, celebrating his birthday without him, too.

But now . . . now he couldn't reach his brother if he wanted to. And he did.

The difficulty in life is the choice.

He'd stumbled across the quote by Irish novelist George Moore several years ago, typing it in the yellow virtual notepad on his iPhone.

Was the difficulty in making the choice—or living with the consequences of the choice? Being estranged from Sam was some bizarre emotional version of a phantom limb. How did doctors explain it? A leg or arm is amputated—but a person feels as if the limb is still a part of the body. But it's not. An itch—with nothing to scratch. Pain that can't be eased.

He may have stopped talking about Sam for a dozen years—but he'd never stopped thinking about him. There was the ache of missing his brother—the knowing that Sam was still there.

Somewhere. Even believing he'd made the right choice—though he sometimes mourned the cost.

Memories skulked around the edges of his mind, but Stephen ignored them. He would not remember birthdays of the past, filled with shared laughter, shared presents, shared cake and ice cream. Which left him with the stark, unrelenting solitude of this birthday. He'd let his dad's phone call go to voice mail and left his mother's annual birthday card unopened on his desk. He might as well open it, read the usual "Happy birthday, love, Mom" inscription, and then let it get lost in a pile of papers on his desk, until he found it several weeks later and threw it out.

When he retrieved the envelope and settled into his chair, Stephen noticed it felt heavier than her usual birthday cards. What had his mother sent him? He slit the envelope open with the edge of his silver letter opener, pulling the contents out and depositing them onto his desktop. A birthday card. A couple of photographs. And a piece of folded, lined school paper. What was all this?

He opened the card first, surprised that his mother had actually written a message inside the front cover. He'd left a brief voice mail saying he would be attending Sam's memorial—but hadn't heard back from her.

Dear Stephen,

    I was going through some old books the other day, putting together things to give to the church garage sale. I found something tucked into a copy of *My Side of the Mountain* that I thought you should see.

    Happy birthday.

                                   Love,

                                   Mom

Stephen picked up the first picture, recognizing the photo of him and Sam sitting with their dad around the campfire during one of their family vacations. Curls of smoke obscured their faces. They'd enjoyed learning how to build a fire and lighting it with one match. Roasting marshmallows for s'mores. Falling asleep in the tent after hiking and swimming.

In the second photo he and Sam were standing, arms slung across each other's shoulders, celebrating winning some of their middle school wrestling matches. Same height. Same grin. Same dark hair slick with sweat. Those were fun times. Exhaustion and elation, all shared with Sam.

On to the piece of paper.

Would he see a penciled math equation? An English essay? When he unfolded the paper, he read the words *Dear Stephen*.

His brother wrote him? When? There was no date at the top of the page. Stephen skimmed the scrawled lines that filled only about a fourth of the page.

Dear Stephen,

I've thought about writing you a few times. While I was at basic training. When I graduated from army medic school. But I didn't know what to say. It's hard to figure out how to get past the silence. It's not that I don't want things to change. I just don't know how to change them.

Stephen heard his brother's voice as he reread the too-few lines of the letter. There was no way to determine when during the estrangement Sam had written to him. He stared at the words until they blurred.

He'd written Sam a letter.

Sam had written to him.

Both letters went missing. Stephen had no idea if Sam ever

received the letter he wrote, and now he held Sam's partial message. And there was nothing he could do about either one.

Both of them wanted to fix the problem that separated them—and both of them failed at figuring out how to get past the invisible barrier.

He teetered somewhere between regret and acceptance. Somehow he had to learn to shoulder his choices—the good and the bad—and keep living. He'd gotten what he'd wanted so long ago: he was just Stephen Ames. No *and*. But he'd never imagined the so-called freedom costing this much.

Stephen folded the letter, holding it in his hands. "Happy birthday, Sam—and thanks." Maybe if they'd had more time, he and Sam would have figured out a way back to each other. He had to believe that. They had both wanted to—they would have found each other again . . . and forgiven one another.

thirty-two

•••••—•—•••••—•—•••••—•—•••••

The last time Haley had sat in Lily's family room, she'd been a mom-to-be. Thanks to Kit's early arrival, she'd missed the rest of the classes.

"I'm disappointed you didn't bring Kit with you. I'm eager to see your daughter." Lily carried in two tall amber glasses, handing one to Haley before settling next to her on the couch. "I'm so sorry I wasn't there when you needed me."

"It's okay, Lily. I've turned my ringer on my phone off and forgotten about it for a day or two before—it happens. I apologize for showing up like this. Next time I'll make sure to bring Kit. But I wanted . . . I needed to talk with you."

Lily waved away Haley's apology. "Is she doing well? Off the oxygen?"

"Yes. She only used it while she was in the hospital. She's all of nine pounds, and my doctor says for being premature, she's thriving."

Lily moved her long gray braid so it hung down her back.

"Why do I get the feeling you didn't come here to talk to me about babies?"

Haley twisted the glass in her hands, the ice cubes sloshing around in the soda, creating tiny bubbles that fizzed and popped. "I always knew you were discerning."

"What's on your mind, Haley?"

"After your husband died . . . how long was it before you remarried?"

"Ah." Lily settled back against the cushions. "I got married two years after my husband died."

"Two years. That's reasonable."

"Are you asking me what's a 'reasonable' time to wait until you get remarried? I can assure you, my mother-in-law didn't think two years was appropriate. In her mind, I should have never remarried."

"Why not?"

"Because if I really loved Tom, I would never replace him with another man. Her words, not mine."

"Did you know your second husband before your husband died? I mean, was he a friend—"

"My first husband was a pastor." She shook her head, a smile curving her lips. "Jerry, who I'm married to now, attended our church. He led the singles ministry. Ironic, I know."

"How did the church feel about you two getting married?"

"Well, it really wasn't their business, was it?" Lily shrugged her shoulders, a knowing smile playing around her lips. "Although congregations don't always act that way. Some members were very supportive. And some . . . weren't. Jerry told me that he would have proposed a lot sooner if it hadn't been for all the church craziness."

"Would you have said yes?"

"I don't know. Back then, I thought too much about what other people thought about me. I didn't want to upset my mother-in-law. I didn't want to upset the church. I didn't want to upset my little ones." She rested her hand on her heart. "The only person I wasn't thinking about was me."

"Aren't we supposed to consider others first?"

"Well, yes. But that doesn't mean that we never, ever think about ourselves. That we never ask God what his plans are for us, for our future, our happiness." She leaned forward, placing her hand on Haley's knee. "Which brings us to you—and why you look so sad."

"Is that a question?"

Lily reached for her glass and settled back against the couch. "Here's a straightforward one: Have you fallen in love?"

"I can't." Haley fought against the searing tightness in her chest caused by both Lily's question and her answer.

"Your husband's death doesn't disqualify you from falling in love again."

"It's too soon . . ."

"Love often has its own timetable. If this were five years from now, would your 'I can't' be a 'Yes, I can'?"

"No."

"Then timing isn't the obstacle. What's the real reason you can't?"

"I can't fall in love with Sam's brother."

"Ah." Lily pursed her lips. "That makes things interesting."

"Interesting?" Her laughter was short-lived. "It makes things horribly, terribly, what-am-I-thinking complicated."

"Why?"

"Because Stephen is Sam's brother. *His mirror twin.*" Haley buried her face in her hands.

"So Stephen looks just like Sam, right?"

Haley's words were muffled. "So much so the first time I saw him, I thought he was Sam."

"Does he act like Sam?"

"No. I mean, they have some of the same quirky manner-isms—they both like to dip potato chips in ketchup. And Stephen drives a Mustang, which was Sam's dream car. But Stephen is so different from Sam."

"How so?"

Haley sat back. Closed her eyes. "Sam was always leaving me. It wasn't his fault. It came with the job. I knew it when I married him. Sam always told me what a good army wife I was . . . I thought . . . I thought . . ."

"What?"

How did she unravel all the unmet expectations in her marriage from the longings Stephen stirred inside her? "I thought I was getting to be a girl this time . . . when I married Sam. I've always felt like one of the guys—following my brothers around, you know? And that was okay. I thought Sam saw me for *me*. But sometimes he treated me more like one of his army buddies."

"And it's different with Stephen?"

"Stephen . . . Stephen is here for me. He stays."

"Go on."

"This feels traitorous."

"Don't tell me about Sam versus Stephen. Just tell me about Stephen."

"Stephen helps me. I've always been independent. Another consequence of having three older brothers. I learned early on not to complain. To take what life handed me. But Stephen sees past that and takes care of things . . . takes care of me. I can . . . rest with him."

"He sounds pretty special."

"He's Sam's brother."

Lily set her drink on the coffee table and reached for Haley's hand. "Haley, you are not choosing between Sam and Stephen; you know that, right?"

"It feels that way."

"Sam isn't here. You can't choose him." How was it that Lily's smile eased the ache in Haley's heart? "At one time, Sam and you chose each other. But that time is over. When we get married, we think it's going to be forty, fifty, maybe even sixty years. But sometimes you have five years. Or three. Or less."

"What will people think?"

"Oh, Haley—that's no way to live your life. You'll stretch yourself every which way but the way God is leading you if you base your decisions on what everyone else is thinking."

Haley tried to meet Lily's gaze, but she couldn't. "What would Sam think?"

When Lily reached out and pulled her into an embrace, Haley allowed it, resting her head on the older woman's shoulder. "Did you and Sam ever talk about what would happen if he died?"

"No. Never." She pulled away from Lily. "I know most military couples do. I mean, Sam showed me the insurance papers. But that was it. We just . . . didn't talk about it. The only thing he ever said was that he didn't worry about me. He knew I could handle everything when he was gone."

"Well, then that still applies."

"What do you mean?"

"It's obvious Sam trusted you. That he knew you'd make wise decisions."

"But he never expected me to fall in love with his brother."

"He never expected to be killed while he was on that deployment, either. The fact remains that Sam trusted you. Take things slow. Pray about your relationship with Stephen. And don't be afraid to walk into the future God has waiting for you."

•••••◆•••••

Haley walked across the backyard until she stood at the tree caught in the tug-of-war between her and the homeowners' association. She ran her hand along the trunk, the bark rough beneath her fingertips, bits of it flaking off and falling to the ground. When she looked up, the tree's branches spread out against the blue sky, dark and leafless.

Lifeless.

Brushing aside a few small rocks, Haley settled onto the ground, leaning against the tree. She set Kit's monitor nearby and placed the envelope holding the information about Sam's death on her lap.

Was she ready to read the details? The medical what and how and why? She knew the basics: Sam had been administering aid to a small number of troops on patrol who had been caught in an ambush. A sniper shot him. He died quickly. Instantly. During the funeral, she'd insisted on a closed casket, even though Sam looked . . . fine.

She picked up the envelope, causing something to slip around inside. Their wedding bands. She opened the back flap, pulling out the simple gold rings Sam had purchased at the post exchange. She'd told him that she didn't want anything extravagant or fancy.

Setting the envelope aside, she slipped both of the rings onto her forefinger—Sam's ring sliding all the way on and her band stopping at her knuckle. She'd considered having Sam buried with his wedding band but then decided their son might want the ring one day. Who knew? Kit might want to give it to her husband.

She touched the brushed gold. Haley knew some people thought she took her wedding band off too soon. It didn't matter what they thought. She took her band off when Sam stopped wearing his band. It only seemed right—and so, so wrong.

She closed her eyes, inhaling the scent of the neighbor's just-mowed grass mixed with the hickory aroma of someone grilling dinner.

She didn't want to read the report. Didn't need to read it. It wouldn't change anything. Wouldn't bring Sam back.

Haley removed both rings, held them in the palm of her hand for a moment, then closed her fingers around them and pressed her hand to her heart.

Her life didn't make sense. Who fell in love with twin brothers—identical ones, at that?

At first, Haley couldn't see past all the ways Stephen reminded her of Sam. Same height. Same build. Same brown eyes. Same brown hair, although Stephen's was long enough to touch his ears. But now she could see beyond all the physical similarities to how Stephen was so very different from her husband.

Sam was the man who always left her—who was always thinking of the next adventure even when he was with her.

Stephen was the man who always came back to her even when she pushed him away. Stephen was the man who stayed.

When it came to their relationship, Sam kept a barrier up—and she had, too.

Stephen somehow found a way past her defenses, asking her to give more of her heart, more of herself, than Sam ever had.

Sam expected her to be independent, to take care of herself.

Stephen asked her to let him help, to let him care for her.

But just because she saw the differences between Sam and Stephen—would never mistake one brother for the other—that didn't mean she was free to love Sam's brother. That didn't make it right. Or wise. Or best.

thirty-three

•••••—•••••—•—•••••—•—•••••—•—•••••

"Is this what you're planning on wearing to the memorial?" Claire picked the dark plum sheath off the bed.

"I thought so." She continued to fold towels. "You know me and dresses—we don't get along that well."

"It's just because you've ignored them for so long."

"Well, David's wife e-mailed this to me—a picture of it, I mean. I know I should probably wear black, but it's been almost a year since Sam died."

"You don't have to explain yourself to me—or anyone else, Haley. The dress is perfectly acceptable. Are you wearing black heels?"

"Yes, the ones I bought for the funeral."

"So . . . how are you doing?"

"I'm fine. I think I'll have all the laundry done before I leave for Oklahoma—but if I don't, it'll wait for me." She dropped the washcloth she was folding. "I need to move the loads around. Do you want to wait here or follow me to the laundry room?"

"I'll tag along." Claire hung the dress on the back of the closet door, following her in silence until they got to the laundry room. "How are you and Stephen?"

"We're fine."

"What's that mean?"

"It means we're fine—nothing more, nothing less." Haley hauled a load of wet jeans from the washing machine into the dryer.

"Are you going to stand there and tell me you haven't realized Stephen Ames is at least halfway in love with you?"

"Stephen and I are friends. He helps out with things around the house. He's Kit's uncle."

"Uncle Stephen loves Kit's mama."

Haley slammed the dryer door, pushing the needed buttons to start the machine, then started filling the washer with whites. "Enough."

"Do you really believe the man comes down here all the time because he likes doing projects around your house?"

"Not listening."

"Fine. Changing the subject. Is Stephen still going to the memorial service with you?"

"Yes."

"Let me ask you this: How do you think people are going to react when you walk into the memorial service—with Stephen?"

"That's not my problem." The pungent odor of bleach stung her eyes.

"It is your problem, Haley—because you were married to Sam."

Haley faced her friend. "I told Stephen I wasn't sure about him coming to the memorial service. He needed to think about how his mom would feel when he walked into the church. She deserves to mourn her son without that kind of pressure." She shut the washing machine, programmed the proper cycle, and then exited the laundry room with Claire following her. "That was how I felt at first. But then I thought about it. Prayed about it. And I realized Stephen has every right to be at the memorial service. And I'm thankful he's going to be there. I want him there—as a friend. I can't imagine going to the service without him."

●●●●●━━●●●●●

What had he just heard?

Stephen stood on the steps leading from Haley's garage into the laundry room, the silence echoing around him.

"He needed to think about how his mom would feel when he walked into the church. She deserves to mourn her son without that kind of pressure."

Hadn't he and Haley talked this out a few weeks ago? When had she gone from wanting him there to considering him nothing more than "pressure"?

Sidestepping her Forester, he exited through the garage door, which had stood open when he pulled into the driveway. So much for taking off early from Fort Collins to surprise Haley, to check and see if there was anything she needed before she left for Oklahoma tomorrow.

All she needed was for him not to show up.

He backed the Mustang out of the driveway, careful not to gun the engine and alert Haley that he'd been there. He rubbed the heel of his hand against the ache in his chest. How had he misread everything between them? Despite blocking his hopes for romance, Haley seemed so open to him. They talked late into the night, sometimes until two or three in the morning. He came down on Friday nights, making dinner for them and watching a movie before going to his hotel room, and then coming back on Saturday to make breakfast and tackle the next homeowners' association–mandated project on the list. And he always left a bouquet of daisies on her dining room table.

But none of that changed what he'd heard: Haley didn't want him at Sam's memorial service. She was flying out to Oklahoma tomorrow—a few days early, so she could spend some time with his mother. And then he was supposed to arrive the night before the memorial. He'd bought his ticket the day after he and Haley agreed he should attend the service—or so he'd thought.

He pointed the car north, moving into the stream of traffic heading away from the Springs. Should he still show up at the memorial service, knowing how Haley felt?

He had a plane ticket.

He had a right to honor his brother.

But the woman he loved didn't want him there.

And to his mother he was nothing more than pressure.

As he waited for the light at an intersection to change from red to green, he waged an internal debate. Why not go back and confront Haley? Hash out the whole should-he-go-to-the-memorial-service-or-shouldn't-he one more time? He activated his Bluetooth, drumming his fingers on his steering wheel, then grabbing the wheel when his phone rang in his ear.

"Hello?"

"You ready to talk serious business plans?" Jared's voice was a splash of verbal cold water.

"What are you talking about?"

"My friend Joe is in."

"In?"

"He's ready to invest in our business."

Stephen eased through the intersection. "Did you inform Joe that our business is still in the planning stage?"

"I let him know he's getting in on the ground floor."

"Basement."

"Details. He's in town. We're meeting tomorrow night for dinner, which I hope ends with a handshake and him writing me—us—a big, fat check. Can you get here?"

Could he get to Oregon? Yes—if he skipped Sam's memorial. And maybe that was the best thing for everyone.

"Let me see what I can do. I'll call you back."

Stephen voice-dialed Haley, continuing his trek back toward home. He fought against the hope that she'd give him some reason to turn the car around.

"Hello?"

"Haley, it's Stephen."

"How's my daughter's favorite uncle?"

How honest should he be? If he knew one thing about Haley, it was that she liked things straight up. "I'm rethinking a few things."

A moment of silence greeted his statement. "Meaning?"

"I don't know how else to do this."

"Do what? Stephen, what is going on?"

"I was at your house earlier."

"What? When?"

"I drove down tonight—wanted to surprise you, see if I could help you get ready for your trip to Oklahoma tomorrow." Now came the hard part. "I heard you talking to Claire."

"You heard me talking to—"

"Telling her that I shouldn't come to the memorial. That it would upset my mother." He pressed the heel of his hand against his forehead. "I thought we'd talked this out, Haley."

"We did, Stephen—"

"You could have told me how you really felt. I want to be at the memorial—but not by forcing myself into it." He waited a heartbeat for Haley to say something. Insist she wanted him there. Her silence stretched between them. "And then Jared called and the business opportunity looks like it's a go, so I think it's best for all of us if I fly out to Oregon instead of Oklahoma."

There was no sound on the other end of the phone. "Did I lose you?"

"No." Haley's voice inched up in volume. "No. I'm still here."

"The reality is—" Stephen wished the call had been disconnected. He could stop talking. Take back everything he'd said tonight. "—the reality is, I—I pushed things. Got ahead of myself. I wasn't thinking clearly."

"I understand. Well, um, Kit will miss you."

"I'll miss her, too." His throat ached. "Listen, I know you're probably packing, so I won't keep you on the phone."

"Sure."

"G'night."

He disconnected without waiting to hear Haley's response, yanking his Bluetooth out of his ear and tossing it on the dash. He was done talking for the night.

•••◆•—◆—•◆•••

Haley hauled her suitcase over to the curbside check-in desk, weaving her way through the double lanes of cars stopped in front of DIA. She deposited the bag, nodding to the young family in Broncos T-shirts who positioned themselves behind her. "Be right back."

Slipping her purse over her head so it was across her body, she sprinted back to Claire's car. Her best friend had already removed Kit's car seat and held Kit in her arms, rocking her back and forth. "Thanks for driving me to the airport."

"Not a problem." Claire ducked inside the car, reappearing

with the loaded diaper bag. "I don't work until tonight. Don't forget this. You told me it was essential to your sanity."

"Absolutely. I think I stuffed fifty diapers in there and half a dozen bottles."

"It's a two-hour flight, Hal."

"And I'm here two hours early. And I've never traveled with a baby before." She hugged her friend. "Thanks again."

Claire stopped her with a quick clasp of her hand. "You never heard from Stephen again?"

"No."

"Why didn't you explain that he didn't hear the entire conversation?"

"Because he didn't want to hear it." Haley sidestepped a taxi as it skirted around her and parked, the air laden with exhaust fumes. "I don't have time to think about this."

"What's that supposed to mean?" Claire raised her voice over the din of running car motors, honking horns, and shuttle buses shifting gears.

Haley pretended she hadn't heard the question. She checked her bag and Kit's car seat at the counter and walked into the air-conditioned climate of the terminal, weaving her way through security and finally stepping onto the escalator to the train that would take her to her gate.

While she waited for the train, she shifted Kit to her other shoulder. She should have pulled out the baby sling from the diaper bag so her hands would be free, but now she'd have to wait until she was at her gate.

Her phone vibrated in her purse but there was no way she'd get to it before it switched over to voice mail. Probably Miriam wanting to double-check her arrival time. But it might be Stephen, calling to say he was sorry. That he was still coming to the memorial. *Maybe.*

Haley detoured to the restroom, waiting behind two other moms for her turn to use the changing table. After changing Kit's wet diaper, she sifted through her overpacked diaper bag and found the Peanut Shell, sliding it over her head. Before settling Kit into place, she retrieved her phone.

Miriam.

She waited until she was at the gate, Kit snug in the baby sling, before listening to the message. As she suspected, Miriam had left a message asking about her flight. A quick phone call reconfirmed her arrival.

Haley stared straight ahead. The continual stream of people heading for their gates or going in the opposite direction after arriving at the airport blurred into a moving mass of colors. She was on her own. She'd expected that for the flight to Oklahoma. But the thought of Stephen being at the memorial had comforted her . . . strengthened her.

She'd been foolish.

She'd made the mistake of relying on a man instead of relying on herself. *Two men.* And both of them were Ameses. At least with Stephen she discovered the mistake early enough to recover from her emotional misstep. And it wasn't as if her heart was completely engaged. With Sam, she'd spent three years waiting. Hoping.

She was on her own. She'd go to Oklahoma. Get through the memorial service. Come home. And she'd forget about Stephen Ames and his waiting-to-kiss-you-again promises.

thirty-four

·····•····•·····•····•·····•·····

Stephen stretched out along Jared's couch. "We got a lot accomplished today."

"We?" Jared handed him a cold bottle of Killian's before settling into the chair across from him. When Moses, his Great Dane, walked toward Stephen, Jared motioned for the dog to lie down. "I did all the talking. You nodded your head appropriately—or inappropriately. You want to tell me what's going on?"

Stephen eyed Moses, who was inching toward him from his prone position on the carpet. "Does your dog want my Killian's?"

"He just wants attention. Ignore him."

"Kind of hard to ignore when you're being stared down by a hundred-and-fifty-pound dog."

Jared snapped his fingers. "Moses! Come here. Lie down." Once the dog settled at his feet, he focused on Stephen again. "So, back to you. Can you explain the whole 'present in body but absent in mind' act during dinner?"

"Distracted, that's all."

"I knew that—the blank stare clued me in. You could have agreed to start a snow cone business."

Stephen clasped his hands around the glass bottle. "I got off track."

Jared waited for him to continue.

"I went to Colorado Springs to find out more about my brother—not to fall in love with his widow."

Still no reaction from his best friend—or Moses. Did the dog ever blink?

"You're not going to tell me how stupid I am?"

"I think you're beating yourself up enough. I'm not going to throw in a few punches of my own."

Stephen saluted him with his beer. "Thanks for that."

"So, I take it Haley isn't interested in a relationship with you?"

"No. I thought I could wait. Be patient. I planned on going to Sam's memorial service with her."

"Then why are you here?"

"Because I heard her talking to her friend Claire about how my being there was going to stress out my mom—how she tried to convince me not to come. I thought we'd hashed that all out and she understood why I wanted to be there."

"Did you talk to her about what you heard?"

"Yes. And then I told her I thought it was best if I didn't come to the memorial and that I'd decided to go to Oregon for business."

Jared shook his head. "Do you think you're in a soap opera?"

"Of course not." Stephen did a double take. "What do you know about soap operas?"

"I dated a woman—*very* briefly—who watched every soap on network television, thanks to the miracle of TiVo. One key element? People don't talk things out. Lots of misunderstandings. Kept the story lines going for months."

"I know what I heard—and there was no cheesy background music." Stephen held his hand up, halting Jared's reply, when his iPhone vibrated. "Stephen Ames here."

"Stephen? Where are you?"

"Dad?" Stephen sat up. "I'm at Jared's—in Portland. Why?"

"Because I'm in Oklahoma, checking into the hotel that I thought you were staying at while you're here for the memorial service tomorrow. But then I'm told you're not registered as a guest."

"What are you doing in Oklahoma?"

"Gina and I talked about it—prayed about it—and I'm attending the memorial service tomorrow."

"Do you think that's wise?"

"Sam was my son. I'm not going to make a scene. I'll sit in the back and slip out when it's over. But I am going to be there. Now, you want to tell me why you're not here?"

How was he supposed to explain why he wasn't there?

"You are coming, right?"

"I was, but—"

"I can't think of a single reason why you wouldn't be here."

"Haley doesn't want me there."

"I find that hard to believe—and even if that's true, the real question is: Do you want to be here?"

"Yes."

"Why?"

All the reasons he wanted to be in the church tomorrow burned in his chest. "Because I want the chance to honor Sam. I want . . . to say good-bye."

"Then stop talking to me and start looking for a flight that will get you here in time for the service."

"But what about Haley?"

"You'll sit in the back of the church with me. We won't attract attention."

Stephen picked up Jared's phone where it lay on the coffee table. It was after eight. "I'm going to try, Dad. I'll keep you posted."

thirty-five

⁘•⊙•⊙•⊙•⊙•⊙•

"You look nice." Miriam stood in the bathroom doorway watching Haley as she brushed her hair, debating whether to leave it down or pull it back in a ponytail. Miriam had tried to convince her to curl the ends, but Haley wanted to feel normal today—as normal as she possibly could while she sat through the memorial service.

"Thanks." Haley let her hair fall around her shoulders. Normal was not fussing about her hair. "Is Kit still asleep?"

"Yes—I just checked on her."

"Which means she'll be wide awake during the service."

"I'll take care of her."

"No, no. I'll sit on the end of the aisle and slip out if she gets noisy." No makeup. A sniffle redirected her gaze to her mother-in-law, who dabbed at her eyes with a wadded-up Kleenex. "Are you going to be okay?"

"Of course." Miriam's lips, painted a soft coral, trembled. "A lot of Sam's high school friends will be there today. His teachers.

They planted a tree in his honor in the school courtyard, did I mention that?"

"Yes. It's a lovely way to remember Sam." She smoothed the front of her dress. "Ready to go?"

Except for the sound of Kit's soft coos from her car seat, Haley and Miriam rode in silence to the church. They were a good forty-five minutes early, but a few cars were already in the parking lot.

The midmorning sun warm on her back, Haley shifted the diaper bag to her shoulder, adjusting Kit's pale pink pleated dress and sweater, hoping it was appropriate. What should an infant wear to her father's memorial service? Miriam had wanted Kit to wear a bow in her wisps of blond hair, but Haley vetoed the idea. Adding the bow seemed too festive— and today was not a celebration. She rested Kit against her shoulder and followed Miriam into the dim foyer, where a few people milled around and an honor guard stood off to one side.

"Why don't we go ahead inside the church?" Miriam moved toward the sanctuary. "I'm sure they reserved seats for us."

"That's fine, Miriam."

Haley inhaled the faint scent of fresh flowers mixed with the air-conditioning. Several people had already chosen their seats for the service. Two men in dark suits sat on the far end of the last row—and one of the men was Stephen.

What? Why was he here when he said he wasn't coming?

Miriam's attention seemed to be focused down front on a large framed photograph of Sam in his camouflage uniform. Next to the photo was a table set with a bouquet of red poppies and white roses, what she could only assume was Sam's high school letter jacket, and his senior photo. Haley waited until Miriam was ready to find their assigned seats. No need to rush today.

Front row on the right. Haley settled into the padded wooden pew, sliding the handwritten RESERVED FOR FAMILY sign to the end. As she took Kit from her, Miriam nodded toward the photo of Sam.

"I always liked that photo—the military one—don't you? He looks so young and handsome."

"Yes."

"He loved being in the army, didn't he?" She settled Kit into her lap. "It made him so happy."

"Yes, he did. It did."

･･●･･ ━ ･･●･･

If only she could tell her mother-in-law not to talk.

Haley had survived Sam's funeral by not talking—except for the needed *yes* and *no* and *thank you*. The fewer the words, the less she'd had to delve into the whirlpool of shock and grief that swirled into a frightening numbness. Haley was months past shock, and even the grief was abating. But today she still needed to sit in silence.

She closed her eyes, listening for a faint echo of Sam's voice telling her, "*You can do this, Hal.*"

Nothing.

Instead, Stephen's voice—so like his brother's and yet so different—slipped past her defenses. "*I pushed things. Got ahead of myself. I wasn't thinking clearly.*"

Why would he say that and go AWOL instead of driving her to the airport, leaving her to scramble to find alternate transportation, and then show up today?

One thing was certain: he didn't want to be here with her.

Once the service started, her mother-in-law stopped talking—and began crying. With one arm cradling Kit, she wrapped her other arm around Haley's waist and leaned against her, the tears trailing down her face to her neck, wetting the collar of her black dress.

For Haley, the music, the words of comfort, even the memories of Sam spoken by some of his high school friends were muted. Was Kit going to start crying? Would Miriam ever stop crying? How was Stephen holding up?

As she took her seat before the succession of speakers—the mayor, Sam's wrestling coach, one of his teachers—Haley searched the back of the church. Stephen still sat in the last pew, his lips thinned into a straight line, his eyes focused on her, not on the activity up front.

Enough of that.

She was here to remember her husband, not have her emotions twisted around by his twin brother. She would never have met him if Sam hadn't been killed. She needed to unravel loneliness for her husband from any sort of mixed-up longings for Stephen. Somehow she had let the two brothers become interchangeable—and that was so, so wrong. It dishonored both of the Ames brothers. Lily had been right: She could fall in love again. Sometime—but not with Stephen. She'd be replacing Sam with his reflection.

When the memorial ended with the honor guard marching out of the church, Haley closed her eyes, bracing herself to see Stephen again. She gathered up the diaper bag and took Kit from her mother-in-law, who soon became surrounded by friends. Haley couldn't stop herself from glancing back to where Stephen and the unknown man were sitting.

They were gone.

She bit her lip. It was easier this way.

Haley closed the door to the guest bedroom, breathing a sigh of relief. Off duty at last. The memorial service was over. Kit was asleep. Miriam had disappeared into her bedroom right after dinner, saying she had a headache.

The house was quiet. And it wasn't her house, so there wasn't any dirty laundry to deal with or bills to pay or letters from the homeowners' association to open or dishes to load in the dishwasher. She had nothing to do except relax.

Relax.

Did she know how to do that anymore?

She could watch TV. Or lounge on the couch and flip through one of the many magazines Miriam subscribed to. Or maybe soak in the tub. Claire said a long soak in the tub always relaxed her.

A knock at the front door halted her decision.

Or she could answer the door. It was probably another flower delivery for Miriam. She'd add the bouquet to the assorted arrangements set throughout the living and dining rooms, filling them with an overwhelming floral scent, and then go take her long soak.

A tall, broad-shouldered older man with a full head of gray hair stood on the stoop—no bouquet, not even a single flower in sight. In the dim light, he looked familiar. "Can I help you?"

"You're Haley Ames, correct?"

"Ye-es. And you are . . . ?"

"I'm Joe Ames—Sam's father. And Stephen's father, too, of course."

Haley's grip on the doorknob tightened. "You were at the memorial today with Stephen."

"I was. We left just before it ended. I didn't want to create any tension with my ex-wife."

"But you're here now." Haley bit back the "Why?" She was tired of fighting with Sam's relatives.

"I wanted to meet my son's wife—to meet you."

They stared at one another in silence for a few seconds. Haley caught glimpses of Stephen—and Sam, of course—in their father's build, the cleft in his chin, the timbre of his voice. She offered her hand, hoping he saw past the tears in her eyes to the smile on her lips. "Won't you come in? I think Miriam's asleep. There's someone I'd like you to meet."

Sam's father moved into the foyer, his hands stuffed into his pants pockets. "I'm sorry if I'm interrupting your evening."

"No, not at all. I'm glad you stopped by. Wait right here."

When she reappeared a few moments later, Kit rested in her arms, her eyes opening and closing, as if she wasn't certain if she was supposed to be awake or asleep. "This is your granddaughter, Katherine Elizabeth. I call her Kit."

"Kit." Joe Ames reached out his hand and caressed the bits of blond hair that feathered across Kit's head. His eyes were wet, and a single tear ran down his weathered cheek.

"Stephen told me how he and Sam were named after Marvel superheroes. Kit's named after a female Hawkeye. I thought I'd continue the family tradition."

"I like that." The man never took his eyes off his granddaughter. "She has the Ames's brown eyes."

"Yes." Footsteps sounded behind her. Haley stopped talking. The only person it could be was her mother-in-law.

Joe Ames's hand fell to his side. "Miriam. I didn't want to upset you. I just wanted to see Sam's wife . . . nothing more. I'll go now."

"Hush, Joe. I'm not upset." Miriam stayed behind Haley. "I saw you at the memorial earlier. I didn't get upset then, did I? Sam was your son, too—and Kit's your granddaughter. The truth is, we've both been fools—and we hurt our boys because of it. We've lost one—" Miriam's voice thickened with unshed tears. "But we still have Stephen . . . and a daughter-in-law and a granddaughter. Maybe we can do better in the future."

His ex-wife's words seemed to stun Joe Ames into silence. After a moment, he exhaled. Nodded. "I think we can, Miriam. I think we can."

Haley reached back and clasped Miriam's hand. If only Sam could see his parents' halting attempt to make peace with each other.

thirty-six

•••••—◆—•••••—◆—•••••—◆—•••••

Villa Stella's hadn't changed that much since the last time Stephen had been there with Sam and their mom. The same orange neon sign spelled out the restaurant's name in looping cursive letters across the side of the brick building. The white and green awning still covered the outdoor patio, filled with diners sitting at the black wrought-iron tables and chairs. When he walked inside, the back wall still boasted a hand-painted mural of a Venice waterway.

"Do you have a reservation?" The hostess, her blue eyes heavily made up with glittering green eye shadow, stood guard at the hostess station.

"No. I'd like that booth over there, please." He motioned to one in the back corner of the restaurant. Filled now with a family of five, including a rambunctious toddler in a high chair, the booth would easily accommodate six adults. "I don't mind waiting."

"Are you sure I can't seat you at a table—"

"No. That booth, please. I'll wait."

He settled off to the side, waiting for forty-five minutes while the family finished their dinner and then the busboy cleared the table.

He ignored the menu—updated since he'd been there last—that the hostess set in front of him, speaking before the waiter could deliver his "Would you like a drink or an appetizer?" spiel.

"I know what I want."

"Okay." The waiter held a ballpoint pen over his paper pad.

"I'd like two Cokes, light on the ice. An order of your garlic bread. And then two orders of your spaghetti and meatballs—extra meatballs."

"Are you expecting someone else to join you, sir?"

"You could say that."

The memories stayed at bay until the man delivered the wire basket overflowing with long pieces of toasted bread, fragrant with butter and garlic. Stephen took the top piece, nodding across the table. He had the bread to himself tonight—but how many times had he and Sam gone through two baskets of garlic bread after a middle school wrestling tournament?

"What are you having?"

Stephen shrugged, his mouth full of toasted bread slathered in butter. "Spaghetti. Extra meatballs. You?"

"Same. And another basket of bread."

They downed half their drinks when the waitress delivered them; she knew the routine and would return with more garlic bread and a second set of Cokes. Their mom nibbled on a house salad.

"You had a great day out there." Sam leaned his elbows on the table, his grin wide.

"I shoulda pinned that last guy—I just ran out of time."

"You'll get him next time."

"Maybe. Did you see the high school coach watching tonight? Ross said he was checking out the incoming freshmen."

"You'll make the team for sure."

"We'll make the team together."

The waiter disrupted the memory, standing beside the table with two plates piled high with pasta drenched in marinara sauce and loaded down with meatballs.

"You want both of these in front of you?"

"No. One here—" He tapped the wooden tabletop in front of him. "—and one across from me."

"Okay." Setting down the plates, the waiter disappeared, returning with a white grater and a block of Parmesan cheese. "Would you like some cheese?"

"Just on mine, please."

Sam would have laughed until Coke came out of his nose at the look on the guy's face as he grated cheese over one plate of spaghetti.

But Stephen hadn't come here to amuse the restaurant staff.

If he'd been smarter . . . more mature . . . more forgiving when he was eighteen, he would have had dinner with Sam at Villa Stella's the night before he left for boot camp. They would have stuffed themselves full of garlic bread and soda and spaghetti and meatballs. Reminisced. Laughed.

And then he would have gone with his mom and his brother to the airport. Walked him to his gate. Hugged him. Said goodbye.

But there'd been no chance for farewells because he'd gotten angry when Sam announced his decision to join the army during spring break. Not a sulk-in-his-room kind of angry. No, he'd shouted at his brother, grabbing his arm when Sam had tried to walk away. And then Sam had turned around and pushed him into the wall. Before he knew what had happened, they were screaming at each other.

"This is crazy, Sam! What about college?"

"What? You're gonna fight me? This is my decision, not yours!"

The yelling stopped. But the bitterness remained. The hurt. And he'd chosen to stay angry. And so had Sam.

And the day Sam left for boot camp he was back in Pennsylvania. Trying not to think about his brother. And failing.

He raised his red plastic cup. "I'm sorry, Sam. Here's to you. I bet you tore up boot camp."

He set the cup back down and dug into the pasta until the next memory came. "You remember that time you told me you kissed Andrea Saunders up in the tree house? And then I told you that I kissed Mindie Jacobs? Well . . . I lied. I couldn't let my brother think he'd one-upped me with a girl, ya know? I mean, I tried to kiss her, but she ran out of the tree house saying she was going to tell her mother."

He stopped talking as the waiter came back to the table. "Do you, um, need anything, sir?"

"No. Everything's perfect. Just as good as I remember."

The waiter walked back to the drink area that was separated from the dining area by half of a brick wall. He tried to act as if he wasn't watching Stephen. The guy probably thought he was certifiable. Well, he just needed to leave Stephen be so he could finish his long-overdue conversation with his brother. He wanted to talk about the time Sam filled his school locker with white packing peanuts on their thirteenth birthday. And how he retaliated by stuffing every single piece of Sam's clothes—underwear and socks pulled from the dirty clothes hamper, too—into his brother's locker. How Sam did their science homework and he did their math homework when they were in eighth grade—until their mother caught on. How they used to lie awake the night before their birthday so they could be the first ones to say, "Happy birthday!"

He swallowed a bite of seasoned meatball. "You always could

get Mom to laugh when she was all set to yell at us. I never figured out how to do that."

Why hadn't he realized that Sam wasn't against him and Dad—that he was just worried about Mom?

He sat in silence, finishing off his spaghetti before putting the last piece of garlic bread on the plate across from him. "It's yours. I can't eat another bite."

Stephen wiped his hands with a napkin and then settled back in the booth. "So . . . I met Haley. And I can see why you fell in love with her. The thing is, I thought I was falling in love with her, too. She's gorgeous, by the way. Not supermodel, knock-you-off-your-feet gorgeous . . . she's just Haley. Uncomplicated. Her eyes say more than she realizes and her smile—when you can get her to smile—well, she looks like she's sixteen."

Stephen cleared his throat. "Sorry. I lost my train of thought. What I wanted to say was I realized I'm in love with Haley— well, I thought I was. She's a way to feel close to you again, you know? And now there's Kit—your daughter. And I let my feelings get all mixed up. I hope you can forgive me for that."

He hadn't really expected an audible answer. What he wanted was peace. He had his head screwed on straight now, his emotions under control. He was Haley's brother-in-law and Kit's uncle—nothing more.

Stephen looked up as the waiter approached the table again. The conversation was over.

"Do you want me to box this up for you?" The waiter motioned to the untouched meal.

"No." As he stood, Stephen pulled a hundred-dollar bill from his wallet. "This ought to cover it."

"Thank you, sir."

"Don't thank me. My brother was always a big tipper."

thirty-seven

Haley inhaled the faint scent of something floral and sweet lingering in the night air. A walk always helped her relax. The solo stroll through the neighborhood near Miriam's had eased both the mental and physical tension from her body. She paused at the end of the walkway leading to her mother-in-law's house. Someone stood just outside the front door.

The height, the shape of his shoulders, even the ease of his gait as he moved toward her . . . Haley knew it was Stephen even though the streetlight behind her didn't cast enough of a glow to reveal his face.

"I thought I'd missed you." His voice reached out to her—no echo of Sam lingering in his words.

"Just took a walk to unwind." She stopped again so that a few feet separated them. He'd changed out of his suit into a short-sleeved polo shirt tucked into a pair of jeans. And yes, he smelled of his familiar citrus scent.

"Long day?"

"Yes—for everyone. Miriam. Kit."

"You."

"Me, too. It was a nice memorial service. And tomorrow your mom wants us to visit Sam's gravesite. That's important to do, although it doesn't mean anything to Kit. Not yet." An Oklahoma breeze tangled her hair about her face. "I met your father tonight."

"So he said."

How . . . distant they sounded with each other. Short sentences. Brief questions and answers. Had their relationship—their friendship—really come to this? She wanted to explain what he'd heard . . . to fight past the "How could you?" or "Why did you?" questions, but they stalled in her throat. Her gaze skimmed his shadowed face—eyes, nose, jaw, cleft chin . . . mouth. The memory of the kisses they'd shared seemed scorched at the edges, dry and brittle, ready to crumble and blow away.

"Are you staying much longer?"

Haley forced herself to look up, to not break the tenuous eye contact with Stephen. They were just catching up. "A few more days, then back to the Springs. You?"

"Dad and I leave tomorrow afternoon."

She closed her eyes, fighting the squeeze of an invisible fist inside her chest that made it hard to breathe, to keep the conversation light. Casual. "Back to Oregon?"

"Yes. I told Jared I wouldn't be gone too long."

"So the business is a go?" There. She'd sounded interested, but not too much. And she could breathe again. Almost.

"Yes. Designing . . . houses will be challenging." Stephen shifted his weight right, then left. "I wanted to apologize for not driving you to the airport—"

"I managed." Haley's smile felt forced. Could he even see it in the darkness? "Claire got us there just fine."

"Then maybe I could explain about some other things."

．●●●●◆●●●●●

How exactly was he supposed to do this?

The plan had been to come by his mother's house. Talk to Haley. Untangle the past few months. Say good-bye. And move on.

But when he'd shown up, Haley wasn't there. Which gave his mother time to share her hope for better days ahead for Stephen and her—and his dad.

His father had said he'd met Haley and Kit—and that he'd forged the barest beginnings of peace with his ex-wife. But still, this more hope-filled version of his mother rocked Stephen's world.

And then he'd looked in on Kit . . . and wavered from his objective. Stephen forced himself to stand back from the portable crib. Not lean over and inhale his niece's baby-fresh aroma. Or give in to the longing to pick her up, cradle her close to his heart.

That would be his undoing.

He'd whispered a prayer for her and a promise to always watch over her—even from a distance—and a good-bye, his eyes memorizing the outline of her profile: forehead, tiny nose and chin. She'd change so fast, this version of Kit would be outdated within weeks.

And now he faced the final challenge: saying good-bye to Haley.

"When I came looking for Sam back in January, I met you . . . and I got confused." Stephen cleared his throat even as he searched for the right words—the necessary words. "I was broken. You were grieving. I let my emotions get turned upside down. I thought I was falling in love with you, Haley."

She watched him, the only movement caused by the wind sweeping her hair around her face.

"But I realize I was . . . It was wrong. I missed Sam. And you were his wife . . . Kit is his daughter . . . Loving you was a way to be close to him." The words that should have been so freeing left a bitter taste in his mouth. "You still love Sam. Now's not the time for you to be getting involved with anyone else—especially his twin brother. I mean, that's crazy."

Still no response from Haley. Why wasn't she agreeing with him?

"I can understand why Sam fell in love with you . . . and I know I probably confused you, too—"

"At first." Haley shook her head, raking her fingers through her hair, shoving it out of her eyes. "But now I'd never mistake you for Sam."

And what was he supposed to say to that? Of course she wouldn't mistake him for Sam—because Sam was dead. But if Sam were still alive, there'd be no question of who she'd choose. No question of choosing.

Haley's eyes closed for a brief moment, and then she looked at him. "Thank you for all your help with the house projects. The crib. And for, um, being there when Kit was born."

"No problem—"

She waved away his response, her fingers coming to rest on her lips as she paused to catch her breath, as if she were preparing to sprint. "Let me say this. Thank you, Stephen Rogers Ames, for everything. For being you. I—I . . . appreciate you."

"May I call and check in on you and Peanut?"

"Sure. Kit will want to hear from her uncle." Haley's inhale seemed ragged. "Well, I need to get inside before Miriam worries that I got lost. You take care, okay?"

"I will. You, too." His arms stayed by his sides, even as the thought of taking back everything he'd just said, of pulling Haley close—kissing her—flamed to life. He inhaled, forcing himself to swallow the words he wanted to say. He stuffed his fists in his pockets, moving forward and stepping off the sidewalk into the grass so that he wouldn't touch her, his action finally propelling her into the house.

Neither of them said good-bye—not out loud.

thirty-eight

•••••—•—•••••—•—•••••—•—•••••

Seven thirty in the morning? Someone was knocking on her door at seven thirty on a Wednesday morning?

Haley shoved her arms through her gray sweatshirt and pulled it on over her camisole. She pushed away thoughts of grabbing her 9mm from the gun safe. Probably some guy wanting to sell her siding. Or window washing. Or driveway resurfacing. She yanked the front door open and caught Sterling Shelton III midknock, with his arm raised.

"Mr. Shelton, do you know what time it is?"

"Of course I do." He lowered his arm, pulling at the sleeves of his coat. "I wear a watch."

"What do you want?" Haley kept the screen door shut. She'd talk to him—but he wasn't getting in her house.

"I want to discuss your tree."

"The tree next to my garage?"

"Of course not." He held up a sheaf of papers, shaking them so that they rattled. "The tree I've sent three letters about."

"Do you have nothing better to do than hassle homeowners?"

"I am not hassling you, Mrs. Ames. I am ensuring covenants are enforced."

"I can see that. Mis-sized house numbers are a horrible covenant infraction."

"I cannot exempt you from them just because you are widowed."

Haley shoved open the screen door, causing the man to step back. "I have never asked for special treatment because my husband was killed."

Shelton may have stepped back, but he didn't back down. "And I cannot overlook infractions just because you have a baby."

"Mr. Shelton, what do you want from me?"

"Remove your tree, Mrs. Ames. It's a danger to the neighborhood. I've had a tree doctor examine it—"

"You brought someone on my property?"

"Of course not. I had him look at some photographs—"

She'd been awake all of thirty minutes—talking to Shelton for five—and already her blood pressure was jitterbugging through her veins. "Who took photographs of my tree?"

"I did—from the sidewalk behind your house. Nothing illegal about that." He slapped his palm against the papers in his other hand. "I've had a certified tree doctor examine the photographs and verify parts of the tree are dead, while others could be diseased and dying."

"Arborist."

"Excuse me?"

"Nothing." Now was not the time to quibble over proper terms—or to recall a similar conversation with Stephen. "Could I see that report, please?"

"Absolutely." He flipped open a brown folder and pointed

to several photographs clipped to the top of an official-looking report. "I'm sure you'll agree—"

As he handed her the documents, Haley held up her hand. "I am not agreeing to anything until I look at this so-called report."

She shuffled through the photos and then skimmed over the report. Shelton was right—the tree was mostly dead. She slipped the report back into the folder and went through the photos one more time. Stopped. What was that?

When she closed the folder, she left one photograph on top. "You're correct—there is a problem."

Shelton's thin-lipped smile spread across his face. "I'm glad you're finally agreeing with me—"

"Oh, I'm not agreeing with you." She held up the photograph. "I'm talking about this problem."

"It's a photograph of your tree—"

"A rather blurry photo, wouldn't you agree? Look closer. You also managed to photograph *me,* in the privacy of my home. And that is most definitely a problem. A legal one for you, as I'll be contacting the authorities about this."

"This is absurd!" Shelton grabbed for the photograph, but Haley held it behind her back.

"We are no longer discussing the tree. We are now talking about invasion of privacy."

She left him standing on the front porch, sputtering, the click of the door closing as satisfying as the bell at the end of a boxing match. *And the winner is . . . Haley Ames!*

But even as she relished putting Shelton in his place, the victory felt incomplete. She wanted to call Stephen—to share the whole story with him. Hear him laugh. Hear him say he was on his way down to see her and Kit and they'd celebrate with a not-out-of-a-box-or-can meal.

There'd been nothing but silence since Sam's memorial service—and she had to accept that might not change.

........◆........

Later that night, Haley curled up in her bed, waiting for sleep. As the minutes turned to hours, she stared into the darkness and into her future. She'd manage life on her own. No depending on Stephen—or anyone else—to come to her rescue.

"After all, God, isn't that the way you made me?" she whispered. "Strong? Independent? Able to take care of myself—and Kit? I can do this. I will do this. And I won't complain. You gave me Sam . . . and I have Kit because of our marriage. And because of Sam, I met Stephen . . ."

And for all his similarities to Sam, he was so very different. Stephen knew how to stop. To rest.

But she wouldn't be selfish. She wouldn't ask for more.

She couldn't ask for more.

And why not? Am I not the God of more?

Wonderful. Now she was hearing voices. God's voice, to be exact. She'd expect something like this to happen when she was sick—running a high fever, like the time Stephen came to her rescue.

This has nothing to do with a fever . . . and everything to do with the Truth—the Truth of who you are.

Haley lay in the bed, almost afraid to breathe. She didn't "do" God this way. She didn't . . .

I'm past all your boundaries, Haley. Stop limiting me. Stop limiting yourself.

"How am I doing that? You're God. I can't limit you."

Oh, yes, you can. Making decisions without me. Letting other people—like your brothers—determine who you are.

"You know, God, my life's been pretty hard lately. I lost Sam. And I'm a single mom. And while we're talking, I think I'm in love with my husband's brother."

I know.

"Of course you would. I'm sorry about that."

There's no need to apologize. Stop taking responsibility for everything . . .

"I am responsible for everything. There's no one else but me."

Haley, can we get one thing straight here tonight?

"What?"

I'm God—and you are not. I know you're tired. Stop trying so hard.

"I don't know how to do it any other way."

That's why I gave you Stephen.

"Gave me . . . Stephen?"

Yes. Haley, I am a God of relationships. Do you think I meant for you to love only one man in your life? There are a lot of things you think you know. About me. About yourself. About how life is supposed to play out. But sometimes you're wrong.

"I didn't mean to get it wrong. I tried to be right."

Everyone tries to be right, Haley. But I am the right way. Not your way. My way.

"I don't know who I'm supposed to be anymore."

I can help you find your way back to that—to you.

"Back?"

Yes. You left part of you behind . . .

"How far back?"

Don't worry . . . I'll go with you every step of the way. And here's the funny thing—

"There's humor in this?"

I like laughter.

"Me, too."

The funny thing is, you walk forward to find what you left be-hind.

"Forward?"

To what I have waiting for you.

"What's that?"

I think you know.

"What?"

Take another look, Haley. Take another look.

thirty-nine

Stephen had started over. Made peace with his past. Faced reality. And started chasing an unexpected, outside-the-box dream. Then why wasn't he content?

He dumped his satchel on the couch, shucking off his shoes and yanking off his tie at the same time. When his phone buzzed on his hip, he pulled it out of the holster, not surprised to see Jared's face appear. Enough. He muted the phone without answering it. "I just spent all day with you, man. Gimme a break."

He tossed the phone down next to his satchel and tie and headed for the galley kitchen. He'd make dinner and then call Jared back. Talk business. That's all he did these days. Who knew a wild idea could become such a profitable venture? He had no time to explore Oregon . . . or to think about Colorado.

In the kitchen, the *Bon Appétit* wall calendar hanging beside the refrigerator declared it was August. *Wrong.* He flipped the page over to September. He'd been in Oregon going on three months now. Another week and he could call Haley for his

once-a-month "How's my niece doing?" phone call. Talk about
Kit. Brief. Casual.

And then he'd spend the next week trying not to think about
Haley. Her blue eyes. The softness of her hair. The taste of her
lips. He'd work out longer at the gym. Stay later at the office.
Try some new recipes and insist Jared eat dinner for once.

Why not throw caution to the wind and call tonight? Get
a week's head start on untangling his emotions. He retrieved
his phone, pacing the length of his kitchen while he waited for
Haley to answer.

"Hello?"

"Hey, Haley, how's it going?" Good. Just the right amount of
casual in the greeting.

"We're good, Stephen. Just getting ready to give Kit a bath."

"Oh, sorry. I don't want to interrupt."

"No, no problem. I've got time to talk."

"So, how's Peanut?"

"Good. Getting bigger—she gained another pound. The doctor said she's doing great. That she'll probably catch up to all the
milestones by her first birthday."

"I'm not surprised. And you? How are you?" He'd pat himself
on the back later for maintaining just the right amount of de-
tached interest in his voice.

"I'm good, too. Still teaching private lessons at the range and
liking that."

What was it with Haley and the "good" business? It felt as
if she was keeping him at arm's length, trying to convince him
they were doing just fine without him. And they probably were.
"Any more homeowners' association hassles?"

"Not since the tree was cut down."

Stephen stopped with his hand on the fridge door handle.
"You cut it down?"

"It was a tree . . . nothing more. And it was dying. Since I took care of the tree, Shelton's been quiet."

"Did you do anything about those photographs?"

"A law enforcement officer paid Shelton a visit—issued him a warning since I chose not to press charges. I don't worry about him hassling me anymore."

"That's a relief."

"Did I mention my family's coming out for Thanksgiving?"

"All of them?"

"Yes, the whole gang. They want to meet Kit. And my brothers said they'll do some of the projects around the house."

"Sounds like fun."

"Yep. Like I said, we're good." Haley stopped talking as Kit cooed into the phone. "Did you hear that? Kit said, 'Hello, Uncle Stephen.'"

"Tell her that I miss her."

"She misses you, too." Something unspoken hung in the air. "How are you doing?"

"Keeping busy, but that's to be expected when you decide to start up a new company." Stephen realized he'd been standing there, hanging on to the fridge door. He uncurled his fingers.

"It sounds exciting—designing houses."

"It's exhausting."

"I bet you're doing a wonderful job." Kit interrupted the conversation with a sudden bout of protests. "Oh, Stephen . . . I'm sorry. I hate to cut you off, but she's only wearing a diaper and I think she's cold—"

"Never let it be said I kept a woman from her bath. Take care, Haley."

"We will."

Once Haley hung up, Stephen turned to stare at the view outside his apartment—not that he'd see any of it. Was this it, then? Once-a-month phone calls that would eventually taper off to even less frequent ones as Kit grew up? Standing by as Haley met some other guy, fell in love, and got married? What was he supposed to do?

There is no fear in love.

Stephen stilled, closing his eyes. It was as if God had whispered a precious truth to him, and his soul whispered back, "What, Lord?"

There is no fear in love.

If he was honest with himself, he'd admit that fear was woven through his feelings for Haley. He was afraid of what others might think—what his brother would think, what Sam's friends would think, what his mother and father would think.

At least he had Haley's mom on his side—maybe even her oldest brother.

"Haley needs a very special man, someone who sees her for who she is—who she could be. Sam could have become that man, but he's not here . . . and I'm sorry he lost that chance. But now you're here—"

"And I'm Sam's brother."

"I know that, Stephen." Paula moved to the door before she spoke again. Then she paused, the door halfway open, speaking over her shoulder. "Don't let a little thing like that stop you from loving the right woman—if you've found her."

A little thing like that?

Even if he ignored everyone else, would Haley ever see him for himself? Was he condemned to being Sam's reflection for the rest of his life?

Sam was gone . . . dead—and because of that truth, there was no way for Sam and Haley to work on their marriage. Maybe Sam would have realized Haley needed him. Maybe he would have stopped choosing the military over his marriage. There was no way to know.

But Stephen was still alive. He could make his own choices about Haley. He had the freedom to love Haley without guilt or fear. Loving Haley wasn't a sin. If he acknowledged all he felt for her, instead of turning his back on it, he'd be overwhelmed by admiration . . . desire . . . respect . . . longing. He would admit he loved Haley. It wouldn't matter what anyone else thought. Their relationship, their future, was between them and God.

But how did he make the leap from fear to boldness? He had to admit he did love Haley—and not in a brotherly kind of way. And that yes, falling in love with her made things complicated. When had his life not been complicated? Messy? Even crazy at times? And as much as he hated to say it, Jared was right. He was acting like some guy in a daytime soap opera, refusing to say how he truly felt about Haley because of what everyone else might think.

No more. He was going to love Haley boldly—and ask her if she could risk loving him, too.

forty

••••=••••=•••===•••••

Stephen mentally gripped his confidence with both hands, refusing to let go. He'd come this far—he was going to finish it.

He consulted his iPhone. According to the GPS, he should almost be at the shooting range. He was minutes away from seeing Haley again. And he'd face her in an entire building full of guns.

Smart, Ames. Very smart.

If she didn't like his idea, he could only hope she'd say no and leave it at that—not pull a gun on him again.

Once he'd parked outside the range, he closed his eyes and breathed a prayer. "I'm going in, Lord. I'm being strong and courageous, believing this is the way you want me to go. I pray Haley's heart is open to me. Please, God, if it's your will . . . let me have the chance of loving this woman."

He nodded to the two men behind the glass counters. Various guns were tagged and set out on shelves. Protective eyeglasses and earmuffs were on display, as well as gun cases and safes. T-shirts and targets. Now all he needed to do was find Haley.

"Can I help you?" A man with a marines-approved crew cut approached him.

"I'm looking for Haley Ames. I was told she was here."

"She's on the range." The man motioned toward the bank of glass on one side of the room. "Finishing up a lesson."

"Is it okay if I wait for her?"

"Doesn't bother me." The man paused. "Anybody ever tell you—"

"That I look like her husband, Sam? Yeah. I'm his twin brother, Stephen. Nice to meet you."

They shook hands and then Stephen crossed the room, standing by the windows so he could watch Haley. Her back was to him, her honey-blond hair arranged in the usual ponytail, which was pulled through the back opening of a denim ball cap. She wore jeans and a form-fitting white T-shirt that accentuated how she'd recovered her slender figure since Kit's birth.

As he watched, she talked with a teen girl, helping her adjust her stance and reposition her arms. Then she stepped back while the girl took aim on a target downrange and fired. Haley patted her on the shoulder, motioning for the girl to try again.

It was a full ten minutes before the teen packed up her gun and the two of them exited the range through the two doors, separated by a small sound-buffering room, then entered the store.

"You did great out there today, Candy. The extra practices are paying off . . ." Haley's voice faded as she recognized Stephen. A smile curved her lips, her blue eyes shining. "Stephen?"

"Hey."

"What are you doing here?"

"Claire told me I'd find you here."

"O-kay. But why?"

"I wanted to show you something—and I have a proposition for you." He hadn't planned on having the conversation in front of other people, but if that was the way things went down, so be it. He wasn't walking away from Haley without telling her what was in his heart.

"A proposition?" She quirked her eyebrow and then paused, seeming to remember her student. "Wait a minute. Candy, same time next week?"

"Sure, Haley."

"Good. You're doing great. Get back here and practice at least twice before then, all right?"

"Yes, ma'am."

Haley pulled off her ball cap, kneading her forehead with her fingers before repositioning it on her head. "So, what's the proposition, Stephen?"

"Is there someplace we could go to talk?"

"There's a coffee shop halfway between here and home, or we could walk along the hiking path back behind the club."

Sit and add more caffeine to his already overloaded system? Not a smart move. And if he had the chance for privacy, he'd take it. "Walking sounds good."

"I'll need to call Claire and tell her I'm going to be late."

"How do you think I found you? Claire knows I planned on talking with you."

Another quirk of her eyebrow. "O-kay, then. Let me sign off the clock—"

"And I'll grab what I need from my car and meet you out front."

He had all of two minutes to practice what he wanted to say once more. Proposition one. Proposition two. Proposition three. And his success depended on Haley's liking all three of them.

God, I hope I've come at the right time. Not too soon. Not too late. I'm ready. I only pray Haley is ready, too.

A few moments later, Haley led him to the man-made trail. She'd taken her hair down, and it hung in soft waves around her face. Why not just enjoy walking with her in the late afternoon sunshine?

"I saw Peanut when I stopped by the house. She's only gotten more adorable since I was here last. She has your blond hair. Your smile."

"Did you come to see your niece, then?"

"No—although I hoped to see her." He patted the black presentation portfolio tucked under his arm. "I wanted to show you this."

"And that is?"

"A couple of things I've been working on. I wanted to see what you thought about some of my ideas."

"You're the businessman, Stephen, not me."

"True—but I value your opinion, Haley. I care about . . . about what you think."

So much for walking and having some casual conversation with Haley. And really, his heart was racing as if he was in a marathon. If he kept this up, he'd sweat through his shirt before he finished. What was the plan again? Three points. Three propositions. One, two, three. Keep it simple. Be courageous.

Around a slight bend in the path, a wrought-iron and wooden bench was tucked up against a small trio of trees. "How about we sit for a few minutes?"

"Sure."

She settled next to him, not close enough for their bodies to touch, but near enough that the scent of lavender caused him to close his eyes for a few seconds as he breathed one last prayer. Then he slid closer to Haley, positioning the portfolio on his lap. "Like I said, I wanted to show you something."

Haley touched the cover, labeled with the words FAMILY TREES. "What is this, Stephen?"

"You'll understand if you look inside."

•••••—◆—•••••

Stephen traveled all the way from Oregon to Colorado to have her look at a portfolio? Of what?

Haley tamped down the emotions that had surged to the surface of her heart when she saw him in the gun club. She'd wanted to run and throw her arms around him—hold on to him and, even if just for a moment, feel at rest in his arms again. She knew if he held her, the yearning that sometimes kept her awake at night would finally be satisfied. Or would she just want more?

But she forced herself to stand still. To not overreact. Just because Stephen was here didn't mean anything had changed.

Haley turned back the cover and stared at the penciled sketch slipped into a clear protective plastic page. With her index finger, she traced the erased and redrawn lines, flipping the page over and reading the scribbled supply list.

"It's the tree house—your and Sam's tree house."

"Exactly."

"I told you I had the tree in the backyard cut down."

"I know."

"Seeing this makes me wish I still had that tree . . . I mean, a healthy tree for a tree house."

"I may be able to help with that." Stephen tapped the sketch with his forefinger. "Turn the page."

Haley gasped when she saw the color photograph of the completed tree house, updated with prefabricated material that wouldn't warp or dry out, with a sturdy ladder and a Plexiglas window instead of a crooked square opening in one of the walls.

"This is amazing. Who . . . who designed this?"

"I did." The smile on Stephen's face was reminiscent of the ten-year-old boy who'd helped his brother build a tree house in their backyard. "Well, Jared helped, too. And our team."

"Y-your team? I'm confused."

"I went into business with Jared."

"I know you did—but I thought you were designing houses—I mean *real* houses."

"Our clients consider these real houses. We're building one as a guest room. The business we started is Family Trees." He flipped through pages, showing different designs. "We create high-end tree houses."

That's why Stephen had come to see her, after three months? To talk about his new business venture? To show her photographs of tree houses? Haley swallowed the acidic taste building in the back of her throat. She wanted to be happy for Stephen—she *would* be happy for him. He was following his dreams.

"Thank you for showing these to me. They're magnificent. I haven't seen anything like them."

"Do you have a favorite?"

Stephen slid even closer, distracting Haley's attention from the photographs. "A favorite?"

"Yes." He flipped the pages back and forth between different designs. "Which one would you want to build for Peanut?"

"Well, you know I love the original." She turned back to the first photograph, the upgraded version of the brothers' tree house, labeled PLAY IT AGAIN, SAM. She flipped back to another design, one with stairs winding around the tree trunk and a circular stained glass window. "But this one . . . it makes me think of all the stories I've read with adventures and a little bit of magic . . ."

"NEVERENDING STORY—that's one of my favorites, too."

"I'm just sorry I no longer have a tree—I'd want you to build this for Kit."

"That's the second thing I wanted to show you." He turned to the middle section of the portfolio. "What do you think of this?"

Haley looked at the new sketch and back at Stephen. He wore the cologne that always made her want to lean into him.

But obviously the man wanted to talk business. "This is . . . a set of house plans?"

"Right again." Stephen pointed out different details. "Four bedrooms. Two and a half baths. Two-car garage. Unfinished basement. Half-an-acre lot—with trees. I've walked the property, and there's a perfect one for the tree house."

"It's . . . wonderful, Stephen." What was going on? Why did Stephen want to show her any of this? "But if I'm not mistaken, this house is located in Oregon."

"True."

"So you want to build a tree house for Kit in Oregon? What, is she going to play in it when—if—we come out to visit you?"

"Well, that question leads me to my third proposition."

"Proposition?"

"Proposition. Point. Proposal."

"You're confusing me, Stephen."

"Then I'll speak plainly." Stephen set the folder on the bench behind him.

"Stephen, what are you doing?"

"I'm being courageous. Your movie hero John Wayne said, 'Courage is being scared to death . . . and saddling up anyway.'"

Haley leaned away from him, eyebrow lifted. "Did you just quote John Wayne to me?"

"Yes. And here's another John Wayne truism for you: 'Life is hard, but it's harder when you're stupid.' Well, I'm not going to be stupid and walk away from the most amazing woman I've ever met. I'm going to stop being so afraid of what everyone else might think if I fell in love with you. I never stopped and asked God what he thought. I didn't see his hand in all this—that our loving each other could be good and right." Stephen took her hand in his, holding it against his heart. "I know traditionally I should get down on one knee, but I want to look in your eyes

when I say this." His voice wavered for a moment, then strengthened. "Haley Ames, I love you. It's crazy. But it's the truth—and
I want the joy of loving you and Kit forever—in sickness and in
health, for richer and for poorer, until death parts us."

Stephen's declaration left her speechless.

Tree houses.

Real houses—in Oregon.

And now Stephen had come back for her. Quoted John
Wayne as he confessed his love for her.

Stephen couldn't know how many times Haley had dreamed of
his kissing her, but the memory of those too-few moments when
he held her evaporated as he pulled her close, the strength of his
arms a welcome haven. He was going to kiss her again . . . finally.

She turned her face away, pressing both hands against his
chest. "Stephen—stop!"

He stilled, his face turning pale. "What's wrong?"

"You told me that you weren't going to kiss me again until I
admitted I wanted you to kiss me."

His arms tightened around her again, and from the wicked
gleam in the depths of his brown eyes, she knew there was no
chance of escaping. "And do you want me to kiss you?"

"Oh, yes—"

With a husky laugh, Stephen fulfilled her request. Her arms
slid up his chest to his shoulders, pulling him close. The echo of
Stephen's laugh intertwined with the familiar scent of him, the
taste of his mouth, how he cradled her close, making her feel
treasured. Even as he fulfilled her longing for him, he created a
deeper desire, one that would take a lifetime to satisfy.

God had promised her more, and the chance to love Stephen
Ames—to accept that he loved her—was abundantly more than
Haley dared to ask for. But this moment wasn't about asking. It
was about saying yes to all Stephen was offering.

She allowed herself to respond without hesitation, without reserve. Let her kiss be her answer. When he started to end the kiss, she whispered, "Not yet," and captured his lips again.

When he pulled away again with a low moan, Haley hid her face against his shoulder. Stephen's breath rasped in her ear. "Haley . . . you can't kiss me like that and not marry me."

Haley caught her breath, running her fingers through the hair that curled just along the nape of his neck. "I love how you wear your hair long."

Stephen pressed a kiss to the palm of her hand. "Thank you."

"And I love the cologne you wear—it always makes me want to ask you to put your arms around me and pull me close."

Another kiss—so warm—pressed to the pulse beating in her wrist. "I'll wear it every day, then."

"And I love how you protect me—and come back for me. No one's ever done that for me—except my brother David, one time when I was bullied in school."

Stephen's laughter rumbled in his chest. "So you're telling me I remind you of your brother?"

"No—not at all. When I look at you I see you—Stephen Rogers Ames."

He cradled her face in his hands and pressed a kiss just at the corner of her mouth. "I love you, Haley. But you haven't answered my question."

"I never heard a question." Haley tried to hide her smile by placing a quick kiss on Stephen's lips.

"Then let me make myself perfectly clear: Haley, will you please marry me?"

"Oh, that's what this is all about."

"Haley . . ." Stephen's arms tightened around her.

"Yes." She traced the outline of his face. "I love you, Stephen. Now, please . . . kiss me again."

acknowledgments

....

The catalyst for *Somebody Like You* was as simple as this: I am a twin—a fraternal twin. Growing up, my twin sister and I looked so unlike each other we had a difficult time convincing people we were sisters, much less twins. I took my real life and twisted and turned it into the premise for this novel.

What I didn't know was that the thread of estrangement woven through *Somebody Like You* would become a real-life, "God, help me" experience. I'm thankful that while I was surprised by fiction becoming personal, God was not. He was faithful to help me write my novel—and He is faithful to help me walk out the realities of my life, day by day. He is trustworthy, compassionate, and patient.

Like most writers, I strive to balance my real life and my writing life. Sometimes real life wins, sometimes writing life wins, and most days are a glorious, haphazard mix of real life and writing life—and just enough sleep and never enough housework.

I am a better writer because of those who anchor me to the real world: my husband, Rob, and our children:

- Josh and our daughter-in-love, Jenelle
- Katie Beth and our son-in-love, Nate, and our first grandchild, Ali Beth
- Amy and our son-in-love, David
- Christa, our "caboose kiddo," who is plunging us into the teen years again because, well, why not?

And what can I say except thank you, thank you, thank you to Sonia Meeter and Shari Hamlin, who have embraced the role of Preferred Readers? You've both jumped into the deep end of the imaginary world with me—and my novels are better because of your input. Thank you, too, for joining with Barbara Haynes and being my spiritual ground support and praying for me as I wrote *Somebody Like You.*

My writing life overflows with both imaginary people who interrupt my days and nights and very real people who helped me brainstorm, fast-draft, revise, and wrestle into submission *Somebody Like You.*

There are so many reasons why author Rachel Hauck is the 2013 ACFW Mentor of the Year—and I'm over-the-moon thankful that she pours her talent and her prayers into my life via Skype, texts, Instant Messages, FaceTime, and those oh-so-wonderful true face-to-face times. She and author Susan May Warren, also an ACFW Mentor of the Year, have both influenced me greatly as a novelist, but even more I follow them as they follow Christ (1 Corinthians 11:1) along the writing road.

The My Book Therapy Leadership Team—David, Edie, Alena, Lisa, Melissa, Michelle, Rachel, Reba, and Susie—keeps me sane. Every writer needs a "safety net," and they are mine—a safe place to ask questions, request prayers, vent, and find wisdom and encouragement for this journey.

I will be forever grateful for the day agent Rachelle Gardner with Books and Such Literary Agency took me on as a client. She embodies all the best in the word "literary agent."

Being a Howard Books author means working with such talented and supportive people as editor Jessica Wong, art director Bruce Gore, production editor Linda Sawicki, and Holly Halverson as a freelance editor. It doesn't get better than this.

And a special thank-you to Nikki Carroll for helping me develop some of the basic details for Haley working at a gun range. Any literary misfires are mine.

Howard Books Reading Group Guide

somebody like you

Beth K. Vogt

Stephen and Sam Ames had big plans for their lives. Growing up as identical twins, they shared everything from toys to dreams of owning a Mustang. But the painful aftermath of their parents' divorce and the reality of the war in Afghanistan set them on separate paths and changed their relationship forever. As Stephen begins a journey to make peace with his brother, he discovers one more thing they share, which will require him to step out in faith and trust God for the outcome.

Topics & Questions for Discussion

1. Based on the description in the prologue, how would you describe Stephen and Sam's relationship when they were young boys? How would you describe Stephen? Sam?

2. What does Stephen's conversation with his boss about the pending layoffs in chapter one reveal about his character?

3. How would you describe Haley Ames as she enters the story in chapter two? What did you feel toward her when you first met her?

4. What happened that created distance and tension in Stephen and Sam's relationship? In what ways did each of them contribute to the rift in their relationship? Have you ever experienced a similar change in a close relationship? How did you respond?

5. Describe how Haley's family of origin influenced the way she related to her femininity. What were the Jordan family rules (p. 83)? How do they compare with God's design for Haley as his daughter?

6. What do you think Stephen was looking for when he went to visit Haley Ames after his brother's death? Have you experienced the loss of a close family member or friend? What were some of the ways you expressed your grief?

7. In what ways did Stephen and Sam turn out to be identical? In what ways were they very different from each other?

8. What did Haley's growing friendship with Stephen reveal about her marriage to Sam? How did she deal with her pain and disappointment during their marriage?

9. Do you think Stephen and Sam's parents had any responsibility for the distance that developed in the brothers' relationship? How might they have fostered a different outcome?

10. Why did Haley have her heart set on a baby boy? In what ways did baby Kit serve as a catalyst for change in Haley's life?

11. How would you describe Haley's relationship with God in the aftermath of Sam's death? What shifted or changed as the story unfolded?

12. On p. 122, Haley says: "Praying feels like trickles of water coming out of a hose when someone has tied a big knot in it somewhere." Have you ever related to this description of prayer? Explain.

13. What role did Lily, the childbirth instructor, play in Haley's life?

14. What was the misunderstanding that created distance between Stephen and Haley before Sam's memorial service? How could each of them have handled the situation differently? What got in the way of honest, direct communication?

15. What happened to Haley's heart as she experienced Stephen's consistent care? How is Stephen a Christ figure in this story? Describe Haley as the story finishes in contrast with the beginning.

16. How did you respond to Stephen and Haley's developing relationship?

Enhance Your Book Club

1. Spend some time reflecting on your family motto or a friend's family motto. Connections to think about might include money, conflict, gender roles, etc. Consider how your motto either reflects or contradicts God's design for us as His children. Discuss what you learned with your book club.

2. Read Psalm 32. Think about relationships in your life that may have ended abruptly or with an unresolved conflict. Ask God for guidance about how to process any remaining grief or anger.

3. Think about someone within your community who is a widow or a widower (potentially a military widow or widower). Discuss ways to serve and encourage them and consider using the time of

your next book club meeting to provide tangible help and encouragement to them.

4. Invite someone who is an identical twin to talk to your book club. Explore the differences between someone who grows up as a twin and others who have non-twin siblings.

A Conversation with Beth K. Vogt

You have said that your first novel, *Wish You Were Here*, took three years to write and your second one, *Catch a Falling Star*, took three months. How about this one?

Somebody Like You was also written in a shorter time frame—about three months. However, I tore this novel apart in the editing process in a way I've never done with any of my other books. I was challenged by both my mentor and my editors—but even more, the issues within this novel demanded a whole new attention to detail and a willingness to delve into emotion.

What was your inspiration for writing *Somebody Like You*?

The initial catalyst for this novel was the fact that I'm a twin. I took the basic twin storyline and turned it inside, outside, upside down and finally created the story of Haley, Sam, and Stephen.

You've indicated that you like to distill your stories down to questions. What was the main question for *Somebody Like You*?

I started with the question: *Can a young widow fall in love with her husband's reflection?* Hidden within that is the novel's story question, which is: *Is it ever wrong to love someone?*

How did your experience of being a twin influence the story line? Are you an identical twin?

I understand the experience of being a twin in a very different way from Sam and Stephen because my sister and I are fraternal twins. Growing up, we had a difficult time convincing people we were sisters, much less twins. My sister and I were very different and yet we experienced the pressure of comparison from teachers and friends, which pushed us apart for a lot of years. And so, because of that, I can understand the separation Sam and Stephen experienced.

Haley Ames struggles to open herself up to vulnerability and intimacy throughout the story. Why do you think this is such a common struggle for women today?

We each experience events in our lives that create wounds that tell us we aren't good enough, we aren't beautiful enough . . . we aren't *enough*. And then we compare ourselves to others, believing other women have it all together and we're the only one who struggles.

What message did you hope to speak through Haley's gradual awakening?

Sometimes we let others tell us who we are. We forget who we really are. Love, unconditional love—the kind of love that is there, day in and day out—heals our wounds and allows us to be our true selves again.

You've mentioned in other interviews that your husband spent twenty-four years in the military. How did your experiences during those years shape this story?

During our years in the military, several of our friends lost their husbands. Seeing that—and walking closely with one friend through that—changed me.

How did those losses impact you?

I always said my husband was in the military and I was along for the ride. I have the greatest respect for military men and women, for the sacrifices they make—and for the families who love them and support them as they serve.

What did you hope to give readers in the prologue—the brief story of Stephen and Sam's relationship as young boys?

Oh, I debated the prologue with my mentor, Rachel Hauck. Writers are told not to begin a novel with a prologue. But this is one of those "exceptions to every rule" times. I believe readers needed to see Sam and Stephen as young boys—to see what they lost.

What was uniquely enjoyable about this novel in contrast to your first two?

Somebody Like You was so challenging to write. Yes, it's a romance, but it deals with issues of widowhood and estrangement. I believe I stood up to the challenge of writing this story honestly, in a believable way—with the support of my family, mentors, and "spiritual ground support."

Have you ever had a relationship end abruptly or with unresolved conflict? How did you respond?
I never imagined that as I wrote *Somebody Like You* I would also wrestle with estrangement in my own life. It's been painful—heartbreaking, truthfully. I've embraced the truth of the verse in Romans 12: *As much as you are able, be at peace with all men.* I've done what I could . . . and I've had to let that be enough for now, trusting that God is working in my life, even when I don't see anything happening.

What was your inspiration for the tree house? Did you have a tree house as a child?
I think there's something inherently hopeful in tree houses—they are the stuff of childhood, of dreams. And I saw a TV show about tree-house builders, which inspired me to weave the tree house more strongly through the story. I never had a tree house as a child, but I always wanted one.

Do you have a family motto you hope your children remember?
Our family motto is: *There's always room for one more.* It grew out of our time as a military family, when we spent so many holidays away from relatives. We always tried to open our home to whoever needed a place to celebrate.

What can we expect from you next?
I'm one of the authors in the A Year of Weddings series by HarperCollins—I'm the author of the "A November Bride" novella. I'm brainstorming several Colorado romance series . . . so we'll see what doors God opens!

MORE ROMANCE THAT MAKES YOU LAUGH, TEAR UP, AND SIGH!

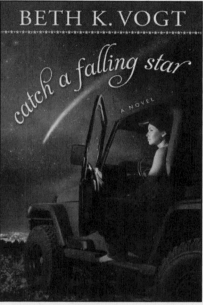

"With equal parts drama and comedy, Beth Vogt's debut romance is as heart-tugging as it is funny and it keeps the reader guessing as to what Allison's *Happy Ever After* will look like up until the very last scene."

—*USA TODAY* on
Wish You Were Here

"Delightful, sparkling romance and a story that is sure to keep you up all night."

—Susan May Warren,
bestselling, award-winning author of
Take a Chance on Me on
Catch a Falling Star

Available wherever books are sold or at SimonandSchuster.com   HOWARD BOOKS
A Division of Simon & Schuster
A CBS COMPANY

The Pleasure of Your Company Is Requested for A Year of Weddings.

A SPECIAL E-FIRST NOVELLA COLLECTION.

RSVP at http://tnzfiction.com/weddings

ZONDERVAN®